DAWN OF THE NEW TEMPLARS

By

Gerhard Plenert

Outer Banks Publishing Group
Raleigh/Outer Banks

FIRST EDITION – January 2021
SECOND EDITION – January 2024

Library of Congress Control Number: 2020952086

ISBN 13 - 978-1-7341687-8-5
eISBN – 978-1-0050312-2-0

DEDICATION

This Book is dedicated to Renee Sangray Plenert

My Best Friend and the Joy of my Life

The One Who Makes Everything Worthwhile

ACKNOWLEDGEMENTS

This book has been many years in the making and there are numerous individuals that need to be recognized. The first being my conscience who validated the flow and identified any holes in the plot, Renee Plenert. Next, my agent who believed in the book and spent numerous years finding the right publisher, Emerantia Parnall-Gilbert from Gilbert Literary Agency, a Subsidiary of Hawkspurr Productions. And last but not least my publisher Anthony Policastro from Outer Banks Publishing.

Although many of the locations mentioned in this book seem fantastical, they are all actual locations that can be visited. The historical stories are based, for the most part, on real events and many of the key characters were real people. It might be fun for the reader to google map some of these sites to see what they look like.

CHAPTER ONE - PART 1

The Attack on Jerusalem
Late Summer, 586 BC, Jerusalem

Brag's panic caused him to stumble on the cobblestones as he ran down the muddy streets. It was a drizzly, gloomy day, which matched his mood and the mood of all the townspeople. Normally he would be careful not to get his robe dirty. His wife had given him such a verbal beating the last time he came home splashed in mud. However today worrying about getting dirty seemed trivial. He was scared not for himself, but for the treasures of the sacred temple.

Jerusalem had been under siege for years and holding back the current attack seemed impossible. Nebuchadnezzar's Babylonian hordes looked as though they were finally going to break through. Most of the King's prophets had been prophesying a successful resistance. But Brag had doubted the truth of their prophesies, remembering how in years past the King Zedekiah, king of Judah, had surrounded himself with supporters and had rejected anyone, including the Lord Jehovah's prophets, that questioned his decisions. Some of the rejected prophets, like Habakkuk and Nephi had warned of the fall of Jerusalem, and now Brag feared that indeed this was finally happening.

Brag had to get to the temple and secure the temple treasures. The king, trusting his chosen prophets, had forbidden the hiding of the treasures feeling that this would be a resignation of defeat. But Brag now feared that it may be too late. In his role as High Priest, it was his sacred duty and responsibility to safeguard the temple site and its contents. This role took precedence over the authority of the king.

Brag was one of only a few 33-degree Masons, the highest Masonic degree. Over the years the Masonic order had maintained its structure as guardians of the temple. Brag would urgently need to find others that could help him secure the safety of the Ark of the Covenant, which was stored in the inner "Holy of Holies" of the temple. Moreover, he needed to accomplish this quickly.

He heard yelling. "They've broken through the North gate. The Babylonian hoards have invaded the city," was the cry heard throughout the city. Fear was rampant. Women and children were screaming and crying in confused resignation. Men were running, but there was no safe place to run. The people were trapped on all sides. They were afraid that their lives would be taken. Fighting seemed futile. Many cried out prayers, pleading with Jehovah to spare their lives. They cried for forgiveness for having ignored the pleadings of the prophets. They begged that if God would reprieve them one more time that they would transform their lives forever. However, it was too little and too late.

Now Barg was on a mission. He had to save the temple treasures. His life was of little importance when compared to the sacredness of the temple and the Lord's emblems within its confines. As he continued toward the temple, he saw Jeru and Jelum running toward him from a side street. These were two other 33-degree Masons. Luckily, they were also feeling the urgency of the situation. They understood the importance of their priestly and Masonic roles. And they were joining Barg to help him secure the temple treasures.

"Come. We must be quick. The Babylonians will know that the biggest treasures are in the temple and they will head there first," cried Barg in a voice of fear.

"Indeed," said Jeru and Jelum simultaneously and with angst. None of the streets were straight. In addition, the rain made the cobblestones very slippery. Jeru slipped and fell to the street as he rounded a corner following Barg. However, no wetness or mud would keep any of them from their mission. Under normal circumstances, none of them would even consider entering the temple in their wet and muddy clothes.

However, the desecration caused by the Babylonian hoards entering and ravaging the temple would be a worse sacrilege than dirty clothes.

The threesome rushed forward, breaking through the fear-filled crowds as they pushed ahead. The shortest route to the temple would take them through the marketplace. As they rounded the corner, they entered the marketplace, which normally was a bustle of merchants soliciting buyers. But today the marketplace was a shambles of overturned benches, with market goods strewn everywhere. People were rushing around, yelling for loved ones, and trying to find some semblance of shelter and safety. But there would be no safe havens in Jerusalem today.

After passing through the market, they finally arrived at the stairs that led up to the temple. And up they ran, two steps at a time, risking the chance of additional slips and falls, and possibly serious injury. But their sacred duty at the temple had now become an obsession, and nothing or no one would deter them.

Arriving at the temple gate there was no one to validate that they knew all the sacred signs of passage. Normally, Barg, Jeru, and Jelum would be challenged. Unless they knew the signs, passage would be denied them. But not today. There was no one to do the challenging.

Once within the temple compound, they did not stop. They continued running right up to the temple and burst through the front doors. Again, there was no one to validate that they had the right to enter the temple. Once inside, they knew where to go and what needed to be done. Plans had been made and rehearsed, and all 33-degree Masons knew what to do. And they rushed to the task.

The temple had two main rooms. The front was larger and contained many of the priesthood implements and many of the sacred writings. Only the members of the Levitical priesthood had permission to enter this room, and only those priests who were pure in both body and soul. Priests with skin blemishes, or missing fingers, or any other type of disfiguration, were unable to participate in the ceremonies of the temple.

The three Masons went through the front room of the temple where the Aaronic and Levitical Priesthood performed their sacred ordinances.

At the back of this room was the entrance to the second temple room, the Holy of Holies. This only had one entrance point, through the main room of the temple. The Holy of Holies was the most sacred place in the world. It was a sanctuary, where only one individual was permitted to enter. It was that person alone, who was then selected annually. This ritualistic tradition based upon a rotation that was determined back to Moses' time, when Moses himself roamed the wilderness with the Sacred Tabernacle.

As they entered the Holy of Holies, the three came to a sudden stop. They were briefly overcome by the sheer majesty of the Ark of the Covenant. Because of the restricted access to this part of the temple, they had never seen the Ark before today, nor had they ever seen any of the other sacred implements that were stored in this portion of the temple, like the staff of Moses. They were emotionally overcome by the majesty of the Ark, its beauty and richness, and its sheer and tangible sacredness.

The Ark was constructed of shittah wood from the tree, which then was considered to be the wood of the Tree of Life; the same Tree of Life that Adam was commanded to avoid. The Ark was 1.5 cubits (2.56 ft.) broad and high, and 2.5 cubits (4.57 ft.) long. It was covered with the purest gold. Its lid was referred to as the "mercy seat," which was also surrounded with a rim of gold. At each end of the mercy seat was a cherubim (angel) facing away from the center of the Ark. Their wings were spread over the Ark, as a type of protecting shield. **(Ex. 25:10-22; 37:1-9)**

The Ark contained the two stone tablets, referred to as the "testimony" of God or His covenant with His people. The stone tablets contain the Ten Commandments written by the finger of God. The Ark also contains a golden jar containing some of the manna, or bread from heaven, which the Israelites' gathered during their trek in the wilderness. It also contained Aaron, Moses' companion's rod. **(Ex. 16:32-34; Heb. 9:4, Qur'an 2:248)**

At the end of each of the long sides were two gold rings, through which two long wooden poles were placed, used for carrying the Ark. The poles were also decorated with gold. **(Num. 7:9; 10:21; 4:5, 19,**

20; 1 Kings 8:3, 6) Physical contact with the Ark had been deadly, and so the poles were the only safe way to move the Ark. And the three Masonic brethren would use these poles to bring the Ark safely to its hiding place in the caves.

Brag ran to open the secret passageway that led into the caves below the temple, while Jeru and Jelum started gathering up the sacred objects they found within the temple. These included the candelabra, the incense burners, the Holy Grail chalice, and many more sacred and revered objects. They rushed these items and temporarily stashed them, only a few short feet into the secret passageway. They would hide them more securely after the secret passageway doors had been closed. Then, all three of them rushed to get the Ark of the Covenant. It would take all three of them to carry the heavy Ark. Normally a minimum of four strong men would be required. During ceremonies, before the Ark was being sequestered in the Holy of Holies, eight men would lift or move the Ark. But today there was no time. The Ark had to be moved immediately. Jelum, being the strongest of the three, quickly positioned himself on one end of the Ark, grabbing the two poles. Barg and Jeru grabbed one pole each on the other end of the Ark.

Brag and Jeru struggled to pick up the Ark. They started to lift the Ark slowly, when they suddenly heard a sound that brought fear to their very souls. It was the sound of heavy booted feet running up the steps to the temple. And they knew this meant that the Babylonia soldiers had arrived.

A sudden surge of un-human-like strength entered their bodies. Their adrenalin had kicked in and they suddenly were able to lift and move the Ark. They worked their way toward the passageway door, Brag and Jeru going first.

The footsteps outside grew louder and closer. The soldiers had reached the top of the stairs and were now running to the temple itself.

In their rush, Jeru slipped, but only slightly and was able to right himself quickly. The threesome moved cautiously yet urgently toward the passageway, entering it just as the soldiers slammed open the outer temple doors.

Barely inside the passageway, they hurriedly set the Ark on the ground. Quietly but quickly, they shut the secret door, hoping they were quick enough so that the soldiers hadn't seen their escape. With the door closed, they felt safe. They pushed a locking bar in place so that the door could not be opened from the outside. They now set about the task of moving the temple treasures to their secret hiding places within the caves.

Within the caves were several chambers, some for the sacred historical records, some for the scriptures, and some for the sacred temple treasures. The three Masons were so involved in hiding the treasures that they didn't hear the scraping and crushing noises above them where the invaders were going about, unceremoniously destroying the temple. The threesome was not aware that that the Babylonian soldiers had accidently blocked the entrance to the underground passageway by knocking large stone blocks on top of the trap door. The Babylonians had blocked the only escape route that Masons knew about. The temple treasures, along with the Ark of the Covenant, would be sealed forever in the secret underground temple passages, accompanied by the three Masons who had protected them with their lives.

CHAPTER TWO

The Deliverance of Jerusalem
Late Summer, 1119 AD, Jerusalem

Huges de Payen, leader of the French Crusaders, sat back on his horse and rested himself as he looked at Jerusalem in the distance. It would not be long now before he would be walking within the walls of the holy city. He was excited about recovering Jerusalem, the land of the Lord and Savior Jesus Christ. He was thrilled to be returning it to Christian control. He was excited about being able to walk in the city where Jesus walked. He would be the first 33rd degree Mason to walk the streets of Jerusalem in nearly 1700 years.

After the Babylonia captivity, followed by the Jewish return to rebuild Jerusalem, very few senior Masons ever went back. They stayed in Babylon, and in Nineveh, and later generations of Masonic leaders migrated directly to Alexandria, Greece, Rome and the other cities of Europe. Shortly after the Roman domination of Jerusalem ended, the city came under the control of the Canaanites, who later became Muslims. Rome had destroyed the last temple, and attempted reconstruction of Solomon's temple. During these interim years, a number of Masons would return to Jerusalem, but never anyone with the advanced degrees. But the vacuum of Masonic power in Jerusalem was about to change.

The day was beautiful. The sun was out, but it was not too hot. It was a perfect day, perfect for a victory. Huges de Payen had received special dispensation from the Pope to organize a special order of the Masons.

This special order would be known as the Poor Fellow-Solders of Christ and of the Temple of Solomon. Later they would become known as the Knights Templar for short. The Pope had commissioned Huges de Payen to identify four or five fellow crusaders, who were also Masons, and they were to organize themselves around the banner of the cross of the Knights Templar. Moreover, he had identified the perfect individuals. This team would be battle hardened, intelligent, and aggressive. However, their true mission would remain a secret. For now, only the Pope and Hughes de Payen would have knowledge of this secret. Outwardly, they claimed their role as the protectors of Christians travelling to the Holy Land.

Huges de Payen turned his attention back to his troops. They all stood in readiness, waiting for the signal to attack. The catapults and trebuchets were being prepared. The ladder teams and ramming beams were positioned for the attack, and the battle would soon begin.

As he scanned the horizon, he saw the signal. The banner signifying battle had been raised in readiness. Looking across the battle line, he could see all his counterpart commanders, raise themselves up on their horses as a sign of attention. He knew that it was just a matter of minutes before the lead banner would be pointed forward, and they would be on their way.

And then it happened. The lead banner was shifted from pointing straight up to pointing forward, and the charge began. Trebuchets and catapults hurled their fiery missiles towards Jerusalem's walls. The Templars had a massive battering ram; which was a tree trunk mounted on massive axels with wheels the height of two men. The ram was pulled by seven horses on either side. The battering ram was sent on its way toward the door of the city. It wouldn't be long now before the doors would be busted open.

Huges de Payen's heart was beating with excitement. He felt like it would burst. The charge was on and he could already see smoke coming from inside the walls of the city. At least some of the fire missiles had reached their mark.

The ladder teams were charging the walls. This, in Huges de Payen's opinion, was the most dangerous assignment. It was easy for the enemy to drop objects from the wall onto the men below. Moreover, once the men started scaling the ladder, there was the risk of having the ladder pushed over.

The Crusaders would position and tie someone at the top of the ladder when it was being erected. This would put someone directly into the face of the enemy at the top of the wall. This Crusader, with sword in hand would be ready to fight, as long as an enemy arrow didn't get him first.

Huges de Payen's Templar troops were assigned to follow the door ram. They were to charge into the city through the city gate. Huges considered this the best possible assignment. The ram and the door would shield them, and they would be the first to enter the city. He could barely control his excitement.

The path to the city gate had a slight uphill grade. The horses pulled the ram wagon, slowly at first because of the weight, and then gradually increasing in speed until they built up as much momentum as possible. The weight and forward movement of the ram would be unstoppable. It would crash through the door as if it were made of parchment. Moreover, Huges de Payen wanted to be the first to follow it into the city.

Huges de Payen turned, to see his men filled with excitement and enthusiasm. He raised his sword skyward and the men cheered in eager anticipation.

Following the ram was slow and laborious, but it did not dampen the spirit of anticipation. Huges de Payen looked around to see how the ladder teams were doing. He saw several of the ladders being push over. He watched the 'ladder men' being shot to death at the tops of their ladders by arrows, before the ladder was even erected. However, he also noticed that several of the ladders had remained upright with crusaders bravely battling their enemies. He saw the Crusaders climbing up the ladders and getting over the top of the wall of the city. He knew that recovering the city was inevitable.

Flames could be seen, billowing up over the walls of the city. The city was burning. And the screaming of women and children could be heard, mixed with the shouting of the Muslim soldiers. Then, his attention was drawn back to the ram as it crashed into the city gates. It wasn't as successful as anticipated. The gates splintered and tore, but the break was not complete. The ram would have to be pulled back and then repeated. In the meantime, Muslim soldiers were throwing rocks, hot oil, and spears from the top of the wall above the gates. Moreover, several of the ramming team soldiers had been struck. Worse yet, in Huges de Payen's eyes, was the death of the two lead ramming horses. Their lifeless bodies had collapsed under the weight of the ram. And now the remaining horses had to haul not only the ram, but also the two horses backwards down the ramp. It was too much weight for them, and they could not move.

Huges de Payen, in a surge of heroism, jumped off his horse, holding his shield over his head to protect himself, and ran to the front of the ram. Using his sword, he started hacking at the straps that held the dead horses to the ram. A shower of arrows and rocks fell on all sides. But somehow, as if guided by a greater power, Huges de Payen only suffered few minor grazings on his arm and legs. His men cheered his heroic effort and then helped lead the ramming team back away from the city gate to a safe distance, where they would again be able to redeploy the ram.

Two of the strongest horses were quickly found to replace the two dead horses and were positioned next to the ram. A strap was thrown under the ram, and over each of the two horses. Two additional horses were used, one at each end of the strap, to pull in opposite directions, thereby lifting the ram so that it would be ready to be secured to the ramming horses. Additional straps were also used to secure the ram, and they were ready once again to attack the city gate.

With an energetic shout from all the men, the ram once again started its climb toward the city gate. This time, Huges de Payen was convinced, they would be successful.

The horses made it to the city gate, nearly at a gallop, straddling one of the fallen horses under the ram. And the crash of the gate was complete. This time the ram went through the gate is if it were kindling wood. The damage of the first ramming had made this second effort almost trivial. And Huges de Payen and his men charged through the crumpled gate, swords drawn, prepared for fierce resistance. However, it didn't happen. Huges de Payen's crusaders didn't know whether to be disappointed, or relieved. But there was no one there for them to battle. The enemy had already retreated and had left the city to the Crusaders.

CHAPTER THREE

Within the Walls
Late Summer, 1119 AD, Jerusalem

Huges de Payen's men stood in the entrance of the city. The roadways were narrow. The city wall stood on the one side and the buildings on the other. They looked up and down the streets to see what if anything they should do next. Their reprieve was short lasting. The attack came from above. And it was vicious. Hot oil fell from the top of the wall and the tops of the buildings. They were trapped. The soldiers screamed in pain as they threw their shields above themselves. Where do they go? Going down the street would run them deeper into the trap. There was only one choice for them. They had to go back through the gate and out of the city. And they did this quickly.

At a secure distance from the walls, Huges de Payen was able to assess the damage to his troops. Between the arrows, the rocks, and the oil, he had lost over half his men and horses. The magnitude of the damage inflicted was devastating. But Huges de Payen was not giving up. Even with his own personal injuries, he was desperate to complete his mission. He had sworn to the Pope that he would secure the treasures of the holy city and keep them from the control of the hoards. Or else he would die trying.

He scanned his options. Going through the gate was out. The only other alternative was to climb the ladders to the top of the wall. He would find their weakest point, a point where the most ladders were standing and where Crusaders were rapidly ascending the wall, and he would lead his men into the city by going over the wall. Huges de Payen had stood within the walls of the city and been expelled, and now he could not be kept from finding another way inside.

He led his men to the section of the wall, which seemed the safest, climbed off his horse, and started up one of the ladders. The rest of his men soon followed his lead.

Once on the top of the wall, he could see the trap that had been set. The Muslim hoards had anticipated a large surge coming through the gate and they were waiting along the rooftops to drop their deadly heated oil on any trespassers.

Huges de Payen realized that the real battle was roof top to rooftop. They would never successfully be able to do battle on the streets. What were his options? What could he do?

Then inspiration struck, Huges started to pull one of the ladders up. His men, having been with him a long time, didn't need to hear a command. They knew exactly what to do and started pulling other ladders up the wall. Once up, holding on to the bottoms of the ladders, they were dropped towards the roofs on the other side of the street allowing one end of the ladder to stay on the city way, and the other end to crash on the roof. Muslims, seeing the strategy, ran to their end of the ladder and started trying to throw it off the roof. But it was too little and too late. No sooner had the ladder landed on the roof; Huges de Payen's men started making their way across the ladder. The weight of the ladder plus the men on it, was offering too much resistance, and seeing there were too many ladders, would make it impossible for the Muslim soldiers to push all of them off successfully.

The Muslims only had the oil. They had no swords to fight with or arrows and rocks to throw at the Crusaders. They realized their impending defeat and they started to run from rooftop to rooftop towards safety.

Once across the ladder, Huges de Payen and his men went from roof top to roof top chasing the enemy. The hoards were in flight. It was only a matter of time before the city would be secured for the Christian heroes.

CHAPTER FOUR

The Order

Late Summer, 1119 AD, Jerusalem

After several days of intense fighting, the bodies of warriors on both sides filled the streets. But, in the end, the Crusaders successfully cleansed Jerusalem of the infidels and returned the city to Christian domination. But Huges de Payen felt somewhat defeated. He had lost nearly two-thirds of his trusted warriors by making the strategic error of entering the city through the gate. In his mind, he considered this the lowest type of treachery on the part of the hoards. However, he would also remember that tactic, and possibly use it himself at some future point.

With the battle won, it was now time for him to get to work on his true mission - the assignment given to him from the Pope. He had to identify four or five fellow Masons and with them he would need to search and find the hidden temple treasures. Unfortunately, only two of the five that he originally planned to select, were still alive. He only had ten remaining Masons to choose from. In a decision that would be a departure from the Pope's wishes Huges de Payen decided to include all the remaining Masons into this new order of the Knights Templar. However, he could not just bring them in without initiation ceremony. There had to be some rite of passage or becoming a Knight would seem insignificant.

Huges de Payen invented an elaborate ceremony, which included entering a newly dug grave, and then coming up out of the grave as a form or rebirth. This would commemorate the death and rebirth of Jesus Christ, considered the true leader of the knights. Then there would be swearing-in ceremony, which included an allegiance to the Pope, and a covenant of secrecy under penalty of death.

Huges de Payen developed his initiation ceremony. Then, he arranged for a secret meeting of all the ten remaining Masonic Crusaders. They met in the Garden of Gethsemane where Huges de Payen had built a small fire. The Crusaders sat around the fire in eager anticipation, not entirely sure why they were there. They quickly realized that they were all Masons and Huges de Payen reminded them of that fact as he began to explain the reason for being there. He started by having everyone repeat the Masonic oath of secrecy. In this way, the meeting would be bound to secrecy, even if they decided not to join the Knights.

Huges de Payen explained that the Pope had commissioned him, to accomplish a secret mission here in Jerusalem. He decided not to divulge to them what the mission was but only tell them that he was to organize and establish a special faction of the Masons; and that they would become known as the Poor Fellow-Soldiers of Christ, and of the Temple of Solomon. Their outward role would be to serve the protection of Christians coming to visit the Holy Land, however they would also have a clandestine role which only the initiated would have knowledge of. With this explanation he asked the Masonic Crusaders, who of them would be interested in becoming a part of his efforts. Almost, as if struck by lightning, all ten Masonic solders raised their swords as a sign of commitment. Percival, one of the more outspoken Crusaders, spoke for them all, when he said, "We have come all this way and fought many battles, all for the glory of the Church and in defense of the Pope, and Our Lord and Savior. We are here to serve the Lord in whatever way he demands. What do we need to do?"

Huges de Payen responded; "First I will need to perform an initiation ceremony for each of you, thereby entering you into the order of the Knights. To do this we will need to dig a grave in the potter's field; the very same field that was purchased with the blood money used by Judas to betray Christ."

"We will perform this ceremony in the potter's field because each of you will need to swear to a life of poverty. All that you come into possession of including if need be, your very lives, shall become the property of the Knights. Moreover, all, as needed for the good of the Church, the Pope, and the Order - shall share all. I will not explain any more to you, until the initiation is complete, and you are all sworn to secrecy within this new order."

The walk to the potter's field was not long, and as was often the case, local graveyard caretakers had already prepared and dug a grave, in readiness for its next tenant. The initiation proceeded along smoother than even Huges de Payen had planned. At the completion of the ceremony, Huges felt confident that these Knights were committed to the success of his mission.

"We will meet weekly, back at the same location in the Garden. Whosoever gets there first, should start a fire. We will need two of you to stand guard, in case of outsiders. We will take turns standing guard. We will meet every Sunday evening, starting next Sunday, when I will explain our mission and distribute the assignments necessary for the completion of the mission. Be prepared to go to work."

CHAPTER FIVE

The Search Plan
Late Summer, 1119 AD, Jerusalem

The first Sunday meeting found all ten Crusaders and Huges de Payen arriving early at the Garden in anticipation of what lay ahead. There had been a lot of speculation amongst the Knights. However, no one felt they could have had guessed the reason for their mission.

Huges de Payen started the meeting by having everyone repeat his oath of allegiance in unity, to serve as a reminder to each of them, that all these proceedings would need to be kept in strictest confidence.

"We are here tonight," started Huges de Payen, "to work together under the commission of the Holy Father, the Pope of Rome." Huges had learned that there were Popes in Alexandria, Cairo, Greece, and Istanbul, and possibly other locations. However, the Crusaders only recognized the Pope in Rome as having taken over the reins of the church from the Apostle Peter, who had received them from Christ. The Roman Pope was the one true leader of the Church of Christ. "The pope has asked us to locate and return to him the treasures of the temple of Solomon. After the temple was destroyed, the Temple Masons were prepared. They had built a secret, underground chamber that would be used to hide the treasures and keep them out of the hands of any infidels. Knowledge about this secret hiding place and how it could be located, was a privilege reserved only for Masons of the highest order. I am the first 33-degree Mason that has set foot in Jerusalem since the days of the Babylonian captivity. We know that the Babylonians did not successfully capture the Ark of the Covenant, or any of the other temple treasures. So, we assume they were successfully hidden."

"It is our assignment to find the Ark and the other treasures and return them to the Holy Father for safe keeping."

The Knights were in awe. It had never entered their mind that they would be looking to find the Ark of the Covenant. Everyone knew the stories, of how the Ark contained the Ten Commandments received by Moses, and how the Ark had the power to kill someone who was unworthy to touch it. And so, their feelings were mixed. Finding the Ark would be a great discovery. But then, what do they do with it? How do they transport it? Many questions would need to be considered as they began their search.

Huges de Payen started drawing a picture of the temple mound in the dirt. "The first problem we have is in identifying the exact location of the destroyed temple. Tradition tells us that it stood in the same location as the current Moslem Dome of the Rock. In fact, it is suggested, that the Dome of the Rock was built in this location so that the Jewish temple could not be reconstructed at that site."

"Then we tear it down," Percival blurted out.

"There is some doubt as to the truth of this location. It seems, in anticipation of the desecration of the temple sight, those who remained in Jerusalem who were expected to know the location of the temple, because of their linage and heritage, intentionally gave out false information about the exact temple location. They anticipated some form of discretion by infidels, who at that time were the Romans. Moreover, it turns out they were correct in their thinking. Except, they were focused on the wrong infidels."

"So where do you think the temple was located?"

Huges de Payen continued; "Why would the temple be located over a large rock outcropping? It does not make sense. It turns out that the Temple of Solomon was located at the other end of the temple mound. Ironically, earlier Moslem Masonic brothers left us with a small basilica to mark the center of the Holy of Holies. They also respected and held the Ark of the Covenant in awe, because of its reported military power, and they erected a small arched dome to mark the spot where the Ark of the Covenant rested in the Holy of Holies of Solomon's temple was built. Today this arch is referred to as the Dome of Spirits. Masonic tradition at the highest level teaches us that the basilica is where we should start our search. Not at the Dome of the Rock."

Christopher, another of the new Knights, had become intensely excited about the idea of a new secret order. He was not sure what the Knights Templar was all about, but just the idea of a new secret order under the commission of the Pope brought excitement and images of grandeur to his mind. He queried; "What clues are we hoping to find that will direct us towards what we are looking for?"

"At the time of the destruction of Jerusalem by the Babylonians, the 33rd degree Masons used a secret, underground tunnel to hide all the treasures of the temple, including, the Ark of the Covenant. We need to find this underground location and recover the treasures, especially the Ark, for the Pope. This will be more difficult than you think since no one has found any clues to an opening to this underground cavern."

"Can't we just go to the basilica and start digging?"

"We know that the Ark was in the center of the Holy of Holies, and so it would not be logical to have the cavern immediately under the Ark. However, I am sure it is somewhere close. Tomorrow two hours before dawn, when the least amount of people are awake; we will go to the Dome of Spirits and begin our search. I will meet all of you there at that time. Two of you will be selected as guards, and the rest of us will begin the search."

"Do we have any clues on what we are looking for?" questioned Christopher again.

"No idea at all!"

CHAPTER SIX

The Search Begins
Late summer, 1119 AD, Jerusalem

The morning was clear and beautiful, but quite chilly. There was no sign of rain, or anything else that would disrupt their search. The morning dew had blanketed the elevated temple grounds creating a layer of slipperiness on the cobblestone rock surface, and the Crusaders had to walk carefully. But there was something exciting in the air which couldn't be dampened by the cold. Everyone was filled with anticipation.

Huges de Payen placed two of the Masons on guard and instructed them to keep everyone from entering the mound area. Then he arbitrarily sectioned off the mound area, starting from the Basilica, and gave each of the remaining King's a piece of the mound. They were instructed to look for anything unusual; or something giving the appearance that a door or cavern had been formed.

The knights searched, carefully looking at each of the pavement rocks hoping to find something unusual. They scraped along the grooves. Then they bashed the tops of the rocks, hoping for a hollow sound. Nothing seemed to work. In a last, desperate attempt to find something unusual, Percival took a couple of the knights and found a long, straight log, cleared it of bark and knots, and made it perfectly round. He then tried rolling it along the surface of the temple mound. He was rewarded for his diligent efforts. An unusual pattern seemed to develop. There was a depression, very slight, and hardly noticeable, but with the straight log, it could be identified.

"Huges de Payen," he shouted out, "I think I found something."

Huges de Payen came running over to investigate. "Tell me more."

"The floor takes a dip here. Maybe the dip is the result of ground settling underneath, either from the entrance or possibly from the cavern itself."

"Excellent thinking Percival! I knew I could count on you to come up with something. Let's start at the lowest point and see if we can dig our way into the cavern".

Huges de Payen called a couple of the other Masonic knights over to help. They would work together to dig their way into the depression. However, it turned out to be harder than they originally envisioned. The pavement stones were extremely tightly fitted together and about six inches deep, therefore their attempts to use wedges and to pry the stones upward went unrewarded. However, it would be Percival who saved the day, once again. He ran off the temple mount in a rush, leaving Huges de Payen somewhat surprised by his actions, and returned a few minutes later with a hand stone masons drill.

"What are you planning to do with that?" asked Huges de Payen. "Drill your way into the cavern?"

"I'm going to drill a small hole at an angle at each end of one of these stones, and then use those holes to wedge up the first stone. Once the first stone is up, the others will be easy to pry up after that. It's just the first one that's the struggle." Percival explained and promptly forged ahead with his drilling efforts.

The drilling was slow at first. Stone was not easy to drill into. However, in time he successfully created two edge holes. Then, with the help of Bors, another one of the new Temple Knights, they were able to slowly, but surely, by using a lot of wiggling and shaking, raise the stone from its resting place.

"Once again Percival saves the day," came the cheerful and noisy response from several of the Knights.

With the first stone out, the knights continued removing stones until they had uncovered an area that approximated a three-foot circle. Then they all started digging. They had brought shovels in the hope that they would be doing some digging, and now the opportunity presented itself.

The ground was packed hard, after many years of walking, and from carrying the weight of the temple above it. Picks were used to loosen the ground, and shovels would remove it and pile it up next to the hole.

Anticipation was high. This had to be the right location. It was near the Basilica where the Temple holy-of-holies had been located. Everything seemed right. And the knights were confident of success.

Then a shovel hit something hard. "What's that?" asked Huges de Payen.

Further scraping and digging identified what appeared to be another stone surface. "Is it possible that the floor we're standing on isn't the first original floor? Is it possible that there is a second floor under the original floor of the temple?" Huges de Payen sounded frustrated, but undaunted.

"Well Percival, I guess you'll have to use your stone-mason's drill again to pry another stone free."

Percival was not to be discouraged. He dug away some additional dirt to give himself a circular two-foot work area, and he started using the drill. It was not long before he was ready to pry a second stone from its secure resting place. This time the stone came up a little easier, which at first seemed surprising. But then, as he looked at the stone, its sides seemed to be slightly cut into a wedge, with the top being wider than the bottom. It wasn't long before he realized what was happening and he yelled out with excitement, "This isn't another roadway. It is the ceiling of the cavern we're looking for. And the ceiling pieces are wedged together to form an arch. I think we may have found what we're looking for."

Discouragement at finding the second stone surface rapidly turned to excitement. More stones were quickly pried away until a circle of about 18 inches in size had formed. Huges de Payen lit a torch and threw it down into the opening. Looking down into the hole he was able to see that the cavern was about six foot high, and four foot wide. And, looking toward the end of the cavern, he sees treasures, golden candelabras, chalices, ornaments, ornamental stands, and more.

Percival, being the smallest of the group, would be the first to enter. Once inside he gave a report of his findings.

"This must be one of the storage areas for the treasures. Off to the side I see an access tunnel. I'm going to explore the tunnel to see what else I can find."

Percival went into the main tunnel. He followed the tunnel to the left and he could see where the tunnel turned upward which he assumed must have been the original access door. He turned around and started heading down the tunnel in the other direction. Poor lighting caused him to trip. Looking down he could see the remains of a man sitting at the side of the tunnel. He was a skeleton draped in rags. And scratched on the wall he could see their epitaph. "We saved the treasures of the temple and the Ark of the Covenant. But we did not know that once you came inside this cavern, and shut the door, there would be no escaping." The temple heroes had sealed the treasure secrets with their lives. Their signatures read; "Jelum, Barg, and Jeru."

By now Huges de Payen had also been lowered into the cavern and he had joined Percival. Going further down the cavern the two explorers came to another cavern storage area. But this time the cavern was empty. It looked as though someone had been digging and moving dirt from the area. It also looked as though looters had taken whatever treasure there may have been. "Why would looters take the treasure from here, but not from the other cave?" asked Huges de Payen. There did not seem to be a reasonable answer.

"The ledge at the end of this cavern is larger than the others. This may have been the resting place of the Ark of the Covenant." Walking into the cavern, the two noticed something lying on the ledge. It was a manuscript of some kind, written on old parchment paper. Picking it up Percival read out loud, "The Gospel according to Saint Mark."

"How is that possible? The Ark was put here nearly six-hundred years before the Gospel of Mark was written. Obviously, someone was down here and stole the Ark, and left us a message. But what could it possibly mean?"

CHAPTER SEVEN - PART 2

Random Act of Violence

Late March 2025 AD, Somewhere in the central Nevada desert

near Elko

"S1 is twenty-seven minutes from approach." It was Greg Tannen, a tall 6-foot 6-inch former Celtics pro basketball player that had the controls of the remote, unmanned Stealth-1 insurgence plane. The aircraft is less than three feet long with a wingspan of 10 feet. It was nearly invisible from the ground without binoculars, and completely hidden from radar. It utilizes the super quiet scramjet engines which can travel long distances at high speeds using very little fuel. The idea behind the scramjet propulsion system, or Supersonic Combustion Ramjet, is that the oxygen needed by the engine to initiate combustion is taken from the atmosphere as it passes through the vehicle. It doesn't use an onboard fuel tank except for takeoff. This allows the craft to be smaller, lighter, and faster. Scramjet speeds could reach fifteen to twenty times the speed of sound. For example, an eighteen-hour trip to Tokyo from New York City takes about two hours. This gives the S1 the capability to perform reconnaissance missions from anywhere to anywhere in the world using Google maps.

The S1 is equipped with a guided weapons system. It can fire from as far away as 3 miles using a variety of guided weapons, and it never misses its target. Today Greg has the S1 configured with a rifle for precision hits, and an S1-V8 missile which is only two inches thick but packs the wallop of twenty grenades. The human target won't see either of these coming until it is too late. And then, using the S1-V8, there will not be anyone left to tell the story. Not even the missile will remain. The casing and all the components are completely incinerated in the explosion, leaving no trace of its source.

Greg is a member of the IOM, which stands for International Order of Mercenaries. This is a fringe group from the historic organization previously known as the Templar Knights. Over the years, the Templars had become extremely wealthy. In an attempt by Kings and rulers to confiscate some of this wealth, the Knights were subjected to unwarranted image and physical attacks. In the end the Knights were disgraced and with their images unjustly tarnished. Eventually, the IOM knights evolved into what everyone branded them as, mercenaries. The Knights realized that their military skills had market value, and they made these skills available to the highest bidder. However, to differentiate the Knights involved with the IOM and to avoid mislabeling the non-IOM Knights, or from disrespecting their mother organization the Masons, they assumed the name IOM. Any member of the IOM had to first be a Knight, and any Knight must first be a Mason in good standing. Hence, members of the IOM were extremely elite.

Ironically, hardly anyone had ever heard of the IOM. Only key individuals, like heads of state, or captains of industry, who had the money to pay for their services, knew of their existence. And, whenever clandestine activities needed to be performed, or when total secrecy was important, the IOM was brought in to do what they did best.

Today's mission was such a mission. Hired by a rich banker family from the UK, the IOM had been tasked to eliminate a political leader in France who opposed the organization and operation of the Federal Reserve Bank of France. This politician had gone so far as to threaten that if he were to gain control of the political machinery, he would nationalize the nation's Federal Reserve Structure. And this brought chills to the bankers who enjoyed controlling the nation's money. They especially feared that a trend of this nature may catch on in other countries.

The Federal Reserve is an independent banking organization that is free from government regulation and which controls the nation's flow of money, holds most of the nation's debt, and controls interest rates. Anyone who opposes the Federal Reserve Bank, opposes a critical source of revenue for the Banks. And Barjet, the French politician who strongly opposed its existence had to be eliminated.

Greg did not care about the reasons or the politics. For him, this was just another job. And his team was the best. Greg was the handsome bachelor that all the girls considered a good catch. But he was the type of guy that was so involved in his work, that he would often miss the passes thrown his way. He loved being the "technical guru" of the IOM. But, unlike most "techies" he didn't dress down or grow a lot of hair on his face. He kept a military appearance, short hair, well groomed, polished shoes, and neatly pressed pants and shirt. He just liked it better that way. When he looked good, he felt good. And when he felt good, his attitude and his actions reflected it.

Greg was a self-made man. He grew up in a broken home, his mother deserting both him and his father to run off with another man. And he rarely saw her after that. His father was in the Air Force, which meant he moved about every two years. His father was stationed in numerous international locations. He had spent time in Germany, Korea, Guam, Alaska, and at several bases on the continental USA. Greg had come to enjoy the travel. Sadly, his father was killed in Iraq, and at age seventeen Greg was left on his own. He was an odd character. He was a sport's jock, because of his father's love of sports, and it was basketball that earned him the scholarships that would get him into the best schools and later onto a professional team. But at age seventeen he buried the sorrow of the loss of his father by diving into books, eventually getting degrees in Mathematics, Physics, and Electrical Engineering. He also became captivated by the secret societies that claimed intellectual superiority, like the Masons and the Rosicrucians. Eventually he settled on the Masons and drove himself to get as advanced as possible. He eventually became a 33rd degree Mason, referred to as the Templar Knight degree, the highest level achievable in the Masonic order. After this achievement he learned about the IOM, the secret order within the Knights Templar, and it became his personal mission to become a part of this group. After retiring from his basketball career, he focused on joining the IOM and eventually worked his way into becoming the lead researcher for the IOM. This role included flying the S1 since most if its missions were scientifically based. However today, the S1 would be an assassin's tool.

This would be a good day for an assassination. Barjet was scheduled to be outside, at a soccer stadium in Southern France near the Riviera. He was presenting his anti-banking message to a large, receptive audience.

The secret to a good assassination was not simply to eliminate the target, but more importantly, that someone else, like Al-Qaida or the Taliban, or possibly the Basque separatists, would be blamed. And the blame had to be credible and reasonable. This would be accomplished by dropping off some "residue." And the S1-V8 missile was designed to carry some "residue" for all its missions. In this case the residue was tell-tale materials left behind that would point a finger. The residue was an explosive trigger like one used in suicide bombings. And the trigger would, of course, contain the fingerprints of a French dissident who has disappeared --- this disappearance also being the earlier work of a separate IOM assignment. As a result, the authorities would be kept busy looking for someone who no longer existed.

"Twenty minutes to target," was Greg's update. Around him were his teammates, each glued to a pair of computer terminals. One terminal was for messages and instructions. The other allowed them to observe progress from a remote camera on the S1.

Greg had the controls that fly the S1. However, the autopilot programming, along with the mapping software, controlled most of the mission and flight activities. Only in the case of an emergency, or in the event of a last-minute change in plans, Greg would then take over the controls.

Dawn, working next to Greg, monitored the targeting and weapons launch systems. She was "built like an Ox," as Greg often said. She was trained as a US Navy Seal, and she had maintained her strength and build. Even though she was only 5' 11", she was a force to be reckoned with, and even Greg, with his 6' 6" frame, thought better of taking her on. But, despite her strength, she was soft spoken and very personable. And Greg enjoyed spending time with her off work as well as on.

Greg often referred to Dawn as being "her own kind of woman." She was independent and free thinking, but she was also wise enough to show sensitivity and dependence when it was appropriate. Her attitude was that there was "a time to lead and a time to be led," and that an individual needed to know how to succeed in either environment.

Dawn had met Greg several years back when Greg was about fifteen and his father was stationed at Hickam AFB in Hawaii, and Dawn was stationed at Pearl Harbor. The two bases shared facilities, and the active-duty personnel would often visit each-other's restaurants or recreation facilities. Dawn was about ten years older than Greg, but he was always extremely impressed with her and they had become good friends. By the time Greg joined the IOM, Dawn had put in her twenty years with the Navy and was ready for retirement. So, when the need came up in the IOM to find someone with both the toughness of a seal and with highly developed analytical skills, Greg thought immediately about Dawn.

Approaching Dawn had to be done carefully. Greg had to ask her about her specific employment interests after her retirement. He told her that he had a need for her specific skills, but that there was a lot of secrecy involved, and that she would need to become a part of a clandestine secret society. Rather than becoming discouraged, Dawn became intrigued. She wanted to know more. And Greg was excited to explain as much as he could without breaking the bonds of secrecy. Eventually Dawn became initiated and trained, and now she was Greg's right hand "woman."

The other teammate on the S1 flying team was Alan, who monitored the surrounding communications systems and networks to make sure there were no surprises. They insisted on avoiding detection. If detected, they would immediately abort the mission. Alan was the true techie-geek of the group. He was an information manipulation genius. And much to the dismay of those around him, he looked the role as well. He lived in a baseball cap, wore glasses, and had the token pocket protector in his shirt pocket where he kept his mechanical pencils. But his abilities had salvaged many a mission, and Greg and Dawn greatly respected these abilities.

Alan got involved in the IOM through his father. His father was a 33rd degree Mason, and he wanted his son to follow in his footsteps. Eventually Alan also became and 33rd degree Mason. That is when he learned about the IOM and he, like Greg, wanted to get involved. But he was not the James Bond type and initially the IOM was hesitant to accept him into their fold. However, Greg emphasized his organization's need to get a computer geek onto his team, and he eagerly brought Alan on board.

"15 minutes."

"Mission hold," Alan blurted out. This meant that he had heard something that may influence the mission, but not necessarily abort it. "I just received communication that Barjet didn't make it to the stadium. He is still en route. Our timing will need to be reset."

"What do you recommend?" asked Greg.

"Let's go up to fifty-thousand feet and circle until we know for sure he's there," suggested Dawn.

"I don't like that," came from Greg. "This area is high in air traffic. We'll get detected."

"If we get detected, then we abort. But let's at least try to wrap this up today. We may not get this good an opportunity for quite some time."

"Good enough." Greg took control and banked the S1 into a near vertical climb until he reached the desired altitude. Then he maneuvered the S1 into a circle around the Riviera.

Then suddenly Greg blurted out; "What's going on? My cameras went completely blank. I've lost visual and all my other sensors as well. It's as if the S1 completely disappeared from existence."

Alan went to work, performing his magic. Using satellites, he zoomed in on a visual of the area where the S1 was last reported. "There's a small airplane right in the vicinity where we were flying the S1." Using altitude detection sensors, Alan quickly estimated the flying altitude of the small aircraft. "And it's at the right height. I wonder if it crashed into us."

"I would have received some kind of indication if that was the case, like a free fall, or some noise. But not just total, sudden emptiness," blurted Greg, showing frustration in his voice. "This is really strange."

Suddenly and unexpectedly a message popped up on all three of their terminals: "THANKS FOR THE PRESENT. IF YOU WANT IT BACK, REPLY TO THIS MESSAGE. WE NEED TO MEET!"

CHAPTER EIGHT

Response

Late March, 2025 AD, South of Alice Springs, Australia

Pine Tree Gap is a six story (all underground) complex in the Australian desert, just south of the Alice Springs airport. This is the headquarters of the IOM. The lowest level is reserved for IOM leadership. This level included an office area, agricultural / food storage, generators, and housing. Everything required in case the IOM team needed to stay underground for up to six months.

An urgent message had come from Greg that the S1 had been hijacked and that the Barjet mission had failed. This news was creating quite a stir.

"We can't respond to ultimatums, blurted Malvika Mishra from across the desk in his office. "That would be an admission of guilt." Malvika was the IOM director general. He was about 6 foot tall, with normally a relaxed demeanor. But he was upset at the idea that their operations had somehow been infiltrated.

Malvika had a strong looking face with fierce eyes. He had a slight tint to his skin. He was trusted and respected as the leader of the IOM order of the Templar Knights, and as the indisputable leader of all IOM activities. He was in his fifties with a head that was bald on the top and had signs of gray around the sides.

Malvika was a lifer, or at least it seemed that way. He had been in the IOM longer than anyone else on the team, and to the team it felt like he was the IOM.

"But we can't let them get away with this either. And if we don't respond, we may never know who they are." This time it was Elliott Schaffer, director of IOM operations. He was slightly taller than Malvika, but this didn't minimize the powerful influence Malvika generated simply with his presence. "I'd like to know how they tapped into our communication systems. How much do they know about us?"

Elliott was about 6' 1" in height, and in his mid-forties. He knew the IOM operations better than anyone, even Malvika. Elliott was the type of leader everyone loved. He was kind and personable, yet firm. When he made a decision, the debate was over and everyone on the team focused on execution.

Like many members of the IOM, Elliott didn't have any immediate family. He had joined the Masons because a college buddy had convinced him that the social order and the internal connections of the Masons would be beneficial for his career development. Elliott was an only child, and his parents had been killed in an airliner crash. Elliott had been married once, but he lost his wife to a car accident. And he didn't have any children. He had developed a strong bond with his wife. She was the eternal companion that he always dreamed of. Her loss affected him greatly. It bothered him that only a few days after her death he was receiving dinner invitations, and social invitations of all types from every single female he knew. He felt like all the unmarried women of the world, and some married, were after him as soon as they learned about his wife's death. And he wasn't in the mood to replace her. He just wanted to remember her. He wanted a chance to mourn. And he resented the meat-market approach to relationships. For him, the Masons became an escape from the complicated social relationships that dating created. The Masons were a relief. Eventually he worked his way to the 33rd degree and, like most others in the IOM, he became fascinated by this organization and its function.

"They've captured the S1 and they were able to break into our communications network. Apparently, they know way too much about us! What do you think?" Malvika had turned to the third person in his office, Stefanie Temple, "Stef" to her friends. Stef was the one that brightened everyone's day. She had the unique combination of being good looking and not knowing it. Her long blond hair and deep eyes acted like a vacuum, sucking up the attention of anyone she talked to. She was a breath of fresh air in this primarily all-boys club. Rarely was a female allowed to work with the Knights Templar brotherhood, but she was an exception. But Elliott and Malvika both knew, given the assignment, she could be ruthless. She wasn't in the IOM by accident. She was an invaluable asset. And Elliott liked having her around as his right-hand-person.

Stef had been brought into the Masonic order by her parents, who were both active in their branches of the Masonic order. Stef, being female, joined Job's daughters with her mother, and became a dominant figure within her organization. She became recognized for her abilities within the Masonic organization, and soon came to the attention of Malvika. He felt there were specific areas where her female talents would be extremely useful. After many meetings and discussions, Malvika opened to Stef and asked her if she was interested in joining the IOM. She eagerly accepted the invitation and has been an integral part of its operations ever since.

Stef had degrees in Sociology and Psychology. She also had an interest in martial arts and had become a master black belt in several art forms. But she wasn't pushy. She had a deep knowledge about relationships and how to optimize performance. But she didn't drive her opinions on anyone. Elliott found her non-forceful approach very refreshing. Initially he used her as a go-for, but soon found out she was much too talented for that role. He brought her into more and more of his operational activities, until today they worked together; so closely that they seemed "connected at the hips." Finally, there was a single woman who had gotten close to Elliott, and he actually enjoyed it. Probably because she didn't have the same agenda most of the other single women in Elliott's life had possessed. Stef just wanted to do her job, and do it well, and wasn't interested in catching the man.

"First we respond," recommended Stef. "Then we destroy them. But we also need to rebuild and tighten up our security. In fact, I think we should start revamping our security immediately. They don't need to know about it. We need to identify and cover up the holes."

"I guess I've been outvoted," said Malvika. "Send Greg a message to respond and have him link all communications here to us so that we can monitor the activity and take control of the conversation. Also, set up some kind of tracking system so we can identify the source of the messages." Malvika was exceedingly stubborn to where he ignored the advice of those around him. But security penetration caused him a great deal of concern.

Elliott immediately typed the message to Greg in his hand-held Blackberry. His second message was to the IT tech support group that told them that all messages from and to Greg's terminal should immediately be displayed on the video conferencing display screen in Malvika's office. It was a matter seconds, and the display was on the screen. From half-way around the world in an office in the center of the desert of Australia, three people watched as Greg, in the middle of the Nevada desert, finished typing his response.

Elliott's third text message was to the satellite tracking and support team. This would be a little more challenging, but he asked them to drop everything and try to identify the source of the messages coming into Greg.

It was only a matter of seconds before a response to Greg appeared on the screen in Australia.

"RESPONDING IS A WISE CHOICE. WE WANTED TO CHECK YOUR VULNERABILITY AND SECURITY. AND WE FOUND YOU TO BE VERY CHALLENGING, BUT NOT IMPENETRABLE. WE ASSUME THIS WEAKNESS WILL BE PLUGGED AND WE WILL NOT BE ACCESSING YOU THROUGH THIS COMMUNICATION METHOD IN THE FUTURE. WE NEED TO SET UP A BETTER METHOD TO COMMUNCATE.

BUT, ON TO OUR REASON FOR THIS INTRUSION. WE HAVE A GLOBAL MISSION. TO COMPLETE THIS MISSION, WE NEED THE POWER OF GOD ON OUR SIDE. AND WE NEED YOU TO HELP US ACCESS THIS POWER. SUGGEST A TIME WHEN WE CAN TALK DIRECTLY."

"What's this 'Power of God' stuff that this guy wants? Is he nuts?" was Elliott's response after reading the message.

"I'm intrigued," replied Malvika.

Elliott also received a text message on his mobile from the satellite communications people; "This message is coming from a rapidly moving object, probably on an airplane, somewhere over the mid-Atlantic." Elliot relayed the news to his colleagues.

"For now, let's keep all communication through Greg and assume that he is their only point of contact," suggested Stef. "Have Greg set up a phone bridge that we can link into. Let's have a talk with this guy and see what's behind all this." She looked across the desk for approval.

A quick nod from Malvika triggered a text message from Elliott to Greg, and Malvika's conference screen lit up with Greg typing his response to the intruders; "How do we contact you?"

The response from the intruders seemed instantaneous. "CALL 01-530-233-9751 AND CONNECT WITH BRIDGE 1234. I AM RELEASING YOUR S1. IT'S NOT TOO LATE FOR YOU TO COMPLETE YOUR MISSION."

"I'm sending a text message to Greg to let us know if the S1 is on its way to the target, and to complete his mission," Elliott commented. "He should let us know immediately if it is successfully completed. No need for Greg to be on this call. This is something the three of us in this office will need to handle."

Malvika had a secure line, which linked directly outside of the complex, and after a few satellite exchanges, calls were made to look like they were coming from somewhere in Mongolia. This line was purposely set up specifically for communications outside of the IOM. He dialed the number just as Elliott finished typing up his message to Greg. Malvika put the call on speaker phone and waited.

A voice started speaking; "Hello my friends. My name is Kres Brokard. I am the neo-Fuhrer, the leader of the NNRL which stands for Neo-Nazi Romarian League. Who am I talking to?"

Malvika appropriately took the lead in the conversation. "We are Hewey, Dewey, and Louie. We are curious about your methods and approach. What do you hope to achieve by using these cloak and dagger methods?"

"Please don't play games with me. I trusted you with my name. Please give me yours. I know about the IOM. But I did not know how to contact you. I have observed your activities, especially with the S1, and now I am soliciting your help. Our mission is a serious one. We are re-inventing the New World Order, with an emphasis on the word Order. We will be the savior of the world in a millennial state. We are installing a better form of world-wide government. Our last Fuhrer, who you know as Hitler, recently died. Don't act surprised. The cover-up surrounding his supposed suicide was cleverly faked. And we have had him in hiding ever since, mostly because he has been seriously afflicted with disease. He was hoping to recover and was waiting for the right moment to take over. He was counting on another World War where he could step in as the returning leader. But now he is gone. And we of the NNRL who remain behind are not as patient as he was. It is time for us to force the issue."

Malvika jumped in, "What's all this about the Power of God?"

Kres responded with a question; "I am a 33-degree Mason, are you?"

"Yes, but there are others in the room that are not."

"Please ask them to leave." Stef knew the rules, and she respected them. She didn't need to be asked. She stood up and headed for the office door. Elliott's eyes were glued to her as he watched her stand up and walk to the door. Stef had long hair, down to the center of her back. Unfortunately, she usually had it tied up in a bun or a ponytail. Today was not one of those days. And her hair looked perfect, clean, and straight, the type of hair that made other ladies jealous. And Elliott couldn't take his eyes off of her. He loved how she looked when she "let her hair down." And he loved to watch her. It was challenging not to be too obvious.

Malvika let out a fake cough trying to get Elliott's attention, and then gave Elliott a sly smile as Stef left the office, closing the door behind her. "She's hot!" was Elliott's whispered comment as he turned his attention back to Malvika and the phone call.

At times Stef resented being excluded, but she told herself that she knew all this when she joined the IOM. If she didn't like it, she had no one to blame but herself. She chose this life, and now she would live it despite the exclusions. And besides, she loved the excitement - and there was plenty of it.

Kres, on hearing the door shut, continued; "Who is left in the room?"

"My name is Malvika, and I am here with Elliott."

"33-degree Masons know of the treasure that was hidden on temple mount in Jerusalem. They also know that when the original Knights Templar uncovered those treasures, they found that the Ark of the Covenant was missing. It had obviously been there. The signs in the underground cavern are undeniable. And the Masons that had hidden it there were still entombed in the cave. But when the Knights went in to recover the Ark, it was gone. And there was no sign of how the Ark was removed. Not even a sign of how they were able to enter the cave."

"Yes. We know all this history. But please connect the dots. Why are we going through all this stealth?"

"Because I need the Ark of the Covenant to complete my plan. I need the Power of God that comes with the Ark. The power to win all battles. And your organization, because you are both Masons and Knights, is the only organization that can help me in this quest. You have more knowledge about this history than anyone. You are the Knights, and you have the history and the documentation that describe the hiding and the attempted recovery of the Ark."

Malvika was not impressed; "That's not normally the type of work we engage in. Our slogan is 'Effective and Expeditious Problem Elimination.' Not treasure hunting."

Late March, 2025 AD, Somewhere in the Southern France

Barjet was angered by all the traffic delays. He was late and he hated being late. His chauffeur drove him around the back side of the stadium on which he was to make his speech. After the customary security check, Barjet was driven directly to the steps leading to the stage on which his podium stood waiting for him. He got out of the vehicle and started hurrying up the stairs which caused him to slightly stumble. He quickly recovered and made it to the podium without any further mishaps.

There was someone at the podium offering excuses for the delay. Upon seeing Barjet approaching he excitedly exclaimed; "The man you have all been waiting for has arrived. Let me give you Barjet."

Barjet apologized for the unavoidable delay in his arrival and started in on his presentation. He was ten minutes into the talk when, looking up high, he spied something which looked like a small bird sparkling off in the distance. But it couldn't be a bird because it reflected light.

Barjet didn't spend any time considering this strange bird. He looked down at his notes and continued with his speech. This was important material and it had to be made public. The country was counting on him.

But these were to be the last words he would utter, as he suddenly felt a sharp pain about his right shoulder. Looking down he was shocked to find not only his shoulder, but his entire arm, and a large part of his chest were missing. Then he collapsed.

Late March, 2025 AD, Alice Springs, Australia

Back at Pine Tree Gap Elliott received a text message from Greg; "Barjet mission satisfactorily completed. Messenger returning home." He passed his hand-held over to Malvika to read.

Kres continued speaking, unaware that the message was being passed between Elliot and Malvika; "I know this is not a normal mission for a group of assassins. But there is no one else I can turn to for help. The secrecy of the mission is paramount. And I have the resources to pay you well."

Elliott responded, "We will need to discuss this internally before I can respond. How do I get back in touch with you?"

"Every day, at this same time, the phone bridge will be open. Please get back to me as soon as possible."

"We will respond. By the way, what did you do to our remote plane? How were you able to capture it?"

"We had a small agricultural plane with a trap door underneath, and we opened our 'bomb bay' doors. We simply dropped our plane over the top of the fuselage and left the wings spread out on either side. It took some tricky flying, and we couldn't do it at too low an altitude, so I had to send out the message that Barjet's arrival was delayed, hoping that you would do exactly what you did. Then, we followed your S1, and at the appropriate moment, we did a Star Wars move of dropping over the top of it. Once captured we were able to jam all communications signals coming from and to the S1. We quickly tracked the signal frequency that the S1 was sending out and we used this same frequency to send out our initial messages to you."

"Very ingenious. Can I ask why you are coming to us, when you seem to have the technology and capabilities to search for the Ark on your own?"

"We have technology, but we do not have the Masonic insight that only the Knights have. We need your wisdom. We need your historical documents. We need your journals and whatever else you may have that will help in tracking and finding the Ark."

"Fair enough. We will respond as soon as possible."

The line went dead and Malvika and Elliott stared at each other in disbelief. Malvika spoke first, "We are Knights, sworn to protect the treasures of the temple. And this guy wants to hire us to find the Ark and turn it over to a bunch of Nazis so they can use the Power of God to start another World War. In my best day I couldn't even dream up something as crazy as that. He knows we are Knights. Why would he even ask us to betray ourselves like this?"

But Elliot expressed a slightly different concern. "I'm worried that if we don't join in with them on this hunt, they may go to another source, or maybe even try to find the Ark themselves. Wouldn't it be better if we kept control of the situation by pretending to go along with this scheme? And, if we in fact found the Ark, then we would be able to snatch it up before these crazies got a hold of it."

Malvika gave him a sly look; "I know I kept you around for a reason. That's genius. You're completely right, Elliott, we need to keep this situation under our wing to control it. But you realize that we're going to have to keep tight control of it within our organization as well. This is 33-degree Mason information and should not be disseminated. I'm thinking that you, although it's been a long time since you were out in the field, should personally take on this mission."

That's exactly what Elliott was thinking as well. He had a couple of his own motivators. One was to find out who these guys were so he could eliminate them. And the other was the thrill of finding the Ark -- a Knight's dream. But he suppressed his excitement in his response; "Of course, I'll do whatever needs to be done, for the sake of the order."

"Then it's settled. I'll leave it in your hands. You join the bridge tomorrow and take control of this mission. Go find us the Ark. And while you're at it, find out as much as you can about these guys. Where are they headquartered? How big are they? And what are their goals? We also need to know how these guys tapped into our security system. We're going to have to revamp the whole thing to make sure this type of break-in doesn't happen again."

"And Stef?"

"Of course, she should be involved. I'll leave it to you to decide how much to tell her and what not to tell her. It seems you can't make a move without her any more anyway. I have to wonder if there isn't more than just a working relationship here."

"NEVER!" was Elliott's smirked response.

CHAPTER NINE

NNRL

Late March, 2025 AD, Somewhere 35,000 feet over the Atlantic

"Those guys can't be trusted," grumped Kres Brokard the Neo-Nazi son of Hitler, after getting off the phone. "Right now those IOM guys are scheming how they're going to take my money, find the Ark, and then keep it away from me. But I need them to help me, both in finding the Ark and in our bigger mission. I need them to sell me one of the nuclear detonators that they took from the United States Air Force. We have a bigger mission here than just finding the Ark. And we have a deadline. I want to celebrate my father's birthday in Washington DC. I want April 20 to be a date that no one will ever forget.

"Additionally, my father was always obsessed with the Ark. He believed that if he had the Ark he couldn't lose. And I've heard it so long that he has me convinced as well. I want the Ark. I'll need to stay one step ahead of the IOM the whole time. And then, at the last minute, I'll get to it first."

Kres was a short five foot six, and slightly overweight. He had the look and demeanor of Hitler. In fact, Kres was Adolph Hitler's son and heir, but he had changed his last name to hide the relationship. He was proud of his father, but he found that the "Hitler" last name raised too many questions. He had taken on the personal goal of finishing what his father couldn't finish. He was going to "one-up" his father. He was going to create a one-world order under his dictatorship, ruled by the superior Aryan bloodline. And, like his father before him, Kres believed that the Ark held the key to successful world domination. The Ark held a power of victory. Just like the Jews of Joshua, Saul, and David's time, Kres planned to use the power of the Ark to defeat his enemies. Whoever controlled the Ark, controlled the Power of God. And he was convinced that the reason his father had failed was because he had gone into battle without it.

Kres was talking to Rohit, his right-hand man, who had also been listening in on the call. "You're right, like always," confirmed Rohit. "And we may have to eliminate those Knights when this is all over. But for now, we need their knowledge." Rohit was the perfect specimen of tall, blonde, Aryan perfection. However, unlike the stereotypical images of a "dumb blonde," Rohit was extremely intelligent and highly creative in solving problems.

"Look, Kres, we know that that the Ark went missing during the Babylonian invasion of Jerusalem. And we suspect that the Knights Templar had something to do with the disappearance. But that's about all we know at this point. Your father tried to find the Ark without the help of the Templars, but that turned out to be a wild goose chase. I know you joined the Masons so that you could learn their secrets, but the only secret you learned was that we need to work with the knights to finish this search. We now know that without the Templars, we're out of luck. For all we know, the Templars already have the Ark and are hiding it."

"On the phone call it didn't sound like they have it. It's possible that the Templars are hiding the Ark from their own people. But I doubt that. They would proudly share their success within their organization. I don't think they know where it is. But let's keep our ears and eyes opened so that there are no surprises."

Just then a message came in on Kres' Blackberry from the IOM. "What the . . . . ? How did those guys get my contact information? Rohit, we have to find out how they broke through my security. This is bad.

"Anyway, the message says that they're ready to meet. Elliott, who was on the phone call, wants to get together for a face-to-face at some neutral location as soon as possible. I'm going to have him suggest a location." Kres started typing on his Blackberry. "But we really need to figure out this security breach. I can't maintain the upper hand if I think that they're tracking our activities".

Kres finished typing his location request, and it seemed almost instantaneous when he received a response back. "Cairns, Australia."

Kres started typing his acceptance and requested a specific location and time. Simultaneously he instructed Rohit; "Have the pilot divert our flight. It looks like we're visiting the Great Barrier Reef. Then come back so we can discuss strategy. We need to make sure we play this game to our advantage."

CHAPTER TEN

Report In

Late March, 2025 AD, CIA Headquarters, Langley, Virginia

The phone rang on Marcello Zuniga's desk. He had been with the agency twenty-one years and was quickly getting tired of the bureaucracy. There had to be more to life than shuffling papers for Washington. And what's worse, the American public considered the CIA a parasite, constantly giving bad intelligence to the Washington leadership. The media is still harping about the missing "weapons of mass destruction" in Iraq. The general outcry was that the CIA should be disbanded.

But habit kicked in for Marcello and he answered the phone. "Agent Zuniga here. How can I help you?"

"Agent Sigma-6-Sigma reporting in."

For Zuinga, this was a call he enjoyed getting. A little cloak and dagger always made the day more exciting. "Codeword Snoopy, Respond."

"Phi-Beta-Kappa," was the coded response. Both sides of the call had to make sure who they were really talking to.

"Go ahead Sigma-6-Sigma."

"The IOM has just received a request from the NNRL for mercenary assistance. They want them to find and extract the Ark of the Covenant."

Zuniga wasn't sure what he was hearing. He had to check and make sure. "Are you talking about the Ark that Moses hauled across the desert?"

"That's the one."

Marcello thought for a moment. Stalin and Hitler both wanted the Ark. Both felt that it had some kind of supernatural power. Is it possible that another major clandestine, destructive group was once again out to "rule the world?" Marcello responded, "There has to be more to this than meets the eye. Keep your ears open. We know very little about the NNRL and this may be our chance to learn more. This could be big. Report out every step of the way."

"Will do;" and the line went dead.

Marcello, who was the head of the Task Force on Mercenary Activities (TFMA), immediately set up a meeting of his task force members, and he invited the members of the Task Force of Right Wing Revolutionaries (TFRWR) to attend as well. Truth was, he didn't know anything about this NNRL group and perhaps the "Right-Wingers," as they were often referred to, knew a little more.

Marcello opened up Microsoft Outlook and tried to set up the meeting. It would be over one week before the two teams would be able to meet and there was no way to speed this up without pushing the meeting request up to higher authorities. And driving this request up the food chain would earn him grief, especially if the purpose of the meeting turned out to be nothing. Bureaucracy strikes again. Marcello hoped that a meeting one week out would be soon enough.

CHAPTER ELEVEN

To Cairns

Late March, 2025 AD, Alice Springs and Cairns, Australia

Walking down the hall, Elliott's office was the first office on the right, and Stef's office was the second on the right, immediately next to Elliott's. There was a door connecting Elliott and Stef's offices, since Stef was Elliott's right-hand "man."

Elliott felt embarrassed that Stef had to leave Malvika's office earlier, but "rules were rules." Stef was not yet a 33rd degree Mason and she had to leave when 33rd degree business was being discussed. In the United States Stef, being female, couldn't become a Mason. However, the IOM followed the European, and primarily British rites, which accept females into Masonic ranks.

As Elliott entered Stef's office she spoke first; "I'll bet that Nazi's still reeling about us coming up with his Blackberry contact information. I would have loved to see his face."

Elliott responded, "Thanks for helping me with that. It evens the playing field a little bit. He needs to know that he's not the only kid on the block with technology. We're masters at surveillance and monitoring as well. I want to place us on an even keel, so that he doesn't think he has the power to manipulate us."

"I think you accomplished that just fine," came from Stef as Elliott shut the door and sat down in a chair across from her desk. "So, what's next?" she continued.

The executive offices at the Pine Tree Gap center were more than offices, they were homes away from home. In the back of each office was a door leading to a small apartment, similar to an upper-class hotel room, which included a small kitchenette, a bathroom, and of course a place to sleep. And for Stef and Elliott, neither of which was married, this hotel room was used more often than their downtown apartments in Alice Springs. Often, they would spend the evening together in the same office quarters. They tried to keep this as secret as possible, attempting to avoid the gossip stream. But office gossip was unavoidable, and everyone seemed to know that Stef and Elliott were "an item," even if Stef and Elliott pretended not to be.

Both of them had travel bags that were ready at a moment's notice. Their lifestyles were filled with last minute schedule changes. Their assignments were often "urgent." And they had to be ready at a moment's notice.

"I'm taking you on an island vacation for a few days," Elliott explained. "We're going to Cairns for a little fun in the sun. I'll update you on the way."

"Excellent. I love the beach and the barrier reef." Stef could read between the lines. They were meeting with the NNRL in Cairns and they had to leave immediately.

Stef grabbed her travel bag and followed Elliott to his office next door. Generally, Elliott was the gentlemanly type, letting the lady go first, but Stef liked "her man" to lead occasionally. That's the only way she would get a chance to check out his cute little butt. Elliott grabbed his bag and the two headed down the hallway towards the elevator, ready to go to the airport. They walked toward the center of the complex where the elevators were located. Being on the 6th floor (numbered downwards) meant that they would need to travel the full height of the complex. But this was a short trip on the complex's high-speed elevators and they soon found themselves on the surface. This put them in the false warehouse which was the only indication of any civilization in this remote desert spot. The area was surrounded by nothing but brush and scrubby looking trees, and of course, lots of dust.

From the warehouse they were able to catch a ride with one of the company's shuttle drivers conveniently disguised as a local taxicab.

For the most part, this area of Australia was a desolate desert. It was flat and dusty, punctuated by large dry hills that the Aussies' called mountains. From the sky the hills line up parallel to each other and look like a parade of caterpillars. They had vertical grooves along the sides of the hill, caused by the heavy downpours that would occasionally hit the area. These surges of rain were often followed by long, dry spells. The dry spells caused the ground to become extremely dusty. Occasionally a wind would come blowing across the desert plains and would percolate the earth into enormous dust storms.

Pine Tree Gap was an IOM complex specifically built south of Alice Springs because of its remoteness. This location offered seclusion while still offering easy access to an airport that could handle small jets. It was separated from civilization enough to avoid suspicion as the headquarters of the IOM. Building the entire complex underground added to its seclusion.

Pine Tree Gap was separated from Alice by one of the large, caterpillar-like hills, which kept it removed and of little interest to the people living in Alice. The entire city of Alice was on the north side of this hill, and only the airport was on the south side. The main road between the two locations travelled around the West end of the hill.

Alice Springs is a small town with a remote, country atmosphere. It maintains its culture and ambience of a country town, thousands of miles away from any major metropolis. But it still attracted a continuous flow of tourists visiting the area. The major attraction in the middle of this forsaken desert were the opal mines and Ares Rock, rename Uluru.

Walking the streets of Alice is a walk through Australian history, where Aboriginals seemed to be a predominant part of the population, and where the stores focused on selling opals from the Opal mines, the animal furs, and excursions into the bush.

Travelling around Alice a tourist is barraged by numerous offers of camel rides. Camels were introduced into the Australian desert for their ability to endure long periods without water. On these rides you learn about ranches which are thousands of acres in size, larger than some countries. And you encounter an endless barrage of flies. At times you feel like you're carrying your weight in flies.

Also, in Alice you find an endless number of shops selling hand carved bowls made from tree bark, handmade spears, boomerangs which are indigenous to Australia's North West, but which are now sold everywhere, and of course the didgeridoo, a hollowed-out tree trunk which is used as a musical instrument. The didgeridoo wasn't known to the native Aboriginals until recently. Apparently, an Aboriginal who was out on a "walk-about" (a long excursion into the outback which may last months) was sitting next to a tree and heard the whistling of a hollow tree trunk. His curiosity caused him to play with the trunk and he found that by blowing across the end of the trunk he could duplicate the sound. He carved the sides of the trunk and created a musical instrument, which today, is falsely advertised as something that has been a part of Aboriginal heritage since the dawn of time.

Elliott and Stef enjoyed the remoteness of Alice Springs. Even though they were both born and raised in the United States, they had been in Australia long enough to call it home. Their Aussie passport may be fake, but their love for the place was real. Besides, Elliott had warrants out for his arrest in the United States, and he didn't want to venture back to his home country until the warrants were resolved.

The IOM had facilities all over the world, many of them in similar remote locations like Alice Springs. For example, Greg's research facility was located in the Nevada desert near Elko. The IOM organization was large and far-reaching, made up of about seventy assassins and twice as many researchers and assistants. The entire team had their equivalent of high-level security clearances. The key to a successful organization of this caliber was to build it on a foundation of trust. And because every member was a High Degree member of the Masonic order, this trust is assumed to have already been established.

As Elliott and Stef stepped outside of the warehouse, they found that it was dark, which IOM team members preferred. The IOM used the Alice Springs airport for their travels, but the rule was that company planes stay in their hangers during the day. If you must travel during the day, you use commercial airlines. But at night, when the commercial traffic at the airport was minimal, the company planes were always available.

The IOM taxi drove the three mile drive down the dirt driveway and out onto the main road. They kept the driveway looking rugged and abandoned hoping to discourage trespassers. But they would still get the occasional intruder.

The Stuart Highway ran north-south through the center of Australia. The airport was a short drive along the highway. The taxi pulled out on the highway heading north. Getting there took less than ten minutes. And their plane was ready and waiting for them as they arrived.

The private company jet had twenty seats, each of which could be completely reclined into a comfortable bed. Stef and Elliott picked seats across from each other and prepared for a couple hours of shut eye.

Initially the take-off seemed fine. But suddenly, shortly after they left the ground, the plane was hit by one of the many severe dust storms that come through the area. Storms of this type were rare in the middle of the night, but not unusual. Having them hit at night made them exceptionally serious, because they were not visible to the pilot. These storms were capable of bringing down a plane, and pilots would normally stay on the ground and wait them out if they saw one coming. But this storm was a total surprise as it hit the plane shortly after take-off.

The plane sputtered and surged sporadically. Stef wasn't thrilled about flying anyway, and jerky flights were the primary reason. She was capable of doing physical, one-on-one battle with the biggest and the best, but she preferred to keep her feet firmly planted on the ground where she felt in control. She could drive a car competitively with the best of them, but then she felt in control. Being in the air made her feel helpless. And the jerky flight put her into a minor panic.

She reached across the seats, grabbed Elliott's arm, and started to squeeze. Elliott was used to this type of reaction from her. He knew it was coming. Normally Elliott was able to deal with a little pain, but this was more than a little. Just then the plane dropped for what seemed like an eternity. Then, suddenly, the plane had a power surge, took control, and resumed its climb.

Elliott felt like Stef was going to break his arm. But looking into her eyes he knew that this was not the time to complain. Right now, Stef needed his arm more than he did. And hopefully circulation would come back after she let go.

After 10 minutes which felt like an eternity, the plane seemed to settle down to normal flight. "We must be above the dust storm," Elliott suggested.

"I sure hope so," Stef agreed. But she wasn't ready to let go of his arm just yet.

The pilot got on the speaker and, apologizing for the turbulence, said: "Sorry about that, mate. That was a totally unexpected sandstorm, or we would have waited it out. But once we were committed to the air, it's better to ride it out than to try to circle around and land in the storm. Landing could be even riskier. The storm cost us a little power in one of our engines. But we should have no problem meeting the schedule to Cairns. Then we'll need to check out the engine before we can return. Anyway, the rest of the flight should be reasonably smooth."

"I can't tell if that was good news or bad," quivered Stef as she eased off on her grip. "I could sure do without another experience like that. I hope the damage to the engine won't affect any more of the trip."

"Don't worry. I'll protect you," responded Elliott as he rubbed his sore arm. But Stef wasn't so sure about his ability to protect her from bad weather and from having the plane drop out of the sky.

It took a lot longer to relax Stef than it took to get her nervous. But after about 15 minutes, Elliott had her calm and they both relaxed and grabbed their current novel, Stef with Cussler, and Elliot with Crichton. It would be several hours before they were back on solid ground.

It wasn't long before Stef was snoring. It was inevitable. Whenever Stef tried to read laying down, she never lasted long. Elliott looked on, impressed, not by the snoring, but by the vision of her laying there. She completely trusted her safety to his protection. He had developed a strong closeness with Stef, one he silently wished could always exist. But for now, he would just enjoy the moment.

The landing in Cairns was smooth despite the damaged engine. By now it was early morning and the sun had already risen. Elliott enjoyed looking out the window at the scenery and watching the landing. The view of the coast was beautiful and, no matter how often he saw it, he was always impressed by the rain forest and the mists that hung over the mountains.

The airport was small. The terminal was one large open area where everyone convened to await their transport to town. Cairns was about a fifteen-minutes ride away. Cairns was also small, but still two to three times the size of Alice Springs. The surrounding countryside was a stark contrast to Alice. Here everything was rain forest green, rather than the dry and dusty clay reddish-brown of Alice. It was hard to believe they were in the same country. And the ocean was beautiful.

Once off the plane, they caught a taxi to the ferry port, which was near the center of town. The town center was primarily a collection of restaurants and souvenir shops. The waterfront wasn't the beautiful beach you would expect at the Great Barrier Reef. Instead, it was somewhat muddy, swampy, and uninviting. But the town had a relaxed, comfortable seaport atmosphere; the kind of place you would go if you were looking to escape the cares of the world.

CHAPTER TWELVE

Cairns

Late March, 2025 AD, Cairns, Australia

Stef and Elliott caught a water ferry out to Green Island on the Barrier Reef, where they would stay at the only hotel on the small island. The island had beautiful sandy beaches, in contrast to the beaches of Cairns. And the island was thickly covered with green jungle-like vegetation. It was mostly vines and small trees and fairly dense, making it difficult to walk through. The island was small. Later, when Stef was sunbathing, Elliott would find that he could walk the entire perimeter of the island in less than thirty minutes. Despite its size, over half of the island was thick with jungle that looked as if it had never been invaded.

Their meeting with the NNRL was scheduled for the following day, which gave them a chance for a day of R&R before the work began. The trip to the island was short, about thirty minutes. Once on the island, the two of them walked from the single long dock, which served as the island's port, to the hotel, which was tucked nicely in the trees, just offshore of the dock. Many of the rooms were so well hidden by the brush and trees that you couldn't tell how big the hotel was simply by looking around. This protected the beauty of the island. Pointing to the beautiful sand beaches Stef realized she had forgotten a critical piece of equipment.

"I need a swimming suit," hinted Stef.

"I'd be glad to get you one, if you let me pick it out," responded Elliott with a grin.

"I'm not sure what you have in mind. But I'm willing to take the risk."

There are numerous tourist gift shops near the hotel and around the pool. "That shop up ahead has something similar to what Misty-May wore at the last Olympics. I'd love to see that on you."

"I'll bet you would. But I'm concerned about what that may lead to." Stef was jabbing Elliott, even though she felt complemented by his interest.

"Don't worry, I'm your protector, remember," reminded Elliott, with a sly smirk as he finished checking them in at the outdoor reception desk.

"You go to the room and I'll be right there." Suggested Elliott handing her a room key and turned on his heels and headed to the small tourist shop he had spotted.

It wasn't long before Elliott returned with swimming suits and snorkeling gear for both of them. Stef immediately started to take her clothes off, eager to jump into the new swimming suit. But Elliott was in a daze. Stef's long hair, and her incredibly perfect, firm with no sag, twenty-year old looking butt, gave him urges. Then there were the strong athletic looking legs, and similarly strong looking arms and all he could think about was how he loved getting close to her. It wasn't the first time he had watched her change, but he considered each time an incredible show. She was perfect. He was amazed that she was his partner. All he could do was sit on the bed and watch the show. It didn't matter how many times he saw her naked, it was never enough. He could never get bored with this show. His mind was completely captivated by the view. And he was also a little embarrassed by how quickly she could get a rise out of him. Stef didn't mind. She liked his attention. Still naked, she walked over to him and stood in front of him. She let him run his hands over her ass and then work his way up her side to fondle her breasts. He loved kissing and sucking her nipples. She let him have his fun for a couple minutes, and then she decided that she was ready to go out and enjoy some sun. She gently pushed him off, knowing that he wouldn't mind. She was always available for him and he could complete the execution of his urges later. But now the sun was impatiently calling them. "Aren't you going to change?" Stef asked with a smirk, knowing what he was thinking without him saying a word.

"Of course," replied Elliott. "But I've been a little distracted." Elliott adored Stef and knew that if he let her have what was important to her, some time in the sun, she would also give him the things that were important to him, more naked time. After Stef was done changing, Elliott was finally able to concentrate on getting into his own bathing suit. Afterwards they applied a heavy dose of suntan lotion, and they left the room hoping to take advantage of the beautiful sunny day. Soon they were on the sandy beach exploring the wonders of the Great Barrier Reef.

Stef wanted to lie in the sun for a while, which Elliott knew meant at least a couple of hours. After about 10 minutes, Elliott was tired of sunning and he decided to walk the beach all the way around the island. It would be fun to explore the island, and to get a little exercise. The entire walk took only about thirty minutes and he was back sitting on the beach with Stef again wondering what to do next. So, he decided to go snorkeling for a while, just to see what he could find.

After about one hour of snorkeling, Elliott had become frustrated and he was back sitting next to Stef on the beach.

"There are little pockets of things to see, but this is nothing like Hanaumah Bay in Hawaii where the colorful fish are all over the place. Would you like to ride a glass-bottom boat that will take us further out into the reef?" Elliott suggested, as he remembered spotting the boat earlier when they docked at the island port.

"I'd love it," responded Stef. By now she had put in a couple of good hours on the beach and she was ready for a diet Coke. Getting off the beach and heading back to the dock where the glass-bottom boat was located would give her a chance to get the drink.

They collected their towels and snorkeling equipment, dropped it off in their room, stopped by the snack bar for drinks, and headed off to the boat dock.

They had timed it right, and they only had to wait about 15 minutes before they were off. Elliott was quick to comment that the boat ride was more successful than snorkeling off the beach. There were different types of fish to see, including sharks and an occasional turtle. Stef was enamored with the beauty of the reef.

"I don't know why we didn't come here a long time ago," Stef remarked. "This is truly beautiful. We need to try scuba diving some time so that we can get deeper into the reef and see even more."

After their Barrier Reef boat adventure, Stef and Elliott returned to the hotel room to clean up and wash off the sticky saltwater. Elliott spoke up.

"We need to strategize a little about tomorrow's meeting. We need to make sure we both have the same agenda going into the meeting so that we know what we want to get out of the meeting?

"I'm not sure we have enough to work with," responded Stef. "I think we'll have to play it by ear and see what they're after. But before we do any of that, I want to lay by the pool for about an hour and work on my tan. Fun always precedes work."

Elliott went to the pool with Stef. He sat in the shade and read his book while she continued to bake in the sun. He had to come to the pool with her in case she needed any sunscreen rubbed on. He took it as his personal duty to perform that task. But otherwise, he preferred reading in the shade, thereby putting less strain on his eyes.

The evening was calm and beautiful. The two of them ventured out for dinner at the hotel restaurant, and later went out to watch the sun set over the rain forest. Tomorrow would be another day. They could strategize then. Besides, the temptation of Stef in a bikini took more self-control than Elliott had and he wanted some "alone time" with her. Soon they retreated off to their room.

CHAPTER THIRTEEN

Meeting
Late March, 2025 AD, Cairns, Australia

The following day was another beautifully perfect day. It had rained overnight clearing the air which now had a damp crispness. Stef and Elliott woke up slowly, knowing that it wouldn't be until afternoon before they met with the NNRL.

They tried to discuss strategy, but the best they could come up with was to wait and listen.

Meantime, Kres and Rohit arrived on Green Island around 11:00AM. They checked into the hotel, picked up a note from Elliott explaining that they would meet in his hotel room at 01:00PM, and proceeded to a small hamburger stand to get something to eat. As Kres paid for his meal he explained, "There aren't a lot of good things I can say about the Americans, but I'm thrilled that they came up with hamburgers. And when you give those ideas to the Aussie's, who do the best at barbeques in the world, you come up with something really special."

"I'm glad you like them;" commented Rohit, "but I'm going to stick with the chicken sandwiches. They seem healthier."

By then it was getting close to 01:00PM, which was the appointed meeting time. They finished their lunches and headed for Elliott's hotel room.

Rohit knocked on the door, and Stef answered. The introductions were cordial. Everyone shook hands. Kres felt a little uncomfortable to be working with a woman. He had always thought that the Knights were only men. Maybe this was some new kind of revisionist organizational structure.

The hotel room was a suite which offered a separate "living room" with couches and chairs organized around a coffee table. The couches were on opposite sides of the coffee table, which allowed the Knights to sit across from the NNRL, as though they were preparing to do battle.

Kres was smaller than Elliott expected, but he noticeably had many of the features of Adolph Hitler. All he needed was that toothbrush mustache that Hitler was so famous for and it would be hard to tell him apart from the real thing.

Rohit was of larger build with blond hair, the model of Arian supremacy. He looked like Kres' personal bodyguard. A muscular tough guy.

"Do we have a confidentiality problem here, since we have a female in the room, and we will be discussing 33-degree Masonic secrets?" Kres queried, as he started the meeting.

"Not a problem," Elliott responded. "Stef is an exception to the rule. Her research has put her into a position where she is probably better informed about the Ark than any of us." Elliott lied. He didn't want Stef to leave, but he also didn't want to offend his new "customer."

"We can all talk freely," he continued, "If we discuss anything that Stef should not be involved in, I will stop the conversation and she can step out."

Stef already didn't like these guys because of their attack on the S1. Now she had another reason not to like them. "These sexist pigs," she thought to herself. "Who do they think they are, treating me as if I had no business being here?"

Elliott could also sense her irritation, and he tried to come up with a way to exploit the situation. But he couldn't think of an appropriate dig just then.

"Let's get to the point," Kres continued, "I don't believe in wasting time. The Templar Knights have the secrets behind the confiscation and hiding of the Ark of the Covenant. My organization doesn't have access to your information. We assume you have archives and detailed records which should help you in a search. In fact, sometimes I wonder if you don't already know where it is but have chosen not to use its power."

"Tell me what power you think the Ark has?" questioned Stef. This reference to power wasn't new to her, but she wanted to learn their perspective.

"I thought you knew all about the Ark," replied Kres. "That doesn't sound like the question of an Ark expert." Stef let his dig slide by without a comment so he continued; "Throughout Biblical history, whenever the Ark was brought into battle, the side possessing the Ark would win. The NNRL needs the Ark and its power for the creation of our new world order. We have several battles that we need to engage in, and we need to be ready. The Ark would make our success a 'sure thing'."

"Are you expecting a war?"

"We may be starting a war. But regardless, we want to be ready for any consequence. War may or may not be desirable. But there are times when it is necessary. And we want to assure ourselves of victory."

"I can definitely assure you that we do not have the Ark in our possession," Elliot chimed in, "however, there may be valuable information in our archives that can help us find it. Digging it out may be quite expensive. What are you willing to spend? And how much time should this take?" Elliott was asking about the Ark, but he was more interested in the comments about a possible war. Elliott was an assassin. But that meant that he only killed the guilty. He was opposed to war which left numerous innocent parties victim to the pride and ambitions of their leader. Kres' comments sounded too much like Hitler, and that made Elliott extremely uncomfortable.

"Cost is not a concern. We have enormous resources at our disposal." Kres replied.

What Kres didn't say was that he had access to the enormous art and gold reserves that were confiscated from the Jews during the time of the Holocaust. The irony was that now he wanted to use these Jewish resources to find and identify a Jewish artifact that he hoped to use for the continued suppression of the Jewish race, amongst others.

"But time IS important. We want to move forward rapidly."

"Why is it urgent?" asked Stef.

"Our leadership has undergone a recent change, and the new leadership wants to move forward as rapidly as possible. We are making plans for a major show of force and we don't want anything to delay our demonstration."

Again, what he didn't say was that after his father's death, he had taken over leadership and he was tired of waiting. He was planning for a major show of force on his father's birthday, April 20. He wanted to make this a date that was implanted in everyone's mind, similar to the way 9/11 has been remembered after the attack on the World Trade Center twin towers in New York.

"We need to discuss details." Elliott continued, and proceeded to spell out the timeline and cost of the operation. It would involve five Knights working full time searching the archives. He didn't mention that in reality it would probably only be himself and Stef working full time, and that he would occasionally use the resources of the librarians and researchers employed by the Knights. But, since Kres was so arrogant about his "unlimited available resources," Elliott felt the need to take some of those resources away from him.

Kres readily agreed to all the terms set forth. Agreement came so quickly that Elliott became skeptical whether there wasn't a plan for betrayal before final payment.

"We'll need to receive payment on a weekly basis!" Elliott demanded. Again, there was rapid agreement.

"When can we begin?" Kres asked.

"We can't let you into the secret Knight libraries. We'll have to do that work ourselves. But we can give you regular updates on our progress."

"I understand. But I want to be involved when we go out searching for the Ark. I want to be a part of the adventure." Insisted Kres.

"Definitely;" responded Elliott.

On the surface this seemed like a simple search and recovery effort; much simpler than anything the Knights were usually involved in. But this was a special situation. So special that Elliott wanted to personally be involved in every step of the process. And, of course, he would need Stef next to him to help him out.

With the business part of the conversation finished, Elliott felt the need to delve a little deeper into the organization he was working with.

"Tell me more about the NNRL." he requested.

"What do you want to know?" Kres demanded.

"Who you are. How you got started. How many of you there are? What your goals are. What you hope to accomplish."

"We're the Neo-Nazi Romarian League, which basically means that we are the revival of rulership by the far right. That was the original goal of my father, the Leader of the Nazi movement, but it was disrupted by the Americans, the Russians and the British. The Romarian League means that we want to reestablish the world Reich similar to what existed during the time of the Romans. Our ultimate goal is a unified world order where everyone prospers, free from the suppression and the exploitation of inferior races and sexes. Our goal is a poverty-free, disease-free environment where everyone can achieve their goals and dreams. We want to create a super race of superior Arian beings. We want to create an economic and social structure that does not limit growth."

Stef was fuming. The only thing she heard him say was "inferior sexes," the rest was all a blur, and she was ready to strike blood.

Elliott, on the other hand, became fearful. These guys were seriously deranged and extremely dangerous. He would have to handle these individuals with caution. This could become an extremely volatile situation. Malvika Mishra was correct in his initial impressions. This organization was a loose cannon and could not be allowed to run free. The IOM had to feign a working relationship with them in order to keep their activities in check.

"We are delighted that we can help," was the best Elliott could come up with, trying to keep his shock from being too obvious.

"Oh, by the way, how'd you guys get access to my Blackberry?" Kres queried.

"Just letting you know that we have as good a geek squad as you do," responded Elliott.

"Point made."

"I have one additional request," Kres was now getting around to his primary reason for wanting to work with the IOM. "I understand that you have recently acquired several nuclear detonators or fuses, as the US Air Force calls them. As a sign of good faith, I would like to acquire one of them from you. I have a very interested buyer," Kres lied. He had his own special interest for acquiring the detonator. He had a mission in Washington DC on the upcoming birthday of his father.

"I don't know anything about that," Elliott lied. He knew that the IOM had acquired a box of miss-shipped fuses that the Air Force had sent out by mistake. And the country that received them was more than happy to sell them to the IOM for a healthy profit.

"I'll have to check with my superiors about that. But it doesn't sound like the kind of thing we would want to sell anyway." Elliott was becoming more concerned by the minute. The NNRL was extremely dangerous. And this relationship can become sticky very quickly.

"Please check into it for me," Kres responded as he started to stand up. The four shook hands in pretended cordiality, and parted company.

After they departed and the door had closed behind them, Elliott was the first to comment to Stef.

"Rohit didn't say a word during the entire meeting. He apparently was here for intimidation only. Or maybe Kres felt the need for a bodyguard."

Stef fell back onto her sofa with a disgruntled look on her face. "I'd love to have ten minutes in a room alone with that guy. I'd give him a different perspective on which sex was inferior."

"Calm down Stef," Elliott offered. "You know that we have to play along with these guys. This is an incredibly sticky situation, and we need to keep all communication channels open. We can't lose control here. These guys are shopping for bombs. We have to be extremely careful, so don't let your emotions get control of you."

"I know, but I never realized it would be so hard."

CHAPTER FOURTEEN

Second Report In

Late March, 2025 AD, CIA Headquarters, Langley, Virginia

The phone rang on Marcello Zuniga's desk. "Agent Zuniga here. How can I help you?"

"Agent Sigma-6-Sigma reporting in."

"Codeword Snoopy, Respond."

"Phi-Beta-Kappa,"

"Go ahead Sigma-6-Sigma."

"The IOM has confirmed the contract from the NNRL for assistance in finding the Ark of the Covenant. These NNRL guys are crazy. They want to revive Hitler's dream of world domination. The leader of the group claims to be Hitler's son. They claim they're getting ready for a New World Order, which may translate to war. They're willing to do whatever it takes to push their superior race and world domination agenda. This is serious stuff. The IOM accepted the contract, not because they wanted to do the work, but because they were afraid of leaving these guys unchecked."

"Are there any other details, like names, places, or dates."

"None at this time."

"Report regularly on this one. It could turn into a major terrorist mess."

"Roger."

"By the way, was the IOM involved in the Barjet assassination?"

"Yes. That was an IOM operation."

"Thanks and keep me posted."

"Roger and out."

Marcello hung up the phone and leaned back in his desk chair. His feelings were confused. He was excited about the possibility of being involved in something this big. This was real James Bond type stuff. But at the same time, he was fearful. He knew how much damage an organization like the NNRL could generate. History is full of these types of organizations and their destruction.

Marcello decided to ignore the Outlook schedules of his CIA counterparts. This new situation required serious and immediate attention. The TFMA needed an immediate meeting with the TFRWR. Everyone in the CIA needed to be aware of recent events.

Marcello's next call was to the French Mafia. They would be extremely interested in knowing who assassinated their political mastermind, Barjet. Marcello thought he may as well use their help in dealing with the IOM. If the Mafia took revenge on the IOM it would mean that much less for him to worry about.

CHAPTER FIFTEEN

Rain Forest
Late March, 2025 AD, Cairns, Australia

The company jet that brought Elliott and Stef from Alice Springs was also scheduled to return them. But unfortunately, it was still grounded for repairs. Parts had been ordered to fix the dust storm damaged engine. However, because of the remoteness of Cairns, combined with the uniqueness of the plane, it would still be a few of days before the necessary parts would be available. Flying commercial airlines was a possibility but waiting for the company plane gave them an excuse to stay in the Barrier Reef resort for a few more days.

Elliott and Stef stayed on the island through the weekend, discussing strategy and approach for dealing with the NNRL. They decided the first step would be to thoroughly research all the activities surrounding the Ark for the last three-thousand years. They contacted Greg's team in Nevada and he immediately started Dawn and Alan working on the project. Then they informed Kres that research had been started.

On Monday morning, when the plane still wasn't ready, Stef suggested they go for a drive and see the rain forest.

"We've done as much as we can from here. So, let's do some sightseeing. Hopefully, we can fly out of here tomorrow."

Elliott checked them out of the hotel, and the two of them caught the ferry back to Cairns. It didn't take long for them to rent a car. There were several car rental locations within walking distance of the dock. And they drove off towards the North heading for Cape Tribulation, the place where the only paved roadway ends. Beyond that point were only dirt roads and jungle.

Cairns is too small to be called a city, but too large to be called a town. Shortly after leaving town, you felt like you were engulfed by country. The drive north was beautiful. They decided that their goal was to drive north until the pavement ends, which was only a couple hours' drive. But this drive would take them through some of the most beautiful scenery in all of Australia. It wasn't long before they saw a large group of Kangaroos off to the side of the road in a field. There must have been at least a hundred of them, all sitting around and enjoying the sun and nibbling on the grass. Stef made Elliott pull over so she could shoot some pictures. She was amazed to see more kangaroos here in the jungle, then she encountered back in the bush of Alice Springs.

The road seemed deserted with only an occasional car passing them. The road followed the coastline, and they passed some beautiful beaches completely void of people. The coastline was one of Australia's most magnificent areas where you could see the rainforest meet the reef. The dramatic clash of green and turquoise blue separated by sandy white beaches lined with coconut palms, and void of people, was beyond compare. "Let's stop and lie out on the beach and catch some rays," Stef suggested. Elliott knew this was coming. Stef liked the sun. And Elliott liked the idea as well, not because he liked lying in the sun, but because he enjoyed swimming in the waves. They pulled over at the next beach they found, slipped into their swimming suits, and went out on the beach. It wasn't long before Stef was spread out on her towel, baking in the sun.

It was hard in many ways for Elliott to leave Stef lying there while he went off for a swim. She was incredibly hard to resist. Elliott watched her for a while. Then, after about ten minutes, he walked out into the waves until the water was about waste height, and dove in. It was a beautiful day, the water was perfectly clear, and the sky was a deep blue.

After about half an hour of swimming, Elliott rested in the water by floating on his back in the waves. He looked back at Stef and as he watched her, he noticed movement behind her in the trees. Normally this wouldn't seem unusual. But since he thought the beach was deserted the movement seemed out of place.

Elliott started to slowly work himself back to the shore, keeping an eye out for further movement, but there didn't seem to be any more activity. After getting to shore, he started walking up the beach to where Stef lay. He could see that she was asleep, because of her mild snoring. He took another look around, to make sure that the coast was clear, and then he went back and knelt down next to Stef. He carefully unfastened the strap on her bikini top, hoping to not wake her in the process. Then he stood up and walked off. Pretending to come up to her for the first time on his way back again, he barked out:

"How are you doing." Much to his delight Stef jumped up, her cute little tits bouncing in the breeze. She didn't have large breasts. They were a little on the small side, much like most of the super models. But Elliott liked them that way. He often said that strong, athletic looking women always had cute little breasts, not big, silicone ones.

Stef gave Elliott an irritated look, as she reconnected her swimming suit top.

"I suppose you thought that was funny?" she asked.

"Actually, it was pretty sexy," replied Elliott. "Actually, I came up because I saw someone watching you in the bushes."

"And you wanted to give them a show?"

"As a matter of fact, I checked to make sure there wasn't anyone there, before I got the idea to disconnect your support system."

"Funny," she sarcastically replied. "Now you have me a little concerned. What did it seem like the guys in the bushes were doing?" she asked.

"I wasn't sure. Probably nothing. But I thought I should check. That's why I came to shore. What do you think we should do?"

"Leave. Let's get out of here. I've had enough sun anyway and I'm ready to continue our drive north."

It didn't take them long to pack up and get back into the car. Out of the corner of their eye they continued watching the bushes, but they didn't see any more activity.

Driving north they soon found themselves leaving the beach area and going slightly inland. The road maneuvered around a small gulf where a river flowed into the ocean. There were no bridges. Crossing the river would require a ferry.

Their timing was just right. They pulled up to the ferry just as it was loading the last vehicles. The ferry looked like a large raft. There was a cable that passed by the side of the ferry and was connected to the shore on each side of the river. A motor pulled the raft along the cable. It held two lanes of cars with a maximum load of eight cars.

Suddenly a fast-moving black Mustang convertible pulled up behind them, squealing its brakes as it came to a stop. The car pulled up behind them onto the ferry, receiving less-than-friendly stares from the ferry master.

Elliott, without moving his head, watched the people in the car behind them. There were two of them and they wore sunglasses and baseball caps pulled low on their heads, so it was difficult to make them out. But there was something familiar about them that made him uncomfortable. But he couldn't quite tie down what bothered him.

The ferry trip was short, and the offload was quick. As they drove on, the scenery became denser and denser, looking more and more like a rainforest. Often, there was a roof canopy which made it seem like you were driving through a long tunnel. The road was still one lane in each direction, but it became narrower and windier. And when two vehicles converged, one would often have to pull on the shoulder to let the other vehicle pass.

The scenery was incredible. Occasionally they would come to a small river or stream. In this backcountry, the rivers didn't have bridges over them. Rather, the roadway went down into the riverbed, requiring vehicles to drive through the river. Normally the water level was shallow. However, during a heavy downpour, the water level would become too high to drive through. It was important to time your travels so as to avoided heavy rains.

Arriving at the Dubuji Daintree National Park, Elliott pulled into a small tourist stop called the Wet Tropics Visitor Information Center, which included a restaurant and gift shops. There weren't any other choices of places to stop. This was also the kick-off point for several rainforest 4-wheeling tours into the Kulki Daintree National Park. This tourist stop was very near the point where the pavement came to an end.

Elliott and Stef parked in the dirt and gravel parking lot and entered the small restaurant to get a bite to eat. "Should we see what the tours are like?" Stef asked. They were debating if they should take one of the tours into the jungle. They weren't sure how long they would take and if they had enough time.

Just then the waitress had come up to take their order and overheard Stef's question.

"I wouldn't recommend the tours unless you're planning to stay the night. There are some heavy rains that are supposed to start in the next hour, and that will continue on through most of the night. Within two hours the road South will be impassable through the riverbeds." The waitress commented.

"What's available here, if we decided to stay?" asked Stef.

"There are some small cottages in back, but they get filled up fast, especially when the weather falls apart. And there are some campsites if you have the equipment."

"Camping is out. We should check the availability of the cottages," came from Stef.

"We can, but I'm not sure we're going to have much fun touring the rain forest in the rain," suggested Elliott, with a somewhat disgruntled look.

"The tours are best in the rain," came back the enthusiastic response from the waitress. "It puts you in the right mood and the lights play differently on the trees in the rain."

"Well then, let's order and while we're waiting for the food, I'll go check out the cottages," responded an excited Elliott. She had aroused his curiosity.

They went ahead and ordered and leaving Stef to wait in the restaurant, Elliott went to the cottages to see what was available. As he left the restaurant, he noticed the same black Mustang that had come up behind him at the ferry crossing. The car was parked away from the restaurant, but the two occupants were sitting in the car, apparently watching the restaurant. Elliot's sharp eye and his training with the Mossad made him keenly aware of things that were out of place. And two guys sitting in a car watching a restaurant, with baseball caps pulled low over their eyes, was out of place here in the middle of the Australian rain forest.

Keeping one eye on the Mustang, he headed over to the cottage rental office. He found out that there was only one room left, non-smoking with one double bed. Elliott preferred a larger bed, but since Stef really wanted to tour the rain forest, he went ahead and booked the room. Then he headed over to the Rain Forest Tours office and proceeded to book a two-hour long 4-wheel drive, through the "hidden back roads of the rain forest."

Returning to the restaurant, Elliott sat down just as the food was being delivered and gave Stef the news.

"But something strange is going on. The two guys in the black Mustang seem to be tailing us. I've been noticing the car off and on since the ferry crossing. I wonder if they were watching us when we were on the beach."

"I've been noticing them as well," Stef conceded, "but I thought I was just being paranoid. But if you're noticing the same things as me, I'm even more concerned. I know we've made a lot of enemies in the past. But no one knows we're here. And I can't understand what they would be after."

"Let's keep an eye out for them and if they continue to tail us, we'll grab them and find out what they're after." Elliott decided.

The meal was good, especially after what seemed like a long day of traveling and the hard work of lying on the beach. They finished just in time to go over to the tourist desk and check in for their rain forest tour. Elliott and Stef both noticed that the two guys in the Mustang were still sitting in the same place and were still watching their movements.

CHAPTER SIXTEEN

Rain Forest Ride

Late March, 2025 AD, Daintree National Park, Australia

"You're lucky. You're the only ones going for this tour," responded the attendant to their inquiry. "You're getting our best driver. And he'll stop whenever you want to take pictures. And the driver can take you wherever you want to go. You can tailor the ride to your interests."

"We're ready to go," suggested Elliott. The attendant handed Elliott and Stef each a thin plastic yellow rain shield and led them over to the four-wheeler which would become their thrill ride for the next two hours. And it was only a few minutes before they were off.

"Welcome to Daintree National Park, the spot in Australia where we have too much rain," came the voice of their cheerful tour guide as he hopped into the driver's seat.

"Hope you enjoy your ride. I'm Kiffin and I'll be showing you a little bit of our heaven on earth here in North-Eastern Australia. Is there anything in particular that you would like to see?"

Elliott had taken the front passenger seat and Stef sat by herself in the back.

"Take us on your roughest roads to your most remote locations, and we'll be perfectly happy," came from Elliott. Stef wasn't so sure that she had the same definition of an enjoyable ride that Elliott had, but she decided to let him have his fun.

The ride started up slowly, as they drove further north along the only paved north-south road. But it wasn't long before the pavement came to an end and the road turned to gravel and mud. They drove through several shallow rivers and soon turned west heading deeper into the thickness of the rainforest.

Kiffin drove slowly, describing the different types of plants and animals. It was easy to see that he was enamored by the beauty of his surroundings. He was pointing out a couple of parrots, high up in the trees, when suddenly a cassowary darted across the roadway in from of them.

"That's a rare treat," explained the guide. "The cassowary is normally very shy and hard to see." The cassowary is a bird, similar in size to the emu, black with a brightly colored head, and standing up to 6 feet tall.

"The cassowary is vital to the ecosystem of the rainforest," Kiffin continued, "It is considered a keystone species. It eats mostly fruits that fall on the rainforest floor. It is an important dispenser of larger rainforest seed. One curious point about the cassowary is that they have their sex roles reversed. After the female lays the eggs, she abandons her mate. And the male incubates and cares for the brood of young until they are up to fifteen months of age."

"So, what does the female do after that?" asked Elliott.

"Party," interjected Stef.

"She goes about finding another mate," responded Kiffin.

"Do you have any dangerous animals out here?" asked Stef.

"Yes. We're coming up to a river here where you should be able to see some crocodile." Kiffin pulled up next to a large river. The undergrowth of the jungle was so thick that, if you didn't know there was a river there, you might have driven right into it.

"There, you can see one now." Kiffin instructed, pointing to a larger pool in the river.

It was hard to see, but Kiffin knew what to look for. The ripples on the top of the water indicated where the crocodile was hiding itself.

"Let's take a little walk and I'll show you some of the smaller wonders of the rain forest," Kiffin suggested. But Stef had no interest in stepping out of the Jeep, now that she knew a crocodile was out there.

Elliott jumped out, knowing that the crocodile was more interested in easy prey, and Kiffin pointed out to him some of the electric-colored butterflies, green tree ants, lizards, and bright green tree frogs. The tree snakes and tortoises were a little harder to find. Elliott was fanatical with the camera.

"Digital cameras are great," he commented to Kiffin. "I can take a million pictures, and just pull out the few really good ones."

Climbing back into the Jeep, Elliott told Stef about all the discoveries.

"I'll just have to see them on your camera after we get back." she replied and had no regrets.

Kiffin started driving back along the dirt road, deeper into the jungle, when suddenly three small holes appeared in the front windshield, starting from the driver's seat where Kiffin sat and migrating up to toward the rear-view mirror. Elliott and Stef instinctively ducked down in their seats, recognizing them as bullet holes. But for Kiffin it was already too late. He slumped over, falling against Elliott who noticed two bullet holes, one in Kiffin's neck and one in his head.

Elliott pushed Kiffin up as he grabbed at the steering wheel and tried to steady the four-wheeler. Kiffin's lifeless foot was planted hard against the accelerator and the vehicle continued to surge forward. Elliott's instincts took over and he turned off the ignition switch and pulled the handbrake. The vehicle bolted, as if it had been violated, and started to slide off to the right off the muddy, slippery road, down a small incline. Just then two more bullets whizzed by and hitting the windshield. This time they were so close that Elliott could feel the gust of their movement past his cheek. Elliott was grateful that the slippery mud caused the Jeep to jerk to the side and causing the shots to miss.

Elliott reached over the driver and swung Kiffin's door open. He pushed his lifeless body out the door and out into the damp undergrowth. The body sunk down into the plant life and seemed to be consumed by the vegetation. Elliott took a quick look around so that he could remember the place when he came back later to reclaim the body. He slid into the driver's seat and started it up. Putting it into gear he tried to move forward, but the wheels had lost traction. He threw it into reverse and moved slightly backwards. Then, turning the steering wheel slightly, he moved forward again, this time slowly. The maneuver worked and he was able to pull the vehicle forward, first slowly, then more rapidly. Looking in the rear-view mirror he could see his pursuers running toward them, closing in the distance between them, with one of them taking aim. He heard the shots but couldn't tell where they landed. He only knew that he had not been hit.

"How're you doing back there?" he asked Stef.

"Just peachy," she responded.

He could see that she had drawn her weapon and was taking aim at the pursuers. One thing you could always count on was that assassins carried weapons.

"Can you hold this thing steadier so I can get off a good shot?" Stef demanded.

She had the habit of always carrying her personal weapon, even when she was on vacation. She fired a couple of rounds, mostly to let them know that she also had firepower. Stef hoped this would keep them from getting too close, but realized that she was outgunned, and could see her enemies had Uzis, the automatic weapons of the Israeli Mossad secret police.

"They have Uzis," she blurted out in frustration, "and they're gaining on us. Get us out of here." Uzis had become very popular and the Israelis sold them openly. They were great as a revenue generator.

"I'm working on it," responded Elliott, as the 4-wheeler surged forward and began gaining speed. Unfortunately, the road was more of a trail; extremely rough, with lots of ditches, roots, and mounds. There was little opportunity to build up speed. But Elliott was trained in pursuit driving, and he bounced and rocked the vehicle over the terrain as quickly as possible.

"They're still shooting at us so keep your head down," yelled Stef.

"It's a bit of a challenge trying to drive this vehicle without a head," responded Elliott.

Their assailants had scrambled back into their vehicle and were now back chasing them. The pursuit vehicle had gotten close enough to where Stef was able to take a better look. "Those are the same guys that were watching us back at the restaurant. They're still wearing the same hats and sunglasses. I wonder why they're after us."

"Maybe we took their favorite parking space." Elliott liked to give a meaningless answer when there wasn't an answer to be given.

They had reached a small clearing where the road was level, giving Elliot the chance to move a quicker. But he soon realized that this route ended with a steep drop-off.

"Hold on tight." He yelled out.

The road took a sixty-degree drop off for about one-quarter mile. Then it took a Y in two directions. One was a sharp left, and the other was a slight right. Elliott would have preferred the left, because it might have thrown off his pursuers, but since the turn came up too quickly, he wasn't ready for it, and he ended up taking the easier route to the right.

After another quarter mile the jungle became dense and tight and started to close in on them. The road became narrower, so tight that they could feel the brush rubbing in on both sides. The road was now very windy, and they could only see their pursuers for very short time segments. Elliott had successfully opened the gap between them with his excellent driving skills.

The jungle seemed to close in on them. The damp leaves were slapping the windshield and the scraping along the sides of the vehicle.

"Keep driving," commanded Stef shortly after they turned a corner and as they passed an exceptionally thick clump of over-grown bushes. She jumped off the right side of the vehicle into a cluster of enormously large leaves. Each leaf was the size of her upper body. And each was soaked by the continuous drizzle that seemed to never end. She fell deep into the clump of leaves and was quickly soaked to the bone. She scrambled to the edge of the leaves and hid behind a cluster of trees, waiting for the pursuit vehicle.

It wasn't long before their attackers came around the corner. She took steady aim at the driver. It was a challenging shot because the vehicle bobbed up and down. But she waited until they were close to her and she was able to maintain a steady aim. She carefully fired off one round, conserving her limited ammunition. The shot rang true and the driver fell forward against the steering wheel, with a small hole in the side of the cap he was wearing. The passenger wasn't ready for the attack. By the time he realized what had happened, the vehicle had veered off the road and had run head-long into a tree.

Stef fired off another couple of rounds at the passenger, but only succeeded in grazing the side of his left shoulder as he ducked down. She saw the side door open up and knew immediately that she was now going one-on-one against a killer with an Uzi. And she only had half a dozen bullets left for her small pistol.

Suddenly the plants and bushes all around Stef started to explode and she realized that the enemy was strafing the area, hoping to hit her with a random round. Stef did her best to hide behind the trees, but it was somewhat risky, since the trees didn't have very thick trunks. In fact, the Uzi round could probably go right through the trunk of the small trees. In desperation, she decided to lay down, in the wet mossy, murky ground cover, just as a strafing round passed overhead. She realized that she had come pretty close to ending it all. Suddenly the wet mess didn't feel all that bad.

She heard someone off in the distance crunching through the undergrowth. She knew it must be her pursuer trying to find her. She laid face-down, motionless, surrounded and covered by the enormous damp leaves and ferns. She hoped that he would miss the direction from which she had fired, since her shots had come when he wasn't ready for them.

The silence was broken only by the constant drip of the accumulated drizzle dripping off of the trees and hitting the leaves that covered her, and by the occasional crunch of the pursuer's footsteps. Suddenly there was another strafing round. Apparently, the killer had been spooked by some animal and he decided to shoot. She remained motionless, hidden under the blanket of leaves and undergrowth.

She felt movement. What was that? She knew better than to move and give away her location. Suddenly she realized what it was, a snake. And she had heard about all the poisons' snakes that lived in the Australian rain forests. Could this be one of them? The snake slithered along slowly. It got to her neck. Then stopped. Apparently, the thing realized that there was something different about this warm body laying here. The snake seemed to be considering its options. Then it started to move again, slowly up the side of her neck and started down her back. Then it turned in a loop and slowly slithered up her back and into her hair. Then it stopped again. It was again considering its options, seemingly trying to understand what hair was. Then it started to slither off the top of her head and down the left side of her skull.

Stef hated snakes. She would rather fight with her pursuers, than deal with a snake. But she lay stiff and motionless. She knew she was outgunned by the Uzi. Unfortunately, the snake wasn't done with her. It circled around on the ground and came back again up the left side of her head, just above her ear. It turned right and worked its way down her neck, squeezing its way under her collar and staying on her back, next to her skin.

'Isn't it bad enough that I'm soaked and chilled? Now I have this slimy, nasty creature spreading its mess down my back!' she told herself, her mind frantically working overtime.

A chill ran down her spine and she had to fight off a shiver, fearing that it would make a noise, alert her attacker, and give away her position.

The snake slithered leisurely down her back, inside her shirt and against her skin. Stef was already soaked, and the damp, slimy snake made it worse. She was unable to suppress a slight shiver and trembled a little bit, as the snake continued to slowly and methodically work its way down her back. When it arrived at her belt line, the snake began to travel its way over the top of her elastic belt line, offering Stef a short spell of respite in letting her think that it was done crawling against her skin. Unfortunately, the reptile was a little more adventurous, and suddenly pulled back. It seemed to like the feel and warmth of her skin and instead the persistent creeping creature slowly wriggled its way underneath the elastic belt line holding her pants in place. It stayed closely pressed against Stef's skin, as the snake continued to work its way down her back. When it had reached the snug place between her butt cheeks, she was about to scream, but she knew she had to hold on and persevere with the grueling situation. Her life depended on it.

The snake continued its journey down the center of her buttocks. It seemed to slow down, possibly investigating what it had found. To Stef the snake's journey seemed to take forever. When it came to a Y intersection, where it had to decide whether to go down the left or the right pant leg, it chose the left side and continued its way on its exploratory journey down's Stef's body. As it worked its way down the left pant leg the motion of the snake's slimy body started to tickle Stef, and again she had to fight to control herself by tightly clenching her teeth, lest she let a scream escape from between her lips, and desperately tried holding her breath for as long as she could. If only to try and gain some control over her body's instinctive reactions to the persistent and interminable assault on her person. By now the snake's head had reached its way to the side of Stef's left knee. The tail end of the reptile touched the top of the neckline of her shirt, and the snake's body was now fully stretched out practically along the entire length of her body. Stef was livid and terrified all at the same time. Should this creature by an untoward chance fancy giving her a deathly nibble with its poison poised fangs, she'd be a 'goner' for sure. This was the grossest thing she had ever experienced. Eventually the snake continued on its journey and made its way out of the bottom of her pants leg, and with an oscillating motion rapidly and silently slipped away from Stef, and out into the jungle foliage.

Suddenly Stef heard a volley of Uzi shots off in the direction where the snake had slithered. She heard the intruder run over to where he had fired his shots and heard him kicking some of the undergrowth. Then she heard a disgruntled complaint; "Just a bloody snake."

Unfortunately for the snake, he met his untimely death at the hand of the same individual that was trying to kill Stef and Elliott. Stef was slightly jealous that she didn't get the chance to shoot the slimy potentially deadly creature. She felt it had molested her, but she knew it was all in her mind. Anyway, it would have felt good to shoot it, even if it didn't know what it was doing.

Relieved from the distraction of the snake, Stef could again focus on the crunch of footsteps. They were getting closer. It seemed like she had been lying there for hours, but she knew that she had to stay hidden longer. She was outgunned and her best defensive tool was stealth.

More footsteps. Extremely close. It seemed like he was almost on top of her. The ground canopy was soft, and somewhat mushy, but the twigs made it crunchy.

More muffled footsteps.... Suddenly, he stepped on her back. She nearly let out a gasp of pain, as the unexpected pressure and weight pushed upon her.

He stopped. He obviously sensed or heard something that didn't seem quite cosher. He stood there, standing on her back. Apparently, he didn't see or sense her bulk underfoot, or he would have shot her, and she'd be a dead woman by now. The canopy had kept her well concealed. And the softness of her body under his feet probably felt natural, just like the rest of the canopy. The unevenness of the canopy hid the presence of her body.

She could feel him turn, putting slightly more pressure on one foot, then on the other. He must have heard something. But he didn't make the connection. He didn't seem to realize that she was right below him at the mercy of his gun barrel.

Then he moved on, slowly stepping forward another couple of steps.

She was relieved to have the pressure off her back. She was left with a sharp pain where he had been standing for several lengthy seconds which had seemed an age.

She knew that if she was going to move, there was no better time than right now. He was close, and his back was turned to her. This would be her best chance.

In one rapid motion she rolled over, sat up, aimed her pistol, and fired three rounds. The first was low and hit him in the butt, the second was higher, striking him close to the heart, and the third was the kill shot that hit him in the spine at the top of the neck. He fell with a crunch in the foliage; never knowing what hit him.

Just then she heard a second set of footsteps rushing through the brush towards the noise of her gunshot.

"You beat me to it," Elliott yelled out. "I was just getting him into my sights."

"Thanks for nothing," exclaimed an aggravated Stef, still sore from the step on her back, and nauseatingly squeamish from the snake.

"I was coming back, but I had to do it slowly and quietly. I should have known that you had the situation under control."

"I'm freezing to death. I can't handle this damp coldness. I've seen all I ever want to see of the rainforest. Let's get out of here."

"I'll go back and get the four-wheeler and then we can backtrack and pick up Kiffin on the way."

"Please hurry", she urged, "I've been soaked, slimed, and trampled on. I'm ready for a hot tub and some peace and quiet."

Stef went to the two bodies and tried to find some form of ID. But they had nothing on them that would help her identify who they were or what their intentions were. She was careful not to leave any identifying fingerprints that could be used to connect her with the shooters.

Elliott drove up and Stef jumped in. After driving a few minutes, they spotted a pond in which Stef threw her handgun. IOM agents knew that they should never leave a ballistics trail. Replacing the pistol was necessary precaution. "They'll never find it in there," she said.

Elliott drove to where he had left Kiffin and loaded him into the back seat. Then they proceeded back to the tourist trap. When they arrived, Elliott dropped Stef off at the cabin so that she wouldn't need to be bothered with the police. Then Elliott asked for the local constable. Finding him he proceeded to turn over Kiffin's body and filled out a police report on what had happened. The police wanted Elliott to go back to the locations of the shootings and explain the events. Fortunately, Elliott had allowed Stef to escape this inquiry by not telling them about her, and she was able to stay behind in her hotel room where she had a chance to get warmed up in a hot bath.

The police informed him that two men had stolen a four-wheeler from the tour company parking lot and that they had a video recording of the theft. From this clip Elliott was able to confirm that these were the same two men involved in the shootings.

Elliott took them to the location of Kiffin's shooting, and to where Stef had done battle with the two pursuers. This entire interview process took several hours. Elliott used one of his fake IDs so that the police would never be able to follow up with him or track him, but he felt he needed to do Kiffin justice and tell his story.

It was a little challenging for Elliott to explain how he managed to get one of the weapons away from the assassins and was then able to shoot them both. He made up a story about running out into the bushes and hiding in a tree, and after one of the men had passed him, he jumped him, took his weapon, and in the struggle shot him. Then he took the weapon and shot the other attacker. For now, the police believed him, but he knew that when they discovered that one assassin was shot in the back, and that both of them were shot with bullets that didn't come from the Uzi, that they would want to ask him more questions. But Elliott counted on the fact that it would probably take them days before they had a real coroner perform an autopsy, and by then he would be long gone.

After claiming ignorance about why anyone would want to kill them, Elliott was released with the recommendation that he stay within the Cairns area in case there were further questions. He rejoined Stef in their cabin. But by then she had finished her bath, had crawled into bed, and was sound asleep. She was exhausted.

CHAPTER SEVENTEEN

Return to Base

Late March, 2025 AD, Cairns and Alice Springs, Australia

Early the following morning Elliott woke Stef and helped her into the car. He wanted to leave the area before any of the police had second thoughts about his story. During the drive back to Cairns, Elliott confirmed that the aircraft would be ready to fly them back to Alice Springs as soon as they arrived. Stef felt refreshed and was ready to go home. She jokingly suggested that they should try another rain forest tour. But the drive back to Cairns was long and they needed to leave the area as soon as possible. The rain forest tour would have to wait.

During the drive, Elliott told Stef the story of the police inquisition and how he had to "modify" reality. He explained that there are numerous holes in the story, like why two people went on the tour and only one came back, or why the kill shots weren't from Uzi bullets.

"I know they're going to have lots more questions, and we can't be associated with any of this. We need to get out of here quickly," Eliot stressed.

They both drifted off deep in thought. "I know what you're thinking," Stef broke the silence.

"What's that?"

"You're wondering why we were being attacked."

"Of course. However, being in the business we're in, it's no surprise. We automatically generate a lot of enemies."

"But it's going to drive me crazy trying to figure this out. And how did they know we were here? How did they know we were driving to the rain forest? The questions go on and on."

"I don't have any answers. But I'll tell you what worries me. I'll bet these were only someone's foot soldiers. Where's the commander? Will he strike again? What's his agenda?"

They drove straight to the airport. When they arrived, the aircraft was already waiting for them. It wasn't long before they were on the plane and taking off, on their way back to Alice. They didn't return the rental car because they knew that there would probably be police waiting there for them. The car license was retrievable from the surveillance videos. Instead, Elliott used one of the IOMs untraceable, secure phone connections to send a message to the car rental company, telling them they had left the car in the airport parking lot and that they would have to retrieve it themselves.

The flight was uneventful. The air was smooth, and the view was beautiful. Unlike most people, Stef enjoyed seeing the vast expanses of the Australian outback. It had its own beauty. There are vast horizons of red dirt with blotches of trees, caterpillar-like mountains, and the occasional water holes. And then there is the occasional ranch building which looked lost and forlorn in the wilderness.

The landing was also uneventful. The plane was rushed off to the private hanger of the Templars, keeping it out of the public view as much as possible.

Once safely tucked away, Elliott and Stef were able to get off the plane and into the waiting company car, again disguised as a taxi. They were rushed over to the Pine Tree Gap complex, entered the abandoned-looking warehouse, climbed aboard the elevator, and were zipped down to the 6th floor below ground.

They knew that Malvika would want an update the minute they returned. And since their return had been delayed by aircraft problems, he would be anxious. They dropped their bags off in their offices and went directly to meet with him.

"Welcome back. Hope you enjoyed your vacation," came from Malvika as he looked up from his computer to welcome them. Elliott and Stef quickly updated him on the meeting and on the events in the rain forest.

"So where do we go from here?" Malvika asked.

Elliott outlined a plan of attack which included research into the Templar archives, to see if there were any additional clues on where the Ark may have traveled, research into the Gospel of Mark, hoping to find the reason why it was left where the Ark should have been, and re-entering the temple mound hiding place where the Ark had been stored to see if there were any additional clues. The third item would be highly controversial and would need to be a clandestine operation. If the Israelis learned about an attempt to enter the temple mound, they would be on the alert to prevent it from happening. This was sacred territory, and they were constantly plagued by treasure seekers, who wanted to dig up the mound for their own riches and glory.

"We need to find the Ark before the NNRL does," Malvika said stressing their need for secrecy, especially when it came to digging into temple mound, "they're going to be looking for it as well, and we need to prevent it from falling into their hands. That would be a major tragedy."

Elliott and Stef left his offices and went back to Elliott's office.

"Let's put Greg's team to work on researching the Templar archives. And we'll visit Israel's temple mound." Elliott suggested.

"I agree. Let's make the call right now," Stef said, as she picked up Elliott's phone, put it on speaker, and began dialing Greg's number.

"Hello, Greg here," came across the speaker.

"Greg, this is Elliott and I have Stef here with me. I have a priority one task assignment for your team." Translated, this meant drop everything and focus solely on the task you are about to receive until it has been completed.

"This is a follow-on to the message I sent you a couple of days ago. I need two things. Stef and I are heading for Jerusalem. We're planning to go into the Temple Mount and revisit the hiding place of the Ark of the Covenant. First, we need help in locating the cave, since we're going to have to do this clandestine. Neither the Israelis, nor the Muslims, are going to let us dig around on their sacred mound. So, I need you to equip the S1 remote plane with earth penetrating radar and give me a least three different perspectives on the mound. Perhaps from above, North to South, one East to West, and one on a 45-degree angle. This should allow us to generate a three-dimensional perspective of the interior of the mound. We need to be able to triangulate a precise location for the caves so we know where the access points should be located. Do this ASAP so that when I get to Israel I can get right to work."

"Second, this was also part of the message I sent you about a couple of days ago; I need you to dig through the Templar archives, libraries, letters, whatever, and identify every reference to the Ark of the Covenant. Go back in time as far as possible. I'm particularly interested in the time period from about 50 AD, just prior to the time the Gospel of Mark was written, till about 1000 AD. So, find out the time frame when we think the Ark was taken from Temple Mound and moved to some other location. Start with that time frame, and then work backwards and forwards from there. Let me know anything and everything that you come up with. Also search Jewish, Israeli, and Palestinian literature during that time frame. I will need two more things. First and foremost, I will need any clues on where the secret hiding place of the temple treasures, including the Ark of the Covenant, may be located on temple mound. Get that to us ASAP because we're going out there to do some digging. Secondly, and just as urgent, I'm looking for anything that may hint at the location of where the Ark may have been moved to."

"Does this have anything to do with our mystery caller last week?" came a question from Greg.

"It has everything to do with it. We're working a contract for them. Please send me a summary each day of what you learned. And send it more often if you find something significant. It may directly affect what Stef and I do. We're traveling out to the region in the next couple of days to do field work." informed Elliott.

"Will do. This sounds interesting. It'll take a couple of hours to get the S1 ready, but then, once we're airborne, the S1 can get over there and do the job quickly. We'll have scrambled images to the 3-D imaging available through our secured share-point web site before you get there." reassured Greg.

"That's all for now," said Elliott as he disconnected the call.

"Do you really think they'll find anything?" challenged Stef.

"I have no idea," responded Elliott. "But we'd be foolish if we didn't check it out and ended up missing a major clue."

"What do you have in mind for us?" Stef asked, her curiosity building, unable to conceal the obvious hint of excitement in her voice.

"I guess we're going to go to Jerusalem and start digging up Temple Mound." Elliott suggested.

We're going to have to do this really carefully. There are always people around there. Muslims, Jews, and Christians, it doesn't matter which, they're all going to be upset if they catch us digging around on the mound. How do you plan to accomplish this little trick?" Stef proposed.

"I have no idea. I think we'll have to go there and investigate the situation before we can fully pinpoint a plan. Let's go there and take a look." Elliott suggested.

"Like always, I'm with you. You seem the keep it exciting. Let's go home, replenish our travel packs, and get some rest. We can head out tonight. I'll check to see if there's a plane we can use. I'll come back to your office as soon as I'm ready." Stef replied, all fired up now over the challenging prospect of the task that lay ahead.

"I feel kinky. Can we spend 30 min. at the gym before we head out?" Hinted Elliott with a subtle smirk on his face, addressing Stef in his occasional suggestive manner, to try and throw her off guard.

"I'll see what planes and flight crews are available and I'll be right back." Stef advised him, very much used to Elliott's ways, who was always hoping against hope to find her in a receptive mood towards his playful innuendos. And left for her office, right next door to Elliott's', and called the air traffic office.

Then she stepped back into the small hotel room, which included a bedroom and bathroom, immediately behind her office, which was a benefit that all the senior IOM officers had available to them. She quickly changed into her gym clothes. Fifteen minutes later she was back in his office with scheduled flight information, ready to head to the gym.

During this time, Elliott had also changed into his gym clothes, and he was ready to go. The IOM gym was on the 4th floor, two floors up from the 6th floor executive offices. The gym had a full quarter mile track, which encircled the central office complex. At one end of the gym were the usual bicycles, walking pads, stair steps, weights, etc.

Elliott enjoyed working out with Stef. They would jog around the track together or lift weights together. Stef didn't enjoy working out with Elliott as much as he did. Stef often complained that she felt she was holding Elliott back. She often urged him to run ahead and lap her just to put some stress on his body. And when they did jog together, Elliott wasn't much of a conversationalist. Stef felt that if she was going to exercise with Elliott, they should at least be able to hold a meaningful conversation. Otherwise, she may as well be exercising alone.

But Elliott didn't see it that way. Just being in Stef's presence made him feel good. They didn't have to talk to be connected. He actually enjoyed the silence because it gave him time to think. And he loved thinking through numerous scientific issues. He was convinced that out there somewhere was Einstein's unifying model of everything. And he hoped that someday he would be able to help identify that model.

Stef and Elliott jogged together, talking briefly about what to expect from the NNRL. Then they jogged together in deep thought and in silence. They ran for three miles, then they lifted weights for another 15 minutes. Elliott has the tendency to sweat profusely when he exercised. He always came away soaked. Unfortunately, he loved to hug Stef. But she pushed him away when he came close to her. She didn't sweat, and she had no intention of sharing Elliott's sweat. She liked staying dry.

After exercising, they both went back down to the 6th floor to their office apartments, showered, changed, grabbed their travel bags, and met back in Elliot's office. It wasn't long before they were on their way to the elevators. At ground level they jumped into Elliott's car and drove down the gravel drive to the Stuart Highway. In spite of the complaining, and the occasional rock marks on the car, this driveway would never get paved or improved in any way. Its rough appearance kept tourists away.

It was early afternoon. The day was beautiful, bright, and sunny, a little on the warm side. They pulled on to the Highway heading north to Alice Springs. The city grew up as part of a railroad project. It was built up just north of a narrow pass between the Macdonnell Ranges, which was used for the rail line. Later the Stuart Highway used the same pass for its long north to south run, going all the way from Darwin in the North to Adelaide in the South. The town of Alice Springs grew up entirely on the north side of the pass. And the airport was built later on the south side of the pass, east of the highway. Pine Tree Gap was just a little further south of the airport off of the Highway to the west.

Elliott opened the sunroof and cracked the back windows in order to let the warm breeze flow through the hot car. As he passed the airport, he heard a car spin gravel, pulling off the shoulder and out onto the highway.

"Don't tell me," was his frustrated comment.

"Don't tell you what?" asked Stef.

"Don't tell me we have another tail pursuing us."

Stef looked in the passenger rear view mirror, intentionally not turning around so as to avoid giving away that they had detected their pursuer. They were being followed by a black sedan. It looked like a Toyota, but she couldn't be sure. Both of them knew what to do. They would keep an eye on the car while performing some meaningless routings to see if indeed they were being followed. They drove through the pass at the south end of Alice Springs. Coming into the city the road squeezed between the railroad tracks on the left and the Todd River on their right. Then the highway immediately went into a roundabout, which offered three different exits for traffic continuing north through Alice, and a fourth option that veered off to the left into some housing developments. Elliott picked the center road, Gap Road, since it was the fastest road, and headed off toward the center of Alice. About halfway to town (about five city blocks) he took a sharp right turn onto Hayes Street, and almost immediately took another right onto South Terrace, sending him back south toward the roundabout. The car behind them followed the same pattern. This route wouldn't make sense if you were heading to a specific location, since they were no heading back south toward the airport.

"Looks like we are being chased again," said Elliott. "This time let's try to keep them alive so we can learn what their problem is."

Stef grabbed the phone and put out the alert message to the IOM team.

"We have a 666 on South heading south."

This radio message alerted the team, many of which were in camouflaged taxis. They all knew that a 666 was a pursuit vehicle, and they immediately changed direction to join in the chase.

Elliott turned left on Stephens Road, over the Todd River, which took them out into the country toward the north-east of the city while Stef kept the team updated on their location. The eucalyptus trees were beautiful out this direction. They passed some camel farms, primarily used to give tourists a camel riding experience. Heading out into the bush would be safer than trying to deal with their pursuer in the busy down-town area. And it would result in fewer questions.

Stef gave an update on the radio. "Stephens Road heading north just past Barrett."

"Apparently these guys haven't figured out that we're leading them into a trap."

"They must not know this area very well or they would know we're not exactly taking the best route."

Elliott saw a couple of company cars coming south towards them and he knew that the trap was about to be sprung.

"Even if these guys behind us figure it out now, it's too late."

The two cars passed. Traffic was very light in this area and it wasn't hard to figure out which vehicle was in pursuit.

Elliott and Stef maintained a steady speed in order to not give anything away. When the two IOM cars came to the pursuit vehicle, one pulled directly in front and the other directly behind, boxing it in. They were too tight to allow any maneuverability.

As soon as Elliott saw them box the car in, he did a quick U-turn and headed back. He arrived just in time to see one gunman poke his head out of the sunroof, Uzi in hand, and he started firing off a hail of bullets at the two company cars.

The company men were well trained, and each had crawled out of their vehicles on the opposite side of their opponent. They got out just in time, as the bullets exploded the windows of their vehicles.

The two men in the pursuit vehicle jumped out of their car, one on each side, and took off running in opposite directions. Elliott took off after one and left the other for his teammates to pursue. He knew that he wasn't on a motorcycle, and that his vehicle was taking a beating. If he were going to catch this guy, he would have to do it fast. But he wanted him alive, so shooting him wasn't an option. He decided to try to run him down with his car. He may break a couple of legs, but he would still be alive. But his plans were foiled when the man stopped, turned, and started firing at him. Elliott and Stef ducked down as the windshield splattered over the top of them. He kept his foot on the accelerator. The firing continued for a couple more seconds. Then they felt a bump, and a crash. The firing had stopped. Here in the bush, it was hard to tell if the bump was from a clump of brush, or from hitting the assailant. Elliott looked up and realized that the car had crashed into a Eucalyptus tree, but it had also managed to run over one of the legs of the shooter. He had tried to jump out of the way and had been unsuccessful.

Just then the shooting started up again. Apparently, a broken leg was not enough to discourage their attacker. A couple of pistol shots rang out, and then it was quiet once again. Looking up Elliott realized that one of the company men, not knowing about the urgency to keep these men alive, had shot him with two pistol rounds. They wouldn't be getting any information from him.

"Are you to OK?" asked the company man.

"We're great," responded Elliott. "We were hoping to keep him alive. But he didn't offer us a lot of options. What happened with the other guy?"

"Same thing. He kept shooting and we valued our life over his. Sorry."

"No problem. I'm sure this isn't the last time we'll hear from these guys. Will you be able to take care of the cleanup?"

"Will do."

"In that case we'll be heading off. Can we use one of your vehicles, since ours is out of commission?"

"Good on you Mate," agreed the company man without hesitation to Elliott's suggestion.

Elliott and Stef climbed into one of the well-ventilated taxis, with windshield spattered all over the front seat, and headed off toward town. They shared an apartment at the Aurora Alice Springs Resort. For them it was a perfect location. It fronted on the Leichhardt Terrace, which was a continuation of the South Terrace, and the back side of the hotel was on the Todd Mall, a section of Gap Road that had been closed off and turned into a down-town walking outdoor mall. The hotel was in the center of town, right in the middle of the action, which wasn't much.

Their room was more like a hotel room with a kitchen. But for them it was perfect. On the back side of the hotel, facing the mall was the Red Ochre Grill, where they often stopped for dinner when they didn't feel like cooking. And today had been another exhausting day.

CHAPTER EIGHTEEN – PART 3

Jerusalem

Early April, 2025 AD, Jerusalem, Israel

Stef received a call that confirmed their flight arrangements to Israel, but they wouldn't be able to depart until 04:00AM. She gave Elliott the news and they decided to catch as much sleep as possible, and then head out at around 03:00AM.

The departure from the Alice Springs airport was uneventful. This time there were no dust storms. There wasn't much of a moon. It was pitch black as they headed north-west. They would travel non-stop over Indonesia, then India, heading North to avoid the Persian / Arab nations, traveling West over the Baltics, and over several of the old Soviet Bloc countries, on towards the Mediterranean. Flying in this region was somewhat tricky. You couldn't take a direct route. There were several countries that would not give fly-over permission for any reason, like Iran, and then there were other countries that wouldn't give fly-over permission if you were heading to Israel, like Syria. In the end you had to fly past the region by going to the north until you were over the Mediterranean, then go south to the Mediterranean, and then come into Israel from the west.

Eventually they landed in Israel, comfortably rested and ready to go to work. They caught a cab and went directly to the Hotel Imperial, close by the Jaffa Gate. This was a favorite spot for Elliot, who loved to walk around the old town markets and experience the culture. It somehow made him feel closer to God, being in a city that was revered by the world's three most prominent monotheistic religions, Christianity, Judaism, and Islam. Ironically, all three believed in the same God, who was a loving and caring God, and at the same time all three religious groups hated and mistrusted each other. It was an irony that had often plagued and frustrated him.

Originally, Christians were composed primarily of Jews, and they worshiped together in the same Temples and synagogues. Similarly, Jews and Muslims were "brothers" during the early years of the Muslim faith. But pressures for the control of Jerusalem, amongst other things, had left each group with a large amount of animosity towards the other. First the Jews controlled the land, then the Arabs, then the Christian Crusaders came in and the Christians took control, then it went back to the Muslims, and now it was back under Jewish control, but the Palestinian-Arab influence was still very strong. Everyone seemed to have their own justification for control, and each is willing to fight to the death to keep that control.

Stef preferred the Scheda Hotel in the Sheraton Plaza. It was a high-rise hotel which was "modern" and had the amenities that you would expect in a Westernized hotel. But she understood Elliott's love of the "old town." She had enjoyed herself back on the Gold Coast, just a few days earlier. Now it was his turn.

Early April, 2025 AD, Elko, Nevada, IOM Research Lab

"We're about ten minutes away from Temple Mount," Greg announced to both Dawn and Alan on his team. He was referring to the arrival of the S1, the same one they had used a couple days earlier for the Barjet assassination. However, the weapons systems had been removed and in its place was a high-intensity scanner which included X-ray, Ultra-Violet, and Infra-Red capabilities. With this scanner he would be able to penetrate about 20 feet into the Mound, which hopefully was enough to identify the caverns and caves that held the Ark and the other temple treasures.

Greg instructed; "We'll take three North-South passes and three East-West passes. The first pass will be at a 45 degree angle off to one side.

The second pass will be directly over the center, and the third pass will be at a 45 degree angle off to the other side of the mount. With those six passes, they should be able to identify every dent in the mount."

Greg was the remote pilot of the S1. Dawn would be responsible for operating the Scanning equipment. And Alan handled the data capture and recording piece of the mission. Afterwards, Alan would then assemble the six scans into a three-dimensional projection of the mount.

"Data capture is ready," reported Alan.

"And the scanning equipment seems to be operating correctly as well. Let's do the first run and then validate that everything was captured correctly," suggested Dawn.

"Good plan," came back from Greg. "First scan starts in 10 seconds, 9, 8, 7, 6, 5, 4, 3, 2, 1, equipment on."

The entire first scan took less than 15 seconds. The data transfer occurred as planned, and the team moved forward with all six scans.

"Heading home," reported Greg. "Send the data to Stef and Elliott as soon as possible."

"I'm building the mount projection and will be sending it off to our data share-point shortly," responded Alan.

Early April, 2025 AD, Jerusalem, Israel

It wasn't long before Elliott had the internet connected and was viewing the share-point files that Greg and his team had generated. The quality was excellent, but the images were confusing. It appeared that there were several caverns in the mount. And some of the caverns seemed to have interconnections. He would need to enhance the resolution of these images before he could identify which cave, they needed to enter.

"Stef, this is going to take some time. There are several caverns in the mount, and they cross each other and go at all different angles. I don't have any idea which cavern we're interested in. I'm going to look through each one of them carefully to see what they contain and hopefully we can narrow down the options from that."

"Elliott, let me take the first crack at analyzing the options. I'm more experienced with it and besides, I can see that you'd much rather take a walk and explore some of the city. And I'm not as excited about walking around out there."

Elliott was hoping she would volunteer. She was better at the software tools than he was, and she was right about his wanting to get out and stretch his legs.

"Excellent. Thanks for the offer. I think I'll take you up on it." Elliott stood up to leave and Stef sat down at the computer and went right to work.

"I'll be back in about an hour or so." confirmed Elliott.

"See you then. Please be careful. You know someone is hunting for us." Stef warned him.

"Will do," was the response as he went out the door, being careful to lock the door behind him. He cared more about Stef's safety than his own.

Stef could quickly see what Elliott was talking about. There were about seven or eight caverns, and several of them seemed to be interconnecting. She started by separating out the caverns. Each of the four views that Greg had sent them would be repeated for each of the caverns. A specific cavern would be highlighted and visualized in each set of the views. Once they were separated, then each cavern could be analyzed to see if it was viable as hiding place of the Ark of the Covenant.

Two-thirds of the caverns were quickly eliminated. They were either too deep below the surface, or too rustic to fit the description of the Ark's hiding place. Two of the caverns were obviously drainage or water canals. Another looked like it was an escape tunnel from within the town from the West side of the mount, to outside of the city on the East side of the mount.

After going through a process of elimination, Stef had narrowed the options down to being one of three. Two of the tunnels looked as though at one time they had access from the surface. They appeared to have numerous storage locations along their walls, all of which were bare. These two caves fit the requirement of being surface accessible hiding places for the temple treasures.

The first cave appeared to have its access point near the northern end of the Temple Mound, close to a small above-surface six-sided gazebo or vestibule, made entirely out of stone with arches on each side. It was called the Dome of the Spirits or Aubbat el-Arwah. It seemed out of place on the mostly barren temple-mount. It had a bit of a haggard look about it, showing signs of weathering. It didn't have the brightness of some of the other buildings on the mount.

The Dome of the Spirits was wrapped up in temple lore, which claims the possibility of three sites for the original Temple of Solomon. The first, most likely site, is where the Dome of the Rock now stands. The second likely location is where the Dome of Spirits stands. Lore claims that the Dome of Spirits was erected to commemorate the location of the original "Holy of Holies" from Solomon's temple and the third most likely location is south of where the Dome of the Rock stands.

The access point for the first cave is immediately north of the Dome of Spirits. This made it a very likely candidate as the hiding place of the Ark of the Covenant which would need to be accessed through the temple's "Holy of Holies."

The second cave was a little more of a problem. Its access point was toward the south end of Temple Mount which was dominated by the Dome of the Rock. The Dome is the third most sacred shrine to Moslems all over the world. The main building was an eight-sided structure about 30 feet in height, above which is a gold domed roof. It houses the rock from where Abraham tried to sacrifice his son to God, and from which Muhammad later ascended to heaven to received God's commandments. The Dome of the Rock was constructed around 691 AD by the Umayyad Dynasty.

Within the Dome, and under the "Rock" is a cave, which is a restricted place of worship for Moslems only. Stef's second cave was directly under a cave that was under the Dome of the Rock. Tradition claims that the Dome was constructed in the same location where Solomon had built his temple, making Stef's second cave another possibility as the original hiding place of the Ark.

The third possible tunnel was also near the surface. It looked like a large, circular room, with cubby-holes on its side walls. It had no identifiable access point from the surface, or from any of the other caves. It appeared to be a large cavern directly in the middle of the mount, about 15 feet below the surface. This cave appeared to be full of "stuff", but the resolution of a radar scan into the earth was so poor that it was difficult to identify anything.

Stef sat back in her chair, feeling highly successful and clearly satisfied with the results of her research. She took a look at the clock and noticed that she had been working for about three hours. Her feelings of success shifted immediately to concern for Elliott. Where had he gone? It was unusual for him to have been gone for so long. She reached for her cell phone and gave him call. No response. It clicked immediately to the message machine without ringing. This meant that either the cell phone battery was dead, something which Elliott was very careful about, or it meant that the cell phone was deliberately turned off, which made no sense if he was just going for a walk. Now she was really worried.

CHAPTER NINETEEN

Travis AFB
Early April, 2025 AD, Fairfield, California

The Templar archives were located at an Air Force Base. Originally, they were located beneath the George Washington Masonic Museum in Washington DC. However, the visibility of that location forced templar leaders to search for a more secure location that no one would suspect. The Templars felt that the most secure place in the world for their library and archives would be on a US military base. Bases were secure. And bases tended to be so busy, and were layered with so much bureaucracy, that the left hand didn't always keep track of what the right hand was doing. If you label your activities with a three-letter acronym, it seemed official. And no one wanted to admit that they didn't know what an acronym stood for, so the Templars became very successful at hiding their activities in plain sight.

In this case, the base of choice was Travis AFB, located near Fairfield, about one hour's drive east of San Francisco Bay Area in California. Travis was located in the middle of no-where, surrounded by flat farmlands growing sunflowers and a variety of grains.

Greg, Dawn, and Alan drove about two hours from their IOM base in Nevada to Elko, Nevada, where they took an East-bound Delta flight from Elko to Salt Lake City. There they connected to a West-bound flight to Sacramento, California. In Sacramento they rented a car for their one-hour drive towards the Bay Area. They hopped on Interstate 5 South, and then took Interstate 80 West toward the Bay. At Exit 57 they headed South on Leisure Town Road and eventually arrived at the Travis AFB main gate. Travis was the home of the 60th Air Mobility Wing. As they approached the gate, off to the right, they passed the 60th's new Air Force training hospital, the David Grant Medical Center, which had a reputation for being one of the best training hospitals in the world. It was the second largest medical facility in the Air Force, and with the planned renovations it would soon be the largest.

Greg, who was driving, presented his CAC (Common Access Card) to the guard at the main gate, and was waved through. Since the CAC card system had been implemented, it was now possible to access all US military bases anywhere in the world, simply by showing this one card. Separate permissions were no longer necessary for each base. And the IOM was tied into the CAC imaging system and was capable of creating CAC cards as needed.

As the threesome entered the base, they could see a large C-5 cargo plane slowly taking off on the runway to the right. These planes were so large they appeared to sit in mid-air and just float.

The threesome drove straight ahead, staying on the main road, Travis Ave, through the middle of the base. They passed the Travis Credit Union on the right, crossed Skymaster Drive, and followed a row of beautiful Eucalyptus trees on the right. They passed the AAFES gas station, which has the curious distinction of having gas pumps on both sides of the street but only servicing them on the north side of the street. Then they passed the fitness center on the left, a large and impressive new complex, followed by the AF Inns, a hotel for temporary military visitors.

At the end of Travis Avenue, directly ahead of them in the middle of the base, is a small, man-made hill, on top of which is a large building, commonly referred to as the "old hospital." This hill stands out, amongst the mostly flat surroundings.

As Travis Avenue goes up the hill it becomes Burgan Boulevard. Going straight ahead put them on the driveway up the hill to the hospital. They followed the drive around to the back side of the old hospital and into a parking spot. They climbed out of the car and headed to a set of double doors on the back side of the building. Entering the building, they proceeded to a stairway that led down to the basement. In the basement was, what appeared to be, a storage closet, locked by a combination paddle lock. Greg set the combination to 2012, the year that the Mayans and Nostradamus predicted the world would end. However, instead of opening the door, this combination opened the wall around the door, and the three stepped through. They could hear the fake combination lock resetting itself as they stepped into the closet.

The wall closed itself, clicking to a locked position, and the floor beneath them started slowly, then more rapidly, to descend. It went down about 20 feet. Then one side of the wall slid aside and opened up into a large 10 feet. by 10 feet reception area. The walls were barren. The entire room seemed drab. Directly in the center of the room stood a small table with a telephone. There was no dial or buttons on the phone. Picking up the receiver, Greg put the phone to his ear.

"May I help you?" Came the question from the anonymous voice at the other end of the line.

"We need to look at the records relating to the Crusader visit to Temple Mount and any information relating to the Ark of the Covenant," responded Greg.

"And where does your authority come from?"

"Malvika," was Greg's one-word response.

A panel at the far end of the room slowly slid aside and someone was waiting inside the door. "I can show you where the Crusader journal records are located."

"We'd also like to see the Gospel of Mark which the Crusaders took from the temple mount."

"That's impossible. That scroll is kept in darkness to avoid erosion. It can only be brought out on special ceremonial occasions, every ten years."

Greg insisted that they must see the book, but the librarian explained that he couldn't show it to them even if he wanted to. "It was in a darkened, sealed container and could only be opened by the reigning Templar High Priest of the 33rd order. And then only when special occasion permitted, like every tenth anniversary of the resurrection of Jesus Christ. And that won't occur for another year."

The librarian continued leading the group to a large filing cabinet and, opening a large drawer stated, "Here are all the journals, written in Latin. You will need to be extremely careful with each of them."

Greg and Dawn, who were versed in Latin, began pouring over the documents, hoping to find some small clue that would help guide them to their next step. Alan, who was not trained in Latin, had the librarian show him to the maps that were drawn during the time of the Crusades.

Early April, 2025 AD, Fairfield, California

"I have good news and bad news. Which do you want first?" asked Greg of Stef. Greg was on speakerphone so Stef could hear the conversation. It was early evening in Jerusalem, but it was just short of noon in California.

"Good, of course," answered Stef. "By the way, the scans of the mount were terrific, and I've identified three possibilities that need further investigation."

"I'll bet I can tell you which they are," jumped in Alan. "One under the Dome of the Rock, one under the Dome of Spirits, and that large circular cavern that's a little lower and near the center of the mount."

"Exactly right. I'm glad you confirmed my analysis."

"I wish I could be there to share in the exploration experience with you."

"Tell me your good news."

"Actually," this time it was Dawn talking, "what we found in the journals seems to support the likelihood that the cavern near the Dome of Spirits is the one we're looking for. I think you should investigate that one first."

"Thanks. That also looks like it may be the easiest to get to. It's the closest to the surface and has the least obstructions. So, what's the bad news?"

Greg explained why they were restricted from accessing the Gospel of Mark that was found in the cave. The librarian won't permit them to even look at it for another year. Not even when Greg dropped some high-level names. The librarian didn't care. The library was his turf, and no one else would be able to tell him how to run it.

Stef was frustrated, "We need to see it. It may hold clues to the location of the Ark. Or why else would someone place it specifically in that location?"

"What do you suggest?"

"Steal it!"

"Say again? I thought you said steal it."

"That's right. Steal it."

"You don't just steal things from the Sacred Archives of the Templars. Add to that the fact that we're in the middle of a military base. You can't just run away from here. The cops around here will give you a ticket if you even look like you're thinking about going more than 25 miles per hour. And if you drive toward the North Gate, which is the quickest way out of here, you drive past a housing area where the speed limit drops to 15 MPH. Its nuts."

"Figure it out," said Stef with exasperation. She had already worked herself into a frenzy over Elliott's absence. Now, add the bureaucracy of the Templar librarian, and she was taking her frustration out on Greg and Dawn.

"Will do," came back the report. And the line went dead.

CHAPTER TWENTY

Escape from Travis AFB
Early April, 2025 AD, Fairfield, California

Greg, Dawn, and Alan knew what to do. They started to scrutinize the library, looking for alternative exits, potential hiding places, and any other means that they might use to abscond with the scroll. Then they took a close look at the security systems surrounding the scroll. The scroll was locked in a secure vault. They found it challenging, but not impossible.

They formulated a plan that involved disabling the security system, especially the security cameras. Then they would drug the librarian and his assistants with sleep inducing darts. After that they would break into the vault, take the scroll out of its container, and return the container to the vault. Then they would return everything to its normal operating condition. They hoped that they could make it out of the library without anyone knowing what had happened. Everyone had simply taken a small nap. No one would even question that something had gone missing.

The plan went off like clockwork. From initiation to completion, the theft took about 15 min. And they were safely in the car, starting their drive off the hill. They took a left turn on Burgan Blvd, heading for the North Gate. Suddenly, and unexpectedly, an alarm went off. It wasn't long before police and emergency equipment were racing in from all points of the base toward hospital hill.

Ahead of them they could see that the gate exit had been blocked. They weren't going to get out that direction. Greg turned right and pulled into the parking lot of Building 1307, which was a single adult housing unit. The three climbed out of the vehicle and started walking toward the park across the street. Alan had the scroll tucked under his left armpit, inside his coat. All three realized that they needed to get back to their Nevada lab as soon as possible, so they could proceed with their analysis of the scrolls. And any delay answering questions or being detained by the police, would cause them to be discovered and could affect the success of the mission.

They stepped out on the jogging trail and started to walk the trail. The jogging trail circled a small man-made lake which opened up on the back side to some family housing units. They walked past the housing units and headed to the North-East corner of the base housing complex. The housing complex had a cement wall all around it. Fortunately, it was hidden from the security check point, so that, by going to that corner of the base, the three could climb the cement block fence, going over the metal bars and razor fence pointing outward, intended to keep people from climbing into the base, but not from climbing out. Once outside the base wall, they walked across the cow pasture, staying off the main road in order to avoid detection.

Following parallel to North Gate Rd., which was the name of Burgan Blvd. after exiting the base. They continued walking until they intersected Canon Rd. At this point they took a left and walked on the road toward Vanden Road.

Greg had used his cell phone to call a taxi, which caught up to them just a little after Canon met Vanden. The taxi took them down Vanden, turning right on Leisure Town Road heading toward the freeway. The cab would take them directly to the Sacramento airport, about a one-hour drive.

Greg called the car rental company and told them where they could find their vehicle. He had used one of his many aliases, which included a temporary credit card. Using false identification and credit cards was a common practice in the IOM, and the car would not be traceable back to him.

They changed their flight reservations so they could leave on the next available flight, and they were off, heading back to Salt Lake City, and then to Elko.

CHAPTER TWENTY-ONE

Followed in Jerusalem
Early April, 2025 AD, Jerusalem, Israel

Elliott loved being in a different culture. It brought out a sense of adventure and presented an opportunity to learn. Elliott recognized that every culture had a set of beliefs upon which it builds its society. Elliott had Christian roots, but the people he was venturing out into today exhibited strong Palestinian / Arabic / Muslim roots. What made Jerusalem fascinating was that within a short walk he could cross between a variety of Christian sects, including Roman Catholic, Eastern Orthodox, and numerous Protestant denominations. He could also cross several Muslim, and Jewish sects. And each group had their own delineated territory. Each had a strong belief system to which they would testify as being the one total and complete truth. This caused skeptics to declare religion to be a confused hodge-podge of ideas and doctrines. It was this same hodge-podge that fascinated Elliott about Jerusalem.

"Wouldn't it be great if someday God came down here and set them all straight," he mused. "What we need is another prophet, like Moses or Mohammed." Looking up into the sky he whispered, more to himself than to God; "I think it's time for God to come down and set man straight."

Elliott walked through the markets, studying the various trinkets and artifacts that were being sold. He wished that somehow, he could justify collecting these small treasures and taking them home with him, but his lifestyle made that impossible. He had to keep his possessions mobile and to a minimum. He crossed from one cultural zone to another, finding each as fascinating as the last. He enjoyed searching through the artifacts and identifying the symbology that made each culture unique.

He had only been out about thirty minutes when he realized that someone was tailing him. This made him more careful. He soon realized that it was not one, but three individuals, two men and a woman that were watching his movements. They didn't seem to be aggressive, only watching. So, he decided to keep an eye on them without letting them know that he had marked them.

Elliott continued working his way through the busy streets. He had designed a circular route for himself as part of his exploration of this part of the city. He continued on the streets that would eventually lead him full circle back to his hotel. But then, he wondered, would it be wise to show his cohorts what hotel he was staying at? Or did they already know? He decided to give them the slip before he returned to the hotel just in case they didn't know. His mind continued to race, trying to create the optimal plan without knowing the intentions or the level of knowledge of his pursuers.

He continued on his exploratory journey while, at the same time, keeping an eye on his new associates, and simultaneously planning his disappearance. He would occasionally step into one of the many tourist shops, not so much to admire their wares, but more so to confirm the intentions of his tails. But his charade taught him very little.

He had worked himself about three-quarters of the way through his route, and was slowly heading back to the hotel, when he tired of the cat-and-mouse game and decided to put an end to it. He ditched into an exceptionally large open market area, which was much like a blend between a shopping mall and a flea market of tourist shops. This area had several entrance and exit points and was large enough to allow him to zig-zag his way into a route that would be impossible to follow. He began his diversion, feeling confident that his pursuers didn't stand a chance of keeping up with him.

After 10 minutes of misdirection, he noticed that his pursuers were having trouble keeping up with him. It wouldn't take a lot to lose them. He made several quick corner turns in rapid succession, and then slipped through a couple of shops that had multiple entrances. That was all it took. He had successfully given them the slip. He exited the market unto a side street, and quickly worked his way to the closest main street.

Elliott had an excellent sense of direction and it wasn't long before he was back on the road leading to the hotel. But then he made a crucial mistake. He spotted a shop that had a collection of hand carved birds that were native to Israel. He knew that Stef had a small bird collection and he wanted to get her the national bird of Israel, the Hoopoe. He picked a carving that he thought was exceptionally well done, negotiated an appropriate price, paid for the bird, and headed out of the shop. But just as he was leaving the shop, he spotted one of the three tails, standing just inside the shop across the street. How had they found him? And why were they following him? He was going to try to find out by cornering his tail. He headed down a quiet side street and made a sharp turn around the side of one of the buildings.

He ditched behind the corner, hoping that his tail would suddenly come around the corner so Elliott could catch him by surprise. The plan worked as anticipated. The potential assailant came rushing around the corner and Elliott smacked him with a length of board that he had picked up. The assailant dropped to the ground, out cold. Unfortunately, Elliott was not the only person in the alley and his actions had drawn some attention. He was starting to collect an audience. Elliott quickly searched the unconscious assailant, taking his gun and looking for some kind of identification. But this individual was obviously a pro. No identification could be found. Only a throw-away cell phone, and Elliott took it. Later he would track the numbers.

Elliott quickly left the area, went back out on the main road, and tried to hide himself by getting mixed into the crowd. He kept an eye out for the other tails but couldn't see them anywhere. They must have split up and tried to catch him by following different routes. He tried calling

Stef to let he know what had been going on, and he found his phone was dead. He couldn't even give her a call to let her know he was alright.

It wasn't long before Elliott had made his way back to the hotel. As he approached the front of the hotel, Elliott noticed the two other individuals that had been tailing him. Apparently, they knew which hotel he was staying at and must have started following him from the hotel. Elliott ditched into a small shop where he pretended to shop, but at the same time he formulated a plan to go back around to the back side of the hotel and sneak in from a side where his tails couldn't see him. He wanted to check and make sure that Stef was OK. His first concern was about her. Then they could work together to solve the mystery of their pursuers.

Elliott came around back as planned. He decided to try calling her on the disposable phone he had taken from his attacker, but quickly realized that without his pre-programmed phone, he had no idea what her phone number was. It irritated him to be dependent on technology, especially when it caused him to change his habits, like not remembering phone numbers. So, he quietly snuck to her room and listened at the door. Not hearing anything he went ahead and knocked on the door.

Stef responded with; "Who's there?"

"Santa Claus," was Elliott's predetermined coded response.

"Get your butt in here," said Stef in her excited voice as she swung the door open. "You had me a little freaked out, taking so long to get back. And I couldn't get a hold of you on the phone. What's that all about?"

"My phone died. Sorry."

"So, what happened to you anyway?"

Elliott told her of his adventure. "We need to go back to the lobby and see if those guys are still there. I wanted to learn what they are after and who sent them."

The two left the room and headed to the lobby from the back side. Stef went in first, assuming that they may not know her. She looked for the guys that Elliott described, but could not find anyone that fit the description.

Giving up on the search, they decided to return to their room. They headed back using a new routing in case the intruders were laying a trap for them. As they rounded the corner in the hall to where their room was located, Elliott suddenly pulled back.

He whispered to Stef; "Someone's trying to break into our room. I see a couple of people trying to jimmy the lock. I'm going to keep an eye on them and after they made it into the room, we'll have them cornered. Wait, they're in. Let's go."

They quietly worked their way to the room and rushed in, pistol in hand. "Hold it. Who are you guys and what are you doing?" The French couple threw up their hands with expressions of total shock and fear.

Stef, turning red, pocketed her pistol and said, "This isn't our room Elliott."

"Oops," said Elliott, pocketing his own pistol. "Crazy Americans got confused."

The French man, putting down his arms, initiated a spew of vulgarities. He was obviously quite angry. Fortunately, Stef and Elliott didn't know what they were saying. But it sounded serious.

Elliott and Stef apologetically left the room and headed off in a different direction. "I was sure that was our room," said Elliott.

"Well, it didn't have any of our stuff. I think we went to the wrong floor."

Elliott pulled his room key out of his pocket and they discovered that they were one floor lower than they should have been.

Arriving back in their room, and verifying that it was indeed their room, Stef updated Elliott on the information that she had received from Greg.

"Let's go over to temple mount tonight and take a look at what we're dealing with," suggested Elliott. "It looks like we need to figure out a way to get into the cave that's by the Dome of Spirits. We need to look at the security in the area. And what kind of a digging project we're dealing with."

Stef readily agreed. "What about those guys that were trying to follow you. I wonder if they're the same group that we encountered back in the Rain Forest. And who are they? And are they trying to disrupt our search, or is there something else that they're after? I wish we could have a conversation with one of them."

"I agree. In the future we'll need to be really careful and keep an eye out."

CHAPTER TWENTY-TWO

Temple Mount
Early April, 2025 AD, Jerusalem, Israel

At 02:00AM Stef and Elliott were in the lobby of the hotel, heading for the front door. A taxi had just arrived and was dropping someone off, so Elliott quickly grabbed the taxi, and they were off towards the temple mount.

Traffic was extremely light, as would have been expected at that time of night. The night air was cool and slightly breezy. It didn't take long before they had arrived at their destination and were walking up the stairs to the mount.

Once on the mount, they walked around the side of the Dome of the Rock, in search of the Dome of Spirits. Normally it might have been hard to spot, but the lighting of the Dome of the Rock, and the full moon, made it easy to spot. They headed over to the Dome to take a look.

"We may need to take out the lights, to make it harder to identify us," suggested Stef.

"But that may just cause the opposite effect of what we're after if it draws attention to us."

"So, what do you suggest? We just start digging here on the mount?"

"That may be exactly what we'll have to do." Elliott had stooped down to look at the ground. "It seems that the Dome of Spirits is built on top of solid rock. But just off to the side of the rock there seems to be cobblestones. According to the map we generated, the cave should be about 10 feet East of the actual dome. We'll have to peel away these cobblestones and dig down about 5 or 6 feet to hit the cave. I don't understand how a cave that close to the surface hasn't caved in or at least shown some sign of a depression in the surface. Unless we're in the wrong spot."

"I'm sure we're in the right spot. I guess we'll find out when we start digging. I don't see a lot of guards posted in the area."

"Let's walk around a little more and investigate the area. I want to make sure we've covered all our bases. One thing I'm not sure of is how we're going to be able to get in and out of here quickly. And we'll need to get some tools together as well. We're going to need some help if we are expected to do this fast." Elliott concluded.

"Where are we going to get help?" proposed Stef.

"I'll have to do a search for any 33rd degree Masons that may be in the area to help us out. We need them to be Templar Knights in order to be involved in this dig." Elliott punched in the number for their offices back in Alice Springs and asked the secretary to search out the names of any Knights in Jerusalem. It may be 02:30AM in Jerusalem, but it was shortly before lunch in Alice.

They continued to case out the area, making sure there wouldn't be any surprises. The plan was to come back the following evening and go to work. As they were heading off the mount, Elliott received an e-mail. Checking his Blackberry, he saw that his office had sent him the contact information for three individuals who were reasonably close to Jerusalem. He would give them a call bright and early in the morning. But for now, the two of them were heading back to the hotel to get some rest.

Early April, 2025 AD, Jerusalem, Israel

In the morning Elliott learned that the local Templar Knights were available and willing to help in the dig. And they had the necessary tools. They set a time to meet on the mount at 2 AM.

Elliott and Stef did a little sightseeing, but this time, rather than exploring the culture the way Elliott liked to travel, they did its Stef's way, on a tour bus. After that they went out for a nice lunch/dinner, and then sat in the hotel room and flipped channels for a while. "We never can find anything worth watching in hotels," complained Elliott. "I don't know why they put TVs in here. It must be to frustrate the guests."

"Do you have any better ideas," asked Stef.

"Oh definitely!" responded Elliott in his solicitation voice, which was a little high pitched. And he added a wink and a smile to spice up the comment.

"I withdraw the question," returned Stef. "I should have known better than to ask that question," as she flipped through all the channels one more time.

Elliott had resigned himself to reading a book. He lay on the bed next to Stef and became completely engrossed.

Stef put the TV on mute, hoping to see if a movie was going to start on that channel, and picked up her book to start reading. It would only be a few more hours before they were heading back out to the Temple Mount.

Early April, 2025 AD, Jerusalem, Israel

They arrived at the Dome of Spirits about 10 minutes before two AM and found four other individuals standing close by with shovels and picks in hand. Following protocol Elliott stepped forward, presenting himself as the leader. In return one of the other four stepped forward to present himself as their leader. They gave each other the secret identifying handshake and Elliott asked the code question; "Why haven't we seen you?"

The leader of the four gave the appropriate response; "Because I've been in Tibet. And where have you been?" The secret passwords were dependent on the date, and the time of day, so they had to think carefully about their questions and the responses.

Remembering the appropriate response Elliott said, "Studying bird migrations in Malaysia."

With the formalities over, they were free to let their questions fly. Elliott's new friend started off with; "What's going on here? Are we really going to dig up Temple Mount?"

"We need to find the location of the cave where the temple treasures were hidden."

"Does this have anything to do with the Crusades and what the Knights took out of here?"

"It has more to do with what they did not take out of here. But we can't explain any more than that. Sorry."

"I understand. My code name is Restov, and my friends are agents Questradis, Whiskey, and Novacane."

"And you are?" Restov demanded, after he had identified all of his associates.

"She's Bravo," said Elliott, pointing to Stef, "and I'm Zeta. We have identified the spot where we need to dig. Yesterday, using our high intensity scanning equipment, we found what we suspect is the location of the cave. It should be about 10 feet East of the Dome of Spirits." Elliott walked over to the spot where he thought they should start digging. "Right about here," he pointed out.

"Very well," responded Restov. "Let's get to work."

In addition to the tools, the Templars had brought barricades and construction cones. They hoped to make it look official so no one would bother them. They quickly set up the barricades and went to work on the hole.

The team grabbed the pickaxes and started to pry up the large cobblestones that covered the mount. The first one was a struggle. They scratched away around the edges, getting rid of all the loose dirt. Then they tried to wedge their picks into the edge of the stone. Unfortunately, the rocks were fit together quite tightly. After several attempts, Restov was able to use his shovel point to get a slight hold on the edge of the stone. He was able to move the stone up slightly, less than one centimeter, but it caused the point of the shovel to be bent. Restov continued to hold up his side while Questradis tried prying with his shovel on the opposite side. He was able to lift the rock just slightly higher than Restove's. Now Whisky stuck his shovel next to Restov's and used it as a wedge to pry Restov's side a little higher. And so on, back, and forth, a fraction of a centimeter at a time, until finally the stone broke free.

With an enormous sigh of relief, they rejoiced at freeing the first stone. Once the first stone was pulled up, the rest were much easier. They could wedge a pick under each joining cobblestone and pry it up from the bottom. It wasn't long before they had cleared an area of about 5 feet by 5 feet. Then they commenced digging.

They took turns, two at a time, digging. There wasn't enough room for more than two. They dug quickly, always hoping that no one would challenge their activities.

Upon reaching a depth of five feet Restov looked up questioningly at Zeta; "Shouldn't we have hit something by now?"

"I would have thought we were close."

Just then Whiskey, who was in the hole with Restov, swung his pick into the ground and everyone heard a thump. "What was that?" asked Whiskey.

Restove and Whiskey started digging rapidly in the area of the sound. It wasn't long before they started uncovering a wooden surface. It looked like a series of beams laid out side by side.

"You'd think that wood would have rotted away by now," said Whiskey. "But this wood doesn't show any signs of rotting at all. They treated it with some type of sap or tar. I've never seen anything like this."

"How are we going to break through?" asked Elliott.

"Let's see if we can find a seam." Restove and Whiskey started digging in opposite directions, looking to find the full length of one of the beams. It took a while, but eventually they each found the opposite ends of a beam. Unfortunately, they found the ends of two different beams. Questradis and Novacane jumped in to relieve them and continued searching for beam ends.

Eventually they did find both ends of one of the beams. The next trick was to pry this beam out of its resting place. Like everything else in their excavating project, this turned out to be challenging. The beam would not pry up. It simply wouldn't budge; not even a little.

"Any other suggestions?" questioned Questradis.

"Let's chip away at one of the ends and see if we can figure out how thick these beams are," suggested Stef. The suggestion seemed like a good one, so Questradis grabbed his pick and without saying a word, aggressively started chopping at the end of one of the adjacent beam's ends. The hope was that if you chopped at the adjacent beam, then you would be able to wedge a pick into the end of your beam and pry it up.

After several minutes of chopping Questradis suggested; "These beams are quite thick. If I remember my history correctly, this cave was accessed quite quickly and easily by the Crusaders."

"That's because they didn't complain as much," quipped Whiskey.

Eventually they had chipped away enough of the adjacent beam so they could stick the pick into the end of the beam that they were trying to get out. After a hearty swing by Whiskey, the pick was in the end of the beam and the prying began. After several minutes, the beam started to slowly lift its way out of its resting place.

Each time a pick had slightly lifted the beam, new pick would be stuck into the beam, just a little lower than the last pick, and the beam would be pried up just a little more. Eventually the beam broke free, and the team celebrated by giving each other high-five slaps.

Elliott grabbed a flashlight. He leaned over the mount and into the cave hole and looked around. "It looks pretty barren in here," was his only comment.

The new gap was about eight inches wide, just enough for someone who was quite thin to slip in. Elliott's adventuresome side came out. He couldn't resist the adventure and quickly wedged himself through the opening. "Hand me a lantern," he requested.

Restov, who was the thinnest of his group, also pried his way into the cave. "What do you see?"

"Not much. This cave is large enough that we can only see one section at a time. We need a brighter lantern. But since we don't have that let's work our way around the cave and see what we can find."

They hadn't gone more than 10 feet when they heard Questradis yell down into the cave. "Someone's coming. It looks like police."

"I'm going up to handle the situation," explained Restov, hinting that Elliott help him get back up out of the hole.

"I'm staying down here," responded Elliott. I'll keep scouting out the cave and see what I can learn. If you have to seal me in for a while, go ahead. I should have plenty of air here for several hours."

And that's what happened. Restov came out of the cave and said, "Quickly, put the beam back in place and cover it with a little dirt so they can't see what we're doing. We'll just tell them we're a utility company looking for pipes."

One of the police yelled out; "What are you doing? Do you have a permit to dig here?"

After they got closer, the Knights realized that these weren't police. They were Israeli military.

"We are searching for gas lines," responded Restov.

"I need to see your papers."

After a pretended search for the non-existent papers, Restov pleaded forgiveness and said he would send his assistant to get the papers.

"We had an anonymous call that there were terrorists plotting something destructive on temple mount. Are you terrorists?" The guard was half joking and half serious. "Regardless, without papers, you need to stop immediately. Put the dirt back in the hole and come back tomorrow when you have the proper documentation."

The Masons realized that they didn't have any choice, so they proceeded to fill in the hole and place the stones back in place, but they did it in a way that would allow them to quickly reopen the hole after the military patrol left the mount.

However, the military didn't leave the mount. They continued to stay on the mount and after waiting around for two hours, Stef questioned; "Do you think Zeta is going to be OK down in that hole."

Rostov was quick to respond, "That cave was quite large, and he should have enough air in there for at least a day if not more. His problem is going to be light. He's going to be taking a long nap."

"Are you sure?" asked Stef. She had pulled out her cell phone and tried giving Elliott a call just in case he could receive a signal. But it was a waste of time. The call went directly to message, an indicator that communication with Elliott's phone wasn't working. She tried a second time, and a third time, but the results were the same each time.

"Are you positive that he's safe?"

"Then I don't think we have any choice but to leave him down there and come back tomorrow night."

"I think you're right. I guess we'll see you back here tomorrow, same time, same place."

"Excellent. See you then."

The Knights left the mount heading off toward the north, staying away from the area of the Dome of Spirits. Stef headed South around the Dome of the Rock, back in the direction from where she and Elliott entered Temple Mount and caught a cab back to the hotel. She was sure Rostov was correct and that Elliott was safe, but it bothered her to leave him buried in that cave not knowing the situation.

Stef's concern was magnified, wondering who had made an anonymous call reporting their activities. Who knows about our efforts here on Temple Mount? Was it one of the Knights that had come out to help them? That seemed unlikely, but it was a possibility. And if it wasn't one of them, who was it? Was it connected to the events at the rain forest and/or Elliott being followed in Jerusalem? And how was this going to affect their over-all mission?

CHAPTER TWENTY-THREE - PART 4

Temple Mount Cave

Early April, 2025 AD, Jerusalem, Israel, Inside Temple Mount

Elliott heard the beam drop in place over his head. And he heard them throw some dirt over the beam in order to hide it. He wasn't bothered until he heard a concerted effort to fill in the hole above him. Apparently, he was in this cave for the long haul. But he was used to being in tough positions. But this would be the first time he was buried alive.

He quickly tried to make a call to Stef on his cell phone, but it was already too late. There was no signal.

Not easily discouraged, Elliott started to carefully work his way along the wall of the cave, watching for any marks or clues that would help him solve the mystery of the lost temple treasures. It wasn't long before he encountered a shelf cut into the side of the cave. This shelf was obviously a storage area for temple treasures, possibly even the Ark of the Covenant.

Elliott had carried his pocket camera with him, a small Cannon with a 4X zoom and 10 Meg pixel count. Elliott took a picture of the shelf but found no marks or anything unusual.

Continuing on, around the wall of the cave he found another, similar shelf. And then another. Each time he searched carefully for any marks, and each time he found nothing significant.

Shortly after passing the fourth shelf he encountered a skeleton, sitting peacefully against the wall. By the disintegrated clothing, still hanging on the shoulders and arms of the skeleton, Elliott could identify robes, suggesting that this was one of the Masons that had been charged with hiding the temple treasures during the siege of Solomon's temple.

He took a picture and moved on.

At this point Elliott encountered a tunnel. This surprised him. There wasn't any indication of a tunnel in the Temple Mount scan that Greg had done for them. Looking into the tunnel, he quickly realized why. The tunnel went down at an almost 30-degree angle, which would have taken the cave out of range for the scanning equipment.

Elliott made note of the tunnel but decided to finish working his way around the cave before exploring the tunnel. If his lantern held out long enough, he would explore the tunnel as well.

He continued on around the edge of the cave and found several more shelves, most of which offered no clues. However, one of the shelves had scratches on the flat surface, indicating that something heavy had been pushed on the shelf. The Ark was heavy enough that it needed to be carried by four individuals. Elliott concluded that this shelf was most likely the resting place of the Ark. He took pictures and was about to move on around the cave when he noticed something scratched which looked like Sumerian Cuneiform stick writing, faintly on the wall, nearly unnoticeable. He couldn't make it out, but it looked like numbers. He studied the markings carefully and took extra pictures. He scanned the rest of the area carefully to make sure he hadn't missed anything.

Weren't there already enough mysteries involved in his search for the Ark? Masons, Crusaders, Lost Knight Templar Treasures, the Gospel of Mark, attacks in the Rain Forest, people tailing him in  Alice Springs and now Jerusalem, and now Sumerian writings. How do they all fit together? Or do they fit together?

Realizing that battery life was limited and that he couldn't spend too much time focused in any one area of the cave, he moved on and found himself back at the starting point, which he recognized by the new dirt on the ground that had fallen when they removed the beam from the ceiling.

Considering his options, he decided to explore the ceiling and floor in the central areas of the cave, hoping that he might discover some additional clues. This search was fruitless. So, he proceeded to the tunnel hoping to explore as much of it as possible while the light lasted.

Finding the entrance to the tunnel was quick and easy. His sense of direction brought him directly to the opening. Once he started down the tunnel, he was surprised at its steepness. Almost immediately he encountered a small mound of dirt. Looking up he could see where the ceiling had been broken through at some earlier point in time. "This must be where the Knights came into the cave," he said out loud to no one in particular. He again took several pictures to document what he had found and moved on down the tunnel. It continued to move down quickly. The it took and abrupt 180-degree turn, heading back in the direction of the original cave, but apparently under it.

Elliott carefully explored the walls, ceiling, and floor of the tunnel, hoping to find some additional clues. Nothing presented itself. At one point, when he was sure he was directly under the original cave, he was surprised by a dead end, or what he thought was a dead end. After approaching the end of the tunnel, he realized that he had hit into a second tunnel, and that the tunnel he was in was an access point which struck a T with a different, main tunnel.

Close to the T, sitting on the ground, leaning comfortably with his back to the side of the tunnel, was a second skeleton, very similar to the first except that this time the skull had fallen off and was resting peacefully in the skeleton's lap. Again, Elliott took several pictures, studying the figure to see if there were any clues to be found, but there was nothing out of the ordinary.

"Now what do I do?" Elliott asked his headless friend, not really expecting to receive much help. "Do I go back and sit in the cave and wait for them to dig me out? Or do I go left or right down one of these tunnels and possibly not hear them when they come for me?" But his sense of adventure got the best of him and he continued his exploration of the tunnel, heading off to the right with no hesitation.

Rather than help him out, this new tunnel added to the confusion. Elliot encountered still another tunnel heading off in still another direction. Consistent to his method, he again stayed to the right. He realized that he had a silent sentinel sitting guard and waiting for him and that the last skeleton would direct him back to the original tunnel and the original cave.

But this time he was in for a surprise. This tunnel ended in a small cave, similar to the previous cave in that it had numerous shelves dug into the side of the cave, but much smaller. And this time the cave was not empty. It was filled with numerous relics and religious paraphernalia that appeared to be a mixture of what would be considered to be sacred by both Christian and Jewish. It included Jewish items like candelabras, oil lamps, and breastplates containing twelve stones, each of a different color stone, most likely representing the twelve tribes of Israel. This was mixed in with Christian items like a large staff that was carved out to be a snake, and at the top of the staff was a small cross, obviously of Christian influence.

The cave didn't contain anything of major monetary value, but Elliott was sure these items had enormous religious significance. Again, Elliott went wild with the camera. He knew the capacity of the camera's memory cartridge would easily handle several hundred pictures, but he wasn't so confident about the length of the life of the camera's battery. The most treasured was the parchment scrolls that he found mixed amongst the treasures. He didn't want to move them in case there was some significance to their location or placement. He couldn't pass up the chance to record these finds. This was a magnificent archeological treasure.

Elliott started to leave this cave, going on to his next adventure, when his lantern flickered, and then went dark. "I guess I'm done exploring," Elliott mused out loud. Then he realized that he had a second source of light, his cell phone. Opening his phone gave off a minimal amount of light, but it allowed him to see his way around.

Elliott worked his way back down the third tunnel to the intersection with the second tunnel. He had the option of returning back or going on. However, even with the poor lighting, Elliott decided to press forward. He couldn't resist the possibility that there may be even more treasures to be found. Staying true to his code, Elliott kept turning right, hoping he wouldn't end up on the road to oblivion from which he would never be able to find his way back to the cave. But his sense of adventure got the best of him, and he moved deeper towards being lost forever.

Early April, 2025 AD, Jerusalem, Israel

After returning to the hotel Stef went back to bed. She couldn't fall asleep for a couple of hours, still confused, and conflicted about the experience at temple mount, and worried about Elliott's safety. Her imagination got the best of her. What if there are poisonous snakes in the cave? What if a part of the cave crashed in when they filled in the hole, and it fell on Elliott? Her imagination was running away from her.

Eventually she fell asleep and, once she was out, she didn't wake up again until 11:00AM. Staying up most of the night and the time zone changes caused her to sleep longer. Stef, being less interested in the culture than Elliott, didn't feel like exploring the surrounding city. Stef decided to stay in her room until it was time once again to return to Temple Mount.

CHAPTER TWENTY-FOUR

The Gospel of Mark

Early April, 2025 AD, Templar Research Center, Close to Elko, Nevada

The trip from Sacramento to Salt Lake City was uneventful. Unfortunately, the connection to Elko was not as nice. It was quite rough. A weather system had built up in the north-central Nevada and the small dual-propeller commuter plane wasn't the most stable. The roller-coaster ride toward the runway made Greg, Alan, and Dawn a little queasy.

Elko was a pony express stop that became a small rancher town. Now it primarily exists to service the mining community. It is known for its remoteness and its country atmosphere. It's also known as the biggest speed-trap in Nevada. The speed limit along Hwy 80 across Nevada is 75 miles per hour, but in Elko it unexpectedly drops to 65 for a short stretch, just long enough for the Highway Patrol to earn some revenue for the city.

"I definitely prefer flying the remote drone plane to riding in one myself," commented Dawn.

"I'm with you on that," responded Greg. "I feel like kissing the ground after we land."

"I've got to see that" joked Alan.

Safely off the plane, they jumped into Alan's car and headed east on US Interstate 80 toward their base camp. A few miles out of Elko at Halleck they exited the freeway and headed South on Hwy 229 toward a small group of mountains just north of Arthur. To anyone driving along the highway, this seemed like an isolated area in the middle of nowhere. As they came closer, they exited off the main road, and started driving down a deserted farm road. Soon it became a paved one-lane road after it was out of site of the main road. The farm road appearance kept people from becoming curious about the area. The Templars wanted the area to have the look and feel of a ranch or farm. They even kept a ranger / security guard working some crops and caring for cattle on the land thereby maintaining the illusion.

Eventually the road entered a tunnel into the side of the mountain. Once in the mountain, they went through a security check, where they passed their ID badge through a card reader, causing a gate to open. Once through the gate they found themselves in a large underground parking garage, where Greg quickly pulled into his assigned slot.

From the car it was a short walk to the entrance of the underground Templar Knight research compound. The entrance was also camouflaged by looking like a metal door to a storage shed. But a quick swipe of the ID badge caused the door to slide to the side, opening the way into the central compound. The entire underground compound had once been a large Gold and Silver mind, which had been abandoned and forgotten. It was sold off when Gold dropped to around $200 an ounce around 2000 and 2001. It was reworked and reinforced, and now it was an entirely self-contained facility, complete with power generation, water purification, and all the conveniences of life above ground.

The compound was the Templar's world-wide research facility. It included a housing unit, a grocery store, and numerous labs. Greg's lab was one of several technology labs where his team worked with the latest and greatest in eavesdropping, transmission, flight, and weapons. Their lab specialized in the activities of the S1 Supersonic Combustion Ramjet, the remote stealth plane used for the Barjet assassination and for the scanning of temple mount. The S1 was considered one of the best tools in the Templar arsenal.

It was unusual for Greg's team to leave the compound on assignment. But Elliott had worked with Greg on numerous occasions and they had developed a strong working relationship. They rarely met face-to-face, but that didn't detract from how well they worked together.

Most of the work of Greg's team was performed underground. So, they were excited about the trip to Travis and welcomed the mini adventure that it had become.

After arriving back at the base, the team had decided not to go to their underground lab until the following day. Today had already been a long day. Greg and his team arrived back at the complex late in the evening, too late and too tired to start their analysis. But the excitement of the investigation kept Greg from getting a good night's sleep. He wondered what this mystery had in store for him.

The following morning Greg arrived at the lab ahead of Dawn and Alan. He had retained possession of the Gospel of Mark, and he was eager to get to work. Like any good investigator, he started by photographing and cataloguing the scroll carefully. He was just starting to open the scroll when Dawn and Alan entered the lab.

"How's it going?" asked Alan.

"Great. I'm already finding some curious markings. On the outside of the scroll is Latin writing, identifying this as the Gospel of Mark. Dawn can help me with the photography, and why don't you take the photographed images and process them."

"Will do." Alan was running a translator. As the photographed images came through to his computer, Alan input them. The inputting of a language that was unknown to Alan was slow, but once in the translator was quick to come back with a translation.

As Greg and Dawn finished photographing, he instructed Dawn, "See if you can run some scans on the scroll. Let's do ultra-violet, infra-red, and x-ray for starters."

Alan continued entering the scroll information into the translator. This work went on for several hours. It would be evening before they had discovered anything useful.

Around 06:00PM Alan had the entire document converted to English. Then he started comparing the newly translated version of the Gospel of Mark against the one in the King James version, the NIV version, and several New Testament translations, to see if there was anything uniquely different in this new translation. He was not just looking for inconsistencies between the two documents, he was also wondering how accurate these later translations were when compared to an original document.

At around 10:00 PM, Alan was about two thirds of the way through the verification, and he encountered an interesting deviation in the translation. In the verse that is now **Luke 12:21, the King James Version** says; "he that layeth up treasure for himself and is not rich toward God." But in the newly translated version that was in the scrolls, it read; "he that layeth up God's treasure in Ethiopia, protecteth the riches of God." Alan made note of this stark deviation and continued on in the hope that there might be other clues.

Alan was coming to the last verses of the Gospel, and becoming somewhat discouraged, when he finally encountered a second clue. In **Luke 24:47**, the **King James Version** reads; "repentance and remission of sins should be preached in his name among all nations, beginning at Jerusalem." However, the scroll translated this version by adding on the words; "and proceeding on to where God's treasures have been hidden and where His temple now resides."

Ideas rolled around in Alan's mind. "Could this possibly mean that the Ark of the Covenant is now hidden in Ethiopia?" It was now midnight. He finished out the comparison work and eagerly woke up Greg to tell him the news. He knew it couldn't wait. It may be valuable information for Elliot and Stef.

Greg agreed that this was significant and typed out an email to Elliott and Stef's Blackberry, hoping the information would prove to be useful. He also asked them what he should do next.

CHAPTER TWENTY-FIVE

Report In
Early April, 2025 AD, CIA Headquarters, Langley, Virginia

Marcello Zuniga heard the beep on his Blackberry. His mind was programmed to wake himself up when that particular sound occurred. He wasn't exactly sure how he became "programmed" to that sound. But he was glad it worked that way. A message coming through in the middle of the night usually meant something urgent. And it would require his immediate response.

Marcello looked the role of an international cop. He was well built and worked out regularly to keep up his strength. He was born in the United States with Columbian parents. But his love for the US was undeniable. His Latin roots gave him dark hair and dark eyes which gave him the look of a Jason Bourne or James Bond.

Marcello was married to his childhood girlfriend, and he was very committed to her. He had two children, a boy, and a girl, both rebellious teenagers, but they were his pride and joy. Both of them idealized his role in the CIA and wanted to follow in his footsteps.

Marcello was CIA all the way. He had copies of every CIA movie ever made and every book ever written, good or bad. It always amazed him how much misinformation existed. His father had been a police officer, and Marcello wanted to follow in his footsteps. He had always been interested in travelling and seeing the world, and he decided that by joining the CIA he would be able to achieve both goals. But it turned out to be tougher than he thought. He had to be top of his class in college, and then the CIA training had been a struggle for him as well. But hard work brought success, and he was now in his dream job leading an espionage task force.

The message on his Blackberry read, "IOM on MT. X NNRL. 911. Egypt/Ethiopia." He knew what this meant. The IOM was still exploring Temple Mound looking for the Ark of the Covenant. The NNRL had minimal or no involvement in the search. The 911 code meant that the search team was coming under attack of some sort. And that the team would shortly be heading for Egypt or Ethiopia. But he did not understand why they were going down there. What had the team learned?

He responded with the message; "CK N" which was code for Check In. Almost immediately the phone rang. After going through the normal verification protocol required for a call-in, Marcello asked; "Why are they going to Ethiopia?"

"They have broken the code in the Book of Mark that was left in Temple Mount which says that the Ark had been taken down to Ethiopia. But they don't know where. It gets confusing because the entire region was referred to as both Ethiopia and Egypt. So, it could be referring to anywhere from the Mediterranean to the middle of Africa. They're just not sure."

"And who is attacking them?"

"Unknown."

"And where's the NNRL in all of this?"

"Also, unknown. Actually, the IOM hasn't kept them in the loop the way they promised. They don't really trust them. And I wouldn't be surprised if the NNRL is going to come after them in the near future because they're the ones that started all this."

"Are there any other details."

"None at this time."

"Keep reporting regularly on this one. There may turn out to be a lot at stake."

Marcello hung up the phone and lay back down in bed. His feelings were more confused than ever. He was frustrated that he still was not able to get the TFMA and the TFRWR together. Bureaucracy strikes again.

Early April, 2025 AD - Somewhere 35,000 feet over Germany, heading East

"Those guys definitely can't be trusted," grumped Kres Brokard to Rohit, not that he ever trusted anyone. "They had agreed to stay in touch, but they have yet to send us any kind of message. If we didn't have a team trailing them, we wouldn't have a clue what was going on."

"Maybe they've caught on to our tails and they're bothered by it."

"But our guys haven't encountered them, not like those other idiots that keep shooting at them. Have we figured out who they are?"

"No idea. They think its CIA, but they're not sure."

"What's the deal with them getting kicked off of Temple Mount? What's that all about?"

"No idea."

"What have you learned from our spies?"

"Apparently the Ark was moved from the cavern in Temple Mount down to Ethiopia or Egypt at some point in time. The Book of Mark says Ethiopia, but that could include anywhere from what we currently know as Ethiopia to Egypt. I think that's where the Knights are going next, if they can ever get Elliott out of that hole."

"Let's head down to Egypt and meet up with them. Can you contact those guys and push them to give us a status check? And remind them that we would like to be more involved in the process."

"I'll get back to you."

CHAPTER TWENTY-SIX - PART 5

Waiting in Jerusalem
Early April, 2025 AD, Jerusalem, Israel

Stef was just getting comfortable, dressing down into just a t-shirt and a pair of shorts, when she received both a phone call and an e-mail at the same time. Both beeped their message, begging for a response. She took the call and left the message for later.

"Stef here, how can I help," was her standard way of answering the phone.

"This is Rohit of the NNRL. We haven't heard from you in several days now and Mr. Brocard wanted to get an update. I tried calling Elliott, but he didn't answer."

Stef knew this call was coming and she was dreading it. She would have preferred Elliott take the call. But that was out of the question. "We have two activities going on. One is back in the US where the team is exploring the Templar library to see what they can learn from the Crusaders and from the Gospel of Mark. At this point, we haven't learned anything from them. Elliott and I are in Jerusalem trying to learn what we can from inside Temple Mount. We're trying to re-enter the site where the Ark was hidden, to see if there are any additional clues. Other than that, there's not much to report. When we learn something, we'll let you know our next steps."

"Mr. Brocard is concerned that you're not keeping him in the loop as agreed." Rohit was skeptical because he already knew about the Ethiopia connection and he thought she was hiding information from him. He was starting to share Kres' mistrust. "Please stay in touch on a regular basis. Remember that he wants to join the search when you start getting close."

"Tell him that we are dedicated to giving him what he needs, and we have his interests in mind. We'll keep him updated as we go along." Stef said the words, but neither she nor Rohit believed them.

The call ended and Stef breathed a sigh of relief. She hated lying. For some reason it bothered her more than killing. This was a confusing ethical dilemma for her. But her conscience bothered her when she lied, even when it was part of her job.

Stef checked her Blackberry for the e-mail message. It was from Greg, giving her an update and asking her for next steps. It was quite long, giving details of the analysis and discoveries. But it all made sense. The Gospel of Mark was the clue that the Ark had been taken to Ethiopia. But where in Ethiopia? And which Ethiopia? The borders had changed numerous times over the years. And by whom? The trail headed southward, but it still left a lot of loose ends.

Stef responded to Greg and explained how Elliott was currently buried in Temple Mount. And that they hoped to get him out tonight. She instructed him to hold tight for now and she would get back to him as soon as she had a chance to discuss everything with Elliott.

Stef responded to a few additional personal e-mails. Also, her other projects back at the Knights headquarters had to be monitored so they continued moving forward.

For Stef, working for the Knights was very much like being in the military. You had a day job which is what kept you busy most of the time, and then you had a "combat ready" job where you dropped everything and pursued an assignment. For Stef, her day job involved researching the latest and greatest in new technological ideas and identifying ways to incorporate these new technologies in ways that would give the Knights a strategic advantage. She had a large team which included spies at many of the major research centers around the world. This team would identify and assess the viability of the research projects. And Stef had received several messages from various team members eager to share their discoveries.

After taking care of her day job, Stef could once-again focus on her current activities, which focused around getting Elliott out of his grave. But first she would try to take a nap and rest up for what would probably turn out to be a long night.

Early April, 2025 AD, Jerusalem, Israel

Stef woke up around 11:00PM, plenty early for her 2:00AM rendezvous at the Dome of Spirits. She would have preferred sleeping a little longer because now, being awake, she started worrying all over again, worrying about Elliott's safety. Logically, her job should have hardened her from feeling these kinds of emotions about anyone, but Elliott was different somehow. And she couldn't quite figure out how. She grabbed her current novel and started reading, trying to get her mind off of Elliott.

Shortly after 01:00PM Stef got dressed and headed out to the front of the hotel to catch a cab. At that time of night, catching a cab wasn't easy and the hotel desk had to call one for her. Once in the cab, she headed off to the Mount.

About fifteen minutes into the drive the cabbie asked; "Is someone following you?"

"Not that I know of," responded Stef, looking out of the back window of the cab. There was a car behind them, but that wasn't unusual. "Why do you think they're following us?"

"They've made the last two turns with us. It's just unusual at this time of the night. It didn't seem like a coincidence. I'll keep an eye on them and let you know if they keep following us."

"If you double back around the next block and they do the same, then we'll know for sure."

"I'll give it a try." The driver turned left, and then left again. The car behind them took the first left, but then thought better of it and went straight at the second left. "I think they realize we're on to them."

"Can you confuse the route a little more so they can't figure out what we're doing."

"Will do!" The driver pursued a route that had numerous turns and even a couple of full loops. Eventually they arrived at Temple Mount. It was a little later than anticipated, but Stef felt it was necessary. There were no additional sightings of someone following them.

Stef was starting to get annoyed by the constant tails. She knew there were far too many of them to be isolated events. There had to be a connection between them.

It was five minutes before two o'clock and Stef hurried up the stairs toward the Dome of the Rock. Then she ran around the left side of the mount towards the much smaller Dome of Spirits. Off in the distance she could see that her four Templar companions had already arrived, and they were starting to put up their makeshift construction barriers. As she started getting closer, she heard a rifle shot. Then there was a cry of pain. One of the Templars fell to the ground, holding his leg.

Then there was a second shot, which ricocheted off the ground. Stef could see the sparks where the bullet hit the rock surface. Fortunately, this bullet did not hit its target. The Templars quickly took shelter behind pillars of the Dome of Spirits, away from the on-coming shots. The injured Templar had also managed to pull himself out of the line of fire, with a little help from one of his friends.

A third shot rang out, another miss, but this time the miss seemed intentional. It seemed more like a warning shot.

Stef got the message and stayed away from the Dome of Spirits. She stayed in the shadows and worked herself back to the Dome of the Rock, hoping the threat would go away.

"They're trying to scare us off," yelled one of the Knights to Stef. "And unfortunately for Elliott it's working."

After about five minutes of no additional shots, Questradis ran toward Stef in a crouched over position, with a zigzagged running patter. He was trying to avoid being shot. But it didn't seem to matter. No additional shots rang out.

"I think they're just trying to scare us off," whispered Questradis to Stef. "And I think they quit shooting because he didn't want us to ID their location."

"I'm sure you're right. But what about Elliott? We can't go after him if we're going to get shot. We also can't leave him in that hole."

"I think we're just going to have to wait one more night."

"I don't think Elliott will make it. How about we act like we've given up and get out of here. Then we come back again in a couple of hours. Hopefully, the shooter is long gone, and we can dig Elliott out."

"Excellent plan. That will give us enough time to get Restov to the hospital. Unfortunately, we'll have to make up some story about him getting accidentally shot or we'll have to answer a lot of questions. I'm sure the shooter will think we've given up for the night, and he'll plan on coming back tomorrow. But before he gets back, we'll be done. Now that we've lost one of the Masons and we'll have to work a little harder to get the work done."

"Excellent. I'll leave the area as well, and the shooter will think we're gone for sure."

They moved forward with the plan. Questradis walked straight back to where his three companions were, not bothering to zigzag. He was sure that the shooter wasn't out to kill anyone. And he proved himself right.

The three Knights had tied off Restov's wound to stop the bleeding. They helped him up and headed off to the North East of the mount, where they would take their car to the nearest hospital.

Stef headed back around the Dome of the Rock and headed off the mount to see if she could find a taxi that would take her back to the hotel. Fortunately, this time finding a taxi turned out to be a lot easier, and she had a quick, uneventful trip back to the hotel. But she was now bothered more they ever by the people that were tailing her and shooting at her.

Once back at the hotel she typed out an email to Greg which said, "We're being tailed and shot at, almost on a daily basis. Do you have some kind of locator, or use some kind of surveillance tool, to try to figure out who's after us? When we were at the temple mount, we got shot at, but we have no idea by whom, or why, or even from where. Could we use the S1 with some kind of scanning mechanism to follow me around and identify anyone who is following or shooting at me?"

Early April, 2025 AD, Jerusalem, Israel

Stef knew Greg. He would figure something out, probably without even leaving the comfort of his $3,000 massaging desk chair that he had in his office. And she would be right; 02:30 AM in Jerusalem was 04:30 PM in Nevada, and Greg was sitting at his desk, looking forward to a distraction from his busy-work. He loved the excitement of the chase, which was a pleasant break from his research heavy day job. And Stef gave him the perfect distraction. Why did she have to do it thirty minutes before quitting time?

Greg called Dawn and Alan into his office, which was more like his own private technology lab, and he presented them with Stef's concerns. "Any suggestions?" he asked the team.

Dawn was quick with, "Let's send out the S1. It still has the scanning equipment attached from the Temple Mount flyovers. We can use it to track Stef. And if anyone starts shooting at her, we can use infrared to track the source of the shot and get an image of the shooter without the shooter even knowing we were there."

Alan suggested, "There is a military satellite that is recording images of Jerusalem on a continuous basis, primarily because it's such a volatile area. We have tapped into its data feed. I'll bet we can go back a half an hour and see images of the Knights getting shot at. It may give us some clues to what's going on."

"Excellent. You've each given yourselves an assignment. Dawn, if there's any way we can get the S1 over the mount before 04:00AM, that would be great, because they're planning on going out there again at that time. Additionally, I'll do a computer track and search through the wireless communications that have been going on in the area to see if there is any hint of what's been going on." Then, with a smile on his face he said, "I think we need to prepare for a long night."

They each eagerly headed off to their new assignments. This would indeed become a long workday for everyone.

Early April, 2025 AD, CIA Headquarters, Langley, Virginia

Marcello Zuniga heard the beep on his Blackberry. It was just before 08:00PM in Virginia. The message read; "The IOM is setting up sophisticated tracking and surveillance equipment to catch whoever is tailing them and shooting at them. If you're involved, I suggest you stop immediately." Marcello deleted the message.

He sent out a message of his own. "Stop the attacks and the tails. We're being tracked."

CHAPTER TWENTY-SEVEN

Return to Temple Mount

Early April, 2025 AD, Jerusalem, Israel, Temple Mount

It was 03:30AM and Stef was heading out to find another cab that could get her back to Temple Mount. This time she went directly to the hotel desk and had the clerk place the call. And a taxi arrived within five minutes.

The taxi driver added a new twist to her frustration. He started with, "How much did you make tonight?"

"What?"

"You're a good-looking babe. You must be worth a good penny. How much did you make tonight?"

"Are you crazy? I'm not a hooker."

"Of course. You're a comfort specialist. A recreation engineer. An alternative living facilitator. A socialization specialist. Whatever. Fine! If you don't want to tell me, I'll let you keep your secret. I was just trying to make conversation."

"Do I look like a hooker to you?"

"What does a sophisticated escort service consultant look like? They look like a hot sexy babe. They look like you!"

Stef was just getting angry. She saw that this was a conversation that she didn't want to encourage so she quit talking. And the driver didn't say any more either. One thing was for sure; this guy wasn't getting a tip.

Stef kept an eye out to see if anyone was trailing her, but there weren't any other cars around at this time of night. Other than the cab driver hitting on her, the drive was uneventful.

Stef climbed out of the taxi, and started making her way up the stairs, when her telephone rang. It was Elliott's phone. How on earth was that possible? A sudden shot of confused excitement surged through her body as she answered the phone.

Early April, 2025 AD, Jerusalem, Israel

Elliott kept moving to the right, not sure how long the light of the phone would last. He could see the time on the phone, and he had been in the cave about eight hours so far. He followed the latest tunnel into a third cave which looked looted and ravaged. Cave treasures were thrown around. It looked like the looters took what they could and discarded the rest. It was painful for Elliott to see the waste and damage to genuine historic artifacts.

Elliott took a picture of some of the damaged historical treasures. As the camera flashed, and he looked at the image on the viewing screen, he realized that he had another source of light. He quickly shut the phone in order to save its battery and started using the light of the camera viewing screen.

This time the cave wasn't a dead end. The tunnel continued through the cave and out the other side, and Elliott continued to follow the tunnel. It went on for quite a while, the tunnel winding back and forth as if it had lost direction.

By now Elliott was starting to get very tired. He looked at the clock on his phone and realized it was now 11:00AM. He also realized that there would not be any effort to dig him up until tonight. He decided to sit down, right where he was at, and take a nap. There wasn't much sense in getting stressed about his situation. He had to make the best of his situation.

Sitting down in a relaxed, reclining position, it wasn't long before he was fast asleep.

Early April, 2025 AD, Jerusalem, Israel

Elliott woke with a start. It took him a second to remember where he was, and why it was so dark. Once he realized his situation, he pushed the on button on his camera and using the light of the camera he looked around to see what had woken him. Seeing nothing he assumed that he must have dreamed the noise that woke him. He looked at the clock and realized it was now nearly 07:00 PM. He had slept for eight hours, which was unusual for him. He must have been extra tired.

The big question of the day was "Which way was he going?" Did he sit down on the left side of the tunnel, or on the right? In his drowsiness he wasn't sure. So, he just sat there for a while waiting to get back his bearings. Eventually he was pretty sure which way he was going, but he was never one hundred percent sure. He moved forward in his adventure through the tunnels of temple mount. He realized that there was an enormous network of tunnels, much more so than he would have anticipated. Some of the tunnels were roughly dug out, and some had very smooth, almost polished sides. It was obvious that the tunnels were dug at different times with different tools and with different levels of urgency.

Suddenly and abruptly the tunnel came to a dead end. He wondered how that was possible. Why would someone build a tunnel that went nowhere? This just didn't make any sense. He felt around the end of the tunnel, hoping to find some type of door or hinge, anything that would explain the dead end. But he found nothing. Just then the light on the camera started to flicker. Elliott decided to turn it off and save some of the light in case of an emergency.

He turned and started to head back through the tunnel, keeping his hand on the right wall, thereby assuring that he would always keep to the right if the tunnel made a turn or broke up. About 20 feet from the end of the tunnel, Elliott's hand felt an edge. Feeling around the edge, Elliott found it to be in the shape of a large circle. Elliott used a little of the light of the camera to take a look and found a door. Apparently, the dead end was intentional; a diversion to keep any would-be looters off track. The real tunnel headed through this circular door.

He investigated the door carefully, looking for some mechanism that would open it, but could find nothing. He stepped back in frustration. "How does this door get opened," he said to no one in particular. He sat down on the floor to think. Leaning back against the wall he looked up and noticed something in the ceiling. Taking a closer look, he realized it was a leaver of some type. Pulling the lever did nothing. Pushing was the answer, and the door gave a click. Pushing on the door opened it to a short tunnel and followed by an enormous cave. Looking back at the opening, Elliott saw a similar lever on the inside of the door. He pushed the door closed, not really knowing why he needed to, other than to fulfill the original intention of the door.

Elliott came into a cavern that had obviously never been found before. He could tell this immediately because it appeared to be completely intact, with historical treasures galore on shelves throughout the cavern. These treasures had the markings of ancient Judaism, very similar to the treasures found in the earlier cavern. However, this cave still had the gold and jewels from the ancient kingdoms.

Elliott wanted to take pictures. Unfortunately, the first time he tried to take a picture, the camera went dead. His light was gone. And he would never be able to share the new-found discovery with anyone.

Then he reflected on his loss of light, and his potential fate. "I'm not going to be doing much sharing of any type if I don't get out of here;" Elliott said to his nonexistent companion. Suddenly Elliott felt very lonely and became concerned about being stranded in this hole forever. He decided it was time to go back to the original cavern. Doing it all by touch and feel was difficult. He made his way back to the hidden doorway, pushed the lever to open it, and moved through it. He closed the door and crossed the tunnel, placing his left hand on the side of the tunnel. And he started to work his way back, doing the opposite of what got him to this point; this time always keeping to the left.

Elliott took a quick sighting on his watch. The glow-in-the-dark dials told him it was nearly 11:00PM, three hours before they would try to dig him out. He kept the phone off saving its limited remaining light for an emergency. But it didn't matter. He had been here before. He already knew what to look out for.

He stumbled into and through the first cave, continuing on along the edge of the tunnel, but never really knowing how far he had travelled. He switched tunnels, found the second cave and, remembering that it was a dead end, went to the other side of the tunnel and continued on his journey.

It wasn't easy travelling in pitch black darkness. He tripped several times, especially if the tunnel made a slight rise or decline in slope. He also tripped over the skeleton that he had found sitting in the tunnel. But he had no other choice than to hurry along and try to get to the main cavern before Stef and team broke through the surface.

He arrived at 02:15AM, a little late, but he wasn't worried since it would take them some time to dig him out. But what worried him was that he couldn't hear anything. It was completely silent.

Elliott became slightly frustrated. He was confident that Stef would be doing her best to get him out. If no one was digging, then there was trouble of some kind. Someone was blocking their efforts. And this frustrated him. He wished he had nabbed one of those people following him through the marketplace to find out who they were and what they wanted. Now he had dumped the problem on Stef. But it would become his problem if he ended up buried for real in this cave.

Elliott sat in the cave and his mind started wandering. Did he come back to the right cave? Of course! He had tripped over the slight mound of dirt caused by their previous exploration. Did his clock get reset since he couldn't get a signal in the cave? No, it would remember the last time zone it had synchronized to. No, he was in the right cave. And he needed to tough it out and wait it out.

At about 03:00 AM he gave up. Apparently tonight was a bust and he would need to spend a second night in the cave. But Elliott was too stir-crazy to just sit there. He decided to adventure out, this time following a "keep to the left" policy. He started out in the same tunnel, but at the first intersection, he veered off to the left. The tunnel took a sharp turn to the left, then to the right. By now Elliott had lost all sense of direction. He had no idea which direction he was going, just that he was following a new tunnel off in a new direction. He had no idea if he had passed any side tunnels, only that he was staying to the left.

Suddenly the wall veered off to the left and Elliott, trying to stay with the wall, fell onto a shelf. He had crossed into another cavern. He decided it must be a cavern because only caverns had shelves. This particular shelf had nothing on it. Elliott assumed it was looted out like the previous caverns he had encountered.

He followed the edge of the shelf and continued on along the edge of the cavern, back into what he assumed was a tunnel. This time he decided it was a tunnel because he noticed a difference in the sound. There was more of an echo to his footsteps, unlike the cavern where his footsteps were duller. Continuing on he felt a draft of air on his head. How was that possible? He decided to risk the use of some of his cell phone battery. He lit up the battery and looked toward the source of the air. At about shoulder height he discovered the entrance to another tunnel. The entrance was a small hole, only about 3 feet across at the largest point. But more interesting than finding the new tunnel was that there was a source of the air flow. Did this tunnel have access to the outside?

Shutting his phone off to preserve what little battery he had left, he climbed up into the new tunnel and fumbled his way toward the source of the air. Once in the tunnel, he found it took several turns and climbed steeply upward. It took two more turns, and then Elliott could see a small glimmer of light. It was the moon, just barely making enough light to shine through the small round hole of less than six inches across. Looking through the hole, Elliott could see that the location of the hole was hidden from outside view by several bushes. Looking closer, it looked as if this was not the end of the tunnel, but rather, it was a small cave-in in the ceiling of the tunnel, at a point where it must have gotten too close to the surface.

Holding his phone close to the hole Elliott found he had a signal. It was weak, but strong enough to make a call. And he immediately placed a call to Stef.

CHAPTER TWENTY-EIGHT

Escape from Temple Mount
Early April, 2025 AD, Jerusalem, Israel

"Hello," answered Stef. "Is it really you Elliott?" She assumed he was calling from inside the cave, and she was partially right.

"Did you forget about me that quickly?"

"There was a sniper shooting at us earlier, so we had to abandon our excavation efforts. We're back now to dig you out."

Elliott cut her off and said, "I have to talk fast. This phone may die any second. I have found a small hole somewhere along the edge of temple mount. Too small for me to crawl through. But it should be less visible to snipers, and security guards, and whoever else may be after you. There's a bush in the way so I can't give you a clue where I am, but I can see the moon through the bush. Can you get someone to track on my cell phone to find me?"

"Definitely. Shut down this call to save battery, but don't shut down your phone, and we'll try to track in on you."

Stef's heart beat fast. She was so excited that she could hardly contain herself. She had become extremely concerned about Elliott's safety. And it was a big relief to hear his voice.

In her excitement she was conflicted. What should she do first? She immediately sent a text message to Greg telling him about the need to track Elliott's cell phone, and Greg responded immediately that he would get right on it. Then Stef went up to the top of the mount and headed around the Dome of the Rock over to the Dome of Spirits. The

Templers weren't there yet. She hoped that nothing had gone wrong with the injured Knight.

Now she was on hold, waiting for the Knights to show up and for information from Greg on Elliott's location. In her excitement, she didn't fully comprehend all that Elliott had said. But now she had time to think. Elliott said he could see the moon. Which side of the mount would have a view of the moon? The West side, of course. It was a slightly steep and ran the full length of the mound. It was a sloping side with a lot of brush that had grown in. It would be nearly impossible to find a small hole somewhere along this side of the mount in the dark.

Time to think again. What can she do to help find Elliott?

Just then a message beeped in from Greg. "We triangulated his location using two towers of the cell phone tracking system. This gets us within about 15 feet horizontally. But that won't help very much on a sloping hill which only registers as a few feet across. Another option, which may get us closer, would be for Elliott to shine a light through the hole and we'll try to pick it up with our S1 scanners. The S1 is already in the Jerusalem area. Let us know what you think."

Wow thought Stef. How'd they get the S1 out here so fast. "Position the S1 over the West slope of the mound so you get a really good look at the 15 feet of area. I'll call Elliott and tell him to shine a light through the hole. Hopefully, we can pick up the light. Let me know when you're ready."

It was only a couple of minutes when the message came back, "We're ready for Elliott's light."

Stef gave Elliott a call and described the plan to him. "My cell phone is weak, but I'll stick my hand out of the hole and wave it around as much as possible. Hopefully, they can spot it through the bushes."

Stef sent Greg a text telling him, "The candle is lit."

Within a few minutes Greg responded with, "We have him. But how do I get you to him?"

"Can you track me?"

"Yes."

"Tell me if I'm getting closer, etc."

"Excellent. We'll play a little game of red light, green light. Start by heading North West. Elliott is located in the middle of the Northern half of Temple Mount."

A short walk got her in the vicinity of a large brushy area.

Greg called her and started walking her through toward Elliott; "We have you. Go further North. We'll tell you when you're across from Elliott's location and when you should head into the brush."

Stef started moving North. Greg coaxed her on until she came to a spot where he told her to stop. "Now turn left into the brush and take about ten steps."

Stef slowly worked her way through the brush. Her mind generated images of snakes and bugs crawling up her leg. She didn't enjoy the experience. However, for the sake of Elliott, there was no question that she needed to do this. "Am I getting close?"

"About halfway there," responded Greg.

Stef kept moving forward, cautiously, one gentle, scratchy step at a time.

"You're almost there," encouraged Greg.

She took one more step and crash. Stef fell through the ground. She had stepped directly into the Elliott's hole. "Ooww!" she cussed. She was wearing pants and a short- sleeved blouse, leaving her hand and arms exposed. But the brush had no sympathy for the covered parts of her body and scratched right through them as well. "Couldn't anybody warn me?" Her right leg had come crashing through the hole and she had scratched up her leg as she came through. Additionally, she fell to the side and scratched herself in the brushes.

"Nice of you to drop in," came a voice out of the hole. "This gives me an entirely new look at you."

"Real funny," barked Stef. She was not amused. "Couldn't you warn me that I was getting close?"

"I've been hearing noises all the time. There are some critters running around out there. I'm not sure what, but they sounded pretty big. You just sounded like another critter."

This didn't make Stef feel any better. Now that she was somewhat stuck in the hole she had to worry about "critters" that might run into her. She struggled to quickly jump up, but all she did was scratch herself up some more.

Her phone started ringing. She had dropped it into the brush somewhere, and now she struggled to try to find it. It stopped ringing before she could locate it, but then it started to ring again. Scraping around in the brush, knowing for sure that a snake or something else would grab her hand any second, she finally found the phone and answered it; "Hello."

"Are you OK?" asked Greg."

"No! I'm not OK. I fell into the stupid hole and I'm all scraped up."

"Well at least you found him." Stef could hear a trace of laughter in his voice, even though he was obviously trying to suppress it. This angered her even more.

"I guess you could say that. Now I just need to figure out how to get myself out and then him out."

She hung up the phone and returned to fighting her way out of the hole. Elliott pushed up on her leg from underneath. Eventually, with a little more struggling and complaining, Stef was finally released from her prison.

Stef yelled down into the hole. "I'm going back to the dome to see if the Templars have arrived. If they're there, I'll get them over here to dig you out. I'll be right back."

With that Stef left Elliott's hole and headed off to find the Knights with their picks and shovels. She hoped that nothing had happened to them and that they had arrived.

Her scratches were extremely painful. She felt like her entire body had been shredded. And she worried about infection. She wanted to go back to the hotel and get herself covered with triple-antibiotic ointment and then bandaged up. But first she had to once again do a woman's work and rescue Elliott.

She was glad to finally get out of the brush. She stood there for a few minutes dusting off and checking the scratches on her hands and arms. Then she headed off to the Dome of Spirits to find her companions.

As she was heading off in that direction, she spotted them coming onto the mound from the North. She stopped walking and waved them off toward her direction. As they came close, she asked, "How's our injured Knight?"

"He's doing great. We had more trouble explaining how he got shot, then we had getting him fixed up. The police are always called in on a gunshot wound, and we were interrogated pretty thoroughly before they let us leave. We had trouble convincing them that this was all an accident."

By the way, have you learned anything about the sniper?"

"No idea," was Stef's response. "I wish I knew. Then I could do something about it. Not knowing is pretty frustrating."

"Anyway," Stef continued, "getting Elliott out has taking an interesting turn of events. Elliott was wandering around and he found a small cave-in. This cave-in gave him enough of a hole so that he could get cell phone reception and he gave me a call. I've located the cave-in and now we need to make the hole bigger so we can get him out."

"Show us where to dig," came the quick response. "I'm glad to hear that he's OK. I was getting a little concerned."

Stef led the way back to Elliott's location. After cordial greetings, the Knights went to work.

"Do you have an extra shovel?" asked Elliott.

"Sure," responded Questradis as he handed a shovel down to Elliott.

"Push as much of the dirt down into the hole as possible. I need it to cover up another access point that I don't want any looters discovering. There are a few things down here I want to save for a later trip, when we're done with our current assignment."

As the knights pushed dirt down into the hole Elliott would shovel it over to the location of the small hole he had crawled through. He wanted to seal up the main tunnel and make it look like the tunnel ended there. He didn't want anyone finding the caverns with the historical treasures that he had stumbled into. He would make a point of hurrying back to this location in the future and pulling out these treasures.

It wasn't long before the knights had expanded the hole so that it was large enough for Elliott to escape. At about the same time, Elliott had satisfactorily covered up the crawl hole and padded it down so that it looked just like a normal part of the cavern. He didn't even want the Knights to know where the access point was, just in case one of the Knights had anything to do with leaking information about their efforts in Jerusalem.

Elliott handed up the shovel and quickly scampered out of the hole. He was thankful to be free of his temporary prison.

"Were you getting worried down there?" asked Questradis.

"Definitely!" responded Elliott. "I was wondering how long it was going to take you to get me out of here."

"We were getting shot at when we came to dig you out last night. Restov ended up in the hospital with a gunshot wound."

"That's too bad. I hope he's doing OK."

"He'll be OK. But it will take him a little while to recover. What did you find down there anyway?"

"I took lots of pictures. I found where the treasures had been hidden and there was some Sumerian writing that didn't make any sense. But I can't show you any of it because the camera died on me. I was using it as a light source until it ran out. I'm glad I didn't kill my cell phone too, because I was using it as a light source for a while." He didn't tell him that there was still treasure in a couple of the caverns. He wanted to save that intact so he could investigate it later. Besides, it may have relevance in finding the Ark, so he didn't want the site disturbed.

They left the hole wide open. There wasn't any good way to cover it up. Any dirt that they had dug out ended up in the hole, and Elliott use a lot of that to cover up the other access point. It was time for them to get out of the area. So, Elliott's escape hole would have to remain open.

Then Stef, Elliott, and the three Knights bid each-other farewell and thanked each-other for their efforts. They were off. The Knights headed back North, off the mount and Elliott and Stef headed South to the staircase that led up to the Dome of the Rock. Descending the staircase, they soon found a taxi and were headed back to the hotel.

They decided to wait till they were alone before they discussed their ordeal and each other's findings. However, after getting back to the hotel, they were both so exhausted that they decided it would all have to wait until after they had a shower and some rest.

Stef was the first in the shower, where she complained the whole time about how the scratches stung. After she got out and got dried off, Elliott rubbed some first-aid cream into the deepest of the cuts. He always enjoyed any excuse to work on her naked body. Then he tucked her in bed and kissed her on the cheek. He knew there was little chance of her still being awake when he got out of the shower.

Then it was Elliott's turn to get cleaned up. He washed off quickly because he felt exhausted and wanted to get to bed. Besides, he knew Stef was waiting for him and, asleep or not, he enjoyed cuddling up to her and holding her.

CHAPTER TWENTY-NINE

Leaving Jerusalem
Early April, 2025 AD, Jerusalem, Israel

Elliott and Stef didn't get up until nearly noon. Both were exhausted from the ordeal over the last couple of nights. Stef was sore from her battle with the scratchy bushes, and she was exhausted from her sleepless worry about Elliott. Elliott didn't sleep at all the first night in the hole, and then, the second night, sleeping in a sitting position on the hard ground was also uncomfortable and he woke up several times during the night. The hotel bed wasn't the best, a little too soft for Elliott and a little too hard for Stef, but when you get as tired as they were, it worked just fine.

They got up, took showers, got dressed, and decided that they needed food. Elliott usually put a lot of effort into what he wore. He would open the suitcase and take whatever was on top, and that would be his outfit for the day. For today it would be shorts and a t-shirt quoting Einstein; "Insanity is continuing to do the same thing and expecting different results." Stef was more meticulous. She went through the few items she had packed, holding each up against herself and looking into the mirror before she made her selection. Today she selected a dark green knee-length skirt and a matching halter top. She loved halter tops because they were appealing to Elliott. He always complemented her when she put one on, and he seemed to want to grab and hold her more. Her loose hanging breasts under that thin piece of cloth seemed to drive him crazy. And today was no exception. She no sooner had it on then

Elliot came up from behind, pulled her against him, and slipped his hands under her armpits and into the sides of the halter top fabric. He whispered into her ear, "You are incredibly hot," as he kissed the back of her neck and squeezed and fondled her breasts. Stef felt the rise of something hard pushing against her butt and wondered how his middle leg could stand at attention so quickly. She wished she could get excited that quickly, but it just wasn't that fast for women. Stef gave him her classic "not now" look in the mirror, but she was delighted that the halter top still did the trick. She pulled his hands free from her breasts, headed quickly to the door, and opened it. She knew he would restrain himself once the door was open. But it would take him a minute or two to get the bulge in his pants under control.

Neither felt like leaving the hotel and going exploring so they headed directly to the hotel restaurant. The dining area was a small room, with only a dozen tables, and it looked like it hadn't been updated in the last century. The décor was dark and some of the paint was peeling on the walls. It attempted to take on a mixture of Arabic and Israeli culture, in an attempt to satisfy all. The hotel restaurant wouldn't serve breakfast at noon, so they defaulted to having lunch for breakfast. Stef had a BLT, which she thought was disappointingly tasteless, and Elliott selected a local dish that the waiter recommended. They were both glad to get something to eat. After the meal they headed back to their hotel room to discuss the last couple of day's events and to plan next steps. As they approached the door of the room, Elliott had a funny feeling that they were being watched. He looked around and didn't see anyone, but he had learned to trust his feelings. He grabbed Stef's arm. And she responded by punching him.

"That hurts," she complained. "You grabbed me right on one of my scratches."

"Sorrryyy!" responded Elliott. "Anyway, what I wanted to tell you is that I have a funny feeling about going back into the room and discussing what we learned. I'm thinking we should find some neutral place to talk."

"Sure," responded Stef. She had also learned to trust Elliott's feelings. It had saved their hide several times. "Let me grab a few things from the room and we can take a walk."

Entering the room, they both looked around carefully, checking to see if they could spot a listening bug of some kind, but they found nothing. However, just to stay on the safe side, they decided to leave their room before they had their discussion. Elliott grabbed his recharged camera, cell phone, and computer. Stef grabbed the information she had received from Greg. They left the room and headed out the front door of the hotel and on to the street to see what they could find. Heading left seemed the better choice, if they were going to find a small outdoor café where they could sit and talk without being monitored. They didn't have to go far. There were lots of perfect curb-side restaurants.

Stef selected a small café which wasn't very busy. Stef said that she thought it was cute, but Elliott knew it was because of the pastries they had on display. There was a chocolate cake that he knew she couldn't resist. They were able to get an isolated table where no one sat close to them. The metal chairs and table weren't comfortable, and there was traffic noise and dust, but they felt more secure at this location than in their room. The table wasn't set evenly on the ground and it wobbled every time it was touched. As expected, Stef ordered a piece of the chocolate cake. In his mind Elliott thought; "I knew it," but he wasn't brave enough to say it out loud. Elliott picked a lemon-lime pie that he thought looked interesting. And Stef, in her mind, thought, "I knew he'd pick something weird," but she also didn't voice her thoughts.

As they started eating, Elliot started the discussion. He went through his discoveries in detail, stressing that most of it was not relevant to their mission of finding the Ark.

Elliott kept talking about the writing on the wall in the first cave. He speculated about its relevance since that seemed like the obvious choice for the storage location of the Ark. It was a little hard to type it in and send it off to Greg for further research. As they talked, he downloaded the picture onto his computer and sent it off to Greg.

Then it was Stef's turn. She discussed Greg's retrieval of the Book of Mark scroll and about the differences between the scroll and the more traditional translations of the Book. The obvious references to Ethiopia left her confused. Why would the Jews send their most prized treasure down to a land that was obviously non-Judaic?

"Do you have any idea why the 'Gospel of Mark' plays such an important part in all this," asked Stef. "And why does Mark care about the Ark?"

Elliott explained what little he knew, "After Jesus died, each of the Apostles was sent on a missionary assignment. They were to go out and spread the Gospel of Jesus Christ. Geographically, Mark appears several places. He goes to Babylon with Peter, and he was in Greece with Paul. But Mark is the Apostle whose specific missionary assignment was Egypt. One of his writings was intended to be a kind of missionary pamphlet that was to be read to the congregations inside and outside of the church. This missionary tract later became one of the Gospels in the New Testament of the Bible. He stayed with Peter in Rome until Peter was martyred. Then he travelled to Egypt to do his missionary work there and to establish Christ's church in that part of the world.

"Mark keeps popping up because there seems to be a strong connection between him, Egypt and Ethiopia, and the location of the Ark. Apparently, from what I can figure based on what we know so far, the Ark was hidden inside the Temple Mount at the time of the invasion of Jerusalem. Then, at some point after the death of Christ, the Ark was taken out of temple mount and moved to the Egypt / Ethiopia area by the Christian Coptics. They would have been the ones who left the Gospel of Mark behind where the Ark had been. I think this was a clue that the Ark was taken south to Ethiopia. That seems to be confirmed by the text changes that Greg's team discovered. Later, when the Crusader Knights dug into the mount, the Ark was already gone and what they found in its place was a hint in the form of a Scroll containing the Gospel of Mark. I suggest that we go South to the area known as Ethiopia during the time when Mark would have been there. We need to retrace where the Ark was taken and right now the only clue, we have is this information that Greg's team was able to glean out of the scroll. Unfortunately, the area we're talking about is quite large. It covers the

Nile valley from the Mediterranean halfway down the African continent."

"What's a Coptic anyway?" was Stef's next question.

"Coptic is just a language. And the Coptic Christians are a very large group, today about 12 million people, who follow the Christianity that Mark taught. Of course, they also distorted the original teachings of Christ, the same way as all the other Christian churches did. The reason they are called the Coptic Christians is because they do all their services in the Coptic language. This is very similar to the Roman Catholics who still see Latin as their Holy language. In fact, it was only a few years ago that religious services were allowed to be held in any language other than Latin."

"So, what's the difference between the Coptic Christians and the Roman Catholic Christians. Did the apostles teach different doctrines?"

"Another excellent question. The Apostles all had the same doctrine. They were taught by Christ. It's the centuries of church leadership that created disputes. The Coptics and the Roman Catholics were very close in the early years of the church. They worked together and met together regularly. They had joint meetings, called councils, where they discussed doctrine and came to agreements on the intentions of Christ's message. For example, the Nicene council created the Nicene Creed as a joint statement of belief. This is where concepts like the Trinity were developed. But over the years, these councils also developed rifts. Specifically, the different Christian groups strongly disagreed on things like the nature of Jesus. Was He both spiritual and human, or just human, or just spiritual? Was He different before He was born from after He died? What was the difference? Another major rift between the churches was over the role of Mary. If Jesus were God, then was Mary the Mother of God as the Trinity would support, or just the Mother of the Son of God? But in either case, if she was the mother, who was the father? Could God make within His Trinitarian Self, His own Son? And why did He need Mary at all? If he was God, couldn't he do anything? Did he need a woman? The Calcadonian council is where this came to a head, and the rift created at this council has survived ever since. This confusion of doctrine generated many heated debates which resulted in a split between the Roman Catholic Christians, the Coptic Christians, and Christian Bishoprics centered around Greece which today are known as the Orthodox Christians. It has only been in the last couple decades that the various Christian organizations have tried to reconcile some of their differences. But still today there are some fundamental differences that will keep these groups from ever being fully reunited."

"Getting back to the Ark, there are still a lot of questions that are unanswered in the information we have collected so far," continued Elliott. "We need to think through the history of the Ark to see how we arrived where we are today. Chronologically, we had the Temple of Solomon built around the mid tenth century BC. At that point they built an underground storage vault for protecting the temple treasures.

"Now, historically, there are two points where the Ark could have been removed. The first occurred in **Kings 14:25** of the Old Testament, where it reads; 'And it came to pass in the fifth year of king Rehoboam, that Shishak king of Egypt came up against Jerusalem: And he took away the treasures of the house of the LORD.' Rehoboam was the son of Solomon so this would have occurred somewhere during the 9th Century BC. Does this include the Ark of the Covenant? Was it taken to Egypt at this time? Or was the Ark hidden in the cave at this time, and possibly restored to its rightful place in the Holy of Holies after the attack?

"Then, the second point where the Ark may have been moved was around the late sixth century BC when the temple was sacked and completely destroyed by the Babylonian troops. But, by then, the Ark was either buried in the ground, or already missing." As Elliott was talking, he plugged his computer and camera together so he could download the pictures into the computer.

"Which do you think it was?" asked Stef, interested in hearing what Elliot had come up with.

"I'm not sure. I think it was buried because I saw the skeletons of a couple of individuals whose clothing would date to the right time as the sacking of Jerusalem. But I would think that either Shishak, or the Coptics took the Ark down to Egypt. I'm going to forward the pictures to Greg so that he can check it out to see if it looks about right." Elliott typed a quick e-mail to Greg attaching the pictures as he did. He used his cell phone as the internet dial up link for sending the email.

Elliott continued, "Our next data point was the early 12th century AD, when the Crusaders came through and all that was left was the scroll of the Gospel of Mark lying on the shelf where we think the Ark was stored. There are two millenniums over which all of this could have happened. The only clue we have is that the Gospel of Mark did not exist until about the second century AD, which cuts one millennium out of the picture. But that has a huge assumption with it; the assumption that the individuals who left the Gospel of Mark were the same people who took the Ark of the Covenant out of the cave.

Continuing the thought process. I'm struggling with the time-line." Elliott said, and drew out a timeline on a piece of paper as he talked. He marked items which included:

10th Cent. BC	Building of Solomon's Temple
9th Cent. BC	Shishak king of Egypt takes Temple treasures
6th Cent. BC	Babylonian invasion and hiding of Ark
1st Cent. AD	Gospel of Mark written
12th Cent. AD	Crusaders dig Temple Mount; the Ark is gone

"I see evidence of the hiding of the Ark because the keepers of the Ark are still there. I also see evidence of the Crusaders digging into the tunnel leading to the cave, because there was a pile of dirt on the ground where they broke through. But I can't find any evidence of anyone taking the Ark out. It would have been difficult to take the Ark out through the tunnel that I came through, since that would have been too small for such a large object. The tunnels are just wide enough to walk through. So, whoever removed the Ark, removed it through the cave that we broke into. But there was no evidence of anyone else coming into the cave."

"How about the reverse?" asked Stef. "Did you see how the keepers of the Ark were able to bring the Ark down into the cave?"

This question made Elliott sit back in thought. "That's true," he said. "How did they bring the Ark down? I didn't see any sign of anyone coming down into the cave."

Elliott started slowly flipping his way through the pictures that he had taken of the cave. He started looking for any clue that might be a hint of how the original keepers were able to bring the treasures down into the cave. He went through them once, then again, a second time. "There has to be more to this story. Based on the evidence we have so far, we would have to conclude that the Ark was never down there. I think we're missing something. I have to go down there again and make a more thorough search. I'm not seeing any hint of how they got the Ark in or out of that cave."

As he slowly started going through the pictures a third time, Stef slid over next to him and looked at the pictures as well. "Maybe we're looking in the wrong place," she suggested.

"What do you mean?"

"Maybe there was another way they brought the Ark in or out. What if there is another access to this cave through a tunnel that is now covered over."

"I've been looking for anything on the surface of any of these walls that may indicate a break in the smoothness of the walls. I don't see anything."

But Stef's thoughts were heading off in another direction. "What if the recessed shelves were actually connecting tunnels that are now covered over?"

Elliott went back to the picture of the shelf where he found the markings and where he assumed the Ark had been stored. "I guess it's a possibility," he suggested as he stared at the picture. "The sides of the shelf don't have a clean, smooth surface like the other walls in the cave."

"Pull up Greg's scan of temple mount," suggested Stef.

Elliott knew where she was going with her thought process. He pulled up Greg's over-flight scans and started looking closely at the area surrounding the temple treasure cave. Sure enough. Next to Elliott's cave, behind the location of the assumed Ark shelf was located, there was a secondary, very small and nearly unrecognizable cave, which looked like a stairway. It was difficult to distinguish it from the primary cave, since the wall between the caves appeared to be very thin. But there it was. A separate access to the caverns.

"I guess I am going to go back down into the tunnel tonight and see if I can break into that second cave. The Ark may be hidden right under our noses and we didn't even see it."

Stef didn't want anything to do with going back to Temple Mount, but she knew that Elliott was right. He would have to go back. "Great," she suggested, "as long as I'm not going down there with you. I'll stay on the surface and be the lookout."

"Great idea. I'll need someone to watch my back. And let's not walk over there by going over the top of temple mount. Let's get there from the side streets so that we're less obvious."

They sat there deep in thought. Several minutes of silence went by, both of them reflecting on what they had gotten themselves into and what they would need to do next. As they sat there, a young Jewish girl wearing a pair of tight jeans and a halter top walked by. Elliott's eyes drifted to the girl and followed her movements.

"Do you really need to be so obvious, especially when I'm sitting here next to you?" questioned Stef.

"What are you talking about?"

"You couldn't get your eyes off that girl's ass. You were staring at it for the last five minutes. Do you have any idea how incredibly rude that is?"

Elliott was stunned. He didn't even realize he was staring. "I'm sorry, I didn't do it consciously. I didn't even realize what was happening."

"That makes it even worse. You're checking this girl's butt out and you don't even know it. What is it with guys anyway? Can't they keep their mind on anything but sex?"

Elliott was stumped. He had no idea how he got into this mess, and even less of an idea how he was going to get out of it. "I'm really sorry! I don't know what to say."

"You could start by saying you like my ass better than you like hers."

Elliott got the queue. This was about jealousy. "Stef," he started, trying to think what would be the politically correct thing to say, "when I met you the first time, I was immediately blown away. I thought you were incredibly hot. You were the perfect woman. It would be indecent to say what I thought the first time we met."

Stef wasn't ready to leave it alone. "What is the perfect woman? What makes you say that I'm the perfect woman? It just sounds like some kind of ploy to get me in the sack."

"One guy's perfect woman is not another guy's perfect woman. There isn't just one answer to that question. Some guys really get hot on tits. Other guys like butts. Some guys like thin body shapes. Other guys like husky girls so they have more to hold on to. So, defining the perfect woman is strictly in the eyes of the beholder."

"What is your definition of the perfect woman?" Stef was now curious to see if she fit the model.

"Well, what I like in a woman is an athletic look. I like a girl that looks well put together. I don't like them boney, and I don't like them husky. I like a girl that looks like she takes care of herself."

"What about tit size?"

"It's interesting, but it's unusual to find an athletic girl with big boobs. Nearly all of them have smaller boobs. It seems to go together. There are some notable exceptions, but in general, I don't care too much about boobs. I like a strong, sexy pair of legs connected to a sexy butt. But, even if the girl has the right body, I can easily get turned off by her appearance. For example, if she doesn't take care of her hair, and it looks snarly and dirty, I'm left with the impression of laziness. Or if she walks slouched over and shuffling her feet rather than upright and with energy in her step, that's also a turn off. I love beautiful long, clean, straight hair. That's a killer for me."

Stef started to get skeptical. "I think you're putting me on. You're describing me, and I think you're just trying to get on my good side. I don't think you're really telling me what you think at all."

"Stef, to me you're totally hot, almost to the point of being obscene. When I met you the first time you were wearing an obscenely short, tight skirt. Your legs were killer, and your butt was perfect. And you had long blonde, straight hair which went down to the center of your back. I was probably drooling."

"OK, I'll let you off the hook. You're being real sweet, even if you're exaggerating. But can you do me a favor?"

"Anything."

"Don't check out other girl's butts when I'm with you!"

"Done. But I'd like to ask you for a favor too."

"What's that?"

"I'd like to have another look at your naked body to reaffirm my opinion. In fact, I'd like a little hands-on time to explore my options with an emphasis on 'explore'. Do you think you can help me out? I'd need you to be intimately involved."

"Of course. But first we have a little planning to do."

Elliott, trying to get the conversation back on the task of finding the Ark, mentioned; "I'll need a small shovel to dig back into the tunnel, and I'll need batteries and maybe another lantern so that I don't run out of light."

They both now knew what they had to do next. They would get ready for one more trip to Elliott's tomb, and hopefully get some additional, useful information from Greg. They paid for their desert and drinks, folded up their laptops, and got up to leave.

"I remember a small hardware store from my previous walk around the city," suggested Elliott." And he and Stef headed off toward that little shop. It wasn't a long walk, but it was a paranoid walk, with both Stef and Elliott on the lookout for anyone watching or tailing them. Once at the shop, they quickly found what they were looking for. Elliott picked a small camping lantern that he would be able to set on the ground. He also purchased a couple extra sets of batteries and a small folding shovel. He was ready to return to his earlier grave.

They walked with a heightened awareness of the possibility of being tracked, Stef raised the question, "What do you think about all the attacks on us? It seems like we're constantly under attack and we have no idea why or by whom. First at the Rain Forest, then again at Alice, and now in Jerusalem when you were walking and again at Temple Mount. We need to do something different. Like your shirt says, we keep doing what we do, the same way we always do it, and we keep getting attacked. I'm getting a little tired of it. There must be a better option. Who do you think these guys are?"

Elliott was at a loss, "I've been wondering that myself. Could it be the NNRL? But if it's them, wouldn't they wait till we were a little closer to finding the Ark. It's almost as if someone is getting inside information about our location, which the NNRL doesn't have."

"Then who could it be?"

"I have no idea, but you know the old saying; 'Keep your friends close and your enemies closer.' I think we need to limit who we share location information with. Let's restrict who we send information to in the hope that it will either stop the attacks or at least help us narrow down the source of the leak."

"I'm with you on that," responded Stef. "I sure hope it isn't someone within the IOM, but it wouldn't be the first time we've had an internal leak."

Now that they had a plan of attack in searching for the Ark, Elliott and Stef felt settled in their plan for next steps. They would go back to the cave in the early hours of the morning and Elliott would try to explore the hidden cave that they discovered from the S1s surveillance scans. Feeling comfortable about his direction ahead, Elliott's mind strayed back to a more interesting topic, Stef's halter top.

CHAPTER THIRTY

Back Down the Rabbit Hole
Early April, 2025 AD, Jerusalem, Israel, Temple Mount

Elliott and Stef took an early nap and set the alarm for around 01:00AM. They caught a cab which took them to the middle of the West side of Temple Mount. Getting out of the cab, they pretended to walk off to one of the nearby housing units until the cab was out of site. Then they tried to estimate the approximate location of the rabbit hole that Elliott had crawled out of. Their first couple of guesses was wrong, but on the third try they found the hole, with Stef tripping over one of the small mounds of dirt left behind from when they increased the size of the hole.

Elliott quickly dropped himself down into the hole, and Stef lowered the shovel and lanterns so he could go to work. Stef found a place to sit down thereby keeping a low profile in the bushes. She didn't want anyone seeing her and wondering what she was doing in this overgrown, scrubby location in the middle of the night.

It wasn't long before Elliott informed her that he had dug his way back into the connecting tunnel and that he was on his way back to the original cave under the Dome of Spirits. He was always really good at directions and he easily remembered his route even though last time he had very little light.

Once inside the main cave he turned on all his lanterns and took a detailed, close-up video of the entire cave, turning himself slowly for a panoramic view. He similarly shot pictures of the ceiling and the floor.

Now that he had pictures of the full cave, he shot close-ups of the area where he believed the Ark was stored. He reshot the scratching on the wall. Now he felt he was ready to break through to the other side where the small cave was believed to exist.

Kneeling on the ledge where the Ark had been stored, he took the point of the shovel and hit the back wall hard. At first it seemed solid. But after his fourth hard hit he felt the back side give-way. He hit a few more times and the shovel blade now easily passed through the wall. He started digging the wall away and, using a flashlight, shone a light through the hole to see what this stairway looked like. He couldn't make anything out, so he continued digging until he had a hole about six inches in diameter. Looking through again he saw a dirt stairway leading up to a solid ceiling. Obviously, this was the stairway used for bringing down the temple treasures. He also saw a third skeleton, obviously the third guardian of the temple treasure, who sacrificed himself to seal the inside of the wall. But there was nothing else. No sign of the Ark.

Elliott opened the hole until it was slightly over one foot in diameter and stuck a lantern through. He set the lantern on one of the steps, took out his camera, and videotaped the entire cave. He could see no markings, only the skeleton. He wondered how this man must have felt, volunteering to starve his way into oblivion, all for the sake of a treasure. But he knew it was more than that. It was the "temple treasure." And this sacrifice was about not allowing anyone to desecrate holy emblems, and not about a treasure.

Then he noticed a small mound of dirt on the bottom of the stairway. All the other stairs were perfectly formed, except for the bottom stair. It had a hill of dirt in the middle, which was hardly recognizable without a close look. But there it was. This caused Elliott to look for the possible source. He could see in the ceiling where one of the ceiling planks had been disturbed. Apparently, someone had come down here using these stairs after the original hiding of the Ark.

Early April, 2025 AD, Elko, Nevada, IOM Research Lab

When Greg arrived at work in the morning, he received the emails from Elliott and Stef and immediately went to work. It didn't take long to confirm that the clothing on the skeletons was of the vintage and timing of the Babylonian attack on Jerusalem. But the marks on the cave wall were challenging. The first part of it was obviously Cuneiform and represented the number 18. But what did the "A3" represent? He couldn't understand why they would use the oldest written language for the first part of a message, and then use modern script for the second part of the message. He couldn't make the connection. He tried to see if he could recognize a difference in the etchings, thereby indicating that the makings were made at different times. But that also didn't seem to be a reasonable explanation.

When Dawn and Alan arrived, he presented the problem to them to get their ideas on a possible solution. All three of the team members wore their usual dress code for the lab, sweats or shorts. They looked like they had just come from the gym. Dawn had a favorite set of white sweats, and sandals, Greg wore a black set, and Alan, the rebel, wore camouflage shorts that he claimed kept him hidden from the rest of the team.

It was rare event when the three team members found anyone else in their lab. They were on their own, and they were happy with that. If there was a problem, they would be sure to have visitors, but if there weren't any problems, they were left alone. They were a special response team that worked in the background in support of the field workers. They were the techies that everyone needed and appreciated. They took care of the S1, and a variety of surveillance tools. They were the IOMs hackers that knew how to break into any high technology system, from the comfort of their lab. They were extremely familiar with Elliott and Stef who were a couple of their regular customers.

The lab itself, wasn't much to look at. It looked like an electronic techie's nightmare. A barrage of computers and monitors, cables, were scattered along the four walls of this square 20 feet by 20 feet room. The equipment along the wall was used as needed. One section comprised the guidance and monitoring systems for the S1, and, when the plane was in use, the team would be heavily engaged with this section of the room. In the center of the room were three oversized desks which consisted of the central workspace for the team.

The S1 had a maintenance hangar of its own on about five floors up from the lab. It had its own hidden cave entrance from which it exited for its missions. The hanger contained all the additional equipment which made the S1 effective, including missile launchers, long range precision targeting rifles, and an unending variety of surveillance equipment. The needed equipment could quickly be attached to the S1 and it could be refueled and mission ready in a matter of minutes.

The S1 had already seen service helping Stef and Elliot analyze the interior of Temple Mount. And the team was sure this wouldn't be the last time the S1 would play a role in this mission. But today, the focus was on the markings that Elliot had found in the caves under the old temple.

"What could "18A3" represent?" asked Alan.

"Maybe they're not supposed to be combined," suggested Dawn. "Maybe they mean two different things. Let's tie them to the scroll of the Gospel of Mark. Would it mean anything in that context?"

They pulled out the pictures of the scroll and Greg started looking at that. Alan pulled up his translation of the scroll and tried to see if there were any meaningful connections. He looked at the two areas where the significant translation changes occurred and tried to tie them back to the scroll. But nothing seemed to connect.

Dawn attacked the terms "18A3", "18", and "A3", trying to find significance in any of these.

Around 02:00PM Greg called the team together to do a status check. Everyone seemed frustrated and discouraged. "I'm beginning to think that these symbols don't mean anything," said Alan. "We need some kind of Rosetta stone to translate what this means."

When Alan said "Rosetta stone" it sparked an idea in Dawns head. Maybe these were two different terms that were pointing at each other in some way. What would A3 represent in other languages? What about near-Eastern languages like Hebrew, Palestinian, or Coptic? And then the answer popped in front of her eyes. These marks were a type of Rosetta stone pointing the team in a specific direction. Excitedly Dawn exclaims; "A3 is the number 18 in the Coptic language!"

"Really," comment Greg. "Great catch. I would have never thought to look at the Coptic language. So, what we have here is the number 18 represented in two significant ancient languages. The 'A3' isn't using modern script, it's a secondary ancient script. I wonder if there is any significance in the number 18? Or were they simply trying to point us toward the Coptics? This seems to be a common theme or message which is saying, 'Go to Egypt and Ethiopia and visit the Christian Coptics.'"

Alan looked at the possibility that 18 was a religious or holy number in some way. This exercise had proven fruitless. Alan was busy experimenting on the numerological aspects of the number 18, but with little luck. There seemed to be a limitless number of variations to what 18 could represent, depending on which numerological structure he would choose. Eventually he found a connection. By writing Mark in the Coptic script and valuing the letters in the name of Mark using the Coptic alphabet he was able to come up with "A3" or 18 as the numerical value of the name Mark.

But Alan wasn't ready to leave it alone. He was convinced that there had to be more here than just the number 18 written in two different languages. He knew that the Coptics were heavily involved in numerology, so he went back to the ancient Coptic language and search out other words that broke down to the number 18. It took him several hours of analyzing Biblical names against the Coptic numerology, but eventually he came up with one significant parallel; Egypt. From this he concluded that one of the 18s represents Mark, and the other represents Egypt, the message being that Mark went to Egypt.

Continuing with his analysis of the numerology, Alan took Mark, and broke it into two pieces, "M" and "ark". Applying modern numerology on these Westernized names, he was quick to realize that the "M" represented the number 13, and the Coptic "A3", if translated to Western numerology, also represents 13 (the A equals 1 and the 3 equals 3). Which caused Alan to wonder if the "A3" was specifically selected because of its dual meaning. The Coptic number 18 had a Western numerology equivalent 13, which also represents the first letter of Mark's name. He also wondered if it was a coincidence that Mark's name had the word "ark" in it. In fact, the name Mark could represent M-ark, or the numerological equivalent, "M – Egypt" (Ark and Egypt having the same numerological value).

With these connections made, the scribbling on the cave wall finally made sense. The clue was pointing the search to the South, to Egypt and the Christian Coptics, where the Apostle Mark was the patron saint.

The team was convinced that they had solved this numerological nightmare. And Greg, in his role as team lead, sat down at the terminal on his desk in the center of the room and typed out a text message to Stef and Elliott.

CHAPTER THIRTY-ONE

Back From the Rabbit Hole
Early April, 2025 AD, Jerusalem, Israel, Temple Mount

Stef was keeping watch along the Western hillside of temple mount. She kept herself low in the brush so that she couldn't be spotted. She wished there was some way that she could check on Elliott, but the cell phone connection into the mount didn't work. She was getting chilled. She had shed the halter top before they came to the mount and replaced it with warmer clothing, knowing the night was colder. But even here jeans, warm shirt, and sweater didn't do the trick. She wished she had opted for a jacket. And sitting on the cold ground didn't help.

Fortunately, there wasn't any activity on Temple Mount or in the surrounding streets during that time of night. Occasionally a car would pass on one of the nearby streets. Otherwise, the evening was uneventful.

This gave Stef time to think. What had she gotten herself into with the IOM. When she was young, she loved the James Bond and Jason Bourne movies, and she idolized the lifestyle. But now, sitting here on the cold ground in Jerusalem, she wondered if she had missed the boat completely.

When she first heard about the IOM, she learned that it was an organization that dated back to the Knights Templar. These were the knights that protected the Jerusalem temple grounds during the times of the Crusades. They were sponsored and supported by much of the wealth of the middle ages and eventually became richer than many of the kings of Europe. The difference was that they didn't live the lavish lifestyles of the kings, and their wealth grew. Some of the kings, like the king of France, saw them as a potential source of money. King Philip IV of France petitioned the Pope, suggesting numerous trumped-up charges, and convinced the Pope that the Knights were a threat and needed to be eliminated. Stef was taught that the knights were betrayed by the Pope and the French King because of their riches. On Friday the 13th, a day that is still remembered today as a bad omen, the Knights were attacked and executed in all corners of the domain of the Roman Catholic Church. Officially the templar extermination occurred Friday the 13th of October 1307, but Friday the 13th is forever since remembered as a day of evil.

Most of the Templar Knights escaped from France on a fleet. In spite of all the secrecy, the Knights had received word that an extermination order had been given. Many of them fled France on ships carrying the treasures of the Knights. Some set sail to Scotland with the largest part of the fleet. They took the templar library, and most of their treasures. In Scotland, Robert Bruce, king of Scotland had no interest in fighting the enemies of a church which had excommunicated him, and he invited the Knights to take sanctuary there.

In 1446 Sir William, the patron and protector of the Templar Knights, organized them under the name they had carried since the construction of Solomon's Temple. They now become known as the Scottish Masons. Sir William started construction of Rosslyn Chapel and set up Rosslyn as a haven for Masons escaping persecution on the mainland.

Over time, the Masonic order reestablished its code of honor and dignity, and the 33rd degree of the order was the Order of the Knights Templar. And that's where Stef comes in. With such an interesting history, how could she resist. She had to become a part of this greater work, the work of the IOM. And now she had worked her way up in the ranks into about as high a position that she would ever be able to attain.

And with all the honor and glory of the Knights to encourage her on, she wondered why she was sitting on the cold dirt, on the side of Temple Mound in Jerusalem, freezing her butt off, and praying that there won't be any snakes. At least the sky was beautiful. It was clear and smog free, thanks to the breezes blowing off the Mediterranean. And the night was filled with stars that were visible in spite of all the bright lights in the area. It really wasn't a bad night to be out.

Stef hadn't completely recovered from her experience with the snake at the rain forest in Australia. Sitting here on the ground in the midst of all the brush made her nervous. She didn't want another snake encounter. She started to regret having chosen to stay out of the cave and wait. She might have been warmer and safer in the cave with Elliott. But that option was no longer available to her. She didn't want to go down into the caves and get lost. She would just have to wait it out. She hoped Elliott would hurry.

She received a beep on her Blackberry, which signaled a message. It was from Greg informing her about the clothing of the skeletons in the tunnel, and about the significance of the scratching on the wall of the cave.

"I guess we're off to Egypt," Stef told herself. Everything pointed toward the Coptic Christians and to the Egyptian and Ethiopian portion of the African continent. "Get your butt out of that hole Elliott."

From their earlier discussion about the attacks on them, Stef and Elliott had decided that they needed to keep closer tabs on NNRL. They were concerned that they may possibly be the team that was tracking and possibly even attacking them. As a consequence, they decided to communicate with them more often. Stef proceeded to send off a text message informing Kres and Rohit that all clues point to Egypt and the Coptic Christian Church and that they would be heading down there next.

Early April, 2025 AD, Alexandria, Egypt

Kres didn't come away from the IOM meeting on the coast of Australia with a lot of confidence that the IOM was committed to helping his NNRL team find the Ark. He was left feeling that he would need to do his own investigative work. He had his own team, and he would utilize them as much as possible.

Kres Brokard, whose original family name was Kres Hitler, had an interesting history. At the end of World War II his father Adolph conveniently faked his own suicide in 1945. He used one of his loyal and unfortunate staffers, who was approximately the same size, to fake his death. He talked him into putting on some of his own clothes, and then he strangled him. He similarly faked the death of his wife of 40 hours, former girlfriend Eva Anna Paula Braun. Then he set the place on fire so that the bodies would be burned. At that time forensic science wasn't what it is today, and there was never a positive scientific confirmation that it was really Adolph Hitler that had been killed. The only proof of his death came from a couple of witnesses who claimed it was him.

Adolph and Eva dramatically changed their appearance. With Adolph it wasn't hard. He had to shave off his mustache, which already made him unrecognizable because everyone had been so used to seeing him with it. He also placed a cap on his head to make himself look bald and put on fake glasses with no lenses. He looked like one of the many scientist geeks trying to escape Germany before the onslaught of the Russian troops.

Hitler's lady had performed a similar transformation. The disguises were sufficient to get both of them into France and down to the French Rivera where they were met by a boat.

Once on the boat, they headed toward South America. The destination was Paraguay. They travelled to Uruguay, and then took a smaller boat the rest of the way. At that time, it was an undeveloped part of the world, which meant anonymity would be easy. Hitler had sent a team to Paraguay earlier in the year, as a backup, just in case he needed an escape plan. And now he was glad he had planned that far ahead.

The trip on the boat was long. Hitler maintained his disguise during the entire trip in order to not leave any trail of his escape. He was now Adolph Brokard. This false persona unfortunately left him in quarters that were less than what he was accustomed to. He knew that if there was any hint that he was alive he would be relentlessly pursued by all the Allied countries. He needed seclusion in order to plan his strategic comeback. It would be on his schedule, when he was ready, and when he had rebuilt his army. This time he wouldn't be as aggressive and try to take over the entire world all at once. This time he would be more subtle. He would infiltrate the world's power systems and then strategically create international conflicts. Rather than take over using his traditional approach of an invading army, he would use spies to create world chaos, hitting the world where it hurt.

Hitler planned to use Western weaknesses to formulate their own downfall. And he knew where these weaknesses were located: in the economic structure, in the political structure, and in the belief structure. The economic structure could be controlled by establishing a series of Reserve Banks, which would be private banks in each country, and which would control the country's money flow and interest rates. This, in turn, controlled inflation and recession and gave him the ability to run the world through a series of economic ups and downs, always take advantage of the cycles to gain economic strength. Economic control fed political control. Administrations could be manipulated and changed simply by creating an economic downturn near the end of an administrative cycle.

The last focus of Hitler's plan involved turmoil in the belief systems, both nationally and internationally. For example, pitting the belief systems of science against those of religion would be a natural and easy conflict. Similarly, the religious belief systems would create numerous opportunities for conflict. For example, the Jews had always been a great scapegoat for the troubles of the world. And now, with their migration into what had formerly been Arab territory in the Middle East, they would create an excellent opportunity for additional conflict. This time Hitler would let someone else, like the Arab nations, solve the Zionist problem for him. He would help both sides become stronger, and in turn cause resentment, and hate. The Arab-Israeli conflict would blossom, and all the other countries of the world would soon be forced to take sides.

The transition to Paraguay was smooth. Hitler's plan was working. It wasn't long before he was able to establish his foothold. A large number of SS storm troopers were secretly given information about where Hitler had relocated, and they slowly transitioned to Paraguay to be with him. It wasn't long before they controlled the national police force and military, and from there they worked their way into several of the leading government positions.

But progress was slow. Infiltrating countries like the United States and the countries of Europe didn't move along as rapidly as it had in Paraguay. It took longer than he had hoped, but he insisted on patience. He had learned his lesson during World War II, that some things couldn't be rushed. He wanted all the pieces to be in place before he made his presence known to the world. Then he would retake his place as world leader.

During his years in Paraguay, Adolph and Eva had a son and named him Kres. Kres Brokard learned all his father's lessons well except one, patience. He wanted to be the world leader following in his father's footsteps. But it wasn't happening quickly enough to suit him. He wanted it now! And, with his father's death, he no longer needed to be patient. His father had accomplished a lot. His father had the Reserve Banks established, and they were performing their function of economic dominance in countries like the United States and in most of Europe. His father had also successfully manipulated the political leadership in the United States on several occasions.

Adolph had also established a strong rivalry between belief systems, like the Muslim-Christian-Jewish conflict had reached a pinnacle of success with events like the destruction of the Twin Towers in New York and the never-ending Palestinian-Israeli conflict. Another belief system conflict which Hitler had been able to magnify was the political conflict between the "big brother" protectorate approach of the Democratic Party opposed to the "self-help – earn your own way" approach of the Republicans. Then, of course, there was the religious right in conflict with the freethinking, scientifically minded left.

What had his father been waiting for? Kres felt that his father had lost his edge. It was time to strike. And with his father gone, the time to strike was now. With Kres in charge, he moved forward with his plan to make another, large 'demonstration' in the Washington DC area which would make the 9-11 fall of the towers seem small. To accomplish this, he needed two things; the Ark of the Covenant because his father convinced him that control of the Ark would guarantee victory, and the second was the need for the nuclear detonators.

There were three things that were necessary to build a nuclear device. The first was the fuel, and he had the nuclear fuel. That was easy to get on the black market from numerous Baltic countries that had nuclear processing facilities. The second was a delivery system, which everyone always thought was some kind of missile or rocket. But Kres' delivery system was a man walking with a suitcase. No one would ever suspect an innocent looking tourist. And radical Muslims seemed to have a willing supply of suicide bombers ready to do the delivery work as needed. The third piece he needed was the detonator. Without the detonator, the nuclear reaction could not be started. And this was the hardest piece to come by. Fortunately, the United States had accidently shipped several of these detonators (or fuses as they called them) to unsuspecting countries. And NNRL spies had learned that the IOM had acquired these detonators.

Kres had hopes of building a trusting relationship with the IOM. This relationship would serve the dual purpose of giving him access to the detonators, and of finding out what information the IOM, and in particular the Knights Templar, had about the location of the Ark. But he was starting to doubt the strength of this relationship. He wasn't sure that the IOM was interested in building a relationship with the NNRL. He had infiltrated spies into numerous organizations, including the IOM and the CIA. These spies had been extremely reliable in filtering information to Kres, but that's all they could give him. He already knew that Stef and Elliott were going to travel to Egypt to follow up the lead on the Coptic Christians. And that's why he was travelling there now. Unfortunately, his spies couldn't tell him where the detonators were or where the Ark was, only that the IOM could help him with it. He would have to get the details by working directly with IOM leadership.

Kres felt he needed to be more aggressive and involved if he was going to achieve his goals. He needed IOM trust and a closer relationship. This would start by him travelling to Egypt to join up with Elliott and Stef.

It was a bumpy landing as Kres and Rohit's plane landed in Cairo. Just then a text message came in from Stef. "Those guys are definitely not rocket scientists." grumped Kres Brokard to Rohit after reading the message. "Now they tell us they're going to Egypt. What a surprise. We already figured out that this would need to be the next stop. Let them know we're already here waiting for them. They need to get moving or we'll finish the job before they even get down here."

Rohit laughed, more out of courtesy to Kres than because he thought the comment was funny. Then he proceeded to type Kres' comment out to Stef. Before he could finish typing, he received a signal that a second message had come through. This time it was from their informant.

The message read; "Team found several additional clues which specifically linked the Ark search to Egypt, the Apostle Mark, and the Christian Coptics. We'll meet up with you in Alexandria."

"Well, I guess I know where we need to go next," commented Kres.

CHAPTER THIRTY-TWO

Departing Jerusalem
Early April, 2025 AD, Jerusalem, Israel, Temple Mount

Elliott had more questions than he had answers. Finding the hidden staircase had answered the question about how the cave had been accessed in the past. But now he had an entirely new collection of unanswered questions, which included: Did these guys come down here to steal the Ark? Or to protect it from some other adversary? And how did they get the Ark out and reseal the cave, leaving no other clue than a tiny mound of dirt at the bottom of the stairs? There was no other feasible option for bringing the Ark into this cave, except by using the stairs. These intruders must have taken the Ark. Nothing else made sense. But who were they, and where did they go?

Elliott wanted to take a closer look. He increased the size of the small hole that he had made in the wall separating him from the hidden staircase. He climbed through the expanded hole, attempting to see if he had missed any other possible clues. He walked up the stairs and videotaped the walls, ceiling, and floor, trying to document the area in detail. But he found no writings or markings of any type. Even the skeleton at the bottom of the stairs gave no clues.

The stairs were dirt steps, with dirt walls, much like everything else that he found in the caves. They were about five foot wide, wider than was needed for someone to walk up and down the stairs, but probably still a tight squeeze for the Ark. The ceiling was also higher than normal, again making extra room for the Ark's Cherubim, the angel statues that were on top of the Ark. The top of the stairs ended in a rock floor. It appeared that several long, flat rocks made up the ceiling of the staircase, and these rocks were the floor of the destroyed temple, which now composed the floor of temple mount. The rocks fit together tightly. Elliott wondered how the three guardians were able to remove the stones, move the Ark to its resting place, and then replace the stones. It must have been a strenuous effort.

After the Ark had been brought down into the cave and placed on its resting place, the wall separating the stairway and the secret chamber was built up. It was about one foot thick and built entirely of earthen clay. The back wall at the bottom of the stairs showed signs of where the dirt had been removed and then used to construct the wall. The obvious goal was to set up another diversion, keeping any intruders from knowing where to go next once they reached the bottom of the stairs. Apparently, this diversion didn't work, because someone was still able to access the cave and remove the Ark.

Discouraged at not finding any additional clues, yet excited at being so close to the resting place of the Ark, Elliott climbed out of the staircase and back into the original cave deciding that he had learned all he was going to learn. He made no attempt to reseal the hiding place of the stairway. He carefully navigated the dirt-walled tunnels, worked his way back to where Stef was waiting for him.

He sealed up the small tunnel entrance connecting the Ark cave from the rabbit hole that he had crawled into, doing his best to conceal any existence of a connecting tunnel. Arriving at the rabbit hole, Elliott found Stef deeply concerned about snakes, and when Elliott stuck his hand out of the hole it surprised her and made her jump. Elliott had no intention of scaring her, but when she jumped, Elliott started laughing and couldn't stop laughing. Stef couldn't understand what was so funny, and no amount of explanation by Elliott could convince her that it wasn't intentional. It took a while before Elliott could stop laughing enough to crawl out of the hole. He climbed out of the rabbit hole to find Stef a little grumpy, tired of waiting, shivering, and still anxious about snakes. With her forceful and irritated encouragement, they got off the side of the mount quickly, caught a taxi, and made their way back to the hotel, Elliott snickering the whole way. Stef mentioned that they would need to go to Egypt in the morning. Beyond that they agreed to not discuss what they were doing until the following morning. They didn't trust the listening ears of the taxi driver, and they were still concerned that their room was bugged.

Early April, 2025 AD, Jerusalem, Israel

Arriving at the hotel, Elliott, and Stef both took warm showers and crawled into bed exhausted. Stef whispered to Elliott that Greg's team had found specific proof that the scratching in the cave tied their search to Egypt and the Coptic Christian Church. They both agreed that they would need to follow this lead.

They planned to sleep in because of the early morning adventure on Temple Mound. Late the following morning Stef and Elliot caught a taxi and headed for the airport to catch a plane to Egypt. Based on the email from Rohit, they decided to meet up with their NNRL customers in Alexandria.

The morning was cool, but clear, and the trip to the airport was uneventful. Both Elliott and Stef had a heightened awareness about being followed and they were constantly on the watch. But no one seemed to have an interest in them today.

Travel to Alexandria from Jerusalem was extremely complicated. First, they had to drive from Jerusalem to Tel Aviv, about a 30-mile drive. Then they had to purchase a single ticket from Tel Aviv to some neutral country, in this case Istanbul, Turkey. Arab countries would not accept travelers from Israel. Next, they purchased a separate ticket from Istanbul to Cairo, avoiding any airline ticket trace of them having been in Israel. They had to pull out a second passport which they only used for Arab travel and which had no Israeli immigration stamps on it. They used this second passport for the flight from Istanbul to Cairo, Egypt. Once in Cairo, they caught a taxi for the long ride to Alexandria, Egypt. This was a 2 ½ hour drive and normally when they travelled, they would have rented their own vehicle. However, in Egypt, the roads are rarely marked, and it was easy to get lost. So, they always used a taxi. In the end, they only travelled a distance of about 400 miles, but the trip took them one and a half days.

Arriving in Alexandria was like entering another world. It was hard to believe that this was once the intellectual capital of the world. At one time it included the world's most impressive library containing the world's largest storage of knowledge. Intellectuals would come from as far away as Babylon, Rome, and France to learn and share in this university setting. They would read, study, and debate with some of history's greatest thought leaders. However today, this city looked like it belonged to a repressed, developing country, a far cry from its former glory.

As they started getting close and Elliott finally picked up a phone signal, he sent Kres a text message asking him where he was staying. Waiting on the response, Elliott and Stef instructed the taxi to head to the center of town. Working their way through the suburbs, the received a message from Kres telling them he was staying at the Sofitel Cecil Alexandria, which was a beautiful hotel, right on the Mediterranean. Elliott gave the information to the taxi driver and they continued directly to the hotel, hoping they would be able to get a room there as well. But if not, there were several other hotel options within a couple of blocks.

Stef wasn't usually squeamish, but the winding sharp turns of the Alexandria streets was starting to make her car sick. And the long hot ride didn't help. "If we don't get there soon, I'm going to need a bag," she whispered to Elliott. Elliott was trying to be tough, but now that Stef brought attention to being car sick, he started feeling it himself.

Arriving at the hotel they gave the bellman their luggage and took a walk along the waterfront, just to shake the car sick feeling. The street vendors and old buildings gave the area a flavor of returning to an environment and culture that was centuries old. They walked out on the sandy beach, which was beautiful this time of year. The beaches sloped off gradually, which made this an excellent beach for swimming. And there were a large number of people out enjoying the warm waters.

They returned to the hotel and went into the restaurant to grab a bite to eat. They preferred not to partake of any of the typically ethnic cuisine that was on offer from the various food stalls owned by street vendors; parked at random about the place. Hopefully, they would avoid getting sick from any of the food that their stomachs might not be used to. After eating, they both started to feel significantly better. Elliott left Stef in the restaurant as he went to get them a room in the hotel. It turned out that there were plenty of rooms and it wasn't long before the two of them, including luggage, were safely tucked away.

Elliott waited until they were settled in before he gave Kres a call. Rohit answered with; "Are you here?"

"Yes, we've arrived, and we're settled in at the Sofitel Cecil. Should we get together and discuss what we've learned, and next steps?"

"Absolutely. We're looking forward to it. You deserve a slight break before we get together. How about in an hour or two?"

"Let's make it an hour from now down in the lobby."

"We'll see you then."

After getting off the phone, Elliott turned to Stef and said, "They were cordial enough. They don't seem too upset with us. We'll let them do most of the talking so we can get a feel for their perspective."

Early April, 2025 AD, Alexandria, Egypt

After an hour of unpacking and getting comfortable, Elliott and Stef headed down to the Lobby to meet up with Kres and Rohit, who were already waiting for them. After cordial greetings, and some comments about the weather and the view, they went to work discussing their research.

Elliott started by asking Kres if he had learned anything new.

"Not a thing," responded Kres. "We were waiting to see what you came up with before we made any decision." This left a question in Elliott's mind which he left unspoken; "Why did they come to Alexandria if they weren't on the trail of these guys?"

Elliott continued, "We searched the Templar archives. We've gone through the manuscript left behind in the cave centuries ago. We've also searched the cave. From these three sources we get pointed down here to Egypt and Ethiopia and to the Coptic Christians. There seems to be a connection to them, but we haven't worked out all the details. Have you learned anything new that brings you to Alexandria?"

Kres spoke up, "We've concluded that the Gospel of Mark must somehow point to Egypt. What specifically did you find that pointed you down here?"

"We found writing in the cave that was in Coptic. We found the manuscript itself which was written in Coptic. And we found hints in the archives of a very close relationship between Solomon and the Queen of Sheba, and that this relationship endured for millennium. We see that Jesus Christ went down and spent time with the Coptics as a child. We see that Mark was sent by Jesus as a missionary to the Coptics to preach the Christian message to them and to organize them into a church. And we see active Coptic involvement with the Roman church until 451 AD during the Chalcedonian Council with its resulting rift. I think the Coptic Christians have valuable information about the ancient Christian church. They may also have information about the Ark."

"I think you're right. I've set up a meeting with some of the Coptic leadership for tomorrow. Are you interested in joining?" asked Kres.

"Definitely." They settled on when and where they would meet prior to going out to the Coptic leadership.

Then Elliott broke into a topic that was bothering him. "Do you know anything about people following and attacking us? Someone seems to know every step we make, and they've tried several times to disrupt our efforts."

"No idea," lied Kres. But Elliott could sense that he wasn't being fully honest.

They engaged in a few additional pleasantries, but neither group was interested in socializing together. Neither invited the other to get together later in the evening. Elliott gave some additional details about his time in the cave but held back pieces of information that he preferred to keep confidential. They finished discussing the logistics of the following day, and then broke off the meeting.

Early April, 2025 AD, CIA Headquarters, Langley, Virginia

Marcello Zuniga heard the beep on his Blackberry. He popped up quickly in bed and looked at the message. His mind had been set to register a message from his Blackberry, no matter how sleepy he was.

His apartment was close to CIA headquarters so as to avoid a long commute. And he preferred it that way because he enjoyed his time at home.

The apartment was part of a restored old red brick barracks that had the flavor of being from the revolutionary era. It was classy and tasteful. Vines grew all over the building, which added another layer of historical authenticity.

The message read; "IOM and NNRL together in Alexandria, Egypt." He knew what this meant, trouble! He had hoped to create a rift between the two organizations by letting the IOM think that the NNRL was spying and attacking them. But this was apparently not working. He would give up that strategy.

He was also concerned that there seemed to be unknown players. The team that he had sent out to disrupt the relationship had also identified other unknown individuals that were tracking the Templar's efforts. This confused him. Why were so many people interested in the IOM and NNRL's search for the Ark?

He responded to his Blackberry with, "Their plans?"

A few seconds later the response came back, "Meeting with the Coptic leadership."

Marcello decided not to respond. The idea that these two radical organizations were working together put fear into him. He decided that this was enough information to finally arrange the CIA-internal meeting that he felt was critically needed. Tomorrow he would get the TFMA and the TFRWR together. He hoped that this meeting would result in giving some direction on what his next steps should be.

CHAPTER THIRTY-THREE

Coptic Leadership
Early April, 2025 AD, Alexandria, Egypt

Late the following morning Stef and Elliot had finished their breakfast and were headed down to meet Kres and Rohit. They had no idea what to expect from this Coptic Christian leadership that they were about to meet. They had performed some internet searches on the Coptics, but it was very vague about current day practices and behaviors. They felt like they were going into this completely blind.

The greetings between IOM and NNRL were cordial but reserved. Rohit hailed them a taxi, and they were off. Kres sat in the front seat and Stef sat in the back between Elliott and Rohit as they wound through the streets of Alexandria, heading for a Coptic Christian monastery located near the site of the original Alexandrian library.

Twenty minutes into the journey Elliott whispered to Stef, "I think we're being tailed again."

In spite of Elliott's attempted stealth, Rohit overheard Elliott and quickly turned around to see if they were indeed being followed. "Who do you think it is? The cab right behind us or someone further back?"

"The car behind the cab, the grey Mercedes has been one or two cars behind us ever since we left the hotel. For as much twisting and turning as we're doing in these streets, I don't think it's a coincidence."

Traffic had slowed to a crawl. The streets seemed very busy and there didn't appear to be any immediate change in the traffic flow. Elliott opened the door of the cab and stepped out, in spite of the protests of the cab driver.

"What the heck are you doing?" blurted Stef in concerned protest.

"I'm going to try to learn something about those guys following us," responded Elliott, as he closed the car door.

Kres turned to Rohit and said, "go with him." Rohit quickly jumped out of the cab and followed Elliott.

Elliott walked up to the car and noticed a driver and a passenger. The occupants of the car looked surprised and slightly fearful. Suddenly shots rang out. The passenger of the car had reached out of his window and taken a shot at Elliott, grazing him on the shoulder.

Stef heard the shot and was out of the cab in less than a second, heading back to the location where Elliott and Rohit had gone. She wasn't going to leave Elliott out there on his own if shots were being fired. She could see that Elliott and Rohit had dropped down on their knees and had taken cover. The occupants of the car following them had now taken shots, apparently to scare off Elliott and the rest of the team. Stef saw that the shooters had jumped out of their car, abandoning it because of the jammed-up traffic, and they were running away in the distance. Apparently, they were not in a talking mood.

Stef could see that chasing them was futile, so she turned her attention to Elliott and his wound. Stef ripped off one of the sleeves of Elliott's shirt at the location where the bullet had penetrated and then exited. It was merely a minor surface wound, nevertheless the cut was bleeding badly. Stef proceeded to take the sleeve and tie it tightly around the wound, stopping the flow of blood. Elliott protested in pain but knew this was necessary. Neither he nor Stef were interested in going to the local medical centers, unless critically necessary, and they didn't consider this critical.

After being bandaged up, Elliott took pictures of the car, the license plate, and the contents. Then he proceeded to forward the pictures to Greg along with a text request to trace the source of the vehicle and find out what he can about it, and why they would be following him.

Climbing back into the taxi, Rohit asked, "What was that all about?"

Elliott and Stef recounted the events in Carnes and Jerusalem. "Frankly," Stef offered, "I thought you guys might have been behind all of these activities."

"Why would you think we're behind this?" questioned Kres, as he turned in his seat to look back at Stef and Elliott. "Don't answer that!" he blurted out with a smile on his face. "Actually, we did follow you for a while. We are interested in your activities, but not in obstructing your progress. We saw other people following you and we tried to figure out who it was - but with no luck. For them to take shots at you makes this serious."

"We can handle ourselves," commented Elliott, indicating he didn't want their involvement. "But we need to corner these guys when we get the chance so we can find out why they are after us."

Traffic slowly started moving again. They watched to see if anyone was following them. Apparently, the abandoned car that was behind them, remained abandoned and blocked the traffic. A harmony of car horns started blaring, as if their noise would somehow bring life to the obstruction and cause it to move out of the way so that traffic could once again start flowing.

The foursome continued winding their way through the streets for another thirty minutes, eventually arriving at an overly ornate and decorated church. It had beauty of its own, majestic looking with numerous arches and steeples. It was mostly white, except where the streams of acid rain had placed black streaks down its sides. Architecturally it seemed overdone to the Western tastes of Elliott and Stef, but it had a beauty that they could appreciate, given the amount of work that was involved in its construction. The taxi dropped them off at the front entrance. Kres paid the driver as they stepped out and started climbing the large stairway that led to the enormous, 20-foot-high front doors. The doors were decorated with elaborate carvings representing the Apostle Mark and several of his successors.

Upon entering the church, they were greeted by a priest who introduced himself as Jano Odulio. He wore the traditional robes and hat of a Coptic priest. The robes looked like he could have been a Roman Catholic priest, but the rounded dome hat gave him away as a Coptic.

He was quite handsome, in spite of the clerical garb which gave him a mystique of inapproachability. He was slightly taller than most of his countrymen. He welcomed them and offered to lead them to the office of the Pope. He explained that the term Pope was a term used by the Egyptian Christian church long before the term was picked up by the Roman Christian church. The term means father. The Church in Egypt used the term as a title of reverence for their presiding Bishop, who was considered to be the father of their congregation or religious community.

Jano noticed Elliott's injury, "What happened? You're bleeding. Shouldn't you be going to a hospital?" His English was strongly accented but understandable.

"I'll have it looked at when we get back to the hotel," was Elliott's response.

"Unacceptable," responded Jano emphatically. "We have excellent medical facilities here and we'll have that looked at straight away."

They walked down the center aisle of the church. Looking off to the left side in a vestibule which was an alcove, used as a side alter for personal prayers, Stef noticed a replica of the Ark of the Covenant and pointed it out to Elliott. Their guide, noticing their interest, commented; "Every Coptic Christian church or Coptic Jewish synagogue has a replica of the Ark. History tells us that it was turned over to the Egyptian church for safe keeping. The Ark was brought down here by Solomon's Son, David."

Elliott gave a surprised look to Stef. This was a new twist to the history of the Ark. This priest was suggesting that the Ark was already gone, long before the Egyptian attacks of the 9th Century BC by Shishak king of Egypt, or in the 6th Century BC during the Babylonian invasion. "I've never heard of a son of Solomon named David. I always thought David was Solomon's Father," commented Elliott. "Where does he fit into the story?"

"Solomon and the Makeda, known to Westerners as the Queen of Sheba, were very close, much closer than suggested by your Old Testament. David, known to us as Menelik I, the first King of Ethiopia, was born of this relationship. The Queen visited Solomon and spent quite a bit of time with him. David was born after the Queen returned to her homeland here in Africa. Later, as a young man he came to visit his father Solomon, who took a strong liking to the boy and they developed an immediate and strong bond. During this time, Solomon became concerned about attacks on Jerusalem from the North. He was also concerned about his sons. In his wisdom he could see that there would be a conflict between his sons over who would be the next king. He also saw that all of his sons were following after the gods of their mothers, rather than following the one true god. Solomon decided to send his David back down to Egypt with his greatest treasure, the Ark of the Covenant. He felt that the Ark would be better protected by David and by his mother, the Queen of Sheba, both of which had a strong testimony of the reality of the one true God. They had a greater respect for the Ark and would keep it safe. Ever since then the Ark has been under the protection of the Egyptian and Ethiopian Churches."

Elliott continued, "Help me understand the time-line here. You're saying that the Ark came down to Egypt long before there was a Christian Church here. They how did the Coptic Christian Church end up with the Ark?"

"It was inherited through church linage. What was originally the Jewish church, converted to Christianity and became what you refer to as the Coptic Christian Church. The hard distinctions between Christians and Jews didn't exist down here. Most of the Jewish followers converted to Christianity as a very natural next step."

Elliott had to think this through. He was struggling with the over-all timeline and couldn't quite make sense of it all.

As they arrived near the front of the church, nearby the altar, they headed off to the left toward a door. Through the door they entered a hallway which led to a collection of offices on either side of the hall. About three doors down, they entered an office area which was obviously a medical center. A nurse was there in attendance and, without saying a word, she sat Elliott down and started immediately unwrapping his wound. Jano spoke to her in Coptic, obviously asking her to take care of the wound.

It wasn't long before she had the injury cleaned and was injecting Elliott with a needle. "She's numbing you. She says you need stitches," explained Jano.

Ten minutes later she had him stitched up and was wrapping up the wound with clean bandages.

"Incredible service," was all that Elliott could say. "What do I owe you?"

"Please," responded Jano. "It would be insulting for you to pay us. Let's go on. The Pope is expecting us."

Stopping near the end of the hall, their escort knocked on one of the unmarked doors. They heard something which must have meant "enter" in a language that none of them understood. Their guardian opened the door and they all walked through into an office which was less ornate, then expected for someone who is the head of the church. The desk and all the other furniture were bland and unimpressive, made from strong, thick beams of wood, but nothing ornate. The only elaborate decorations were those on the walls, which all appeared to be original drawings representing Christ, the Apostle Mark, and other significant past leaders of the church.

Jano provided introductions in English, which eased the concern that the Pope would not be able to understand them. Elliott further introduced the four of them and, after some cordial comments about the beautiful art and about the weather Elliott brought the conversation to the purpose of their visit.

"We wanted to discuss the Ark of the Covenant with you. We're very confused about the sequence of events and where the Ark is now. I understand that Solomon's son brought the Ark down here to protect it from invaders in Jerusalem. But that would have happened around 500 BC, before the actual invasion of Jerusalem and the destruction of the temple by Babylon. Why would the Masons, the protectors of the Ark, allow the Ark to be taken? What did the Masons who were protecting the Ark at the time of the invasion, hide in the cave under the original temple? And how did a copy of the Gospel of Mark end up in this hiding place if the Gospel wasn't even written until nearly 600 years after the Ark was moved?"

The Pope, speaking in heavily accented and broken English, started explaining; "The original Ark was replaced with a decoy, and everyone was left to believe it was the real thing. The Masons were involved in moving the Ark to Africa. Menelik I was a Mason of the highest order and his foot soldiers were also Masons. Menelik considered it his greatest achievement to bring the Ark here and to be trusted with its safe keeping.

At the time of the Babylonian invasion, the history of the true Ark had been hidden from the Jerusalem guardians, and they thought they had the real Ark. Actually, there were numerous attacks on Jerusalem, some by Egypt from the South and by Syria from the North. Each time the Masonic guardians moved the Ark, and numerous other treasures, down into the secret cave, later returning them back to their rightful place in the temple. However, during the last invasion, the one by Babylon, the temple was completely destroyed, and the temple treasures, including the fake Ark, were sealed into their tomb forever.

Later, about the second century AD, numerous organizations started to become fascinated with the Ark, believing that it would give them some kind of superpower. The Coptic church became concerned that these organizations would try to get access to the Ark. The Alexandrian Pope at the time decided that the temple treasure cave should be broken into and the fake Ark recovered. This was accomplished by one of our own Coptic Christian Masons. He took the decoy Ark out of the cave and burned it, and he left the Gospel of Mark scroll as a pointer. Leaving the Gospel may not have been a good idea, but nevertheless, it was left. Only Solomon and his Son actually knew the full story of the true Ark. Even today the location of the Ark is a heavily guarded secret. Every Coptic church or synagogue has a replica of the Ark, and there are numerous false locations for the Ark, all of which were designed to misdirect searchers."

"As you know, we also have a special interest in the Ark. Is there any information you can give us that would help us in our search?" Elliott suggested.

"As I said, the location of the Ark is a heavily guarded secret ever since the day it was placed into our trust. We will do nothing to compromise that trust. However, I would be very interested in learning why you are searching for the Ark." the Pope enquired with more than a mild curiosity.

Kres jumped into the conversation at this point and did his best to put forth a convincing lie; "We are also extremely concerned about the safety of the Ark. We have learned of organizations that are planning to use it for military purposes, hoping that it would give them some type of superiority. The Bible talks about how the Israel had military superiority if they possessed the Ark. Do you believe any of this?" Kres wanted to get confirmation of the power of the Ark.

"We have never used it in that way," commented the Pope. "We know nothing about its power in battle. Our only concern is that we keep the wish of Solomon and Menelik I and protect the Ark. You don't have to worry about it. We will keep it safe."

Elliott and the team could see that there was very little hope of them learning anything new from the Pope. He was clamming up tighter and tighter.

As they were guided out of the church, Stef thought she would give it one more try by asking their escort; "Where did the Queen of Sheba live during the time of Solomon, or, more specifically; where would her son have taken the Ark?"

Jano Odulio offered a suggestion; "I'll give you some suggestions that may help you in your search. You'll find this out eventually anyway. But let me tell you that there is no way that you will get close to the Ark or even be able to take a look at it. No one, including the Pope, has actually been able to see the Ark except the caretaker who is responsible for its care. Very few people even know of its location. There are numerous theories about its location, but very few people know anything for certain.

I'll give you a couple of possible leads. These leads are long shots to some extent. First, there is a holy mesa which holds the Debra Damo Monastery. Only men are allowed to enter. It is a sacred monastery set aside for priesthood ordinances. A Templar Mason would be allowed to enter the cave and go to the monastery. Within the monastery are the historical scrolls which tell the story of how the Ark was brought down here to Egypt and then moved on to Ethiopia. You will need a Coptic translator to read the scrolls, but these scrolls are considered to be the only authentic historical record of what happened to the Ark. If you go there, you will have to show reverence to the church and to the caretaker of the sacred writings. You may have to spend several days living and working in the monastery to gain his respect and trust. Only then might you get a chance to look at the scrolls or books.

Another lead that you may want to pursue, which is also a long shot, is the compass."

Kres jumped in, "A compass? What type of compass do you have?"

Jano continued; "It's not a compass as you think of a compass. It's more complicated than just a magnetic pointer. It's actually an extremely complex piece of machinery, a mechanical computer that was developed by Menelik I's scientists. It was designed to always track the location of the Ark. Melelik devised some type of mechanism similar to clockworks. It tells time, the phases of the moon, the rotation of the planets, and numerous other tidbits of information. But it also works as a compass and a pointer and, by entering specific codes, it can tell you the current location of the Ark. I realize that scientifically this sounds a little farfetched. But the reality is that the intellectuals around Menelik's time had technologies that we cannot replicate, even today. They had the technology of the ancients which built structures like the pyramids, or the sphinx. And, for the most part, this technology has been lost. However, the compass does utilize some of this technology as a guide to the Ark."

It was Elliott's turn, "How do we get this compass?"

"We have a couple of them within the archives of the Coptic Church. But, quite honestly, it will be harder to find and get access to these than it will be to find the Ark. However, around the 1900s a fisherman outside of Greece found one of the compasses amongst a ship's wreckage at the bottom of the Mediterranean. This device is now located in a museum in Greece. I hear that a few years back some university attempted to reconstruct the device and that they may have actually gotten it to work. But they obviously do not know the device's purpose. I'm not sure about the accuracy of the reconstruction of the device, so I don't know if it works correctly. However, if you find out the location of where the device was found, you'll have an excellent chance of finding a second, similar device. Rarely were these devices used in isolation. Most of the time they came as a pair, thereby allowing confirmation of the message that comes from the device. So, if the reconstruction does not work, you can try finding the twin of the original, and perhaps that will give you the information that you need to find the Ark." Jano suggested.

Elliott came back with more questions, "How do we know if it's working? Does anyone know how to use it? Where is it located?"

"I have been a life-long student of the device and would be willing to help you test it to see if it works. It has become known by the name of the island where it was found. It is now called the Antikythera Mechanism. The internet will help you find the museum where it is located and the location of the reconstructed device." Jano advised.

"Why would you help us when the Pope was so strongly opposed to helping us?" Elliott asked his curiosity aroused.

"Strictly personal interest. There is no official church ruling against searching for or finding the Ark. And the excitement of the search makes me want to join your search. However, since I have my duties here, and I cannot leave, perhaps I can be a remote participant in the search." Jano admitted, with an undercurrent of excitement to his voice...

"I'm sure we will need your assistance as we learn more. We would greatly appreciate your help." Elliott revealed, gratefully.

"Another option that you may want to pursue is to talk to the Bishop of the Ethiopian Orthodox Christian Church in Jerusalem. He has developed a name for himself as the expert on the movement of the Ark. And he loves to share his knowledge. So, sitting down with him for a couple of hours might turn out to be extremely valuable." Jano further suggested, obviously eager to assist Elliott and his team where he could in their common endeavors.

Elliott and Jano exchanged contact information and Elliott promised that he would keep Jano informed of any findings.

Rohit jumped in; "Can you copy me on any information exchanges between the two of you? I would like to stay better informed than I have been in the past."

They parted company, Jano going back into the Church while Elliott and the team headed down the stairs. "That was quite interesting," commented Kres. "Who would have guessed that the servant boy would be our greatest asset."

"If it wasn't for him, we really wouldn't know where to go next," injected Stef. "How are we going to handle this new information? Do we go after the historical documents, or do we go to Greece on a device hunt?"

Kres jumped in aggressively and adamant. "This search is urgent, and we don't have any time to lose. This is not an either/or option. I insist that you pursue all leads and do it right away!"

The ride back to the hotel had everyone buzzing. They were amazed at how this search had taken such a decisive and dramatic turn. So far, they had stolen Templar archive documents, been shot at, been buried in the temple mount. Now they were going on a search through some ancient monastery caves for historical scrolls, return to Jerusalem to talk to more Coptic priests, and chasing some ancient device with unknown technology that no one has ever heard of. The excitement of the search was overwhelming to everyone.

Suddenly the back window of the cab exploded, with shards of glass flying everywhere. Then the cab driver fell forward, his body pressing down on the car's horn causing one continuous, loud blast. The back of cabbie's head had been replaced with a glob of gushing blood.

The car veered right into the oncoming traffic, narrowly missing several cars, and slamming into a parked car on the far side of the street. Elliott, Stef, and Kres reacted quickly. The damage wasn't severe. The front left fender and headlight were smashed in, but the damage didn't keep them from opening the doors. As soon as they car came to its sudden stop, they threw their doors open and jumped out. Rohit was trapped in the middle of the back seat but tried to crawl out behind Stef as quickly as possible.

A volley of shots came ripping through the roof of the car. Apparently one of the shooters was somewhere above them. Unfortunately, Rohit was not able to escape as quickly as the other three, and two of the roof shots ripped through his shoulder and out his chest and stomach. He collapsed to the floor of the car. Everyone could see there was little to be done. Rohit was squirming, but there wasn't any hope. The damage was too severe. He was gone.

Elliott and Stef worked their way down the street to the North, dodging between parked cars as they ran. They knew they had to get out of the shooter's line of sight as quickly as possible. Stef ducked behind a minivan just as one shot kicked up rocks next to her feet. She felt the sting of one of the rock chips cutting through her pants and into the flesh of her leg. Initially she thought she was shot, but after closer inspection she could see that it was just a flesh wound caused by a rock. Elliott kept up with her and ducked into the entryway of an apartment complex close by. A shot being fired was their queue to move to their next location. Stef slouched down and worked her way around the parked car behind the minivan, staying on the side that was away from the shooter. But the gunman saw her, and the windshield of the car exploded.

Elliott tried to work his way from one entryway hiding place to the next entryway. Unfortunately, it was further than he originally estimated, and the shooter got off a shot, narrowly missing him. Elliott could see the bullet hit the wall next to him, and a second close shot left a hole in the pavement about six feet up ahead of him. The next time they ran for it they both ended up around the corner and down a side street. Apparently, that was sufficient to get out of the shooter's line of sight. There were no more shots in their direction.

Stef and Elliott could hear shots being fired off in other directions and were sure that these shots were aimed at Kres. They continued slinking along for another couple of blocks, taking protection behind whatever, they could find, until they were confident that they were safely out of range. Elliott made a make-shift bandage from his shirt sleeve and successfully stopped the blood flow on Stef's foot. Then they found another taxi and headed back to the hotel.

Kres wasn't as lucky. Unfortunately, he decided to head South, which ended up bringing him closer to the shooter. He similarly ducked behind cars as he ran. Initially he thought that he had made the right move because all the shots seemed to be aimed at Stef and Elliott. But then the tables seemed to turn against him, and he drew all the fire away from Stef and Elliott. Apparently, he continued to be in the visible line of fire and Elliott and Stef had moved out of the line of fire. First a shot hit the ground next to his foot. Then a second shot came so close to his ear that he could feel its warmth and the rush of air. Kres turned left at the intersection, but apparently this did not get him out away from the visibility of the shooters. He continued to see and feel shots narrowly missing him and hitting the cars or the pavement beside him. But he couldn't successfully escape all the shots. Eventually one hit his leg, going through the flesh behind the shin, as he ducked behind a parked truck. Luckily, no bone was broken, and he was able to move. He decided to stay hidden behind the truck, taking a close look at his wound and doing his best to stop the bleeding. He wished he had the benefit of the help of the Coptic nurse that Elliott had experienced. He took off his shirt and used it to tie off the wound and stop the blood flow. The truck he was hiding behind continued to be riddled with bullets for another ten minutes. The shooting abruptly stopped as police started appearing on the scene, sirens blaring, blasting in from all directions. Apparently, the shooter had given up the fight now that someone was on the scene that could shoot back. Some of the police headed for the roof top where the shooter was believed to be located. Others secured the area. And several attended to Kres. After another ten minutes an ambulance appeared and Kres was loaded into the ambulance and rushed off to a nearby hospital to get stitched up.

The hospital was more like a clinic, with none of the sanitary precautions that he was used to. It was a two-story building, with an indoor parking lot on the ground floor, and the medical facility on the top floor, which looked more like an apartment complex. There was a large open-air section in the middle of the building where the fumes from the cars was able to filter upstairs. Kres hoped he wouldn't end up catching anything.

It would turn out to be a long evening for Kres. First the hospital people took their time patching up the hole in his leg. Then the police spent over five hours interrogating him on what happened. They questioned him about why he was in Alexandria, and he explained that he was meeting with the Pope of the local Coptic congregation. He claimed he was doing religious research. Then they asked about Rohit, and he explained that he was a travelling companion. When asked why anyone would start shooting at him, he explained that he was at a loss to understand why anyone would attack a pair of religious envoys. They must have mistaken them for someone else.

The police seemed to have missed the fact that Elliott and Stef were also in the car, and Kres didn't bring it up because he didn't want to raise additional questions and add to the confusion. He just wanted to get out of this hellhole and back to his hotel. He also didn't want Elliott and Stef to give a different story than he had told. It was better to leave them out of it and not complicate the situation.

It wasn't until the following morning when Kres was finally released from the hospital, and from police custody, and was able to return back to the comfort of his hotel room. The first thing he did was place a call to Elliott and Stef.

Early April, 2025 AD, Alexandria, Egypt

There was a knock at the door of the Alexandrian Coptic Christian Church's Pope.

"Enter," came the reply.

Jano opened the door, stepped inside, and closed the door behind him. "They bought it completely. They're going to include me in their search. They're going to follow up on all three leads. Some of them are heading to Jerusalem to talk to the Bishop there, others are going to the Debra Damo Monastery, and they're also going to try to bring the replica of the Antikythera Mechanism here for me to test it and see if it works."

"Excellent work. Keep me informed about any communications. This way we will be able to stay on top of their activities, and, if needed, we can divert them off the trail. You'll be my personal secret agent. We'll have our own little Coptic Christian underground. Isn't that exciting?"

"Yes sir," responded Jano, bowing slightly and leaving the room.

CHAPTER THIRTY-FOUR

Leaving Alexandria
Early April, 2025 AD, Alexandria, Egypt

The drive back to the hotel was quiet, with Elliott and Stef deep in thought. Neither of them wanted to discuss the recent attack in the cab. But both of them were extremely frustrated. Arriving back at the hotel, Elliott and Stef let some of the emotion control them. Stef gave Elliott and angry look and started with; "Who in the...#?!!! is after us?"

"I have no idea, but let's not go back to the room, just to stay on the safe side. Who knows where they're planting bugs? Let's take a walk down the beach." Without agreeing or disagreeing, Stef started walking across the street toward the beach, and Elliott followed. He caught up with her and they were walking together on the sidewalk on the opposite side of the street. Elliott continued; "We'll need to activate the S1 to monitor what's happening. The S1 can watch our movements and track anyone that attacks us."

"I just hope we live long enough to learn the results."

Elliott motioned Stef over to a bench along the Mediterranean Sea and went over to sit down. He took out a small note pad and a pencil, which he always carried with him, and started building a list of who would be interested in their search. "I can't believe that there would be anyone so concerned about our Ark search that they would try to kill us," he said to Stef. "This is beyond ridiculous. Obviously Kres and Rohit aren't behind it. So, who else could be after us?"

"This list could be large," responded Stef, "if we go beyond this project. Then we have lots of enemies. But if we limit ourselves to the search for the Ark, I don't know anyone who is interested in our efforts, except for the NNRL. And at least one of them, or maybe two, was killed today in the attack. So, I doubt it was them. Who else could it possibly be?"

"It just doesn't make sense. If Kres was killed today, we may not have a project anymore. This may be the end of our search."

"Have you tried calling him?" asked Stef.

"Yes, and his phone is either dead or turned off."

"Whoever's attacking us seems to know every move we make. Is it possible that this is an inside job, originating within the IOM? Who else would have that level of detail about our movements? Maybe we shouldn't bring in the S1 surveillance unit. Maybe we should go stealth for a little while and not let anyone know our whereabouts."

"Now that we're talking, I tend to agree. I'm thinking we should run quiet as well. At least then we'll know if there is some kind of leak. It may not be within the IOM, but someone is tapping our communications, and we need to figure out the source of the leak ASAP. Next time they may be successful. We may not be around much longer if we don't. So, from now on we communicate as little as possible with anyone, both inside and outside the IOM. Then, we'll start bringing pieces of the organization back into our circle of trust, and by the timing of another attack, we'll know where the leak occurred."

"I like it except it sounds like it's going to take some time before we figure this out, and I don't want to give these guys too many more chances to take us out. And I don't like being the bait. I wish there were a better way to accomplish, but I don't know what it would be."

"It sounds like a plan;" said Elliott. "Back on the search for the Ark, what are your thoughts? I vote we continue looking for it." With or without the NNRL, Elliott wasn't ready to give up easily. He was going to continue his search for the Ark. And Stef could sense his commitment. He didn't have to say anything. She had worked with him long enough to know he was hooked. He flipped to a new page in his small notebook and started reworking his timeline:

10th Cent. BC	Building of Solomon's Temple – moving of Ark of the Covenant from tent Tabernacle to Temple
9th Cent. BC	Moving of the real Ark to Egypt and/or Ethiopia by Menelik I, the first King of Ethiopia, Son of Solomon, and the Queen of Sheba, and replacing it with a false Ark in the Temple
9th Cent. BC	Shishak king of Egypt conquers Jerusalem and takes Temple treasures to Egypt (Coptic history has the Ark already removed at this time)
6th Cent. BC	Babylonian invasion and destruction of Temple - hiding the "false" Ark into the temple mount
1st Cent. AD	Gospel of Mark written
2nd Cent. AD	Coptics enter the mount to destroy the false Ark, thereby hiding its existence and the existence of the real Ark, and leave the Gospel of Mark Scroll in its place as a clue for the worthy
12th Cent. AD	Crusaders dig into Temple Mount to find temple treasures - Ark is gone, replaced by Gospel of Mark – Gospel and remaining temple treasures removed

"This is a story line that is three Millennium old," was Elliott's comment to Stef. "And it continues to get more confusing. Now that we're involved in this, it has completely captured my interest and I'm not sure I can let it go, with or without Rohit and Kres. Now that we've met with the Coptic leadership, we have three more clues to chase. Number 1); some ancient Greek artifact with the capability of pointing to the Ark. That sounds like something out of a fantasy novel, but we'll have to pursue it. Number 2); historical scrolls hidden in a cave in a monastery in Ethiopia detailing the history of the Ark. And number 3); a Coptic Christian Bishop who is an Ark historian back in Jerusalem. I hope we're not just running off on a wild goose chase. Hopefully at least one of these leads will give us direction."

"Me too. I agree and I'm with you. Can we go back to the room? I'm too worn out to think." Stef had calmed down after talking and walking with Elliott. The events of the day had proven to be extremely draining, and that was catching up with her. "You figure it out and let me know what we're doing in the morning. The excitement, and all the travelling, has me completely exhausted." Stef knew that planning their strategy for next steps was something Elliott loved to do, and he was very good at it. She wasn't trying to separate herself from the process. But she also knew that she was better at execution than at planning. Besides, she trusted him fully.

The two left the bench, crossed the street, and went into the hotel, heading back to their room. Stef went directly to the bathroom, took out her contacts, pulled off her shoes, socks, jeans, shirt, and bra. She crawled into her side of the bed and rolled over on her side. "Good night," was all Stef could say as she lay there with her eyes closed. She was exhausted, still feeling the loss of sleep from the long nights in Jerusalem, and the roughness of the trip to Alexandria, adding to that the excitement of the day. It wasn't long before she was sound asleep.

But Elliott's mind was still racing. He was struggling with all the recent events. Who was attacking them? How does he deal with three new leads simultaneously? What is the Egypt and Ethiopian connection? How did the Ark, which was a Jewish temple treasure in Jerusalem, end up under the control of the Coptic Christians in Africa? He decided to break the decision to maintain "a code of silence and secrecy" in order to send a message to Greg. There were some things that he just couldn't do alone. He needed Greg's help. He texted a message: "Two requests: (1) What is the connection between Jews and/or Christians, and the Ethiopians / Ethiopian Orthodox Christian Church, and (2) What is the Antikythera Mechanism and how do we get a hold of it?"

After another two hours of thinking and analyzing, and listening to Stef snore, Elliott was also losing his battle to stay awake. The arm wound had drained some of his energy. He was confident that it was well taken care of medically, but the loss of blood, and the adrenalin rush of the attack on the cab, had sapped him completely He was out of energy. He kept playing with his timeline, trying to make sense of where the Ark may have gone. But it wasn't long before he lost his battle to stay awake, and he fell asleep, sitting at his desk, his head resting on the pad of paper that contained his scribbling.

CHAPTER THIRTY-FIVE

Planning Next Steps
Early April, 2025 AD, CIA Headquarters, Langley, Virginia

Marcello Zuniga sat slouched in his chair, flipping through a large pile of reports that seemed to grow on its own. He dreaded this part of his job. These reports were always ten times larger than they needed to be. They always overplayed the good news, and the bad news was hidden somewhere between the lines, and he hated digging out the bad news so that he could get a true picture. Today was a slow day and he had some time to catch up on his backlog of reading. He had just started reading an Air Force report on ICBM inventory discrepancies. The report had been sitting on his desk for months. But he noticed something that abruptly brought him to attention.

The ICBM (Inter-Continental Ballistic Missile) Wing of the Air Force out at Hill Air Force Base in northern Utah, was reporting a clerical shipping error and some inventory discrepancies. They reported that one box of four cone-shaped fuses for ICBMs was accidentally shipped from North Dakota to Taiwan. The Taiwanese had ordered Helicopter batteries. However, when they opened the box of parts, they couldn't identify the contents, and, in contacting the USAF shipping office they realized that their intended shipment was inadvertently replaced by a box of ICBM missile warhead parts. The US had shipped nuclear detonators (fuses) out of the country. Fortunately, Taiwan was a trustworthy friend. These parts could easily have ended up in the hands of someone not so trustworthy.

The miss-shipped parts were quickly recovered and returned home. But upon further investigation the Air Force realized that this wasn't the only box of missile warhead fuses that was missing. And they had no idea where the other boxes of parts had been shipped, because it was obviously a misdirected shipment. They went back and checked all their orders, especially those which looked like they may have received the wrong parts, but there were no clues to help them in their search. It was obvious that the miss-shipped fuses were either still unidentified and sitting in boxes somewhere, or worse, they were identified for what they really were and had now become the possession of someone who didn't want the United States Air Force to know they had them.

Marcello's concern was increased when he encountered another report that expanded on the missing fuse story. This report went on to say that CIA agents out in the field had recently received unconfirmed reports of the sale of missile parts to the IOM. Thinking out loud Marcello said to himself; "Is there any significance to this report and the IOM's current work with the NNRL? This is too big a coincidence to be a coincidence."

The NNRL was an organization high on the CIA watch list. It was a group that the CIA considered extremely dangerous. And the only pieces missing to create an active nuclear bomb would be the nuclear fuel and the delivery system. The nuclear fuel could be acquired from any number of nuclear processing plants around the world, many of which were extremely unfriendly to US interests. And the delivery system didn't need to be a rocket. The bomb could be delivered in the trunk of a car, or any number other ways. Bottom line was that if the NNRL was able to get nuclear fuses from the IOM, the damage could be incredible.

Early April, 2025 AD, Alexandria, Egypt

Elliott jumped up with a jerk. He had fallen asleep, with his head on the table, and the ring of his phone gave him a rude and sudden wake-up. He answered the phone with a gargled and sleepy; "Hello!"

"How are you guys? Did you get away OK?" asked Kres.

"We're fine. We got away safely and returned to the hotel. Since we didn't hear from you, we were starting to get concerned that you also got killed. We tried calling you but couldn't get an answer. What happened to you?"

"I just about got killed. Shortly after the shooting started, the local police came pouring into the area and the hit man ran for cover. Otherwise, I may not have made it. He came pretty close to taking me out. I ended up with a bad leg wound, which prevented my escape and landed me in a hospital surrounded by half the city's police force. They badgered me with questions all night, like: 'Who was shooting at you? Why were they shooting at you?' And on and on. Anyway, I just got back from getting patched up and interrogated. So, I'm not in a very good mood. I want to know who did this! I want to know who killed Rohit and shot me in the leg! Do you have any idea who that was? And how did you manage to escape without a scratch?"

"We have no idea who is doing this. And the bullets through the roof could easily have hit any of us. I'm not sure the shooter really cared who he hit. I think he was after all of us. Up to now we suspected that the source of these attacks had something to do with you guys. But obviously that's not the case. Stef and I have been trying to guess who may be after us, but we have no idea. It's also bothersome that these gunmen constantly seem to know where we're at and what we're doing. It's almost like they have a tracking device on us or that they're getting inside information on our movements."

"Well, I'm thoroughly mad," barked Kres, and he sounded like it too. "I didn't just loose an employee today; I lost a close companion and a good friend. And whoever it was that attacked us today has become the primary target and focus of my effort. I will root them out and destroy them. They're messing with the NNRL and that's the wrong group of people for them to get mad."

Elliot had no doubt that he meant every word he was saying. Kres continued, "I assume you two will continue following the leads that we've come up with. Please keep me informed. I'll get back to you when I've avenged this attack." Kres' passion made Elliott shudder. Elliott was fully capable of handling himself, but Kres' anger sent out waves that could be felt through the phone.

"Do you guys have any missile systems, or missile parts, some kind of delivery system, that I could get from you?" Kres asked. "I think it would be helpful in my search."

"I really don't know what we have," Elliott lied. He knew about the ICBM parts, and he knew his IOM team had nuclear experience. They had access to all three of the key pieces in a nuclear warhead, the detonator or fuse, the refined nuclear fuel, and the delivery system. But he wasn't going to let Kres know about it. This guy was scary, especially when he was angry. The NNRL leader was too aggressive and revengeful. Who knows what he would do with that type of fire power? "I'll check into it and get back to you." Elliott hoped this would stall Kres and later he would tell him that he didn't have anything to offer him.

Elliott also promised Kres that he would do a better job of keeping him informed. He promised that he was in the process of developing a plan of attack to follow all three leads simultaneously, but, at this point, he still wasn't quite sure how he was going to accomplish the feat. Elliott stressed that they do not discuss the specifics of any of the leads or of any of their travels over the phone. He also informed Kres that he and Stef were getting rid of the cell phones and getting throw-away phones and he would keep Kres informed of the numbers. Elliott wanted to eliminate any possible means of being tracked. They ended the call with Elliott still wondering who could possibly have attacked them, and why Kres was suddenly interested in nuclear warheads.

As he got off the phone, Stef stirred and turned over on her side, which was her signal for Elliott to crawl in behind her and wrap himself around her. He knew his queue, took his clothes off, and quickly crawled into the bed. At first Stef squirmed. Elliott was cold and she had warmed her spot in bed. And when he put his hands on her, she butt-bumped him, which was her signal for him to back off until he warmed up. Elliott spent five minutes on his side of the bed, rubbing his hands together to get then warm. Then he returned to Stef, again testing his hands against her skin. This time there was no butt bump, so he knew he was OK. He moved his hand up onto her soft breast and kissed the back of her neck. "It doesn't get any better than this;" was the thought that went through his mind. And it wasn't long before they were both snoring.

CHAPTER THIRTY-SIX

Nukes

Early April, 2025 AD, near Asunción, Paraguay

The Asunción NNRL warehouse is a river-front warehouse north of Limpio, a small suburb north-east of Asunción, Paraguay. Krank Markal and Lefty Leviticus are Paraguayan born citizens of former German-Nazi parents. They managed this top-secret location for the NNRL. Krank is the perfect image of a tall, white Arian with blue eyes and blond hair. He enjoyed physical fitness and worked out regularly. Both of his parents were imported Germans.

Lefty was the opposite with short, black hair, and dark eyes. He looked a lot like the local indigenous population, taking these features from his mother who was a native of the country. His father was a German immigrant who married after his arrival in Paraguay.

The warehouse was part of a large, multi-warehouse manufacturing complex, situated here to hide its true identity. The facility was known as 8-42, the numbers coming from the coordinates 25°06'08" S; 57°29'42" W. It was a tin roofed, tin sided box about the size of two

two-car garages, which made it extremely noisy when it rained. But it was well disguised, looking similar to all the other warehouse buildings that surrounded it. Without close inspection, no one would identify it as a NNRL storage facility for weapons and equipment.

The facility was along a main road which facilitated truck access. It also had its own dock, which was used for clandestine nighttime shipments. The dock-river access went all the way to the ocean.

Two months earlier, a night-time shipment was received from a plutonium processing plant in the Balkans. The materials had been loaded into a cargo container whose manifest was identified as coal. The actual plutonium was encased in a box, which was buried in coal in the center of the container. From the Balkans the container travelled on a barge across the Black Sea, past Istanbul, and into the Sea of Marmara. From there it was transferred from the barge onto an ocean-going cargo ship and continued its long journey, travelling down the Aegean Sea between Greece and Turkey, and out into the Mediterranean Sea. No one questioned why coal was travelling so far. They assumed it was a special type of coal that would be utilized for a specific purpose. And no one detected the radiation being emitted from the container. The crates had some shielding, and the coal provided additional shielding, but these weren't perfect shields, and some radiation was able to escape the container.

After crossing the Mediterranean, it was clear sailing through the Strait of Gibraltar, across the Atlantic, and on to South America. In Montevideo, Uruguay, the container was again transferred to a smaller barge, to continue its journey up the Rio de la Plata, past Buenos Aires, Argentina, and on toward Paraguay. The river traveled along the borders of Argentina, Uruguay, Brazil, and eventually past Asuncion the capital of Paraguay. The river continued its northerly journey until it took a sharp Eastward turn, signaling to the river captain that they were closing in on their destination of Limpio, Paraguay.

After arriving at the NNRL dock, the container was quickly off-loaded and transferred into the warehouse, where Krank and Lefty went to work. They emptied the coal and the plutonium out of the container and transferred the nuclear fuel into a lead-lined trunk. The coal would be saved and used to heat the warehouse. Then the container was removed from the warehouse and was left outside in the storage yard in case it would be needed at some later date.

The shipment contained enough plutonium for ten 20 kiloton nuclear weapons, each similar in power to the bomb dropped on Nagasaki near the end of World War II. And now, one of these nuclear payloads needed to be smuggled into the United States for a special celebration of the Adolph Hitler's birthday.

Smuggling anything into the United States was tricky, especially nuclear fuel. The borders of the USA were plagued with detectors, and weapons grade plutonium would quickly be identified. So Krank and Lefty had to make special arrangements for the transfer. Neither wanted to travel with the plutonium for long distances, realizing that the radiation from the materials could have serious and possibly even deadly effects on their health. After drawing straws, it was decided that Lefty would be able to stay behind to take care of the 8-42 warehouse, while Krank would travel with the payload on its journey toward the United States.

The process for getting the plutonium into the United States was complicated. First it would require taking the plutonium into Brazil. The material was loaded into a three foot by three foot by three-foot cube crate, which fit nicely into the trunk of a car. The whole thing weighed less than 30 pounds and was easily carried by one individual. Krank loaded the crate into the back of his old Ford Pinto, which was held together by bailing wire and tie straps, and he was off. He threw a lead blanket, which he had stolen from a dentist's x-ray technician's office, over the top of the crate, hoping it would shield him from the radiation during the upcoming long drive. Additionally, he wore a second dentists x-ray blanket hoping this would further protect him. He thought he was ready to go, he just needed the word to go-ahead with the mission.

Krank received word via a phone text message from Kres that the "Birthday Celebration", as the mission had now been labeled, was a go. Krank loaded up his car and proceeded immediately East toward the Brazilian border. The roads were rough and long, especially on the back roads. However, once he arrived at the East-West freeway, his travel time greatly improved. It was beautiful, scenic country. He travelled through large regions of farmland, through larger cities like Luque and Emboscada, and through the smaller cities like Yapacara, Caacupe, and Caaguazu.

The area around Asunción has a tropical, hot, and humid climate. Even though the country is land locked, and in the middle of South America, its altitude is only about 150 feet above sea level. The area has a relatively short dry season that spans from June to September, the remainder of the year being wet.

Halfway through the trip the main freeway ended, and travel resumed on the smaller, rougher farming roads. The 200-mile trip took most of the day, with most of the travel averaging at about 30 miles per hour. Eventually he arrived at Ciudad Del Este, a suburb of the Eastern Paraguayan border town of Presidente Franco. It was now a short jump across the border to Brazil. But first he would find himself a small hotel and spend the night.

The following day, Krank crossed the border into Foz do Iguancu, Brazil. From here he travelled through more beautiful farm country heading for Cascavel, his pre-determined rendezvous point. At the west end of Cascavel, in a NNRL warehouse known as 43-27 for the grid coordinates of 24°58'43" S, 53°29'27" W, in the city of Guaruja, was the staging point where Krank would deliver his nuclear payload. Waiting for him was a container filled with granite kitchen counter tops, headed for the United States. The latest fad for kitchens was to have solid, one-piece counter tops. Granite was one of the few materials which would successfully shield the plutonium radiation and thereby avoid detection. A hole had been made in the center of the counter tops, which was just the right size for the payload that Krank was carrying.

Krank delivered the nuclear material. The center 6 countertop sheets were pulled out of the cargo container using a forklift until the center hole was visible. The nuclear material was placed into the hole, and the countertop material was pushed back into the cargo container. Then the container was sealed. An hour later a truck arrived to haul the container off to the nearest seaport, and from there forward the materials on to the United States.

Krank left Guaruja and started his long drive back for the border and on to Limpio. The truck hauling the cargo container headed off in the opposite direction to the container loading docks of Paranagua, east of the city of Curitiba, along the coast of Brazil. From there, it was a direct shot to any of the many seaport towns of the United States.

CHAPTER THIRTY-SEVEN

The Plan
Early April, 2025 AD, Alexandria, Egypt

Steff woke to find Elliott deep in thought, sitting at the table and scribbling notes. She walked up behind and put her arms around him and whispered; "So what's next boss?" knowing that Elliott wasn't the type of person to be "boss" to anyone or to be "bossed" by anyone.

"I think we need to take a three-pronged approach. I'll go to Ethiopia to the Debra Damo Monastery. You can't go there anyway, only men allowed. So, you go back to Israel and talk to the Bishop of the Ethiopian Orthodox Christian Church in Jerusalem and see what wisdom he can share with you. And I sent Greg a message last night to start working on finding the Antikythera Mechanism. Kres called. He's OK except for being shot in the leg. He spent the night being interrogated by the police. He is in a pretty sour mood, especially after losing Rohit. Kres is off trying to find our attackers. I'd hate to be the one he's after. He sounded scary."

"I was afraid we were probably going to split up. I prefer sticking with you and working together. I don't like it, but it makes the most sense. I guess we're done here. We should start packing and head out. But I dread the long drive back to Cairo."

"We can wait an hour or so. Let's take a walk along the waterfront. We may never be back this way again, so let's enjoy one last look."

"I really don't think I'll want to come back any time soon. But a walk would be really nice, just to get the kinks out."

They got dressed and headed down to the lobby where Elliott talked to a travel desk and asked them about flights to Ethiopia and Turkey. Stef would need to repeat doing two flights, once again avoiding the appearance of traveling between an Arab country to Israel. Then Elliott ordered a taxi for 10:00AM (two hours out) that would take them to the Cairo airport. That would give them an hour and a half to walk along the Mediterranean, and another half an hour to get packed up.

Early April, 2025 AD, CIA Headquarters, Langley, Virginia

The Task Force on Mercenary Activities (TFMA) and the Task Force on Right Wing Revolutionaries (TFRWR) were finally together. Three representatives came from the TFRWR and three, counting himself, from the TFWA. Marcello couldn't help but be frustrated by the incredible bureaucratic nightmare he had to navigate to get these two organizations in the same room. Their offices were in the same building, just down the hall from each other. "You just gotta love government," he said to himself.

Marcello Zuniga started the meeting by explaining the intelligence information he had recently received. He explained the roles of the IOM and the NNRL and how they were working together. He discussed their travels to Israel and then on to Alexandria, Egypt in search of the Ark of the Covenant.

"So why do we care?" asked Quincy Lewis representing the TFRWR.

Marcello was so stunned by the question that it took him a couple of seconds to get his composure. Then he answered, "Any time you have a high security risk organization on the move like this, we should be concerned. And, in this case, we have two of them on the move and moving together."

"I understand that. But who cares if they search for some mythical Ark of the Covenant? Why would this be a CIA concern?"

"This is about more than just finding the Ark. This is about high-risk collaboration. This is about identifying and utilizing a weapon. The nation that possesses the Ark is invincible."

"Don't tell me you believe all that nonsense. You probably think that the 'X-Files' program on TV is real. Do you think we have agents running around chasing spirits and ghosts? This isn't a CIA concern. Not until you convince me that there is some kind of credible threat against the United States. And I don't see any kind of threat here."

"So, you're telling me that the TFRWR doesn't care if the IOM and the NNRL are becoming buddies," said Marcello, the frustration obvious in his voice.

"Of course, we care. But I still don't see a threat against the United States. I see this as an archeological dig and nothing more."

"We've been tracing their activities, and one thing that has become very curious is that they are regularly being attacked by some unknown assailant. Someone's trying to kill them. Does that interest you?"

"Well, if these assassins do their job, then it just means we have a few fewer potential threats to worry about. I still don't see why I should care. Can you tell me that either organization is doing anything threatening?"

"We have an agent in the field working for the NNRL, and he's concerned. He says that he doesn't fully understand what Kres is up to, but he sees the Ark hunt as a diversion trying to draw attention away from the real goal."

"And what does he think that real goal is?"

"A return to the 3rd Reich. A return to Hitler's glory. The perfection of the Arian race. He doesn't know. Any of these are a possibility. He just thinks there's more to this than just an Ark hunt. Did you read the ICBM discrepancy report? The one that talks about the missing nuclear missile head parts. And that some of our field agents suspect that the IOM has picked up these parts? Do you see that as a credible threat?"

"I see this as a lot of speculation and storytelling. I don't see any reason why I should throw resources behind your speculations. Do you?"

"No, I don't," responded Marcello. He had enough and he was ready for these guys to leave. "No. I guess my concerns were unfounded."

Everyone stood up and the TFRWR started filing out of the room. As they left the room, Quincy whispered to his two companions Conrad

Brady and Joe Fanara; "Politics. These guys won't follow the hunch from another department. If the idea wasn't developed by them, then they won't support it. No one outside of their office is considered credible. I want two agents in the air with me tonight heading for Ethiopia! We need to keep an eye on the NNRL and the IOM, even if our co-harts don't see it."

Back in his office Marcello threw up his arms in frustration and told his co-harts, "I guess we don't care about enemies of the state unless they're knocking over our trade center buildings. I'm going to Ethiopia myself to see what's going on over there. I just have a bad feeling about these guys working together and I'm going to get to the bottom of this. I want to know what's going on, with or without the help of the TFRWR. By the way, have we heard anything new from our man in the NNRL?"

"Nothing," replied Conrad, the agent charged with monitoring communications with their agent in the field. "I'm getting a little worried. He missed his assigned call. And usually, if he's going to miss, he at least sends us a text message letting us know. But this time everything is silent."

"Let me know the minute you hear anything."

"Will do!"

Later that evening Marcello, Conrad Brady and Joe Fanara caught a flight for Cairo, which would then connect with a flight to Ethiopia. There still wasn't a message from their NNRL agent in Alexandria, Egypt.

CHAPTER THIRTY-EIGHT

All Roads Lead to Ethiopia
Early April, 2025 AD, Alexandria, Egypt

Elliott shared his concerns about Kres with Stef as they drove back to the Cairo airport. "I'm concerned about Kres' sudden interest in our nuclear capability. I feel stronger now than ever that we have to keep these guys within arm's reach. There's more to this whole adventure than a search for the Ark of the Covenant. And I can't get my arms around it."

"Are you thinking that this is all about getting access to our nuclear capability," questioned Stef.

"I just hope we're not getting tricked into participating in something that we would prefer not to be involved in."

Stef's mind was spinning. She wasn't sure how this turn of events would shake out. "But what about Rohit's death, and Kres' injuries. That doesn't sound like something you would stage."

"I'm probably just being paranoid, but my paranoia has been good to me in the past."

"Is there a way we can test your theory to learn that Kres is really after the nukes?"

"I'm sure there is. But I can't think of anything off hand. I like your idea about some kind of test. But what shape would that test take?"

"How about telling him we have the nukes?" suggested Stef.

"But then we're committed and what if we don't want to participate."

"Then what if we say that we need more information about his intentions before we can pursue this discussion."

"Doesn't that say we have the nukes?" responded Elliott.

"Well, I don't know what the best answer is. Here's an idea. What if we take the opposite approach? What if we tell him we have no knowledge of any nukes? Then, if he leaves us, we'll know his intentions were all about the nukes all along."

"I like your line of thinking. Let me put some time into that idea and see if I can find any flaws. Then, I'll give it a try."

The Kres discussion lasted most of the travel time back to Cairo. When they arrived at the airport, they checked their baggage and headed to the gate. Stef's plane to Istanbul, Turkey would leave in about 90 min., but Elliott had a three-hour wait before he could travel to Addis Abeba, Ethiopia using Ethiopian Airlines. In Turkey Stef would have to purchase a separate round-trip ticket from Turkey to Israel, and she would have to use her second passport for the trip.

Elliott arrived in Ethiopia late in the evening, as expected. He landed at the capital city of Addis Abeba in the center of Ethiopia, which was the only city with an international airport. It would have been a shorter drive for him to travel from one of the neighboring countries to the north like Eritrea, however, border disputes between Ethiopia and its neighbors, made this very risky.

From the airport he caught a taxi to the center of town. There were several nice hotels, like the Sheraton and the Hilton. He called the Sheraton on his taxi ride into town and confirmed that they would have a room available for him.

At the hotel he worked with the concierge to arrange for transportation to the north of Ethiopia. He knew he had a long, all day drive from Addis Abeba to Debra Damo, which was on the northern border of Ethiopia. Ethiopia is about twice the size of Texas, which will make for a long travelling day. The drive was about 700 km over roads that would often seem like a ride in the outback of Australia. The trip would take between twelve to sixteen hours. So, he would need to get as early a start as possible.

After arranging for a driver, he quickly made his way to his room and went to sleep. Sleep came quickly. The drive from Alexandria to Cairo, the wait at the airport, and then the flight to Addis Abeba left him feeling exhausted and worn out.

Early April, 2025 AD, Addis Abeba, Ethiopia

Elliott was up early and eager to get going. The night was uncomfortable, for many reasons. He didn't like the bed. It seemed a little hard. He didn't like the shower. It wasn't as warm as he liked. He didn't like the air conditioning, it smelled. He didn't like the cold, tile floors. But most of all, he didn't like being alone. It wasn't that he didn't know what being alone was like. In fact, in his role as an agent he had spent many nights on the road, alone, and in uncomfortable situations. But it had been months since he had spent a night alone. And he had come to enjoy his time with Stef. Being alone brought out the reality of how much he liked being with her. It just felt comfortable. It just felt right.

But he had to get going. He had a long drive ahead of him. And sitting around feeling sorry for himself wouldn't make it any better. He went down to the lobby and took advantage of the breakfast buffet. He was only there for about 15 minutes when he heard an announcement over the loudspeakers calling out his name. His driver had arrived. He grabbed some fruit, paid his bill, and headed for the front entrance of the hotel.

Elliott was surprised by the driver. He looked like he was about 15 years old. He went up to introduce himself. "Do you speak English?"

"Yes," was the response.

"Do you know the route to Debra Damo?"

"Yes."

"Are you ready to get going?"

"Yes."

"How long do you think the trip will take?"

"Yes."

Elliott grew concerned. He tried another question, "What's the name of a good hotel in Debra Damo?"

"Yes."

"Oh boy. This is going to be fun," said Elliott to himself.

"Yes. I speak English. I bring you Debra Damo. I know good hotel for you. My uncle has good hotel. You like. Long drive. Must go."

"That was a lot better," thought Elliott. "But we're not going to have much of a conversation on our way up there."

Elliott jumped into the back seat of the car. The first hour was spent just trying to get out of the city. Then they hit the open road, going faster in the country, and slower as they passed through villages. But none of it was real fast. For the first hour Elliott enjoyed the scenery. This wasn't a place that he would be visiting again in the near future, so he wanted to see as much of the country as he could. But it wasn't long before the fatigue of the previous day's travel followed by the hard night made him drowsy. Done with the redundant scenery, Elliot couldn't help himself. He lay down on the back seat and fell promptly asleep.

CHAPTER THIRTY-NINE

Back in Jerusalem
Early April, 2025 AD, Jerusalem, Israel

Stef arrived in Jerusalem near midnight. She had called ahead, when in Turkey and had made reservations at the Sheraton. Since Elliott wasn't with her, she decided she would spend the next few days in style. Not that the hotel in Alexandria was roughing it, or that the hotel they had stayed at last time in Jerusalem wasn't nice, it's just that she felt safer in a more Westernized hotel. And that's really what it was all about, feeling safer.

The rest of Stef's night wasn't restful, much like Elliott, but for a different reason. The hotel was comfortable enough. In fact, it was perfect. But Stef always had trouble getting a good night's sleep when Elliott wasn't around. Getting to sleep was difficult. And then, once asleep, she would toss and turn. Every little sound would wake her up. When Elliott was around, she felt safer. She felt a trust; a confidence that he would take care of her. It just wasn't the same when he wasn't there.

In the morning, Stef went down and had her usual egg-white, no cheese, lots of vegetables omelet, which a fitness relative of hers had told her, was much healthier. But she wasn't sure because what was healthy one year seemed to be unhealthy the next. But, for now, until the fad changed, it was egg-white omelets.

Back in Istanbul, Stef had also contacted the Bishop of the Ethiopian Orthodox Christian Church in Jerusalem. He was quite open and willing to talk to her about the Ark and welcomed her visit. They had set up a time after lunch. This gave Stef a chance to catch up on e-mails, and the news.

Stef tried several times to give Elliott a call, but the connection did not work. Either his phone was off, which she doubted, or he was already out of signal range. She knew he wouldn't call first because of her erratic sleeping pattern. He never wanted to wake her. So, she would have to make the first move. But she also knew that he had a long drive today and he was probably already out of the city and on his way to the Northern border of Ethiopia. So, she would just relax. She knew he would call her back after he received a signal and saw that she had called.

After a relaxing morning Stef went back to the restaurant to enjoy a lunch of fruit and vegetables. She dressed conservatively, wearing a long dress and a shawl, so as not to offend the Bishop. Then she caught a taxi to meet the Bishop. The trip was quick. It was overcast, which gave the day a sense of gloom. But the city was bustling with traffic and street vendors. It seemed to have a personality all its own. The whole city seemed to move along in an organized chaos which was hard to describe, but interesting to watch.

The Bishop's church was impressive, filled with numerous art pieces that dated back hundreds, if not thousands of years. Once again, as with the church in Alexandria, she noticed a replica of the Ark of the Covenant off to the side, in one of numerous vestibules. She was received by an escort, similar to the ritual they had gone through in Alexandria, and she was brought back to an office around to the side and at the rear of the church.

Her escort knocked at the door, and a voice at the other side said; "Enter."

He opened the door and, without entering, said; "Your guest has arrived."

"Please, show her in."

He stepped aside and motioned Stef to enter the sanctum of the Bishop.

The Bishop stood and walked around his desk to welcome Stef. He wore a long white robe which reached to the ground. Only his sandaled feet could be seen. And the robe had long baggy sleeves and a hood which hung at his back. His head was bare and bald. He put out his hand, which Stef eagerly shook. "Welcome. Welcome" was his repeated greeting. "It's good to meet someone who is interested in my church and in the sacred Ark of the Covenant which we cherish and protect."

Stef responded with; "I am delighted that you are willing to take the time to meet with me."

"I understand from our phone conversation that you are interested in finding the sacred Ark of the Covenant. Before we discuss its history and location, I need you to explain to me why it is so important for you to find the Ark. What is your interest? Are you some kind of archeologist?"

Stef started to explain; "Nothing so noble. Our interest is strictly selfish. We understand the Ark contains the Power of God, and we what to harness some of that power."

"Most people consider the power of the Ark to be a myth, religious nonsense. Why are you so interested in it? What makes you so sure that it really has any power?"

Stef felt different. She didn't kick into her normal BS mode. She felt as though she could be completely honest. There was something different, and she couldn't put her finger on it. Something that Elliott often referred to as the Spirit of God or the Power of the Holy Ghost. She wanted to be completely honest, but she didn't know why.

"Have you heard of the Knights Templar?"

"Of course. I am quite familiar with the Crusaders and their efforts here in Jerusalem. And I am familiar with their connection to the Ark of the Covenant. But how do you fit in?"

"I am a female, non-priesthood holding, member of the Knights Templar. We are an active organization. We recently learned of an Arian, Nazi based organization who is trying to get the Ark. And, as protectors of all things sacred, the Knights have decided to try to help them find the Ark, not to give them access to it, rather to protect the Ark from having them abuse it."

"I understand," the bishop replied, in a thoughtful, reflective manner. "If you are truly a templar knight, then you are also of the Masonic order, as am I, and as many of my congregation are. And I will require you to give me the sign of the Knights Templar of the Masonic order." The sign was given and received. And all the formal barriers and walls between Stef and the Bishop came crashing down making way for free and open discussions. "The knights that helped you on the Temple Mount were from my congregation. They briefed me on what you were doing, so this is not the first time I heard about your activities."

"One of them was injured. How is he doing?"

"He is doing well. He was glad to be of service. Truthfully, we also wanted to keep an eye on you."

"Thank you for your help," Stef responded. "And we don't mind your watching us and even being involved in what we're doing. I have a question."

"Yes?"

"Do you have any idea who shot your knight? Someone keeps following us and attacking us. They injured two members of our team, and recently they killed one of us. Do you know who they are or what they were after?"

"Actually, I was hoping you would be able to answer that question. I was going to ask you the same question. We don't like having members of our congregation shot at and injured. I was hoping you had some insight into the identity of the culprit."

"No idea; but we do have a couple members of our team trying to figure it out. I'll let you know if they learn anything. It may turn out to be useful information for you. Anyway, what can you tell me about the Ark?"

The Bishop started giving a long dissertation; "Let me give you a little history lesson first. The Ark was brought to Ethiopia by Solomon's son, Menelik the first king of Ethiopia, the son of the Queen of Sheba. It was hidden in a carriage of treasures that Solomon was sending back as a gift, so no one but Solomon and Menelik knew that the Ark had left Jerusalem. Solomon did this as a precaution since Jerusalem was a very volatile city, and he wanted to keep the Ark safe. A replica of the Ark was carefully built and placed in the Jerusalem temple taking the place of the real Ark so that everyone thought it was the genuine item. Even the temple High Priest did not recognize the difference. When the Babylonians finally invaded Jerusalem, the real Ark was never at risk.

"The false Ark was hidden in a secret cave below the Temple Holy of Holies, along with numerous other temple treasures. And there it stayed hidden for centuries. This ruse worked for a long time. But then, rumors started circulating that there was some great temple treasure buried in the temple mount. And everybody was interested in the treasure, including the Arabs, and the Jews, and the Christians. So, as a security precaution, to keep people from searching for the real Ark, the Ethiopian church felt it was important to destroy the false Ark, thereby maintaining the story that the Ark had been captured by Babylon and was lost forever."

"So, you're saying that the Ark does really exist."

"Of course! It does indeed exist and has been under our protection for nearly 3,000 years. And it will stay under our protection for another 3,000 years if necessary, until Jesus Christ, the Savior and Messiah returns to the Earth and we turn the Ark over to him for safe keeping. As we are told, there will be a restoration of all things, including the use of the Ark."

The Bishop continued; "You know from your Bible that Joseph, Mary, and Jesus came to Egypt to hide out from Herod. This wasn't by accident. They stayed here for several years until Herod died. They had friends and relatives down here. And we have several Gospels that teach us about the activities of Jesus as a youth while he was in Egypt. In fact, he was down in that area for several years. Much longer than most gospel historians believe. He was well into his youth before he left Egypt and headed back to Nazareth. And he left his mark."

"How does the Gospel of Mark fit into all of this?" asked Stef.

"First let me continue on with my history lesson. From the time Joseph came to Egypt, until the time Jesus came there, there was always a strong Jewish presence in Egypt and Ethiopia. In fact, you have seen in your Western Bible, that Moses married an Ethiopian **(Numbers 12:1),** and in the book called **Acts Chapter 8**, the story of the Ethiopian eunuch, a high chieftain of the Queen of Ethiopia, going to Jerusalem to worship. During the time Jesus was on the earth the Jews in Jerusalem were very racist. They wouldn't allow the Samaritans, because of their mixed Jewish and Palestinian blood, to worship in the temple. Doesn't it seem strange, in a society that was this religiously closed, that they would allow a black man to worship in their temple? Where is the connection? And then, in your Book of Acts we read how Philip, without hesitation, taught the Ethiopian about Christ and went ahead and baptized him. And this was before Peter the Apostle received the revelation that the gospel was to be shared with the Gentiles. In other words, there were Ethiopian Jews that were an accepted part of the Kingdom of God.

"But one big difference between the Ethiopian Jews and the Jews of Jerusalem is that when the Ethiopians were taught the gospel of Jesus Christ, they readily accepted it as the truth. The Ethiopians readily became Christians. But the Jews in Jerusalem fought against Christ's teachings and eventually killed Him."

"So where does Mark fit in?"

"I was just getting to that. After Christ's death, the Apostles were sent out on missions in all different directions. Peter, the lead Apostle, and Mark were missionary traveling companions. Peter taught the gospel in Jerusalem, then in Babylon, and then across the continent to Rome, where he was eventually killed. After Peter's death, Mark headed to Egypt, where he taught the gospel and wrote what you refer to as the 'Gospel of Mark' in your Bible. Unlike Jerusalem, his message was eagerly received by the Jews in Ethiopia and Egypt and he had large numbers of converts. The majority of the Jewish population was converted. Paul went on to establish numerous congregations throughout the land. He became the patron Saint and hero of our Church, which, as you know, is referred to as the Ethiopian Orthodox Christian Church or 'Coptic Church' for short."

"What does the term 'Coptic' mean?"

"It's the language of our holy records. Much the same as Latin is the sacred language of the Roman Catholic Church."

"This is an incredible story. So where is the Ark?"

"It's been moved several times, but now it is in Aksum!"

CHAPTER FORTY

The Antikythera Mechanism
Early April, 2025 AD, IOM Research Base, Elko, Nevada

Greg received a message from Elliott which read; "Two requests: (1) What is the connection between Jews and/or Christians, and the Ethiopians / Ethiopian Orthodox Christian Church, and (2) What is the Antikythera Mechanism and how do we get a hold of it?"

The first request was easy. A little research into the Ethiopian Christian Coptic Church showed that the Apostle Mark established the Christian Church using the members of the Ethiopian Jewish Church. They were ready and eager converts who already believed in Christ since He had spent several years with them as a youth. They knew He was not ordinary. And they readily accepted His claim to be the Son of God. The Apostle Mark had an easy time of converting this pool of ready believers.

But the second request from Elliott was a very different story. Greg, Dawn, and Alan were excited about their discoveries. The requests sent to them led them in fascinating and interesting directions. Especially interesting was the research around the Antikythera Mechanism. The more they searched, the more fascinating it became. They learned it was some type of mechanical device which looked a lot like the inner workings of a large clock. It was found around 1900 by fishermen off the coast of the Greek island after which it was named. It was turned over to a museum that performed some preliminary research on the device. They x-rayed it and analyzed it in every way possible short of tearing it apart. They concluded that it was a mechanical computer containing about 70 gears with precisely cut teeth and complex gearing. These gears simultaneously served several purposes. The device performed the functions of a calendar and a clock. It recorded planetary motions. It contained the characteristics of astrological symbolism. But the most fascinating aspect was its ability to perform as a compass that would not only point at the poles but would monitor the movement and migration of the poles.

The Antikythera Mechanism was believed to be created during the Hellenistic period either by Archimedes of Syracyse around 200 BC or Tesibius, a Greek and Egyptian mathematician of Alexandria, Ptolemaic, Egypt. It is believed that there were several of these devices in the Alexandrian Library in Egypt before it burned down.

More recently the device was moved to the Bronze Collection of the National Archaeological Museum of Athens. Additionally, several searches for additional copies of the device have been made by numerous individuals, including the famous Jacques Cousteau. There were also a couple of replicas made of the device, based on the scans. One of these replicas was housed in the Smithsonian Library in Washington DC. But the reconstruction believed to be the most accurate was now on displayed at the American Computer Museum in Bozeman, Montana.

The three researcher knights were huddled in their conference room, discussing their findings, and wondering what their next step should be. Greg started; "I can't get a hold of either Elliott or Stef. They must be out of reach. Their cell signals don't seem to work."

"Well, we don't want to take action without their concurrence, do we?" asked Dawn.

"I don't think there's any doubt what we do next," injected Alan. "They had us steal from our own archives at Travis AFB. Why do you think they would have any hesitation stealing from a museum in Bozeman? I think we go get it and deliver it to them in the Middle East, wherever they may be."

"Why do you think they would be able to do anything with it if we did steal it?"

"I would think that their friends the Coptics would be better able to explain how it should be used than anyone else on earth. They seem to be connected with how it was created, and they still claim to have one or two hidden away. Originally these were housed and possibly manufactured in Alexandria. Why not go to the source if we're trying to decipher that device."

"Your logic makes sense. But I'm concerned about Stef and Elliott's feelings about stealing from public museum," commented Dawn.

"We just assassinated Barjet a few days ago. Now you're worried about stealing something from an unknown museum in an unknown town in the middle of nowhere. How does all that make sense? Let's go get it and be done with this," insisted Alan.

"Boy, you're pretty eager for an adventure," jived Greg. "I agree with you. Let's do it. Let's go get the device and then one of us should fly it out there to Elliott and Stef and deliver it and see if we can help in any way to decipher the device and find the Ark," concluded Greg. "I'll send Stef and Elliott a message describing what we're going to do and let them know we're on the way. Now, the only remaining question is which one of us is going to the Middle East?"

Before he could finish the question, Alan's hand shot up. "I'm your man."

Early April, 2025 AD, Addis Abeba, Ethiopia

Marcello landed in Ethiopia with his junior cohorts, Conrad Brady, and Joe Fanara. During the trip, Marcello had updated them on all aspects of the case, expressing his concern that the relationship between the IOM and the NNRL could only lead to more trouble.

Conrad was a country boy, raised in central Montana and named after his birthplace, Conrad, Montana. He was relatively short, 5 foot 7, but strong and physically fit. He grew up in Great Falls where his dad worked as a civilian at Malmstrom Air Force Base. He loved the country, but the economic crunch had resulted in smaller farmers selling off their farms while larger corporations took over the farms and created mega-automated complexes that cut costs in any way possible. The result was that there were lots of country boys vying for the few remaining farm jobs. And he wasn't one of the lucky ones. He had taken a liking to police work, having spent some time as a security guard while attending the University of Great Falls studying criminal investigation. That caused him to be interested in federal investigations and he applied for the FBI and the CIA. The result was his current position at CIA headquarters. But he longed to return to the country and promised himself he would get a reassignment first chance. He definitely wasn't going to marry one of those Eastern girls. He wanted a down-to-earth gal that had a love for the land, horses, back-packing, and fishing. And that wasn't going to be someone in the DC area.

Joe was, in many ways, the opposite of Conrad. He was tall, about 6' 3", skinny, and worshiped New York City, considering it a living paradise. He would rave about how you could find anything and everything within a city block of home. And about how you could order anything from home and have it delivered without leaving his living room. He talked about how you could see all the latest and greatest shows, stars, and concerts. His family was Jewish, and he loved the strong Jewish ties that were in New York. His father was a policeman, as was his brother and uncle. So, he was destined to be part of a police effort of some kind. And the CIA seemed perfect. He often talked about himself as the United States James Bond: a lady's man that was invincible. If only his boss could see how valuable, he was and put him on a meaningful assignment.

Conrad and Joe had gone through some tough times together during their CIA training, and that left a bond between them which, in spite of their background differences, left them connected. They had a trust for each-other beyond reproach. They knew they would always be able to count on each other.

Since the days of President Jimmy Carter, the CIA had lost its clandestine wings. Its ability to do James Bond type secret missions had ended. It was now an organization of paranoid geeks doing data collection. No one wanted to go out on a limb or be at risk. And Conrad, Joe, and Marcello were bonded together by their lust to be Jason Bournes. They wanted to save American lives by identifying and striking potential enemies before they had a chance to strike. And they knew that the time would come when top secret operations would once again be required, especially now with all the terrorist activity in the world.

Marcello, Joe, and Conrad went through Ethiopian customs together explaining that they were adventurers looking for an opportunity to spend time exploring the country and playing the role of tourist. They couldn't let on that they had anything to do with the US government. That would raise a whole stream of questions that really didn't have any good answers.

After making their way through customs, Marcello checked his Blackberry to see what hotel had been reserved for them, and they caught a taxi for the Hilton in down-town Addis Abeba. The ride wasn't fun after the long flight from Washington DC. The sooner they arrived at the hotel, the sooner they would be able to catch up on their long-lost sleep.

During the drive to the center of town, Marcello searched his other messages. He had been expecting a message from one of his double agents that would give him more information about the activities of the NNRL and IOM. He expected a message from his connection with the NNRL. But instead, he received a message from his contact in the IOM informing him that his NNRL agent had been killed. The message read, "NNRL agent lost. Next stop Aksum." The message had come through. He now knew where he had to go next. But making those arrangements would have to wait for the following day. All energy had been drained out of him and he was physically exhausted. Nothing else would happen today.

CHAPTER FORTY-ONE

The Rush to Ethiopia
Early April, 2025 AD, Alexandria, Egypt

Kres hadn't left Alexandria as quickly as Stef and Elliott. He was sore and wasn't ready for the long drive to Cairo. His leg wound made it extremely painful to walk. But he wanted to get back to "civilization", as he called it, to have a real doctor look at his leg injury. But first he decided he had to take a couple of days for recuperation. Then he would venture forward. He also decided it would be helpful to wait until he heard back from Elliott and Stef before he decided what to do next.

Kres was mad. And he didn't hide it well. It all started a couple of days ago when he learned of Rohit's betrayal. And it was completely by accident. He was tracking the communications that he and Rohit were making with Elliott and Stef. He wanted to see if they had really been trying to stay in touch. And he was disappointed in two ways. First that Elliott and Stef had lied to him about trying to stay in touch. And second because he saw several communications between Rohit and a phone number in Virginia. Kres called the number, just to see who would answer, and, after inquiring where the number was located, he found out he was talking to someone within the CIA. He realized that Rohit was supplying information to the CIA.

Because of the betrayal, Kres had organized the hit on Rohit. He contacted the French Mafia. Kres knew about the hit on Barjet because he had intercepted and monitored the S1 that performed the hit. He also knew that Barjet had mafia connections. So, he was sure that they would be interested in making a deal. The deal was that if they would take out Rohit, they could also have the IOM assassins that had orchestrated the hit on Barjet. He thought that by riding in the car, he would be above suspicion.

But it didn't work out that way. Rohit was killed, but Kres was also shot. And Elliott and Stef escaped without harm. And that made Kres mad. He wasn't supposed to get shot. What went wrong?

The deal Kres made with the French mafia was that if they took care of Rohit, he would also give them the information to not only take care of Elliott and Stef, but also hit the IOM headquarters. But he didn't want them to make the hit on Elliott and Stef too soon. He first needed to get the information about the location of the Ark and about the availability of nuclear detonators. And he needed the IOM to give him this information before they took out their revenge.

Kres ordered room service for lunch, trying to stay off of his leg as much as possible. Then he contacted his warehouse outside of Asunción, Paraguay.

"Hola, esta Krank."

"Guten tag, Krank;" Kres responded to Krank's French greeting by speaking German. He preferred his native tongue and he knew that most of lieutenants were familiar with the language. Kres continued; "Has the package been delivered?" He was referring to the nuclear material being delivered to the container in Brazil.

"It has. And it has been sealed and forwarded." This reference was to the nuclear material being sealed within the container load of granite counter tops, and then being forwarded on to the dock-yard in Brazil. "We also have confirmation that the container is ship-board, but the ship will not being leaving the harbour for a couple of days."

"Just so long as it arrives on time at it's destination. Then I'll be happy. Can you stay in touch with the harbour and make sure there are no delays?"

"Will do;" was Krank's reply. "We also have additional information that I'm sure you will be interested in. We have found a second source for part 2." They made an effort to stay coded in their messages, realizing that all phone messages were tracked and searched for key words. Words like "nuclear" or "weapon" would be caught and tracked.

There are three parts to a nuclear weapon. Part 1 is the fuel, which was in route. Part 2 is the detonator, and that's what Krank was referring to. And Part 3 is the delivery system.

"Tell me more," inquired Kres.

"We found someone else who had accidently received material from the same source as the IOM." Krank was referring to the US Air Force who had miss-shipped a box of nuclear detonators and the IOM, learning about it, was quick to go out and acquire the detonators. Now, apparently another load of detonators had also been miss-shipped. And Krank had identified the location or sellers of the detonators.

"Excellent work. Please pursue this second source and try to arrange an acquisition as soon as possible. Please keep me informed of the progress. Maybe we won't need the IOM after all."

Kres was thrilled by the news. He didn't like dealing with the IOM. If he could get the detonators from another source, then he would finish finding the Ark on his own and he would leave Elliott and Stef to the disposal of the French Mafia.

His anger had subsided with this new news. Up to this point his plan had been an execution nightmare. He hadn't received the nuclear information that he wanted from the IOM. And he wasn't supposed to get hurt on the attack. He wanted to be in the car when it was attacked in order to divert attention away from him as the assassin, but there wasn't supposed to be any pain, at least not for him.

Kres proceeded to make a second call. He wanted to find out what went wrong and why he was shot. He had called them earlier, asking for his contact person. Unfortunately, he was connected with an answering machine, and this assassination plot wasn't something he wanted to leave on a recorder. So, he decided to try his call again. But again, there was only an answering machine and Kres hung up the phone. Then, just as he was hanging up his phone, it started ringing. He was sure it was the French Mafia contact calling him back. "Hello."

"Hello. This is Marcello Zuniga," was the response on the other end of the line. "I understand that you were trying to get in contact with me."

"Yes;" replied Kres. "We have a problem." There was something familiar about the voice on the other end of the line. He just couldn't put his finger on it.

CHAPTER FORTY-TWO

The Antikythera Mechanism
Early April, 2025 AD, Bozeman, Montana

Bozeman is a small city in South-Western Montana with less than 30,000 people. It's a university town located on Highway 90, between Billings and Butte. Its motto is: "The Most Livable Place." There are two major universities in Montana, Montana State University in Bozeman, and the University of Montana in Missoula. The Bozeman location is for "cowboys", and the Missoula school is for the "hippies." And there is very little love lost between the two schools. Football contests between the schools are often very exciting events.

The university is the primary industry around which the town exists. Otherwise, it would just be another of the many small farming towns that can be found throughout Montana. Driving through the town gave visitors a sense of the farm culture. It had a roughness about it, built on hard work and connection with the land. And it's obvious that the citizens were farmers and "country folk".

Bozeman is slightly north of the North-West corner of Yellowstone National Park. To the west Bozeman has endless farms. Grains of every kind, and cattle are the staple. And many of the farms were struggling. A combination of reduced government support, and subsidized competition from overseas had made it difficult to maintain the smaller farms. As a result, many of the farms were being bought out and consolidated into larger, mega farms.

To the east, Bozeman rises to the Rocky Mountain Range. This is the same mountain range that runs the full length, North to South, of the United States and Canada. This range contains many of the most beautiful numerous parks in both countries, like Yellowstone Park, Glacier Park, the Grand Tetons, etc., their beauty and distinction.

Bozeman's biggest claim to fame is the <u>American Computer Museum</u>, which had achieved international recognition. It seemed like the most unlikely place for a Computer Museum. Most people would expect to find this museum in Silicon Valley, California, where the computer industry grew up, or in Seattle, the home of Microsoft, or possibly even in Denver because of the large number of computer technology companies that had their facilities in the area. But you don't expect a technology museum in Bozeman, Montana.

There are several cities that are slapped up against the Rocky Mountains including Denver and Salt Lake. A common characteristic of these cities is that flights coming in and out of the city tend to have surges of turbulence. The updrafts or winds generated in these areas can make travel rough. Bozeman was not unique. As the IOM team flew into the city, they also encountered bouncy travel, making each of them wish that they were flying the S1 remote airplane rather than sitting on an airplane themselves.

The trip took them from Elko, Nevada, through Salt Lake City for a one-hour layover, and then on up to Bozeman. The plane on the leg to Bozeman was a small, 20 seat, propeller aircraft which seemed to magnify the turbulence. Luckily, in spite of the roughness of the air, the landing was uneventful, and the IOM team of Greg, Dawn, and Alan were glad to finally get off the airplane.

The flight to Bozeman lands in Belgrade, MT, a small farm town about 9 miles West of Bozeman. The IOM team landed at the airport and were surprised by the size. Greg commented that he had been in living rooms that were larger than this airport. There seemed to be more security and airport personnel than there were travelers.

The trip had taken the majority of the day. It was now 3 PM and they felt rushed to get to Bozeman as soon as possible so they could get into the museum before it closed. They didn't want to spend any more time here than necessary. The plan was to scope out the museum, figure out a way to get the mechanism, and come back in the middle of the night to get it. Then they would catch the first flight back down to Salt Lake. The plan had only one glitch. There weren't that many flights from Bozeman to Salt Lake City and they would have to wait until the morning to fly back. So, they decided to scope out the museum, get hotel rooms, come back in the middle of the night, and steal the mechanism, and then take the first flight out in the morning before anyone even knew that the device was stolen.

It didn't take long to get their rental car, and they were on their way to the big city. Greg took the driver's seat. He liked being in control. Alan had printed out a MapQuest map giving directions to the museum, and he was the designated tour guide in the passenger seat. And Dawn eagerly took on the role of back seat driver.

After exiting the airport, MapQuest took them on a drive down Gallatin Field Road for about one mile. Then they took an 8-mile drive along the freeway frontage road called MT-205 that followed parallel to US Highway 90 to Bozeman. Upon entering Bozeman, they followed the MapQuest directions toward the American Computer Museum at 2304 N 7th Ave. It would seem that three geniuses driving in such a small town, guided by maps, would have an easy time of this simple navigation exercise. But instead, the drive became a war zone. Alan insisted he knew where to go, and Greg criticized the route because it seemed like they were taking all the worst roads with all the biggest ruts, and Dawn kept suggesting they turn here, or park there. Their voices kept getting louder and louder, until it seemed as though they would be coming to blows. The final straw was when Dawn said, "Can't you slow down a little? We're going to drive right past it. And I'm tired of my head hitting the ceiling of this tin can."

With that comment Greg lost his cool, stomped hard on the breaks, which caused everyone to jerk forward, and blurted out; "I'm done with this. Why do I have to put up with this nonsense? Either you guys shut up, or I'm getting out and walking and you can do this on your own!"

Alan and Dawn just looked at each other in disbelief. Then Alan burst out laughing and said, *"Sooorrrryyy!!!* I didn't realize you were so sensitive."

Alan's laughing caused Greg to laugh as well. Between sniggers, Greg responded with; "I'm not joking. I don't need this abuse. Unless you're giving me meaningful directions, I want you guys to shut up. I don't need any more comments about my driving."

Alan couldn't hold back the snickers, but he tried hard to keep his mouth shut. And Dawn decided to keep quiet as well. She didn't like to irritate anyone, especially Greg. She had a lot of respect for him and wanted to stay on his good side.

It was only about five minutes later when they pulled up outside of the museum. It wasn't obvious that there was a museum there. It looked like any other building, and if it weren't for the small sign out front, they would have missed it completely. It was a lot smaller than they expected. It surprised them that this low-tech farming community would contain a computer museum which included a replica of an ancient Greek artifact, known as the Antikythera Mechanism. And soon this artifact would be in the possession of the IOM team.

The team exited their vehicle and headed to the museum to see what it was they were after, and to see what type of security they would need to penetrate. The IOM team was in luck. The museum was in the middle of a move, having selected a more suitable site closer to Montana State University. And moving meant that security would be intermittent at best. All the Knights had to do was locate the replica of the Antikythera Mechanism, grab it, and take off. Hopefully, it wasn't already packed up.

While her companions waited in the car, Dawn used her charm and faked curiosity to convince the museum curator that she needed to see the device for a research report that she was writing. It sounded like a legitimate story, so the curator led her to the device. Unfortunately, her charm was a little too successful because she couldn't shake the curator. He wanted to tell her all about the device and why the museum had a copy of it. Apparently, its construction was the masterwork of one of the university professors who had had taken a strong interest in it.

Pretending to be absorbed in the device, and taking extensive notes, Dawn was able to sketch a map of the room where it was located, its exits, and its security system. All of it seemed extremely lax. Dawn watched carefully where it was stored and how it was protected. Afterwards it would be easy for the team to come back in the middle of the night, break in, and take the device.

With the plan in place for taking the replica of the Antikythera Mechanism, the team proceeded to a Super 8 motel about one-half mile away and checked in. They made plans to reconvene at 01:00AM to execute their plan.

Then Dawn objected; "We can't shut down for the night until we've had something to eat. Now that we have our plan in place, my hunger is kicking in and I'm starving. Either we all go to eat together, or you give me the car keys so I can get something."

"Where would you like to eat?" asked Alan.

"Anything's fine. The hotel mentioned a Burger King on Main Street downtown. How about we go there?"

"Let's do it." They all jumped back into the car and headed off for the two-mile drive for a Burger King style dinner.

During the drive, the discussions continued about what needed to be done to acquire the device. Since Dawn was the only one who actually saw the device, Greg and Alan asked numerous probing questions. Where was the device in relation to the exits? Were there any security devices connected directly to the device? Were there cameras on the device? How was the device attached?

They were surprised by the answers. The device was not secured in any way. It was displayed behind an unsecured glass case, which could easily be broken. And the entire security and camera system was electrical and connected to the main power source, which meant that if you disconnected the power, the security system went off. This should be an easy break-in and escape.

They arrived at Burger King, parked in the nearest parking slot, and entered the building. Alan was obsessed with Burger King's Flame-Grilled Burgers, which Dawn liked as well, but Greg favored the healthier Chicken Burgers. They sat off in a corner in order to avoid being overheard. "Draw us out a floor plan," requested Greg, as he opened his notebook to a blank page and handed it to her along with a pen.

Dawn started drawing boxes on the page and explained; "There are several rooms to this museum. Here is the front entrance. The Antikythera Mechanism is located in this room, off to the side, about right here." She pointed to a spot on her diagram and drew an X. "There are exit doors here and here." Again, she drew Xs on the floor plan. "There are cameras here, here, and here." This time she drew Cs on the floor plan.

Alan spoke up; "I saw the power supply coming into the side of the building, about here." Dawn drew a P on the plan.

Greg suggested; "This seems like a pretty basic grab and go. We need to take out the power source, which requires cutting a couple of wires, then break in, probably through one of the large side windows, grab the device, and take off. We passed a small hardware store on the way here. We'll need to get a couple of flashlights, some gloves, and wire cutters. Alan, you take care of the power, I'll break out the window, Dawn, you go in and grab the device while I get the car ready for the escape. The whole thing shouldn't take more than five minutes."

"Got it;" agreed Alan. "We'll need bolt cutters too. I remember seeing a padlock on the power box. So, we meet at the car at 1:00AM, we do our grab, and then we return to the hotel. In the morning we head out to the airport to catch the first flight back. I think we can handle it."

Having finished off their burgers, they returned to the car and drove off to the small hardware store. It wasn't long before they had the tools, they need to complete their task. And they were off to the hotel for a few hours' sleep.

But plans rarely work out exactly. One AM rolled around, and Dawn and Alan were standing out in the cold next to the car. But Greg, the keeper of the car keys, was nowhere to be found. "Give him a call;" grumped Alan.

Dawn dialed he phone. "Hello," responded a sleepy Greg. "Oh my gosh! It's 01:10AM! Where are you guys?"

"Where do you think we are?" grumped Dawn. "We're standing out here freezing. Get your butt down here and get this car warmed up."

"I'm on my way. I fell asleep watching TV. I thought I'd just stay up till we left, but obviously that didn't work out."

"Stop talking and get down here! It's got to be below freezing out here." Actually, the temperature was in the low 40's, but the breeze made it feel colder.

"I'm on my way."

Greg rushed down the stairs from his second-floor room and ran to the car. "Sorry." He opened the car doors and the three of the got into the car and drove off toward the museum.

They arrived at the museum at about 01:20AM, and quickly went to work. They put on the gloves. Alan took off first, went around the building, and found the power box. He used bolt cutters to break off the lock, then easily opened the power box. It didn't take long to find the main power source. But the job was easier than expected. He didn't have to cut any wires. He just had to switch the main breaker off, and the power systems shut down. He knew he had been successful at shutting the system down, because he saw some lights inside the building flicker off.

When Greg saw the light go off, he knew that was his queue. He went to one of the side windows, and with a couple of appropriately placed hits on the tempered glass, in just the right spots, he was able to shatter the glass. Dawn jumped out of the car, climbed through the window, and slipped on the glass, falling on her rear.

"That was graceful;" chided Greg.

"It's not funny;" responded Dawn. "That hurt. And I think I cut my hands in the process."

"Through the gloves?"

"Yes."

"Don't get any blood on anything. That would leave DNA evidence."

"Too late."

"How badly are you bleeding?"

"Bad enough."

"Get back out here. I don't want you dripping blood all over the museum."

"Gladly." Dawn climbed back out the window, trying her best not to get blood on anything else.

"Get in the car and try to get that bleeding under control." Greg climbed into the museum and, using the flashlight, tried to find his way to the location of the Antikythera Mechanism. After a few wrong turns, he was finally able to locate the device. He grabbed it, assuming it would easily pull away, but that was too optimistic. There was a bolt holding the device to its stand. The stand was about three feet tall and about one foot around. It was wooden and, if it wasn't too thick, it might be breakable.

Greg was frustrated, but not ready to give up. He yanked at the stand. It creaked but wasn't going to give in easily. But he felt it weakening. He yanked again and again until finally he broke it in half. Some big pieces broke, but there was a plywood lining, and it didn't want to release its prize too easily. He had to twist and pull on it until it finally gave way. Taking the device along with half the stand, he headed back out toward the broken window. As he arrived near the window, he saw Alan doing his best to scoop up any glass with blood on it. He was using his flashlight, trying to identify any blood spots, hoping that if he got most of it, they wouldn't even consider the possibility that blood may have been left behind. He was scooping the glass up into the shopping bag that they received at the hardware store earlier that evening, when they purchased the tools they needed.

Looking up Alan said, "I think it got the majority of it, if not all of it. We should be OK."

"How's Dawn?"

"She'll be OK. It's mostly her pride that's hurt."

"Good enough. Let's get out of here." Greg popped the trunk and threw the device, along with half the stand, in the back, and slammed the trunk shut.

Greg and Alan jumped back in the car and started driving off. "How's your hand?" asked Greg.

"The bleeding has stopped. It will be fine. Sorry about that."

"Don't worry about it. We got what we needed." Actually, Greg was bothered by the fact that a five-minute operation took nearly thirty minutes. A bunch of school kids could have done better than that.

The drive back to the hotel was quiet. All three knew that this was not a job that they could brag about to their future children. They were just glad it was over.

After arriving at the hotel, they opened the trunk to take a look. "We're going to need to get this stand broken off. We can't take the whole thing with us just the way you have it here." It was Alan who was commenting. "I'll go get a large towel out of my room and we'll wrap it up. Then we can take it to my room and see if we can break off more of the stand."

"Good plan," responded Greg, as Alan walked off.

Once they had the device in Alan's room, they were able to pound, stomp, kick, and chip at the stand. Eventually they had it to where the device was only connected to the top plate of the stand. This was workable. Greg had brought with a fold-up duffle bag which looked like a large gym bag. The device, along with the top of the stand, fit nicely into duffle bag.

They cleaned up the wood chips into the shopping bag that came from the hardware store, the same one where he had the glass chips. In the morning they would dump the bag in a dumpster somewhere.

"I guess that's all we can do for now," commented Dawn. "What time do we head out in the morning?"

"Let's leave at 08:00AM," responded Greg, planning to make the 09:30AM flight.

"Will you set your alarm this time?" chided Dawn.

"Yes. I guess I'm going to be hearing about this for a while."

"That's right." Each of them headed off to their own rooms to get whatever sleep they could before their early morning departure.

In the morning, having accomplished their mission, Greg, Alan, and Dawn headed for the airport and made the 09:30AM flight to Salt Lake City. Then Greg and Dawn caught a second flight to Elko, Nevada, while Alan headed off to Ethiopia with their newly acquired treasure.

CHAPTER FORTY-THREE

Heading North
Early April, 2025 AD, Addis Abeba, Ethiopia

Joe and Conrad were at the hotel restaurant by 07:00AM, as planned. Marcello had taken a side trip to the hotel's travel desk to make arrangements for a trip to the northern border of Ethiopia.

The hotel lobby was big, but somewhat unorganized. The lobby was interesting, almost like a museum. It was splattered with cultural artifacts from all over Ethiopia. If he had the time, it would be fun to just walk around and study all the artwork and tools. But today Marcello had a purpose and agenda, and he needed help. There were plenty of desks in the lobby area, but it was hard to identify which desk served what purpose. At first Marcello couldn't identify a travel desk. He approached the lady standing at the registration desk; "Who do I talk to if I'm trying to schedule a driver?"

"Do you need a taxi?" questioned the short, dark skinned lady who had obvious Ethiopian ancestry. Her name tag identified her as Alisha. Her English was broken, but of good quality and easily understandable.

"I need transport to the Debra Damo monastery."

"The what?" questioned the receptionist. Elliott repeated the request, wondering if he was pronouncing it incorrectly. "I've never heard of that," responded Alisha. "Is it somewhere in Addis Abeba?"

"I was told it is somewhere near the Northern Border of Ethiopia, close to Eritrea. It is supposed to be a holy place to the Coptic Christian Church."

"Is it near Axum?"

"I think so."

"I know someone, a close friend, who can drive you there," was her helpful response. But Marcello was leery of "close friends." This was a red flag to him, indicating that the receptionist had her own agenda which involved some kind of kick back.

"I would rather use public transportation," was Marcello's response.

"Buses are crowded and very dirty. And they make many stops. The trip will take twice as long and be very uncomfortable. Please, let me call my friend. How soon do you plan to travel?"

"As soon as possible. Go ahead and call your friend and find out how much it is going to cost for the trip. There will be three of us travelling, plus luggage, so make sure he is able to accommodate all of us. Also, ask him how long he thinks the trip will take."

Alisha made the call as Marcello listened, even though he didn't understand the language and had no idea what they were saying. He always wished he had a universal translator implant, like the travelers had on the Farscape TV series, so he could understand any language.

After Alisha got off the phone, she told him that her friend would be at the hotel in one hour and that the trip was all set. "But we haven't discussed cost;" protested Marcello. "I'm not ready to go unless the cost is reasonable."

Alisha told him how much the trip would cost, and Marcello was amazed. It equated to about $50 US for the driver, and Marcello would pay for fuel and hotel directly for any over-night stays. This price included 4 days of travel, the drive North, driving around the area for two days, and the drive back to Addis Abeba. Marcello assumed that he was probably paying twice what he could have paid if he searched around a little more, but how could he go wrong paying this guy what amounted to $12.50 US per day in wages.

Alisha continued; "The trip will take most of the day. Most parts of the road are very slow to travel, and some parts are even dirt roads. But he will get you there safely. But it will take all day. It will be dark when you get there."

Marcello thanked Alisha and headed off to join Joe and Conrad for breakfast. Breakfast was a buffet, elaborately staged with lots of local fruits and nuts. Marcello ordered a vegetarian omelet and then spiced it up with as much hot sauce as possible. He felt uncomfortable eating any type of meat, when visiting a developing country. He also believed that the reason why the citizens of Mexico and numerous Asian countries were so healthy was because they ate their food extra hot. He had convinced himself that their life spans had been increased because of the spices in their food. And so, he wanted his food spicy hot.

"We're set to leave in one hour. I have a driver who is supposedly taking us to Debra Damo. But it seems like most people here haven't even heard of the place. But apparently this is going to take us all day."

How do they know it's going to take us all day;" asked Joe, "if they don't know where we're going?"

"Based on my information that it's on the northern border. That's how they came up with the time estimate. We're going to have to wait till we get closer before anyone is going to be able to give us specific directions to the location of the monastery. "

"Let's do a quick internet search with Google or MapQuest so we can at least make sure we're going in the right direction. We can watch for towns or landmarks that will tell us how we're doing."

"Excellent idea. Go ahead and do it, Joe."

The three finished their breakfast and headed off to their rooms, while Joe headed for the front desk. Alisha pointed him to a desk where he could sit. She gave him internet access and he was off, printing out a couple of maps of their anticipated northward route. He was even able to find the location of Debra Damo and plotted the shortest route from Addis Abeba.

CHAPTER FORTY-FOUR

Debra Damo Monastery
Early April, 2025 AD, Debra Damo, Ethiopia

It had indeed been a long, dusty, drive through the northern half of Ethiopia. At the insistence of the driver, Elliott had spent the night in the town of Axum where the driver arranged a room at the small hotel owned by his uncle.

It wasn't the worst place Elliott ever stayed in. Actually, it was a lot nicer than the cave under the Dome of the Rock in Jerusalem, where he had spent the night a few days back. Now they were traveling east along the Adi Abun-Adigrat road. The driver pointed out Debra Damo off in the distance. It was a mesa (referred to locally as an amba) with steep vertical sides.

The road was dusty from the six months lack of rain. What made it worse is that the best air conditioning relief was received when the windows were opened, and this allowed the dust to be blown into the car, and right into Elliott's face. As they approached a small bridge the driver pointed out a rocky, rutted, dusty and dry dirt road heading north. He indicated that it led to the Ethiopian Coptic monastery of Debra Damo on top of the mountain. A rusty, unreadable, sign with a cross on it was the only indication that this was the road.

Travelling this, connected to a smaller road which was rougher, but that was the only way to get to the monastery. They rumbled through a small village, and then took a steep 150 foot drop down to the valley below. Then they came to a small creek, crossed over, and followed up a steep 20-foot climb, followed by a climb of several hundred more feet using a series of switchbacks back up and out of the valley. They also noticed a sign which read; "No females of any species allowed beyond this point." Elliott later learned that this sign was common for all Coptic monasteries.

Ultimately, they arrived at the base of the mesa. Their timing seemed to be just right. But Elliott sensed that someone had seen them coming. There was a man standing at the top of the cliff wall, in a small, sheltered building, waving, and yelling, "Welcome to Debra Damo. Please, come." A rope was being dropped down for them. It was the only way to get up on the mesa. There was a second rope, a safety rope, which Elliott tied around himself. Then he started ascending the 60-foot wall by stepping in notches etched into the hard dirt cliff sides and which led to the top. This wasn't working very well. He kept slipping out of the notches which were designed for a much smaller foot. His shoes were too big to fit into the notches. He had to be lowered back down where he took off his shoes and tried again, this time barefoot.

The rope man on the top kept the safety rope tight and eventually helped pull Elliott through the, four foot by five-foot opening, at the top. The top of the climb was not the top of the mesa. There was a shelf in the mesa, which was the access point for the monastery. The climb up the side of the cliff landed the visitor to the shelf. Then, there was a trail that led around the side of the mesa and from there he could climb to its top.

The driver seemed genuinely scared to go to the top of the mesa. Elliott couldn't decide if this was a fear of heights, or if there was something about the monastery that scared the driver. In the end, the driver refused to climb the cliff and decided he would wait at the bottom of the mesa. This made Elliott nervous. He did not want to be left behind. Also, the hesitancy of the driver made Elliott wonder what may be bothering him.

Once inside the small building at the end of the shelf, the monk guided Elliott on by pointing to a set of rock stairs and said, "Go here!"

Elliott walked past a variety of hanging vegetation and past several stone buildings set along the path to the top of the mesa. When he arrived at the top, he found a totally flat, desert looking environment. It could be a desert, except that it was surrounded by sheer, downward cliffs in all directions. Looking over the edge he could see river cut valleys followed by more mountains in all directions.

Elliott was greeted by a monk who identified himself as Brother Tesfai. Elliott explained that he wanted to see the monastery and Enda Abuna Aragawy church, and possibly speak to the keeper of the sacred documents or scrolls. Tesfai explained that Abuna Aragawy was the founder of their order and he helped build the great monastery of Debra Damo around 525 AD. He explained that many of the sacred records of the church were kept here because of its inaccessibility, therefore being one of the safest places in Ethiopia.

Tesfai lead the way past several stone buildings to what he described as the "holy church." He explained that there were about three-hundred monks serving here at Debra Damo. He led the way into a building that was constructed of slabs of brown rock, in every shade and color of brown imaginable. Between the rocks were wooden beams, referred to as monkey heads, which seemed to give support to the structure. Such an intense blend of color in the rocks and the wood required design and intention. It could not have been accidental. The building itself was as modern looking as any in the cities nearby. But the guide explained that this was believed to be the oldest Christian church in Ethiopia.

After entering the building, they went through a series of small rooms. The second room had little squares covering the ceiling which contained carvings of animals and plants. Elliott asked the guide if this were where he would find the curator or keeper of the records. The guide responded that it was too late in the day to meet with the curator. That the curator was already in prayers and that Elliott would need to stay the night, and he could talk to the curator in the morning. He explained to Elliott that if he liked he could stay in one of the caves here at the top of the mesa. Or else he could go back down to the vehicle below.

Elliott wasn't thrilled about the climb up, let alone climbing back down in the dark and then back up again in the morning, so he decided to stay on top and see what the caves were like. After all, caves were beginning to seem like home to him. "Can I stay in one of your caves?" asked Elliott.

"Of course," replied Tesfai. He showed Elliott over to the side of the mesa and started to tie a rope around his waist.

"What's this?" asked Elliott.

"The caves are a short way down and dug into the side of the mountain."

"And I have to climb down the side to get to the cave?"

"Of course."

"Do you have any other accommodations? Any place else I could stay that doesn't require climbing down a steep cliff?"

"Of course. The novice monks stay in these buildings. You can stay with them if you like," Tesfai said, pointing to a rock building with a tin roof. "The caves I was offering you, are considered to be our more respected accommodations."

"I guess I'm staying with the novices."

Tesfai showed him into the dormitory style barracks which contain approximately 20 bunk beds. "I hope you will find this adequate."

"Absolutely," responded Elliot, who was delighted to not have to spend another night in a cave.

Early April, 2025 AD, Debra Damo, Ethiopia

Elliott woke up before the sun came up. Actually, he was awake off and on all night. The snoring got so loud at times that he considered going outside and sleeping on the hard ground. He wasn't used to sleeping in so noisy an environment. When he was with Stef, she would occasionally snore. But that was nothing compared to the music he had to listen to in the Debra Damo barracks.

The novices were up early. Their chores started with gardening and meal preparations. Some went out to the gardens at the bottom of the mesa in the valleys below. They grew fruits, vegetables, and grains. And then all of it was hauled up the rope to the top of the mesa.

Elliott would have preferred sleeping a little longer, but his curiosity about the operation of the monastery got the best of him. He was glad he got up because he enjoyed observing the entire process and found it impressive. The novices escorted him to a dormitory style breakfast with long tables. Everyone sat together. There was a blessing on the food, and then everyone consumed their meals in silence. Afterward, Tesfai reappeared and sat down next to Elliott. "Are you ready to meet with the curator of the sacred records? He has heard about you and is expecting you this morning after breakfast."

"I am anxious to speak to him," responded Elliott. Elliott finished eating and brought his eating utensils to the common dishwashing area the way all the other novices did. Then he and Tesfai walked to the same church they visited the previous evening. This time the curator was there, ready and waiting to talk with Elliott.

The curator was old; Elliott guessed he was probably in his 80s. He was similar in height and build to Tesfai, skinny and slightly bent over.

"I have other chores to do so I will leave you here," said Tesfai.

"But who will translate for me?" asked Elliott. He had noticed that Tesfai had to say everything in his native language when he was talking to the curator.

"I will get his assistant to come in and work with you on translations," responded Tesfai. Elliott tried to communicate with the curator, but the only response he received was blank stares. True to his word, it was only a matter of a few moments before one of the novices came in to help out. Elliott recognized him from the dormitory where he had spent the night. He had slept, or rather snored, in the next bunk over.

"I would like to ask the curator what the sacred records teach us about the Ark of the Covenant," Elliott queried the novice.

The novice proceeded to question the curator. Their exchange sounded like a lot of gibberish to Elliott. He hoped that the message was coming across clearly.

The curator got up and started to leave the room and the novice urged Elliott, "Follow him. He wants you to go with him. He wants to show you the records."

Elliott followed faithfully, hoping this would lead to the information that he was seeking. The three of them went down a flight of metal, circular stairs, into the heart of the mesa, and into a cave beneath the church. "This is where the sacred records are kept," explained the novice.

They arrived in what seemed to be an underground library. There were scrolls, and books, and tablets of all kinds. Some of them were obviously thousands of years old. But the curator seemed to know where to go for the information he was seeking. He pulled an old book off one of the shelves. The book had small, wooden planks for its covers. It was a collection of parchment pages, bound together by leather straps. It was obviously even older than this ancient church.

The curator held the book with respect and delicacy. He explained, and the translator translated, that this was the sacred history of the Ark. It told of the rescue of the Ark from Jerusalem, and how it was brought first to Egypt, and then even further into the African continent to Ethiopia for safe keeping. There was the constant fear of attack because other nations had heard about the mystical and magical powers that the Ark contained. Everyone wanted access to these powers.

The book told of how the Ark was taken from Solomon's temple, with the help of Solomon, and a forgery was put in its place. It told of how, Menelik the first king of Ethiopia, used the Ark's power to become the king. It told of how a sacred and secure hiding place was created for the Ark, and how this place was guarded day and night by the keepers of the Ark. It told of how the Ark had been moved several times, each time trying to keep it hidden from any potential threat. It started in northern Egypt, but eventually worked its way down into the heart of Ethiopia.

"Does it tell us where the Ark is now?" asked Elliott, finding the history to be extremely interesting, but also wanting to get to the point.

"Apparently the last move of the Ark left it in Axum."

"I was just there two nights ago. Are you telling me the Ark was there all along and I didn't even know it?"

"Apparently so," was the guarded response.

"Do the writings tell us where in Axum the Ark is located?"

"No. They just say the name of the city."

That was the information Elliott was after. But he graciously continued to listen to a history lesson about the high level of importance placed on the Ark and the respect given to Menelik as keeper of the Ark. The prophets have stated that the Ark would be protected and would not be disrupted until the return of the Messiah.

Elliott was thrilled. The Ark was closer than he ever imagined. And he was anxious to move on. However, Elliott remembered his driver's instructions that the Monks expect to receive presents for their hospitality, and that the presents could come in the form of pencils, paper, gum, or anything else he might be carrying with him. Elliott proceeded to empty out his pockets and give what few things he had to Tesfai. Then he asked him if he would come down the mountain with him because Elliott had something else to give him. In reality, Elliott just wanted company going down the steep climb. But the thought of an additional gift was enough to get Tesfai to tag along.

By the time they arrived at the top of the climb, Elliott had gotten himself so stressed out about the 60-foot drop that he was experiencing tremors in his body. He kept visualizing himself dropping down the side of the cliff, and it wasn't a pretty sight. He was becoming more scared than he had experienced in quite some time. And he was mad at himself. He was supposed to be "mister macho," the James Bond of the IOM, and here he was getting scared of a little climb. His thoughts bounced back and forth, until he was finally able to calm himself down and start the climb. He felt like a total idiot.

He started the climb. Again, he had a safety rope tied around his waist which was supported at the top of the climb and lowered slowly as he went down. He used the main rope to hold on to as he stepped into the small notches used as footholds at the side of the cliff. About one-third of the way down he suddenly slipped, losing his footing, but the tight hold he had on the rope, and the help of the safety rope, saved him for a disastrous fall.

Arriving at the bottom, Elliott was ready to kiss the ground. But he knew that would look extremely stupid, so he put on his macho face and waved his thanks to the rope handler. Then he went to the car, which he was delighted to find had not left him, and he proceeded to pull a couple of notebooks and a handful of pencils out of his bag and gave them to Tesfai. They said their goodbyes, and Tesfai scampered back up the steep incline. It was almost as if he danced his way up the cliff without the use of any rope. Elliott watched in amazement. Then he climbed into the vehicle, greeted the driver, and they were off returning down the same dust road.

"Where to boss?" asked the driver.

"Back to Axum," replied Elliott.

"Excellent," was the response, and they started their slow journey down the hill into the valley, over the stream, and back up the other side.

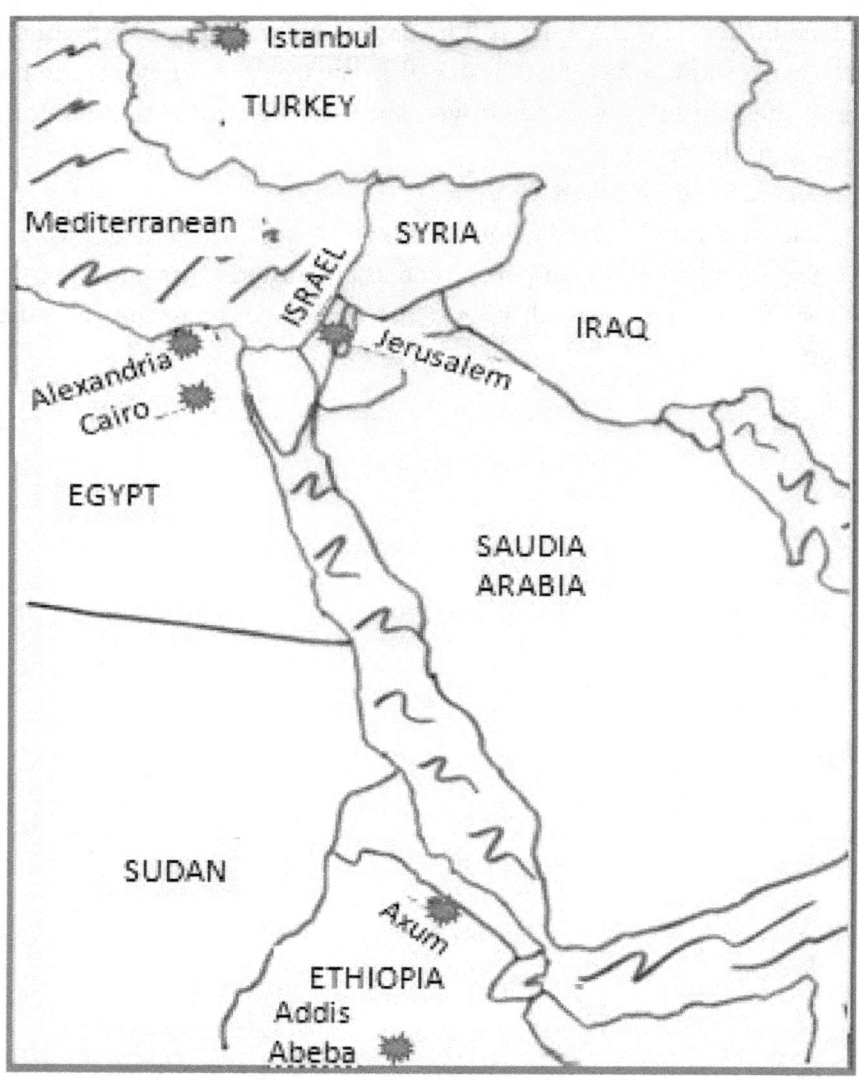

CHAPTER FORTY-FIVE

The Road to Axum
Early April, 2025 AD, Addis Abeba, Ethiopia

Jano and two novice Coptic adherents arrived on the first flight to Addis Abeba, Ethiopia from Cairo, Egypt. The Pope in Alexandria, after a conversation with the Bishop in Jerusalem, felt that Jano should keep a close watch on the events in Ethiopia. He felt Jano should go to Axum and work with the local Bishop to make sure the Ark remained safe. He knew he would receive the help of the Lord in protecting the Ark. After all, the Lord had protected it for over two millennium. How could a few individuals pose a serious threat? But he also knew that the Lord expected him to do everything in his power to protect the Ark. And then, after the Pope had done all he could, the Lord would finish the job.

The three Coptic priests remained solemn in their assignments. They didn't joke or talk much. They believed that silent reflection opened the door for the word of God to freely flow. God can't talk to you if you're too busy talking. And they didn't want to miss any important messages that God may be trying to share with them. A message from God was more important than one hundred messages from man.

The plane trip was slightly bumpy, but otherwise normal. During the trip, none of the other passengers tried to talk to them because they had an aura of reverence around them. No one wanted to disturb their prayers and meditation. Passengers treated the priests as if disturbing them would be sacrilegious and sinful. So, people avoided the three.

Getting off the plane they went directly through the luggage claim area and to the passenger pickup area at the front of the airport. They didn't have any checked luggage. Their only luggage was a small duffle bag that they carried with them onto the plane. Waiting for them in front of the airport was a minivan, also driven by a priest from the local Christian Coptic community. Jano had called ahead to the Coptic Bishop in Addis Abeba and had arranged for the ride north. The Ethiopian bishop became very concerned when he learned about the search for the Ark and he immediately ordered transportation and a guide for Jano and his team. Jano also contacted the Bishop in Axum and arranged to meet with him.

The three Alexandrian priests climbed aboard the minivan without a word of greeting, not even a "Hello." They settled into their seats. The driver, who as a local priest, headed out of the airport and the four of them were off heading to the northern border of the country.

The foursome would be driving for the remainder of the day, and into the night without interruption except for the occasional food or potty break. It would be a long trip, but they wanted to get to Axum as soon as possible so they could prepare for the anticipated onslaught of the Ark searchers.

Early April, 2025 AD, Alexandria, Egypt

Kres was never known to be even-tempered. And his anger had been raised to peak performance. All his best laid plans seemed to be unraveling around him. He had hoped that he and Rohit would be able to achieve the goal of finding the Ark, and of negotiating a relationship with the IOM, which in turn would allow him access to their nuclear weaponry. But the IOM had been very stand-offish and had kept their relationship at a distance. Then he learned from Marcello that Rohit was in fact a double agent passing secrets to the CIA, and possibly other organizations. And, to top it all off, when Rohit was supposed to be assassinated along with one or two of the IOM operatives; it was Kres who gets shot. He was beyond himself with fury as he discussed his frustrations with Marcello over the phone.

"What the...#!??? went wrong?" asked Kres. In Kres' mind Marcello was a member of the French underground. The connection between Marcello and the CIA had not been made. "It was a simple assassination. Was that too hard to handle?"

Marcello had an entirely different agenda. He was also disappointed in the results, but for an entirely different reason. In his role as CIA agent, he wanted to get rid of all of them, IOM and NNRL included, and solve this problem once and for all. However, his ties with the French Mafia went way back, much earlier than his work for the CIA, and he was angered by the IOM execution of Barjet, who was also a member of the French Mafia, and who Marcello considered a minor hero. So, Marcello was delighted when Kres contacted him two days earlier, under the guise that Marcello was a leader in the French underground. Marcello's plan was to use Kres' information to set up an assassination for all four of them.

"For some reason they mistook you for one of the IOM agents," responded Marcello.

"They didn't even go after the IOM agents. They went after me, as if they were doing it intentionally. You guys are the biggest bunch of screw-ups I've ever met?"

"We really shouldn't be having this conversation over the phone. You know that wireless communication is tracked by satellite and that key words are searched and identified. I'd like to meet with you and somehow resolve this face to face. Do you think that would be possible?"

"Definitely possible. Where and when?" In the back of Kres' mind he was looking for an opportunity to take revenge on Marcello, who he considered an incompetent idiot. If they met together, he would be able to carry out the wish. Unfortunately, Marcello was having the similar thoughts about Kres.

"I'm in Ethiopia. Where are you?" Marcello had his own agenda. He wanted to finish the job that his mafia friends had bungled in Alexandria. He wanted to take Kres out, followed by Stef and Elliott. His CIA perspective wanted to rid himself of the headache that the IOM –

NNRL alliance had created. And his French mafia perspective wanted to take revenge on the Barjet assassination.

"I'm in Alexandria, Egypt, but I'm heading down to Ethiopia later this afternoon. Perhaps we can meet there. Where in Ethiopia are you?"

"I'm in Addis Abeba, Ethiopia, but I'll be heading North shortly to Debra Damo, close to Axum."

"Perfect. I'm heading to Axum as well. Let's meet some time tomorrow."

Kres had made plans to go to Axum. He received a message from Stef that she would be heading to Axum based on her conversations with the Bishop in Jerusalem. That Bishop had informed her that the Ark was in Axum. Additionally, Elliott was already somewhere in the area, but out of signal range.

After disconnecting from the call with Marcello, Kres immediately placed a call to NNRL headquarters. His mind was made up. He was going to move forward with his "Birthday celebration" in Washington DC. He kept his phone message as short as possible and gave the order; "Initiate Birthday Celebration." This was the surprise birthday present he planned to give to his now deceased father, Adolph Hitler.

The message "Initiate Birthday Celebration" triggered a collection of activities. The nuclear material was already in route to the United States. It would then continue on to its ultimate destination. But the other two pieces of a bomb still needed to be put into place; 1) the delivery system, and 2) the detonator. These last two pieces were now triggered, and action would be taken.

His second request centered on his difficulties in Egypt and Ethiopia. With Rohit gone, it was time for him to quit trying to handle the search for the Ark by himself. He was going to call in some of his NNRL troops. He ordered 10 agents to make their way as quickly and as secretly as possible to Axum, Ethiopia. They would receive further orders after their arrival. And they were to come armed.

CHAPTER FORTY-SIX

The Fuel
Early April, 2025 AD, Asunción, Paraguay

The message "Initiate Birthday Celebration" was sent out by Kres using text messaging to all the key players in the NNRL network. This triggered the activities of the three independent cells, all three of which would eventually merge together at their delivery point. The details of each cells' activities were kept hidden and revealed on a "need to know" basis.

The effort of the first of the three cell teams was already in process. They started earlier because their process would take longer than the others. This cell included Krank Markal and Lefty Leviticus who were responsible for the delivery of the nuclear fuel. They departed Paraguay as soon as Krank returned from delivering the nuclear material to Brazil. They hopped a plane in Asuncion and headed north to Miami. The flight left Asunción at 06:00AM, connecting through Sao Paulo, and arrived in Miami thirteen hours later at 06:00PM Miami time. From there they rented a car and started their long five-hour drive toward McKay Bay Harbor near Tampa, Florida, where the containers would be unloaded.

Under normal circumstances, they would have taken Interstate 75 across Florida, because it was a faster road. But they had until tomorrow before the container ship arrived. So, they opted for the slower, more scenic route and headed south out of the airport, and connected up with SW 8th Street, also known as Highway 41. Then they followed Hwy 41 west, taking them through the Everglades from Miami on the Atlantic East coast to Naples on the Gulf of Mexico West coast. They continued on 41, working their way north along the coast and got as far as Fort Myers. All the travelling had finally caught up with them and they decided to spend the night. They knew it would still be more than a day before the container arrived, and then it would take time to be off loaded. So, they decided to take it easy, and enjoy the Florida coastline. Hwy 41 took them right through the center of the business district, and there were numerous hotel options for them to choose from.

The following day they continued on their journey on Hwy 41, heading north. They stopped often to see the sights, especially when they arrived in the Venice area. There were lots of signs advertising this area, and Krank and Lefty couldn't resist spending some time in the area. They talked with disgust about the decadence and wastefulness and the richness of the area. But inside they were jealous that they had to live in near squalor in Paraguay, while the hated United States counterparts were able to live in such a beautiful environment. It just wasn't fair. Don't they deserve to live at this same level of luxury? Don't they lead good lives, as good as any of these people? Their jealousy made them want to take revenge. However, at the same time, destroying this beauty was somehow wrong as well.

They ended up spending way too much time walking round and enjoying the sights of Venice. They ended up driving the full length of Casey Key, stopping often to walk on the beach. Paraguay, being a land lock country, didn't afford any opportunities to walk along an ocean beach, and Krank and Lefty were enjoying this opportunity. Eventually they ended up in Sarasota, where they hopped on the faster Hwy 301, which connected up with Interstate 275. By evening they arrived in Tampa, where they found a Super 8 Motel along the interstate. Tonight, they would relax. Tomorrow they would check on the arrival schedule of the cargo ship that held their precious cargo.

Day three of their stay in the United States started with a visit to the McKay Bay Harbor dock management office where they learned that their cargo ship had arrived during the night and that the containers were already being off-loaded. Unfortunately, the off-loading could take as long as three days. They asked if there was a way that they could check on a specific container and they were told that it would be impossible to check on a container without walking around on the dock. They were also told that they would not be allowed access to the dock because it was a dangerous, high risk area when loading or unloading was in process.

Realizing they had learned as much as possible, they departed from dock management office and headed back towards their car. "What do we do now?" questioned Lefty.

"We could break into the container yard and make sure the container arrived. But that seems fruitless since the yard is so large and many of the containers look alike. I suppose we're forced to wait until the container gets delivered to the trucking company."

"But then the trucking company is going to cart the container off to Indiana somewhere, to deliver the granite counter tops. We don't want to chase them that far, do we?"

"Not really. We'll just have to intercept the cargo en route. The trucker has to sleep sometime and then we'll get the goods while he's asleep."

"Do we know which truck we're waiting for?"

Krank made a quick call to the trucking company and then reported; "I called the trucking company that was hired to do the delivery. They are scheduled for a pick-up tomorrow. So, we'll have to watch all the Trans-Pak trucks hauling yellow containers and check the number of the container as it leaves the dockyard. Then, when we see the right container, we follow it until we get the chance to break in. We'll have to open the back of the container and steal the fuel."

"Got it. Sounds like a plan. Let's do a little sightseeing and go back to the hotel." Lefty was enjoying the ocean and wanted to see more. They took a drive along to Clearwater and spent a few hours on the beach. Then they headed back to the hotel for another night of waiting. Tomorrow, assuming all goes well, they should be able to reclaim their prize and head off to the rendezvous point.

In the morning Krank again contacted the Trans-Pak shipping company and pretended to be the buyer of the granite counter tops. He confirmed that the tops were being shipped on that day. After a quick Hotel breakfast-bar breakfast, Krank and Lefty headed off to the dock yards and kept a close watch on all the trucks leaving the area.

As is always the case when you're waiting for something, the truck with the precious cargo was to be one of the last to leave the dock yard that day. Krank and Lefty had waited around for nearly eight hours before the truck pulled through the dockyard gates.

"It's about time," complained Krank.

"The race is on," responded Lefty.

They started following the truck, staying far enough behind to not be too obvious, but not so far that they would lose him. The truck headed for Interstate 275, then connected with Interstate 75, heading north out of Florida and toward the north central states.

Since it was already late in the day, they hoped that the trucker would stop soon and shut down for the night. What they didn't realize was that truckers liked to drive at night because it was cooler and less traffic. In fact, this trucker intentionally picked up his load late in the day. He slept through the daylight hours because he intended to take a late-night drive.

But Krank and Lefty had been awake all day, watching the trucks as they pulled out of the dockyards, and they were hungry and sleepy. But now they had to drive. They didn't dare loose the truck, now that they had finally found their precious load.

The first couple hours were easy. Krank drove and Lefty relaxed. But then Krank started yawning more and more. Lefty found that he needed to constantly watch Krank. On one occasion he noticed Krank had closed his eyes and Left hit him hard in the arm to keep him awake. The punch made Krank jerk and they swerved back and forth across the two-lane freeway trying to get back in control of the car. Krank swore, but he also realized that Lefty had saved his life.

Now the two started to get creative. They opened all the windows and turned the music up as loud as it would go. The option of switching drivers didn't work, because they would have to manage it while driving, and the car was simply too small for them to maneuver one person out of the driver's seat while another moved in. Besides, it didn't matter who was driving, the other person wasn't going to be able to rest anyway. They had to watch out for each other so that they didn't fall asleep.

After a while, it became very theatrical. They looked a little like Laurel and Hardy, constantly punching and yelling in an attempt to keep the driver awake and on the road. At one point they became so absorbed in trying to stay awake, that they didn't realize that two other trucks hauling yellow trailers had pulled up in front of them. And now they didn't know which truck they were following. They had to race to catch up with the trucks and check the tracking numbers on the trailers so that they knew which one was theirs.

As the night went on the theatrics became steadily worse. The punching and yelling seemed to be the only tools they had to try to keep them alive.

"I'm getting a little sick and tired of getting punched. I think sometimes you're doing it just for fun, not because you need to. That hurts!" Krank complained.

"At least you're still alive," responded Lefty.

"Well, my arm is so badly bruised up that it's going to hurt for a month. Can you let off a little?"

Just then the truck turned off into a rest area, and Krank, excitedly exclaimed, "Great. Now you can have a turn at getting punched."

The truck pulled to a stop in one of the rest area truck park stalls, and Krank and Lefty took turns going to the bathroom and buying up as many snacks as their cash flow would allow. They hoped that if they kept eating, they wouldn't be sleeping.

The stop was shorter than expected. The truck started pulling out and Lefty hadn't returned to the car. Krank jumped out of the car and ran into the restroom after Lefty. "We're rolling. Get a move on."

Lefty was in the awkward situation of trying to pull his pants up quickly and zip them as he ran out to the car. As he jumped in, Krank started driving, barely giving Lefty enough time to shut the car door.

"Dang it," burst out Krank. "I wanted you to drive so I could punch you for a while. I......#!??? nearly lost my bloody foothold to haul my arse into this......#!??? car, just because you're in such a ......#!??? hurry to get

going, I was too late to stop you from taking the wheel again. Oh well....
hopefully, these snacks will keep me awake and sane, and at least I
won't have to put up with your over-kill abuse on my poor shoulder any
longer." He mumbled between clenched teeth still puffing and
breathless from their hasty departure and trying his best to keep up
with his somewhat inconsiderate colleague.

The truck driver had no intention of stopping for very long. He had
taken a quick potty break. That would suffice him for the next three
hours. The snacks had been consumed well before that time, and Lefty
was beck to punching Krank in the arm at regular intervals. By now it
was 04:00AM and the caravan was closing in on Chattanooga,
Tennessee. Krank expressed concern; "At this rate we'll in Indianapolis
before this guy takes a break, and that will make it a lot harder for us to
get the payload. We're going to have to think about ways to stop this
truck. The place where it's delivered may be a lot harder to access."

This left Lefty thinking. "I'm not sure what our options are," he
mused.

"Let's just hope he gives us a break real soon."

"If we had a gun, we could shoot a tire out, but Kres stressed that we
carry no weapons in the United States, because that would make us
immediately suspicious. So, what are we going to do? Crash into it?"

"I guess that's an option, but it doesn't sound like a very smart one."
Krank said, twisting his face into a soured look and indicating his
displeasure with the idea. But he didn't have any better ideas to offer.

They continued on following the truck, hoping to get a break sooner
than later. It was the only choice they had. Then, at 06:30AM, after
what seemed like a never-ending night of torture, the truck finally
pulled off the freeway, taking an exit close to Louisville, Tennessee.
Krank and Lefty were excited, hoping that their ordeal may finally be
over. They were rewarded when the truck pulled up to a parking area
near a Motel 6. They pulled off as well but kept at a distance attempting
to remain undetected. They watched as the trucker got out of the truck
and checked in at the reception desk of the hotel. They continued to
watch as the trucker returned to his truck, grabbed a bag, and went off
to one of the motel rooms. The tough part of the job was now done. All

they had to do was to break into the back of the truck, grab the nuclear material, and sneak away. It should be a snap.

They gave the trucker an extra half hour, making sure that he wasn't returning to the truck. Then they snuck over to the back of the truck and tried to break in. But the container was locked, with an extremely strong paddle lock. And they had forgotten to bring any tools with, like a hack saw or bolt cutters. They had plenty of time on the previous couple of days where they could have come up with the tools, but they had forgotten. They had nothing to help them.

"What the heck are we going to do now?" questioned Lefty. "We need to get this done before anyone notices us. There aren't any hardware stores open this time of night. I have no idea how to break this lock."

"We need to think," was Krank's words of wisdom.

"Doesn't our car have a tire iron?"

"Run and get it. It's worth a try."

Lefty ran off and returned with the lug wrench from the rental car. They tried wedging the sharp end of the bar into the paddle lock. Initially they had very little luck. Krank put his full weight against the bar. Suddenly it slipped out and he fell backwards, crashing into Lefty. The two of them hit the ground hard. "That gave me a few more bruises to deal with," complained Krank. "It wasn't bad enough that my arm is so sore that it's going to hurt for a month, now my legs are banged up as well."

They put the bar back into the lock and tried pulling together. Progress was slow, and it took several yanks, but eventually they were able to slowly twist a small gap in the lock, and then more and more of a gap, until the lock finally broke free.

Excitement returned. Now they would finally be able to access the precious cargo that they had successfully smuggled into the United States. They opened the cargo doors and swung them wide. Then they were faced with the next problem. In Brazil, the granite counter tops were loaded into the container using a forklift. Unfortunately, there wasn't a forklift to help them today. But they had anticipated this problem early on and had invented a creative solution. The center counter tops were weak and intentionally cracked. The granite tops were loaded on the truck separated by small, one half inch spacers. This left a crack between each of the tops. And with the weak, cracked tops in the center it wasn't hard to insert the sharp end of the lug wrench between the cracks and start breaking away at the counter tops. The process took longer than they had hoped, but eventually they were able to break their way to the center and open up enough of a hole to pull out the nuclear material. It wasn't an easy process, but it was successful.

They grabbed the nuclear material, and as they were climbing down out of the back of the truck, they heard a yell. "What's going on over there? What are you doing?" It was the truck driver returning to the vehicle.

Krank and Lefty grabbed the nuclear material and took off toward their rental car. They popped the trunk and threw the material in the back. Then they jumped in the car and raced off as quickly as possible. In the rear-view mirror, Krank could see the truck driver taking a picture of the back of their car on his phone. "We've got a problem," he said.

"What's that?"

"The truck driver has our picture and our license number. We're going to have to switch vehicles."

The truck driver immediately called the police and reported the destruction to his truck. He gave the 911 operator a description of the car, its drivers, and that they had taken something out of the truck, but he wasn't sure what it was. The 911 operator immediately dispatched the information to police cars in the area, and the search was on.

However, in spite of all their bungling, Krank and Lefty weren't stupid. They were passing by a 24-hour Wal-Mart parking lot and they pulled in, parking the car in the middle of the busiest area of the lot. Then they went around looking for an unlocked car, hoping that they would find keys under the floor matt or tucked above the visor. It took them three tries, but eventually they found an older car that they immediately started up. They drove it over to the rental car, transferred the nuclear fuel, and headed off toward their rendezvous point.

By the time the police found the abandoned rental car, the two Paraguay citizens had travelled a good 100 miles. The fingerprints gave the police nothing. There wasn't a fingerprint file on Paraguayan citizens. And the car rental was accomplished using a stolen credit card. All leads in the search lead to a quick dead end.

Krank and Lefty found themselves a Comfort Inn near the side of the freeway. They parked their stolen car around back so it wouldn't be noticeable. They rented a room and were asleep before their head hit touched the pillow. It would be dark again before they woke.

The rest of the trip would be uneventful, compared to the last couple of days. They switched cars several times. In Charleston, they rented another car, again using a different stolen credit card. And this would be the vehicle that they used for the remainder of their travels.

CHAPTER FORTY-SEVEN

The Delivery System
Early April, 2025 AD, Ann Arbor, Michigan

Mohammad Abdullah was 18 years of age and Moyad Ali was 19. They had been friends all their lives. They were born in the Iraqi Arab communities of Detroit where they attended school together. Now they are both attending the University of Michigan. Mohammad had Iraqi parents, who had immigrated to the United States shortly after their marriage. They wanted to escape the continual bloodshed that had become a part of the Iraq-Iran war, and there seemed to be no end in sight. When the opportunity presented itself, Mohammad's father quickly accepted a faculty position at Michigan State University. Seven years later they became citizens of the United States.

Moyad's father was also Iraqi, but his mother was Saudi. They met while attending school at the University of Michigan and have lived in Michigan ever since, becoming US citizens shortly after the birth of Moyad.

During their youth, Mohammad and Moyad were taught to love the United States. Both sets of parents repeatedly told them that the US was the "best country in the world." It offered the most opportunities for growth, development, and education, and anyone with initiative could easily be successful. They mocked the suppression of the Iraqi leadership and domination of the Saudi royals. They truly believed that the United States was land of equal opportunity for everyone. They believed this to be God's country and, contrary to what the Middle

Eastern Arab communities claim, Allah would be proud of what the United States has become.

Mohammad and Moyad maintained the religious heritage of their youth, more because of cultural intimidation than because they were true believers. The university had taught them that truth was found in science, not in the teaching of old men and obsolete books. The result was that during their university years they still attended the local Mullah every Friday, but they maintained serious reservations about the reality of God.

The message they heard at the Mullah was different from the teaching of their parents. These messages were new, and they pierced the two boys' hearts. It wasn't the focus on God that touched them; rather, they felt like their eyes were being opened so they could now see the evils of the world in which they lived. They heard the message of sexual abuse, moral degradation, and a Western destruction of values. At first, they didn't take the message seriously. But after hearing the same message month after month, they started to pay attention; they started to believe. They looked at the society around them and they could see the corruption for themselves. They saw pornography available in very public places, they saw women wearing degrading and sexually explicit clothing, and they saw television shows treating sex as a way of life rather than as a sacred act of procreation. They saw alcoholism, drug abuse, gambling, and poor health habits including obesity. Western society was truly the den of iniquity that was being described by their Cleric.

Cults exist in all religions, including Christians like Jim Jones, to Hindus, to Ultra-Orthodox Jews, and Buddhists. Cult leaders take the religion's foundation and distort it, emphasizing a particular goal that they are trying to achieve. One of the main teaching tools of cult organizations is their ability to modify behavior by teaching half-truths. For example, in this case, the half-truth was that the world you live in is degrading everyone who lives in it. Then, from that half-truth they teach excerpts from the Koran that are taken out of context. And before long, the cult leader has his followers believing that the Koran commands us to abolish this type of behavior. What the Koran actually teaches is that we should abolish this behavior in our lives. But the Mullah teaches the half-truth that "abolishing this behavior" requires each of us to go out and violently destroy the evil that surrounds us, even if it means suicide. But he forgets to teach that the Koran strictly prohibits suicide. A cult leader will repeatedly pound this message into the potential believer. Eventually, after months of hammering this doctrine into their brains, Mohammad and Moyad not only started to believe this doctrine, but they started to search for ways where they could make a difference. They didn't want to become someone who condoned the degradation of society by their apathy and lack of action. They wanted to take on an active role in reform.

On this particular Friday, the boys were walking to the Mosque on their way to afternoon prayers with a group of their Moslem friends as they passed a bar. Just then a lady, who was visibly drunk, stumbled out of the bar, tripped, and crashed into Moyad. He immediately put out his hands, trying to catch her. He was sure she was going to hit the ground and hit it hard. He tried to hold her up and help her get her balance. But he was rewarded with swearing and accusations. She started screaming; "This friggin' Arab's trying to maul me. Did you see that? He grabbed me and tried to grope me? HELP!" she screamed.

Moyad pushed her away in disgust and she crashed against the wall. *"HELP! HELP! He's beating me."* she repeatedly screamed. Onlookers did not take her seriously as she staggered down the sidewalk. They could see that it was the drunk and not Moyad who was out of line.

"Can you believe that?" Moyad questioned. "She stinks and can't even walk in a straight line. And she's trying to accuse me of being obscene. Like she'd even be worth groping."

"I can't believe how disgusting this world has become," added Mohammad. "The decadence in this world must be wiped out."

At the prayer meeting they heard the usual rhetoric about the decadence and decay of Western society, and about the need to "abolish this behavior." The memory of the drunk woman stumbling out of the bar was still visible in the minds of the two boys.

Near the end of the meeting, the Mullah asked; "Is there anyone out here who is a hero to Allah? Is there anyone who would commit their life to the truth? Is there anyone who can dedicate their life realizing the impact that they can have by following the teachings of the Koran? If so, we will have a special meeting immediately following today's prayers for anyone who would like to discuss how they can affect the world in which we live. We need to eliminate this Western decay and restore the world Allah intended us to live in."

Mohammad and Moyad looked at each other. They didn't need to say a word. They both knew that they needed to stay after for this meeting.

Prayers ended shortly afterwards and a small group of 10, of which 9 were students, came to the front of the Mosque to hear what the Mullah had to say. He started with; "We have the opportunity to make a difference. I have received information about how we can have a most dramatic effect on Western decadence. I cannot go into detail today, but if you are interested in hearing more; if you are interested in being an instrument to change, please return tomorrow at 07:00PM and we will go into more detail." What the Mullah was really saying was that he didn't trust everyone, and he wanted to see who would come back to learn more.

Early April, 2025 AD, Ann Arbor, Michigan

Mohammad and Moyad arrived at the Mosque at 06:55 PM, making sure they were on time. They wanted to know if there was some way they could help.

As the Mullah expected, the two boys were the only ones that showed up. The others, who had stayed after on the previous day, were just nosey, and had no real intention of committing themselves to the cause. They didn't want to go out of their way to help. But he could see fire in the eyes of Mohammad and Moyad. These were boys who would be willing to sacrifice for the Allah.

"Are you ready to make a difference?" the Mullah started the conversation. "Do you think you have it in you to change the world? Will you make Allah proud?"

How could they resist? Of course, they would want to be heroes to their God. Who wouldn't? Mohammad spoke first; "What do we need to do?"

The Mullah responded, "I have been presented with the opportunity to organize a demonstration of the power of Allah. We can hit the demon of Western decadence and immorality and stab it right in the heart."

"What are we doing?" asked Moyad.

"What we have planned will make the attack on the twin towers of the World Trade Center seem like child's play. We're going to destroy Washington DC, starting with its military power center, the Pentagon."

"How are we going to achieve this wonderful feat?"

"There are teams in motion right now heading for Washington DC who are going to bring all the pieces of a bomb together. Then, when the bomb has been assembled, we have been asked to be the delivery system. We have been asked to pick up the completed bomb and deliver it to the heart of the Pentagon. Is this a mission you think you can handle? You're still rather young." The Mullah was playing on the boys' pride. He was sure he could get them to complete this mission.

"We may be young, but we're committed. Our dedication will assure the successful completion of our mission."

"Excellent." The Mullah was proud to have such dedicated followers. He knew he could count on these boys to do their best to satisfactorily complete the mission. And, even if they didn't get all the way to the Pentagon, they could be as much as fifty miles away, and the Pentagon would still be destroyed.

The Mullah continued with his instructions; "First, we will need to change your names. I have someone who is waiting to create fake driver's licenses with your new names. Mohammad Abdullah, you are now called Joe Smith, and Moyad Ali, you will be Frank Marshall. I have also arranged for credit cards and cell phones under your new identities. These cards will be used to rent a car, get hotel rooms, and for anything else you will need. We have sponsors who will eagerly pay all your expenses. You are to drive to Washington DC and get a hotel room. Then you are to wait until I text you the location where you will be picking up the bomb. You will also receive instructions on where to deliver the bomb."

"How soon do we leave?"

"Tomorrow morning at 09:00AM. Come here and I will have the driver's licenses, the credit cards, the rental car, and the cell phones waiting for you."

"Thank you for your confidence and trust in us," said Moyad as he graciously bowed to the Mullah.

"The pleasure is all mine," responded the Mullah. He had very little interest in going on a suicide mission himself. He was glad he had found someone who was so willing to do the dirty work for him.

The following morning, the boys arrived, picked up their cards, phones, and car, and drove off toward Washington DC. They were excited, as if they were on some grand adventure. Neither wanted to ask the ultimate question, the one which they already knew the answer to. They didn't want to be thought of as weak. They didn't want to disappoint Allah. The question they were afraid to ask was "Will we come out of this alive?"

CHAPTER FORTY-EIGHT

The Fuse

Early April, 2025 AD, Ann Arbor, Michigan

The three key components of a nuclear device are the fuel, the delivery system, and the detonator. The fuel could be acquired at any one of several nuclear processing facilities that existed around the world. The delivery system was traditionally thought to be missile, or a bomb dropped by a plane. But now that suicide bombers have become a reality, a delivery system could be nothing more than the trunk of a car, or a suitcase. It didn't require elaborate technology. The third piece needed for a successful bomb, the detonator or fuse as it is often called, requires a level of technological sophistication that few countries possessed. For most countries, the access to a detonator was beyond their technological capability. However, occasionally, a few simple mistakes and miscalculations can put these critical fuses into the hands of terrorists.

The US Air Force had accidently mistaken four boxes of nuclear detonators as boxes of helicopter parts. One of the boxes was shipped to Taiwan, who immediately contacted the US Air Force, and the detonators were returned. When they were restocking the parts from Taiwan the Air Force realized there were three other boxes missing. The US intelligence community had learned that one of these boxes was shipped to the Philippines. Upon receipt of the parts in the Philippines, a US military consultant was asked what these parts were. This consultant, seeing the opportunity to increase his earnings, said he would take the box off their hands and make sure they were disposed of correctly. What he did was put the detonators on the market, looking for the highest bidder. This second box of detonators ended up in the hands of the IOM.

A third box of the detonators was delivered to Brazil. It took months before the Brazilians opened the box and realized that they had been shipped the wrong parts. The detonators were sent to the engineering department where the engineers quickly identified them for what they were. Once again capitalism kicked in and these engineers saw the opportunity to benefit from the mistake. They offered them for sale individually, rather than selling the entire box. It was in the last couple days that these fuses went on the market, when Kres was arriving in Alexandria. Kres immediately realized that he no longer needed the IOM, but the attempt to assassinate Elliott and Stef failed. But they may still serve a purpose if they find the Ark.

Kres dispatched one of his highest ranking NNRL team members to negotiate with the Brazilian engineers. He wanted to get his hands on one of the detonators. This proved to be successful, and Kres now had control of all three components of a nuclear device. And he was ready for action. He was ready to celebrate his father's birthday in a way the world would always remember.

Kres organized three separate and independent cells for each of the components. The first cell included Krank Markal and Lefty Leviticus who were responsible for delivering the nuclear fuel. The second cell included two Arabs from Detroit, and they would become the delivery system. And the third cell included a high ranking NNRL team member, Joseph Ahuna, the same individual who purchased the detonator from the Brazilians, and Karl Geisenberger, a nuclear scientist that would be responsible for assembling the device.

Karl wasn't the perfect specimen of blond hair, blue-eyed master race German. He looked more like Einstein. He was short, about 5' 6", with dark curly hair and brown eyes. None would mistake him for anything but the geek-scientist that he was. And he made no attempt to be anything else. He enjoyed the mask of privacy and anonymity that his scientist role allowed him to maintain. He was one of several German scientists that were working on the nuclear bomb, at the time the war ended. He was amongst men like Wernher Magnus Maximilian Freiherr von Braun, more commonly known as Wernher von Braun, who later spear-headed the United States space program, or the rocket scientists that were rounded up and later became the leaders of the Russian space program. But he considered himself fortunate to have escaped with Hitler to help him develop his vision for a New World Order in Paraguay. He would be the scientist responsible for assembling the weapon that would be used to celebrate the memory of the Fuhrer's birthday.

Joseph Ahuna was somewhat of an anomaly in the NNRL hierarchy. He was a native Hawaiian, the only one in the NNRL. Being forced to leave Hawaii because of a family dispute, where he had killed a cousin, he chose to move to Paraguay, believing that they would never find him there. He knew that his cousin's brothers would be looking for him. So, he hid out in a land-locked country in the middle of South America. At first it was a struggle for him. He missed the ocean, fishing, swimming, and surfing. But he knew that he needed to avoid travelling or doing anything that would make him visible.

Joseph didn't have any training which would make him employable. It wasn't long before Joseph found himself at odds with Paraguayan law. During one of his prison stays he shared a cell with a member of the NNRL, and from this connection he joined and rapidly moved up in the NNRL hierarchy.

When it came time to acquire the detonator from the Brazilian engineers, Joseph readily volunteered. Negations were quick and easy. Apparently, the sale of the detonators was not well advertised and there were only three bidders that showed up at the auction. Since there were four detonators in the box, and since Joseph was only after one, there were plenty of detonators to go around. Joseph returned to Paraguay within a day with the detonator in hand.

The cell that included Joseph and Karl was tasked with delivering the detonator to the rendezvous point, assembling the bomb, and turning it over to the delivery team. But first they had to camouflage the mechanism. They decided that this would best be done by replacing the inside of a VCR with the detonator mechanism, repackaging the VCR in its original packaging, and placing it into a suitcase along with a video camera and some additional photography equipment. They wanted the VCR box to seem ordinary.

Suitcase in hand, the two members of the detonator cell purchased airline tickets to New York. From there they would take the train to Washington DC and meet up with the other cells.

CHAPTER FORTY-NINE

Betrayal

Early April, 2025 AD, Addis Abeba, Ethiopia

Alan arrived in Ethiopia around 11:00AM, well ahead of Stef. His trip from Salt Lake City had routed him through Europe, where he endured a 12-hour lay-over. But now he was finally in Addis Abeba, exhausted.

Alan had been in communication with Stef and knew when and where she would be arriving. Her trip back from Jerusalem had also encountered delays in Turkey, but she would be in the air soon, finishing up the last leg of her journey. Alan caught a taxi to the Sheraton, which was where Stef wanted to stay, and caught a short four-hour nap as he waited for her to arrive later that afternoon.

Alan had successfully smuggled the stolen replica of the Antikythera Mechanism through customs, even though it did cost him a few dollars to get the customs agent to quit asking so many questions. He couldn't resist taking it out of its packaging and played with it. He had no idea how it worked. He hoped Stef would be able to shed some light on its operation. But he knew that the mechanism wasn't his priority. At this point, the mechanism was the bait, and Stef was the prize he hoped to catch.

As he sat on his bed tinkering with the device, he received a call on his cell phone. "Hello?"

"This is agent Rudolf Westerner from the CIA. Is this Alan, agent of the IOM?"

Alan was startled for a moment. This was an unusual introduction. However, this was not the first time that the CIA had made contact. "This is Alan. How can I help?"

"We need to meet. I have information about the IOM and NNRL relationship that you will need. You may be at risk. But I can't go into any more detail over the phone. When can we get together?"

"Right now, would be fine. I'm in room 1203 in the Sheraton. Can you come now?"

"I'll be there in about thirty minutes. I'll meet you in your room." And the phone went silent.

Alan was left wondering what this big secret was going to be. He had been contacted by the CIA about three months earlier and had started working with them, spying on the IOM. His contact at the CIA made it abundantly clear that he was now working for the CIA, and that his job at the IOM was a secondary, under-cover role that may need to be jeopardized or even terminated at any time. Alan had always dreamed of working for the CIA as a spy, and he wasn't going to pass up this opportunity. They were obviously interested in finding an IOM insider so they could track their activities, and the opportunity to join the CIA may never be available again.

Up to now, spying for the CIA had been easy. All he had to do was send them a message every couple of days letting them know what was going on. But now he was going to meet someone out in the field. His curiosity was peaked.

Since he had thirty minutes to kill, Alan decided to go for a walk around the hotel. This was the first time he was in Ethiopia, and he thought he'd do a little exploring while he waited for the CIA agent.

The hotel was quite impressive. It didn't feel at all like he was in the middle of a developing country. The art and architecture was some of the finest he had ever seen. And the care and keeping of the hotel was also top-notch. He had hoped to get outside and away from the hotel, but there was so much to see on the hotel grounds that his thirty minutes had been used up before he had a chance to venture too far. He had to get back to his room for his meeting with the CIA.

Alan had not been back in his room more than five minutes when the knock came on the door. Answering it he opened the door to two men. One was a tall, strong looking individual who looked like a body builder. The other was medium in height and smaller in build, but also looked like a formidable contestant in any conflict.

"Hello," responded Alan, putting out his hand. "Come on in."

"We'll avoid names," responded the visitor, shaking Alan's hand as he cautiously strode through the door entering the room. The two agents took a quick survey of the room looking around in all directions. One entered the bathroom.

"Clear;" commented the second agent as he came out of the bathroom.

The caution of the CIA agent made Alan suspicious. "Can I see some form of ID?" he asked.

"Not necessary," responded the agent. But now Alan wondered if he was even an agent at all. "You know Agent Marcello Zuniga." Alan nodded his head. "We work for him, and he has a special mission that he wants you to carry out for him."

Alan's attention was aroused. He listened intensely as the CIA agent explained his mission and Alan's role. As he listened, Alan leaned back in his chair. "Wow," was his only comment.

Early April, 2025 AD, Addis Abeba, Ethiopia

After the agents left Alan's room it was starting to get close to Stef's arrival time. And Alan had decided to pick her up at the airport. Using CIA contacts, he made arrangements for a driver that would take him to the airport. He had also sent Stef a text message that he would be waiting for her outside the baggage claim area. He packed up his belongings but left his bag in the room. He knew that his stay in this hotel room would be a short one.

The drive to the airport was long and slow, a combination of bad roads and heavy traffic. Alan didn't like the rough travelling, but he knew that there would probably be a lot more of it before he was finally able to leave Ethiopia.

They were starting to get close enough to the airport to see planes in their landing patterns. Alan's phone beeped, indicating the receipt of a text message. He pulled out his phone to see that Stef had just landed. He knew it would still be another thirty minutes before she was able to get off the plane and retrieve her luggage. He gave this information to the cab driver, who casually waved his hand indicating "no problem."

After killing time by driving around in circles for a while, Alan finally received the text message that Stef was ready to be picked up. They entered the airport arrival area and pulled up to the curb near baggage claim. Alan pointed Stef out to the cab driver, and he drove as close as possible. Alan jumped out of the cab and gave Stef a big hug. "It's so great to see you again," said Alan. "It's been such a long time. We talk often over the various messaging channels, but we rarely get to see each other in person." Alan had always had the "hots" for Stef, but he knew she was Elliott's girl and that was one line he knew he couldn't cross. He needed to stay on good terms with both of them. But, having Stef alone and to himself was exciting for him.

"It's great to see you too," responded Stef, somewhat surprised by his aggressiveness. This seemed unusual to her. This wasn't the Alan she remembered. She wondered what had changed. "I assume you have the Antikythera Mechanism."

"Absolutely. Back at the hotel room." Alan helped the cabbie load the luggage into the trunk of the car. Then he slid into the back seat of the cab next to Stef. "I hope you had a decent trip."

"It was rough, but fine. This is what we do, like it or not. It's just a nuisance going through Turkey to get between Jerusalem and Egypt. And then the flight to Ethiopia was also a little rough. But I've been on worse. And we're here. I can't wait to see the device. I hope we can find someone who is knowledgeable enough to know how to use it. I wonder if it can really pinpoint the location of the Ark.

"I learned from the Bishop in Jerusalem that the Ark was located somewhere in Axum. But he wasn't able to give me any more information than that. Hopefully the Antikythera Mechanism can finish out our search." As she was talking the taxi driver had pulled away from the airport loading area and was heading out on the main road. But instead of heading West, toward the center of town, he started heading East. Concerned, Stef commented, "The center of town is off in the other direction, isn't it? I could see it from the plane, and it doesn't seem like we're heading in the right direction."

The driver quickly responded, "Traffic bad now. I take quicker route."

Alan didn't seem to be concerned, so Stef continued talking. "I learned a lot about the history of the Ark and how it came to be down here in Ethiopia. Apparently, it really exists, which is something I was still uncertain about. I thought we might be on a wild goose chase, as the Americans say. But it seems to indeed be a real thing. And apparently it has a long, complicated, and drawn-out history. I can't wait to see where all this leads."

After about fifteen minutes of driving, they found themselves out in the country, on some back-roads. Again, Stef became concerned. She tapped the driver and asked, "This can't be right. What's going on here? Tell me what you're doing. Where are we going?"

She sat back in her seat and quizzically looked over at Alan. She was shocked to find herself staring at the barrel of a 34-caliber automatic, with the safety off, ready to fire. "What the heck are you doing?" she challenged Alan. "Why are you pointing a gun at me?"

Alan didn't answer. He continued to aim the gun at her. Meanwhile the taxi had pulled over and the driver had gotten out of the car. They were on a seemingly deserted road, with no one around to question them or challenge them. The driver went to the trunk, opened it, and came to Stef's side of the car. He opened the back door. "Hands back!" he commanded.

Stef looked at the driver; "What the dickens is going on here?" Turning back to Alan she said, "Alan, will you tell me what's happening?"

"Put your hands behind your back," commanded Alan, in an entirely new tone of voice. The friendly, cordial Alan was gone, replaced by a demanding and more aggressive tone. "Turn your back to the driver so he can tie up your hands. Hurry!"

With her hands behind her back, the Taxi driver tied them together with plastic tie-downs. Then he slipped a bag over her head and tied it, tight enough to keep her from throwing it off, but not so tight as to restrict breathing.

Stef was beside herself. She started screaming at Alan. *"WHAT THE HELL IS GOING ON HERE? WHAT ARE YOU HOPING TO ACCOMPLISH? WHO ARE YOU WORKING FOR? TALK TO ME...EXPLAIN YOURSELF!*

As the taxi pulled back out on the road, Alan decided to keep quiet. Responding would just generate more questions. The silence managed to enrage Stef even more. She resorted to the only weapon she had left, her feet. She started kicking her feet in the direction of Alan. And occasionally she would strike a blow. But she was unrelenting. She knew she was in trouble, and, at this point, felt she couldn't make things worse. He was probably going to kill her anyway.

Alan grabbed her feet and held on for dear life. One of her kicks had hit him squarely in the jaw, and he was reeling from the sting. This generated an interesting mix of emotions for Alan. Holding on to her feet was also somewhat rewarding. He wouldn't ever have been able to get that close to her in any other circumstance. But here he was, aggressively cuddling the legs of the woman he adored. He had the option of tying up her feet, but this was so much more fun.

They rode the bumpy backroads for another forty minutes and then came to a stop in front of a small adobe mud building with a grass roof. The building had one small door in the front, for which they had to bend down to get through. Once inside, they tied one of Stef's legs to the end of a chain. The other end of the chain connected to a stake. Then they removed the bag over Stef's head.

Immediately Stef took to yelling. "What is going on here? Will you talk to me?"

"No," was the only response Alan would give.

Then she turned to the driver, "Are you deaf mute? What is your problem? Why won't you tell me what is going on here?" She screamed as loud as she could. But then she realized that if they cared how much noise she made they would have gagged her. So, they had to be somewhere out of earshot of anyone.

The taxi driver, in clear and unbroken English, responded with, "I have no reason to talk to you, and even if I did, I wouldn't answer any of your questions." The taxi driver left the building and could be heard opening and closing the taxi door. Then the taxi started up and drove off. The taxi driver's mission was three-fold; to retrieve Alan's bags from the hotel, to get a different vehicle, and to arrange for food. He was getting the three of them ready for the long drive to Axum in the morning. And with Stef's lack of cooperation, he wasn't looking forward to the trip.

Stef resorted to the only thing left for her to do, pout. And pout she did. In fact, she was very good at it.

Alan took Stef's phone, and using it he texted a message to Elliot that said; "I'm in Ethiopia and all is well."

CHAPTER FIFTY

Arrival in Full Force
Early April, 2025 AD, Addis Abeba, Ethiopia

Kres arrived in Ethiopia the following morning, timing it within one hour of the arrival of his ten agent warriors. His agents had come from Paraguay, by way of Ghana, and flew across the African continent. This made it easier to smuggle weapons into the country. They had chartered a private plane to take them to Ethiopia.

At their arrival there were no handshakes or greetings. Their only hello was a meeting of their eyes. Each of the eleven had stern, serious looks on their faces. They had arrived to do a job, and they were ready to get to work.

The ten NNRL warriors looked like Navy Seals; tough, rugged, in great shape, and ready for action. They were all German and had the appearance of Hitler's storm troopers. When they walked together in a group, they were a scary sight to behold. People stepped aside and let them pass. These weren't men that you wanted to challenge.

Kres and his team took four taxis and headed for town. The drive was slow. The traffic was heavy. It was also very quiet in the cabs. This was a group that was not comfortable with socializing and with a lot of small talk. They were focused on the mission, even though they weren't sure yet what that mission was. And Kres was holding off on telling them anything until he had them all together and away from the listening ears of any cab drivers. Eventually they arrived at the Sheraton and booked themselves into three separate three-bedroom suites. After checking in, Kres asked them all to meet in his suite in thirty minutes so that he could discuss their mission with them.

Thirty minutes goes by quickly when you're unpacking and getting organized. After thirty hours of travel, these men wanted to get the details of their assignments so they could take a nap. When the thirty minutes time was up, they were all anxiously waiting in Kres' room to learn why they had travelled so far.

"We have been infiltrated and sabotaged," Kres started. "First, I learn from my friends in the French underground, often referred to as the French mafia, that Rohit is a traitor and a CIA agent. So, I asked these friends if they would help me take care of Rohit for me. In return I would turn over the assassins of Barjet, who had been one of their well-positioned government stooges until the IOM assassinated him. They readily agreed. During the attack, when Rohit and the two IOM agents were supposed to get killed, Rohit was indeed killed. Unfortunately, the IOM agents got away without a scratch and I was shot," said Kres pointing to his leg. "At the time I believed it to be an accident. But the more I think about it the more suspicious I become. Why did the French mafia avoid killing Barjet's assassins? They had a clear shot at the IOM members, but they hit Rohit and me. It all doesn't make sense.

"This all started because I wanted to use the IOM as a source of nuclear detonators under the disguise of finding the Ark of the Covenant. Of course, finding the Ark that my father had long relished, would be an added bonus. At this point we still have a contract between the NNRL and the IOM to find the Ark of the Covenant. But I have found another source for the detonators and the IOM team is disposable.

The IOM is getting very close to the Ark. It appears to be somewhere in northern Ethiopia, somewhere near Axum. So, my approach, at this point, is to let them finish their search for the Ark, and then eliminate them. Here is our mission. First, to carefully monitor the activities of the IOM operatives, Elliott, and Stef, in their search for the Ark. Then after we have the Ark information that we need, we execute them. They are a liability, and we don't want them to share any knowledge of our operations. Next, we execute the French Mafia idiots that shot me in the foot. I asked the mafia guys to come to Axum so they could have another chance at shooting Elliott and Stef, and they're on their way. And last, but not least, to recover the Ark of the Covenant and bring it back to our base in Paraguay. I'm tired of dealing with the IOM. The headache they cause me is not worth it. Let them finish their search, and then let's get rid of them.

Tomorrow morning we're going to all travel to Axum together. Eventually the IOM team and the French Mafia will be showing up there. We can seal this entire deal up in one neatly wrapped package. Once we get to Axum, we'll see what the IOM and the mafia have planned, and we'll send out teams to accomplish our missions. Are all of you ready?"

A resounding "Yes" was heard from all corners of the room.

"Then let's get a good night's sleep. Tomorrow we head north." Kres advised.

CHAPTER FIFTY-ONE

Arrival in Axum
Early April, 2025 AD, Axum, Ethiopia

Elliott could see Axum off in the distance. It had its own appeal and personality. It was different from Addis Abeba, the capital. It was like a country town, more relaxed, with a type of spiritual reverence. After spending a couple days at the top of a Mesa, and endless long drives through the dusty countryside, Axum looked good. A shower, a comfortable bed, and a meal made out of items he could not recognize, sounded pretty good right now.

As they came closer to the city, Elliott's cell phone signal was restored, and he received a barrage of messages. He tried to read some of the texts, but the road was so bumpy that looking at his Blackberry started to make him car sick. He had text and phone messages from Stef, Alan, Greg, and Kres. Between bumps he was able to make out that everyone was headed to Axum. Apparently, Stef had completed a very successful Jerusalem mission and had learned that Axum was the location of the Ark. And she had reported this information to Kres, Alan, and Greg. And, because of that information Kres and Stef were on their way to Axum. Alan was also meeting up with Stef in Addis Abeba, Ethiopia, prior to her drive north to give her the replica of the Antikythera Mechanism.

Elliott felt excited that the information he had received at Debra Damo had been confirmed by a second source in Jerusalem. But he was frustrated that he and Stef hadn't gone directly to the Bishop the first time they were in Jerusalem and saved all these extra steps. But now there was no doubt. The Ark really does still exist, and its location is Axum, the city off in the horizon that he was slowly rumbling closer to.

There was one final test that he wanted to accomplish. Elliott wanted to test the Antikythera Mechanism to see if it would provide any additional clues for finding the Ark.

"We go to my uncle's hotel?" the taxi driver asked, more in the form of a statement.

"Yes," responded Elliott. Even that location sounded good at this time in spite of being less than five-star quality.

"He be happy you come back," responded the driver. The sun was starting to set. It was getting late. The distance wasn't far, but the ride was rough and very tiring.

"I can't wait," responded Elliott sarcastically, but not in a way the driver could detect.

Elliott's driver had become excited when he learned that Elliott was interested in going back to Axum. He had grown up in this city and was very proud of it. His enthusiasm manifested itself in a never-ending barrage of conversation, giving Elliott a history of the city and a listing of tourist highlights. Elliott enjoyed understanding the culture of the areas he visited, and appreciated learning about Axum, even though the driver's English was somewhat broken.

Axum is located in north central Ethiopia, near the border of Eritrea. From about the 4th century BC till about the 10th century AD the city of Axum had been the capital of the kingdom of Axum. This kingdom was a major naval and trading power in the region and was considered the jumping off point connecting Europe to India during this time period.

In its time, Axum was a very sophisticated nation which had its own written language, called Ge'ez. It also developed its own unique architecture, which is exemplified by large obelisks, thought to date back as early as 2,000 BC or even earlier. The largest of these was about 70 feet tall. The driver went into a long discussion of how the Italian Nazi soldiers stole this obelisk and erected it in Rome as an example of engineering excellence in the ancient world. He explained how it took intensive pressure from the United Nations to finally have it returned to Axum in 2005. In 2008 it was re-installed and dedicated, and, according to the driver, Elliott had to go see it because it was one of the world's greatest engineering marvels.

The Axum nation had a strong Jewish and later Christian influence, aligning itself primarily with the Byzantium Empire. Around the 7th century AD, Islamic domination shifted the power structure of the region and the trade routes to Alexandria began to collapse. The Axumite Empire fell into decline and Arab traders began to dominate the trade routes.

Quarrels arose between the Islamic groups and the Judeo-Christian Axumites over religion, national boundaries, and trading rights. Slowly, Axumite populations and power brokers moved further south and further inland to avoid quarrels with their northern neighbors. The reorganized nation became the much smaller, land lock nation known as Ethiopia.

Axum was the seat of influence during the Solomon period when the Ark was taken south. It was also influential when Christ walked in Jerusalem. Still today, seventy-five percent of Axum's population of 50,000 maintains its membership in the Ethiopian Orthodox Christian Church. The remaining population is a mixture of other Christian denominations, Jewish, Muslims, and non-believers.

Unfortunately, today Ethiopia, including Axum, is economically one of the poorest nations in the world, but its culture was extremely rich. According to the driver, it has a lot to offer the history buff, the religious student, and the tourist.

Besides the obelisks, Elliott was informed that he had to visit the chiesa antica di Santa Maria di Sion (Church of Our Lady Mary of Zion). The grounds of this church, referred to as the Tsion Maryam Church Complex, houses the Chapel of the Tablet. Suddenly Elliott perked up and leaned forward in his seat. The driver went on to explain that this was an Ethiopian Orthodox Church and that the chapel housed the Ark of the Covenant in which lays the Tablet of the Laws known and the Ten Commandments. This location was so important and so revered that it was where the Axumite and Ethiopian emperors were crowned. It is the holiest site in all of Ethiopia and its surrounding nations and, according to the driver, the holiest site in the world.

"So, you know where the Ark of the Covenant is located?" questioned Elliott.

"Of course," replied his driver. "Doesn't everyone? No one is keeping it a secret."

Elliott was in shock. He had already been in the city that contained the Ark of the Covenant. And his taxi driver knew where it was located. All the time spent with the Coptic leadership, and up at the Debra Damo monastery could have been saved simply by asking his taxi driver if he knew where the Ark of the Covenant was located. But, overpowering his frustration, he was also excited. "Can we go see it?"

"Absolutely not. It is kept in the Chapel of the Tablet and only the Guardian is allowed access."

"Can we drive by the Chapel of the Tablet?"

"Of course. It is very close to your hotel. We will need to drive into town on the East end and drive along the North edge of town until we get to the hills along the West. The main road ends at the park where all the obelisks are erected, including the large one that I just described. When we get there, the Axum Church and the church grounds will be on our left, in a large park which dominates this end of town. This is the historic and spiritual section of Axum. You need to get out and walk, but you can see all the historic locations."

"Will you take me there and show me around?"

"Of course. But do you not want to go to the hotel first and rest?"

"No. I'd like to see the Chapel of the Tablet first. Will you be able to guide me around?"

"I am at your service. I have been dedicated to your service for the last couple days and I will continue to do so until you have achieved all that you want."

"Then stay with me and help me until I return to Addis Abeba."

"Of course."

Once they entered the city of Axum the road was paved and smoother and the ride became more comfortable. "This is the only paved road in Axum," explained the driver. They drove past mud and stone buildings eventually arriving at the other end of the paved road, which was the location of Axum's historical sites.

Elliott had become extremely excited. After all his adventures, he realized that a couple of days ago he was within walking distance of the Ark and he didn't even realize it.

Elliott sent a text message to Greg and asked him to send their unmanned recognizance airplane, the S1 on a fly-over, over the Chapel of the Tablet. He told him to get the S1 ready and on its way heading to Axum, Ethiopia and that he would give Greg further instructions on the location when the S1 was in the area. He wanted to take x-rays and scans of the chapel, hoping to see what it contained. Does it truly contain the Ark of the Covenant? Could he really be that close?

Greg texted back that he received the message and would get the S1 ready and off even though it was the middle of the night for him.

Elliott also sent messages to Alan and Stef, wondering why he hadn't heard from them. Has the Antikythera Mechanism been delivered? He hoped that Stef had not run into any trouble along the road to Axum. He was also anxious to tell them about the Chapel of the Tablet.

CHAPTER FIFTY-TWO

More Arrivals in Axum

Early April, 2025 AD, Axum, Ethiopia

Stef was sore, frustrated, and tired. The night had been rough. One foot had been tied to a post. Her hands were untied, which made it a little easier to rest. She was left to sleep on the floor as best she could. But between the hard ground, the dusty air, the never-ending flies, and the stress of being captured, she didn't get a lot of sleep.

"Who did you sell-out to?" Stef angrily challenged Alan.

"I didn't sell out. I was a plant," was his response.

"By who?"

"That's a question you may never get an answer to."

"Why? Are you planning to kill me?"

"Not at all. We just need you for leverage."

"Leverage for what?"

"I'm not the person who can answer that question. For now, you'll just have to be satisfied knowing that you'll be safe. Tell me what you know about the Antikythera Mechanism."

"Is that what this is about? You already had the mechanism in your hands. Why do you need me?"

"It's not about the mechanism. I was just curious about it since I was involved with its theft."

"Then what is this about? Why are you holding me?"

"I can't talk about that." Alan kept trying to talk to her about the Antikythera Mechanism. He had found it extremely interesting and wanted to find out what Stef knew. But she had lost interest. She refused to give Alan any information that may help him. And since the Bishop in Jerusalem had confirmed the location of the Ark, it seemed irrelevant. Now that she was a captive, she had even less of an interest in talking.

It wasn't long before the sun rose. Stef was yanked up on her feet and pushed into the back of a windowless van. The van was unfinished on the inside. One of Stefs hands was cuffed to a sidewall of the van, and they were off. The van had a metal floor. It was rough and dirty and had obviously been used for construction. She could tell that this wasn't going to be a fun day. She could not see outside so she had no idea where she was going. And the road was dusty, rutted, and windy. This was going to be a long hard day.

After bumping along for about two hours, Stef could no longer contain her car sickness, and she threw up, making sure to aim for Alan's shoes. Alan wasn't pleased. He thought about hitting her, but he still had an attraction for her and hitting her seemed barbaric. Alan wanted to be a gentleman to the lady he admired, even if he was now forced to hold her hostage. He just couldn't treat her like he would anyone else. Unfortunately, as he wiped her vomit off his shoes, he could see that her feelings for him would probably never be mutual.

The drive seemed to go on forever. And for Stef it just got worse. She was too uncomfortable to sleep, which would probably have been her only reprieve from the car sickness. So, she had to just sit on the hard metal floor and endure. At least the car sickness kept her distracted from the bruises and welts that were building up on her butt.

The drive was taken in three three-hour increments, which seemed like an eternity to everyone, including the driver. When they stopped for a bathroom break or food, Stef wasn't allowed to leave the van. They gave her a bucket for a toilet, and for vomiting. She was too sick to eat anything.

Alan repeatedly tried to make calls or send text messages, but his efforts were futile. He wanted to get updates on what he was to do next. His frustrations came out in sighs and foot stomps. At one point he hit the side of the van, as if that would make the phone suddenly work.

Alan's struggles with the phone made Stef realize that he was not working on his own. He was someone else's puppet. But who? Who had ordered him to hold her hostage? And what could she do about it? Did Elliott know? Was there anyone else in the IOM organization involved? She tried to concentrate on these questions in an attempt to keep her distracted from her sickness, but it only partially worked.

Eventually they arrived in Axum. Stef was relieved to hear the driver's comment; "We're finally here." They pulled into a large garage at the edge of town and the garage door closed behind them. Stef quickly realized this wasn't going to be a stay at the Sheraton. What she didn't realize was that there weren't any Sheratons in Axum, so that wasn't even an option. Here, in Axum, a Motel 6 would be considered a luxury hotel.

Alan disconnected Stef from the side-rib of the van where she had been fastened. He immediately connected her two arms together behind her back using handcuffs. She was a formidable opponent in battle, and he didn't relish any of her kicks to the head, which he had seen her do during training exercises. He helped her get out of the van and brought her to a table in one corner of the garage. He pushed her down into one of the chairs.

The garage was the width of a double car garage, but twice the depth. The back half had been converted into a make-shift residence, with a couple of couches, a sink and countertop that served as a kitchen. There was a small hot-plate stove, and a dining room table. It wasn't much, but it was better than the floor of the van. The garage only had one exit, other than the garage door, which was a door near the center of the back wall.

Along the left wall of the garage were several single beds. They looked like old army cots. None of the beds were made up. They had blankets and sheets strewn on them. There were a couple of men sitting on two of the beds, having a heated conversation about something in a language that Stef could not understand. Other than these two men, Stef, Alan, and their driver, there was no one else around.

The driver brought Stef some bread, and some meat that looked like chicken, a bottle of water, and told her to make herself a sandwich.

Gerhard Plenert

"What do you expect me to do with that?" asked Stef, referring to her hand cuffs.

But Alan already knew what he was going to do. He had the driver hold a gun aimed at Stef, and he took out a second pair of handcuffs and locked Stef's right leg to the chair. He disconnected the handcuffs that held her hands behind her and reconnected the handcuffs back together again in front of her, allowing her enough mobility to make herself a sandwich.

Stef still didn't feel all that great after the rough ride. Her car sickness hadn't completely dissipated. But she decided to go ahead with the sandwich in hopes that it might make her feel better.

"Are you going to tell me what's going on here," she asked Alan.

"You're leverage. That's all. We need you in case things go South."

'Who's 'we'?"

"Can't tell."

"What's happening that might go South?"

"Can't tell."

"What can you tell me?"

"Only that you're going to be stuck here for a couple of day. After that, assuming that everything goes as planned; you'll be free to go."

"So, what do I do for the next couple of days?"

"Eat, drink, and sleep. Enjoy the vacation."

"This isn't the vacation I would have chosen."

"Nor I." Alan would have enjoyed spending his vacation with Stef. But this wasn't the way he would have arranged it.

CHAPTER FIFTY-THREE

Still More Arrivals in Axum
Early April, 2025 AD, Axum, Ethiopia

Marcello wasn't far behind Stef. In fact, his team had seen Alan and Stef's van several times during their drive to Axum but didn't realize what he was seeing.

He pulled into the Yeha Hotel; part of the government run Ghion chain. It was one of the nicest hotels in town, but at the Motel-6 standard. And a one-night stay would run about 37 US$, very inexpensive by USA standards. He sent Conrad into the lobby to arrange for three rooms, which he had reserved earlier in the day when they were still down in Addis Abeba. He preferred the second-floor rooms, in this two-story hotel, because it improved surveillance, if that became necessary.

"Let's get settled in and meet back in my room in about thirty minutes," suggested Marcello. The three each got settled into their rooms and as planned, converged back to Marcello's room.

Part of Marcello's standard equipment, that he had brought with him was an anti-bug, high frequency scrambler. He started it up in the room to make sure that their conversations would be secure. He opened the conversation. "Let's discuss our situation and formulate some kind of plan. What we know for certain is that the IOM and the NNRL are both coming to Axum to locate the Ark of the Covenant. They may be here already. Additionally, the NNRL thinks the French mafia is on their way here to assassinate the IOM team members. Luckily, I have intercepted that process and they think I represent the mafia. We may be able to use that to our advantage.

We also keep getting messages that the NNRL is planning some kind of Hitler Birthday celebration which may be nothing, or it could be something extremely serious. We just don't know. The primary reason we're here is to learn more about what the IOM and the NNRL have planned. I'm concerned that there is something under the surface here that we're missing, and which could have serious repercussions. Does anyone have any thoughts on how we should approach this?"

'Well, I see this as quite simple," Conrad started. "It's all about the Ark. Everyone wants to capture it and steal it. We need to beat them to the location of the Ark, and seal off the surrounding area."

"I agree," interjected Joe. "If we do that, they will come to us. Then we'll just have to wait and see what happens."

"Good," responded Marcello. But at this point it was getting late in the day. "I'm going to visit the location of the Ark. We'll set up eight-hour shifts staking out the chapel where the Ark is located. We'll need to stay in constant contact with each other. I'll take the first shift and then I'll call one of you after my eight hours to come and take over. I'll send the driver to come and get you. I'm anxious to see what we're up against. But I'm also looking for something more. I just don't believe that the Ark is the only reason all these individuals are in Axum."

"I'll take the next shift," Conrad volunteered.

"Excellent. I'll call you when it's your turn."

Early April, 2025 AD, Axum, Ethiopia

Alan received the call he had been waiting for. "Hello."

"I'm here," responded the caller. "Cover her eyes and let me in."

Alan put a pillowcase over Stef's head and tied it loosely at the bottom. He went to the door at the back of the building, opened it, and said, "Come on in."

"Thanks," said Marcello as he entered the garage. Then addressing the entire group, he said; "Do not use names. Did you have any trouble getting her up here?"

"The roads were rough, but we made it fine," answered Alan.

"No kidding they were rough," blurted Stef from within her pillowcase. "My butt bones have been chipped. Who are you anyway? Why can't I see you? Are you afraid I'd recognize you?"

"I'm no one you need to be concerned with," responded Marcello. Then, turning his attention back to Alan, he asked; "Are you going to be OK here for the next couple of days? I need you to keep an eye on her. She may turn out to be critical to our operation."

"No problem," responded Alan. "What's the plan anyway?"

"That's the problem. We're not sure what the plan is. We think there is more to the NNRL Nazis than just an interest in the Ark of the Covenant, but we're not sure what that interest is. Until we find out, we'll have to lay low and just observe."

"Observe who?" asked Stef. "Do you know if Elliott is OK?"

"I'm sure Elliott is fine," responded Marcello. "Now shut up so we can talk."

"Don't you tell me to shut up you coward. Come here and try to make me shut up. Untie me you coward and I'll show you who gets shut up." Stef was at her prime in anger and frustration, and she was taking it out on Marcello.

"Let's go outside," suggested Marcello to Alan.

Stef could hear the door close. It was now very silent, except for the occasional rat that Stef heard running across the floor. She raised her legs off the floor. She was sure that one of the rats would run up her leg if she left her foot on the floor. She wished Alan and his friend would return so that she could be distracted by their conversation. The rats made her nervous.

CHAPTER FIFTY-FOUR

Return to Axum
Early April, 2025 AD, Axum, Ethiopia

It wasn't long before Elliott's driver came to a stop in a parking lot next to a field filled with large obelisks. This was obviously the area that the driver had been describing during the last portion of their trip to Axum. The driver pointed across the street to an area that looked like a park with a large church in the middle. "The church and the Chapel of the Tablet is over there," he directed. "This is the closest parking lot. But we need to go over there."

They got out of the car and the driver now became a tour guide. He pointed out the obelisks, highlighting the one that was "stolen by the Nazis." He then led Elliott across the street to the park grounds. This area was well maintained and had a spiritual reverence about it. "This is where the Church of Our Lady Mary of Zion is located. Actually, there are two versions of the church, the old church is in the back and the newer, larger church is the one that you see."

"Is the Chapel of the Tablet somewhere over there?" quizzed Elliott. That was really the only thing he was interested in, but he pretended to be a good tourist in order to divert attention away from his central focus: the identification and recovery of the Ark.

"Yes, but it is on the back side near the hill."

The guide showed Elliott through both of the churches. The importance of the Ark to Ethiopian Orthodox Christianity was strongly apparent. There were vestibules with replicas of the Ark in every church. And there were murals showing when Solomon's son Menelik, the first king of Ethiopia, and the son of the Queen of Sheba, brought the Ark down to the ruling Axumite kingdom which is now known as Ethiopia. Elliott got more and more excited by the minute. He couldn't wait for what he considered to be the highlight of his tour; seeing the Chapel of the Tablet which contained the Ark of the Covenant. Of course, if no one is allowed into the Chapel except the guardian, how would anyone know if the Ark really existed.

Finally, leaving the second and older church, the guide led Elliott around the side of the building and pointed out a small chapel which was surrounded by a fence. Pointing he said, "That's the Chapel of the Tablet."

Elliott's first impression was, "that's it?" It seemed inappropriately small. It was in the middle of a dry, brush filled area, not kept up any nicer than any other area in Axum. It was surrounded by a six-foot high red metal fence which was about ten feet away from the chapel on the sides and back and about thirty feet away in the front. The area of the chapel was about the size of a two-car garage, but the height was between twenty-five and thirty feet. The walls looked like they were made of solid rock rectangles. The building had a ten-foot-high door centered on the front side of the building. There were also double windows on either side of the door. The windows had shutters and were closed hiding any view of the inside. It also blocked light from getting in. All four sides of the building looked the same except for the door on the front. On the roof, in the center, was a small half globe with what looked like a weathervane on the top.

Elliott wondered how the guardian could live within this small enclosure. It didn't seem adequate to support living quarters for the guardian, let alone also house the Ark.

"The guardian has food and supplies brought to him daily," explained the guide. "He has dedicated his life to the protection of the Ark, and he is the only person who will ever be allowed to see the Ark. He is a monk and that is his life. His bride is the Ark, and his life revolves around its protection."

Elliott noted the lack of security. This one little Ethiopian monk was the only protection afforded to something as historically and religiously significant as the Ark of the Covenant. It almost seemed disrespectful. It would be incredibly easy to break in and snatch the Ark. The trick would be getting out of Axum with the Ark. Anything like a helicopter or small plane coming into Axum would surely be noticed. There would need to be a diversion of some type. He could see that there would need to be some careful planning if the taking of the Ark was to remain clandestine.

Elliott took numerous pictures, trying to document the area so that he would be able to look closely at all the details as he formulated his plan. He couldn't identify any security system. There were no alarms or cameras. He couldn't decide if he was incredibly lucky, or if he was somehow being duped and misled. And being duped seemed like a real possibility.

Elliott and his driver turned tour guide walked around the grounds a little more, the driver pointing out other highlights and features that would captivate the normal tourist. But for Elliott, the curiosity had been satisfied or peaked; he couldn't decide which.

The ride to the Yeha Hotel was quick and uneventful. Elliott checked into the hotel and was given a room on the bottom floor. This put him near the parking lot, which was noisier than some of the upstairs rooms, but he was too tired to object. Elliott was delighted to lay back in a semi-soft, but not necessarily all that clean, bed. It was better than a cave, or a bunk in a dormitory full of monks, or in the back of a clunky old taxi.

As he lay there, he again became concerned about Alan and Stef. He decided to ping Stef once again with a text message. "How is my hot mama doing? Are you in Axum yet? Get up here. I have plans for you." Stef would know what types of plans he had in mind. She always accused him of having a one-track bedroom mind.

After about three minutes a message came back from Stef's phone; "Stef is being held captive. Will not be able to respond. Will be updating you more later. This phone will be turned off and the battery removed. Do not try to respond or to trace."

Elliott sat up in his bed in shock and said, "What the heck is going on here? Held by whom? Why would Stef be kidnapped? Where is she?"

Shortly after this he received a message from Greg; "The S1 is over Africa and is closing in on Axum. Do you have any specific directions?"

Elliott typed back the following instructions: "Stef and possibly also Alan have been kidnapped. Try to locate them by tracking their cell phones or anything else you can think of. Find out if they got to Ethiopia, if they got a ride from the airport, etc. I received a message on Stef's phone one day ago that she had made it to Ethiopia, but I don't know if she sent the message --- the message didn't contain the usual flirty comments that she normally makes to me, so I don't think it was authentic. I think someone else was using her phone. I don't even know if it was sent from Ethiopia. Let me know if you learn anything. Use the S1 any way you can to find out what's going on.

"The Ark is secondary. But, when you get a chance, scan the Chapel of the Tablet which is behind the Church of Our Lady Mary of Zion. I want to know what's inside that building. Then, when I have that information from you, I will give you additional instructions on the Ark."

Within minutes Elliott's focus had changed. No longer was he scheming how to get the Ark out of Ethiopia. His new focus was on Stef, and of course Alan. And he felt helpless. He felt he had his fill of this clandestine circus. He wanted to get out of the business, especially if it started to put someone as important as Stef at risk. He swore to himself that if he got her back safe, he would finish up this mission and quit the business. He found himself on his knees. This was too important to leave to his own capabilities. This required help. And it was in these times of extreme need that he always resorted to prayer.

Elliott wasn't quite finished with his prayers when he heard several cars pull up. Several doors opened and closed in the car, and he heard men talking. This wouldn't have been unusual except that Elliott thought he recognized one of the voices. He went to the window and cracked it just enough to peek out. There stood Kres with an entourage of ten Arian looking musclemen following him into the hotel.

"Oh my gosh," was all Elliott could say. "These guys look like they're ready for war. I wonder if they're behind Stef's kidnapping?" But Elliott knew he had very little chance of taking on this group by himself. He would have to time his actions appropriately.

He carefully thought through and considered his next step. He decided he would send Kres a text message to see if his response was friendly. "I'm in Axum and think I have found the location of the Ark. How are you doing?" was the message.

A few minutes later he received the message back, "I'm travelling to Axum. Tell me what hotel you're staying at and I'll try to join you. Where are you located so we can meet?"

Elliott knew this meant trouble. Why wouldn't he say that he was already in Axum? And what about all these fellow soldiers? Something just did not ring right, and he began to smell a rat. Elliott decided not to answer right away. Instead, he decided to text Greg. "Do we have any listening tools aboard the S1?"

"Of course," came back the delayed response.

Elliott decided that this conversation required too much texting, so he gave Greg a call, "Are you able to spy in on the rooms in Yeha Hotel and pick up the various conversations? I need you to separate out the conversations so that you can pick up on specific clue words or phrases, like Stef, Alan, or Ark of the Covenant?"

"It will take some programming, but 'yes,' it can be done. I'll start the surveillance immediately and start recording all conversations. I'll build the search algorithms and initiate them as soon as I have them ready," was the response. "By the way, Stef, and Alan both arrived in Addis Abeba, Ethiopia and Alan had checked into the Sheraton there. But Stef never checked in. That's where the trail ends. The text from Stef's phone to you was made after her arrival, but I suspect she was already captured at that point."

Elliott's thought process continued as he talked out loud to Alan. "Whoever sent the message must have known that Stef would send me a text as soon as she arrived. They must have known something about our organization. That leaves me highly suspicious about the kidnapper's intentions. It must be someone who knows us. Someone with inside information."

"Agreed. I'll let you know as soon as I learn more."

They hung up the call just as Elliott received another text from Kres, "Are you there? I didn't receive a response."

Elliott responded with, "I'm travelling, and connectivity is hit and miss, but I'll let you know where I'm staying as soon as I get it tied down." Elliott knew that Kres would see through this, especially since earlier Elliott had told him he was already in Axum. But he would rather have Kres wondering than to let him know that he knew they were staying in the same hotel. And if he gave the name of a different hotel, Kres would probably go there and find out soon enough that Elliott was lying.

Elliott was at a loss. He didn't know what to do next. He knew where the Ark was, but he didn't know how to get it out of Ethiopia. He knew that Stef and Alan were in Ethiopia, but he didn't know where. And he had no idea why they would have been kidnapped. He saw Kres enter the hotel with his ten goons, but he didn't know what their purpose was either. And why there were so many of them. He concluded that they must be behind the kidnapping. Elliott felt helpless. He felt like a lone soldier out in the middle of a war with the enemy all around him and no way to get out. His only hope was that Greg and the S1 would learn something that would be useful.

Then an idea came to him like a ringing bell. "Of course," he blurted out. He grabbed his Blackberry and typed in an e-mail message to Greg, "Do you have any fire-power on the S1, or is it completely stripped for surveillance?"

About five minutes later the response came back, "We leave a small caliber weapon on board for emergencies. What do you have in mind?"

Then Elliott texted; "I have an emergency. How small is the caliber? Is it small enough to take someone out?"

"Easily. Who is the target?"

"I'll let you know when I figure it out."

CHAPTER FIFTY-FIVE

The Chapel of the Tablet
Early April, 2025 AD, Axum, Ethiopia

Jano and his two novice Coptic adherents arrived in Axum dreary and worn out after their long drive from Addis Abeba, Ethiopia. They went directly to the offices of the Bishop at the Church of Our Lady Mary of Zion and explained the potential threat to the Ark of the Covenant and to the Chapel of the Tablet which housed it.

"Please wait here," the Bishop, locally referred to as the Pope or Father, told Jano. "I want to confer with the guardian of the Chapel. I'll be right back."

The Pope took the threat seriously. He went out to discuss the situation with the guardian. However, no one, not even the Pope, was allowed within the fence surrounding the Chapel. And yelling was highly irreverent. So, the Pope did what only he was allowed to do. He took a small pebble and threw it against the door of the Chapel.

Nothing happened. He waited for at least fifteen minutes. The Pope was just beginning to bend over to pick up a second stone when the door to the Chapel slowly opened and the guardian came out and walked over to the fence.

"What can I do for you, your honor," the guardian monk reverently asked.

"We seem to have a serious threat against the Ark. Two organizations are teaming up and trying to steal it. And apparently they are quite a formidable force."

"Thank you for the warning," responded the guardian. Then, to the dismay of the Pope, the guardian turned around and went back into the Chapel, closing the door behind him.

The Pope went back to his office where Jano and his associates were waiting. He reported that the guardian is now aware of the situation. Jano asked, "What can we do to help?"

"Nothing," replied the Pope. "Only go to the church and say prayers for the safety of the Ark."

After leaving the Pope's offices, Jano turned to his novices and suggested; "We should be more vigilant. We should set up a watch at the Chapel of the Tablet. We should take turns watching who comes and goes. Perhaps we should get some video cameras so we can record the people that come to the chapel. Then, if there is a problem, we will have a record of it for the police."

"I will take the first watch," spoke one of the novices.

"While you are doing that, I'll come up with some camera equipment and bring it to you. But first we must obey the wishes of the Pope and say prayers."

Jano and his associates left the Pope's office area and went over to the church, lit two candles each, and knelt quietly in prayer.

Early April, 2025 AD, Axum, Ethiopia

Marcello had left the garage where Alan and Stef were hold up. He had instructed Alan to keep their phones turned off with the battery removed. He gave Alan a new cell phone which would be used for future communication. After leaving the building, he walked to the car that was waiting for him. It was the same car and driver he had contracted in Addis Abeba. He had hired the car for the full length of his stay. The driver slept in the car and was always ready and available.

He instructed the driver to take him to the Church of Our Lady Mary of Zion. He wanted to walk the grounds and see the Chapel of the Tablet. During the drive he sent a text to Kres, identifying himself as the French Mafia. The message read; "Am in Axum awaiting further instructions."

There was no immediate response, so he assumed that Kres was sleeping or out of signal range. He needed to maintain his pretended role as the mafia assassin. This may be the edge that he needs to prevent disaster.

After arriving at the chapel, and walking the grounds, Marcello was disappointed. This chapel wasn't much to look at. He expected something more dramatic than just a rectangular box about the size of a one-car garage. It had a limited amount of decorations around it and seemed to be reasonably well kept up, but other than that it was not noteworthy. He knew that this was the place where everything was going to come down, but he wasn't altogether sure what it was that was going to happen. He knew that the NNRL was after the IOM, and that the French Mafia was supposedly after the IOM, and he knew that both the NNRL and the IOM were after the Ark. These were all violent organizations. Nazis vs. Knights Templar Assassins vs. the French Mafia. There was bound to be fireworks. And how it would end up, no one knew.

Marcello's biggest concern was the Nazis. They seemed to be the most volatile of the organizations. And he would love to see their leader eliminated. But to proclaim this as his goal would be unethical. After all, he wasn't supposed to be one of the assassins.

Kidnapping Stef was his security blanket. If everything went wrong, he would use her to help him define next steps. She may be leverage against Elliott. Or she may have useful information that he could use against the NNRL or the IOM. But he didn't want to use drugs or torture on her until it became critical. At this point, he and his team would just watch and see.

He found himself an old wooden splintery bench to sit on. He picked one that was isolated and out of sight of any traffic. He sat and watched. He would take his fist turn tonight and sit out his eight hours. Then he would text Conrad to let him know that the driver was on his way. He would wait for Conrad to get there. Then Marcello would go back to the hotel and try to get some sleep. He was sure that nothing would happen tonight. But he didn't want to miss anything. He anxiously looked forward to getting back to the room so he could fall asleep and get some much-needed rest.

About three hours into his watch, well after midnight, Marcello perked up. There were footsteps approaching, which was very unusual since he hadn't seen anyone during his entire stay. Who would be coming at this time of night unless it was one of the players in this game of espionage? Then he realized there were more than one set of footsteps. Marcello guessed it was at least three men coming up. It was just a matter of seconds before he realized his guess was one short. There were four individuals, and one of them looked like the photos he had seen of Kres.

Marcello silently moved around behind a bush that was close to the bench. He continued to stay even further out of sight, hoping that he wouldn't be seen. At this point, all he wanted to do was observe these guys and follow them. He couldn't believe his luck. One of the "bad guys" had walked directly into his trap.

Kres and his group walked around the Chapel of the Tablet. Marcello could hear one of them say in French, "This is it? This is why we have eleven of us here?"

The man that Marcello thought was Kres came back with, "There's more to our trip here than just getting the Ark. This is just one small step in our over-all objective. But I agree; recovering the Ark looks like it won't be too hard."

The men walked around a little more, and then left. And Marcello snuck out from behind his bush, staying out of sight. He decided to track where they were going. He wanted to see where the NNRL members were staying. It would be easier to keep an eye on them if he could monitor them twenty-four hours a day.

They were obviously walking back to their hotel. That wasn't much of a surprise. Everything in Axum was within walking distance. And the town shut down hours ago so finding a taxi at this time of night wasn't even an option.

Marcello had to be extra careful. His presence could easily be recognized. He couldn't blend into any crowds.

Much to Marcello's surprise, Kres and team turned in at the Yeha Hotel, the same hotel Marcello was staying at. This would become tricky. He needed to stay hidden from them. Even though he had never met Kres, he knew that it was possible that Kres had seen pictures of him. And that would be risky. Also, there weren't that many "white" Western tourists, and he would tend to stand out.

Marcello watched the rooms Kres' team entered and made note of the room numbers. Then he headed back to the Chapel of the Tablet to continue his surveillance. During his walk back he sent texts to all of his teammates telling them that they needed to keep an eye out for the NNRL warriors. He informed them that they were in the same hotel and he gave them the room numbers that he saw them enter. They were amazingly close to Marcello's rooms.

The walk back to the chapel and the rest of the surveillance shift were uneventful. At the appointed time, Marcello sent a text to Carl and sent the driver after him. The shift change occurred on schedule. Carl informed Marcello that they were now taking turns watching the NNRL rooms as well. There had not been any activity after they received his message. Marcello left to go to his room and was delighted to be able to lie down and get some sleep.

CHAPTER FIFTY-SIX

The Chapel of the Tablet Stake Out
Early April, 2025 AD, Axum, Ethiopia

Elliot was awakened by the noise of his blackberry receiving a message. He had fallen asleep in his chair, never having made it to bed. He jumped up with a start, forgetting momentarily where he was.

Looking at the blackberry he saw that it was Greg. He quickly checked to see what the e-mail message was. "No new news on Stef or Alan. There is a lot of chatter about the Ark of the Covenant, but most of it was from tourists. But I did record a conversation that said something about an assassination plot organized by the French mafia to take revenge on the IOM. And I heard something about revenge being taken on the French mafia because they failed in their attempted assassination and shot Kres instead. For which Kres and team were now going to take revenge on them. It sounds like the assassination plot in Alexandria was aimed at you and Stef, and that it originated with the NNRL. I've put those voice prints on constant surveillance to see what else I can learn."

"Interesting," Elliott said to himself. But this also raised a level of concern. Now both the French Mafia and the NNRL had him and Stef in their sights. Had they already taken revenge on Stef? He sincerely hoped not.

Elliott replied with the message; "Thanks and let me know the minute you hear anything else." It seemed strange that Greg, who was half a world away in Nevada, was able to listen to conversations in a hotel room that was just above him.

Just then a second e-mail came in from Greg; "There is definitely something in the Chapel of the Tablet, and it is about the size and shape of the Ark of the Covenant. I've attached the scan images so you can see what it looks like."

Elliott couldn't access the pictures on his Blackberry, so he had to turn on his computer and download the images. They were interesting, but not conclusive. There was definitely something in the Chapel that looked like it could be the Ark.

There would be no rest for Elliott. Another e-mail came in from Greg. "That's a busy boy," said Elliott to himself. This time the e-mail said, "A separate conversation, in a separate room, but in the same hotel, referenced the French mafia and talked about the need to keep an eye on the NNRL and the IOM. I can't make out who they are. But it appears you have someone else to deal with and they don't sound like the mafia boys. They sound like they're just watching what you're doing, rather than trying to assassinate anyone."

Elliott threw up his arms, and said out loud; "What is going on here? How many players are in this game? We have the NNRL, the French mafia, the IOM, and now some spooks, all here at the same time. This is turning into a nightmare. We have the NNRL and the French mafia gunning for us. And Stef and Alan are being held prisoners somewhere. This is totally out of hand." He had no idea what his next steps should be. He didn't even know what instructions to give Greg, other than; "Let me know the minute you learn anything new."

Elliott was exhausted. His concern for Stef was overpowered by his body's need to sleep. He lay down on his bed and, before he realized it, he was asleep.

About one hour later he woke up with a start. Inspiration had come to him in a dream. He immediately sent a text to Greg giving him instructions on next steps. He typed; "I need to even out the playing field. I need your help to reduce the competition. I also need you to follow anyone that comes out of these rooms. They may be able to lead us to Stef. Do you have the ability to track more than one person at a time?"

The response came back; "Tracking only works as long as they are visible. If they enter a building, I can monitor the conversations, and I can identify warm bodies, but I won't know for sure which body is the person I'm following. I can track multiples as long as they're within a reasonable distance of each other. Let me know more about what you mean by 'reducing the competition.' Let me know as soon as you've decided what help you need. I'll update you on any movements."

Just then Elliott heard French conversations and men walking down the stairs of the hotel. He peeked out of his room in time to see three of Kres' team. He quickly sent a text to Greg.

Early April, 2025 AD, Axum, Ethiopia

Morning had arrived and it was Marcello's turn at surveillance, this time in his hotel room, watching the rooms of the NNRL. The hotel was in the shape of an L, and Marcello's room was located in such a way that he could peek through a crack in the curtains and see Kres' rooms along the other inside wing of the hotel. The curtains were converted towels that were nailed above the window. They were adequate, but tacky. It was an ideal location for surveillance. The other two CIA agents had rooms right next to Marcello, one on each side.

It wasn't long before he saw three of Kres' team leave one of the rooms. Marcello recognized one of the men from the previous night. He watched them go down the stairs and start walking down the street. Marcello made a quick call to Conrad, who was back from his stake-out of the Chapel of the Tablet. It was Joe's turn to watch the Chapel. Conrad was trying to catch up on some sleep, but Marcello had a different idea. Marcello asked Conrad to take over surveillance of Kres' rooms because he was going to follow some of Kres' men.

Conrad's room was one room closer to the intersection of the two hotel wings. This made the angle slightly tighter for him to keep watch on Kres' rooms. The biggest problem was that he was so sleepy. It would be challenging to keep his eyes from closing.

After the Nazis had successfully made their way down the stairs, Marcello slipped out of his room and started tailing Kres' soldiers as closely as seemed reasonable to avoid detection. The three men left the hotel complex and turned left, heading down the street. They walked for about one block, then took a left turn into an alley, dropping out of sight of Marcello. It took Marcello a few minutes to get to the corner of the alley. He didn't want to seem too anxious. He wanted to stay anonymous. He started to casually walk past the alley, not sure what he would find in the alley and not wanting to be obvious.

Halfway across the entrance to the alley, Marcello came to a dead halt. He couldn't help but stare down the length of the alley. There, lying on the ground, where the three men he was trailing. Each one had a large, bloody, gaping hole in their chest. Whatever hit them had hit them so hard that it had knocked them backward causing them to fall on their backs to the ground. Their clothes showed large blood stains, looking like they had been hit by a missile, not just shot with a bullet. How was this possible? He hadn't heard anything. He scanned up and down the alley and could see nothing that would indicate a shooter had been present. Yet here they lay, dead in the alley.

Marcello was smart enough to move on. He didn't want to be identified with the shooting. Who would have done this? The IOM are supposedly working with the NNRL. Why would they do this? And it couldn't be the French mafia because he had intercepted control of that avenue of interaction and communication. Apparently, someone else was involved in this game. And he had no idea who it could be.

He had to stay anonymous. He needed to find out more about what was going on. He ducked into a small shop and spent some time there looking at souvenirs. He purchased a few postcards and some stamps. Then he stepped out and continued down the road away from the alley. He decided to play tourist for a few moments and went up to view the obelisks. They were fascinating, in that they had been constructed thousands of years ago, with minimal tooling, and then moved and erected here at this location. How was that even possible?

But he had work to do and he needed to get back to his hotel room. He headed back down the road toward the hotel, making sure to stay across the street from the alley. By the time he arrived across from the alley, he noticed that the police had arrived and were studying the bodies, trying to make sense of what happened. "Good luck," was Marcello's only comment, not to anyone in particular.

Marcello was baffled. What had just happened? How did they get shot? And by whom? And why? The mystery kept getting deeper and more confusing all the time. He arrived back at the hotel and did his best to get back into his room without being detected by the NNRL. He was sure he had been successful.

Early April, 2025 AD, Axum, Ethiopia

"Where are those idiots?" asked one of Kres' team in frustration. "How hard is it to get some bread and cheese?" Apparently the three members of Kres' team that Marcello had been tracking were sent on a mission to retrieve food. And it was taking longer than anticipated.

"Go find out what happened to them," responded Kres. Two more members of his team left the room in search of the three companions. They weren't gone five minutes when they were heard running back up the stairs. Then a stumble was heard followed by the grinding sound of flesh hitting pavement. Kres opened the door to see his two warriors had fallen, dead in their tracks, large gaping bullet holes through their heads.

"Get them in here quickly before we have the police show up and we have to answer a lot of questions," Kres yelled. The two dead warriors were retrieved and pulled into the hotel room.

"WHAT THE...#!!?? IS GOING ON HERE?" Kres yelled. "I suppose the other three were shot as well. We've lost half of our team and we don't even know by whom or from where."

Just then a text message came through for Kres. He read it silently, "Fuels cell has the goods and is heading to rendezvous." Kres had set specific report-in times for his cells. And this was one of those times.

"Wow!" exclaimed Kres out loud without explaining. Everyone stared at him, but he didn't explain. This was on a "need to know" basis.

A couple of minutes later he received another message. "Fuse cell on schedule."

He responded to both cells with the text; "Proceed as per plan." Then he constructed a second text, sending this one off to his headquarters in Paraguay. "I need you to send a small Lear jet to Axum. I have a package that I need to ship back to headquarters."

Little did Kres know that there was an S1 stealth drone plane flying overhead picking up all conversations and communications coming from the hotel.

Kres looked up from his Blackberry and spoke to his team, "Our agenda has just changed. We're getting the Ark tonight. After we get it, we're going to the Axum airport and getting on a plane. We're heading East, over the water. No one will expect that. We'll drop our cargo off at headquarters. Then we'll head to the United States east coast. We have a confidential destiny in Washington DC which needs to be fulfilled. What we do in DC will trigger the re-emergence of the Furor's Reich. The Ark is the power of God which will guarantee our success. Whoever has the Ark will have success in their battles. We need it for that reason. And the demonstration we have planned for Washington DC will be the first step in bringing us toward our role of world domination."

"I don't know who's killing off our team. Besides, there's no reason to delay. We execute tonight."

The team knew better than to ask too many questions. They accepted what he said and planned to spend their last night in Axum. One of the warriors spoke up; "What about the French mafia who tried to kill you?"

"Good point. Let's solve that problem tonight as well."

Kres dialed his phone. "Hello," came from the other end.

"This is Kres. Who am I speaking with?"

"Marcello. How are you Kres? What can I do for you?"

"I need to meet with you some time. Did you come to Axum as planned?"

"Yes. We are here. When and where would you like to meet?"

"How about midnight at the Chapel of the Tablet?"

"Excellent. I'll see you then."

Kres disconnected the call and turned to his warriors. "We're going to literally 'Kill two birds with one stone tonight.'" Kres didn't realize that Marcello was a CIA agent who had infiltrated the French mafia in an attempt to learn about their activities. The hit on Barjet, and Kres' interest in taking out the IOM, had worked entirely to his favor. And Marcello was conveniently able to inform on Rohit and have him taken out as well. It was Marcello, using his clandestine connections with the French mafia that had arranged the hit in Alexandria. Little did Kres know that Marcello was just a few rooms away in the same hotel.

Just then there was a knock on the door where Kres and his men were hold out. One of the warriors peeked out the window and whispered; "Cops. I think they spotted me peeking out of the window."

Simultaneously, without saying a word, everyone looked down at the two bodies on the floor. How are they going to explain that? Then, to everyone's surprise, Kres said; "Let them in."

One of the warriors opened the door slightly and asked the officers what they needed. The officers identified themselves and explained that three men were found dead in an alley one block away, and they had room keys to this room. They needed someone to come down and identify the bodies and to answer a few questions. "Of course," responded the warrior. "Come on in."

As the officers entered the room, the door was quickly shut behind them, and they found themselves in a room with five large burly men, one small wimpy looking man, and two dead bodies. They weren't sure what they had got themselves into and instinctively reached for their weapons, but that turned out to be the last thing they ever did. Before the guns were out of their holsters, their necks were broken.

"Apparently, we're collecting bodies in this hotel room. Let's go to one of the other rooms, in case more police show up. At least then we won't have to answer questions." They peeked out to see if there was anyone else around. Seeing no one, they quickly changed rooms.

From a hotel room, five rooms over, Marcello was peeking through his window and watching all their movements. He saw the death of the two NNRL Nazis, and how their friends quickly pulled their bodies into the room. He searched the roof line but couldn't find any sign of an assassin. He had no idea where the shots originated. He also saw the arrival of the police. He took note of the fact that the police didn't leave. He also noted the sudden and quick change of rooms.

And overhead, the S1 was doing its job, with Greg at the controls in Elko, Nevada, on the other side of the world.

CHAPTER FIFTY-SEVEN

Birthday Plans
Early April, 2025 AD, Axum, Ethiopia

"Five down and six to go," was the start of the phone call Elliott received from Greg. Then he went on the relay the message Kres had received from his cell, and the messages he had sent out. Greg also relayed Kres' comments about going after the Ark tonight. After that Greg added, "It doesn't sound good for DC. Based on the text messages and from what I can read between the lines from the conversations between the NNRL team members, it appears the NNRL is importing the components of a nuclear device into the United States and transferring it to the DC area. It sounds like they're planning something risky."

"Got it," replied Elliott. "Keep up your surveillance and let me know if you learn anything else. Nothing on Stef?"

"Nothing. Their cell phones have been disconnected, probably by the kidnappers, so I can't track them that way. However, I am recovering strange messages and conversations from a Marcello who seems to be an agent of some type. My guess is CIA. I picked up one conversation between him and one of his agents who seems to be in a warehouse somewhere in the outskirts of Axum. I could have sworn the voice at the other end of the line was Alan, but of course it couldn't be. That wouldn't make sense. I'll keep monitoring his communications activities and see what else I can learn. The important thing is that it looks like there are some additional players in this game, and it may be them that have kidnapped Stef and Alan."

"Keep up the good work. I'll send you instructions when I figure out my next steps. Right now, I need to think." They disconnected their call. Then Elliott spoke out loud to no one, "Maybe I'll have another dream."

Elliott was beside himself. He started to think through the process of everything that was happening. What was he going to do now? This project was no longer about identifying and getting the Ark. Maybe the Ark was just a diversion all along and the NNRL had really been after the IOM's fuses. But now that they apparently have fuses from some other source, based on the text message that Kres received, they don't need the IOM. But why are they still going after the Ark? They must really believe the Ark has tremendous superpowers, which they felt they needed in order to assist them in seeing their future conquests successfully fulfilled. Maybe there are multiple goals involved here. The comments about world domination suggest that the NNRL is trying to bring Washington to its knees. Where is all this going? And why does the IOM care? They care more about the Ark then they do about Washington DC. However, if the balance of world power is distorted, that would directly affect the influence of their spies in the super-power structure.

"We can't let Washington fall. And we can't let the NNRL walk off with the Ark," Elliott was again talking to himself. Without Stef around, he didn't have anyone else to listen to him.

"I have to find this CIA agent and work with him. Perhaps he considers us their enemy. I need him to convince him that we are on the same side. I need share the concerns about the NNRL in Washington DC.

Elliott sent a message to Greg asking him to try to locate the CIA agent, if at all possible. He knew he had to be at the Chapel tonight, but he wasn't sure what he could do to prevent the assault on the Chapel of the Tablet.

Elliott loved diagrams and pictures and he started drawing out the various pieces of this puzzle. The major players were:

    The NNRL
    The IOM
    The French Mafia

The Unknown Agent in his hotel

The Warehouse in the Outskirts of Axum

And the major problem areas were:

Stef and Alan's Kidnapping

The Theft of the Ark of the Covenant at Midnight

The Nuclear Activity at Washington DC

And here he was, all alone, with the world's problems on his shoulders. And he probably missed some key player or some important event in the process.

CHAPTER FIFTY-EIGHT

Nightfall
Early April, 2025 AD, Axum, Ethiopia

Elliott had been watching the NNRL activity as they migrated up and down the stairs of the hotel. He noticed that they were hesitant about leaving their hotel room after five of their members were so easily eliminated. He chuckled to think that these big Arian thugs were so easily intimidated. He decided that he needed to be at the Chapel of the Tablet ahead of Kres' entourage. He would find an ideal hiding place to observe their activities. He would take his night vision digital camera along so he could record their activities.

It was easy enough for Elliott to sneak out, since he was on the bottom floor of the hotel, one floor lower than Kres' team. He quickly made his way to the church grounds and found himself a hiding place on the top of a small mound next to the Chapel and behind a small bush. It seemed like an ideal location. He also alerted Greg with the message, "Bring the S1 over the Chapel of the Tablet. Scan the chapel to see if the Ark is still inside. Keep an eye on the area to keep a check on the activities of Kres or anyone else who may be scouting around the area. If they take the Ark, follow it. Don't lose it. Also, be ready to shoot, but do not shoot unless I give you instructions to do so. I don't want you shooting me."

He felt ready. He was in an ideal location, and the S1 was tracking overhead. The S1 had been a formidable weapon, and he was thrilled to have it in his arsenal. All his resources were ready for the events of the evening. And fortunately, there was a full moon so he would have a clear view.

It wasn't long before Elliott heard someone approaching. It turned out to be three individuals. Two of them quickly ducked behind some bushes while the third openly sat on a bench, as if he were waiting for someone.

Shortly after that, Kres and his 5 goons could be seen coming up toward the Chapel. The one sitting on the bench yelled out; "Hello there. Are you Kres?"

"Yes," was the response from the shortest of the group. "Are you Marcello?"

"Yes. We finally meet. Are you here to point me at the IOM?"

"Actually, I'm here to thank you for shooting me in the leg," responded Kres as one of his warriors started to pull out his weapon and take aim at Marcello. But before he could pull the trigger, a shot rang out from a nearby bush and Kres' minion fell dead to the ground.

Marcello didn't wait around for a second queue. He took off running around the side of the old church.

The remaining Nazis pulled out their weapons and started sprayed the bushes near the source of the shot that hit their friend. They fired, not really knowing what or where they were shooting, but hoping they were firing in the right directions.

"Get him," yelled Kres to one of his solders pointing in the direction of where Marcello had run, giving him a push. The man took off running around the side of the church, but his efforts were fruitless. Marcello had hidden himself out of site. He had his pistol ready in case the man came too close, but he didn't need to use it.

The other three solders ventured into the bushes to see if they had hit anything, but there was nothing there. Either their assailant had gotten away, or they were shooting in the wrong direction. "The only thing back here is a dead rat," commented one of the soldiers.

"You obviously shot at the wrong thing," Kres replied, disgusted that another soldier had fallen.

"Should we start a more extensive search?" asked one of Kres' men.

"No. We have no idea how many guys are out there or where they are. Let's just get the Ark and get out of here."

The four remaining team members headed over to the chapel and jumped the six-foot-high fence by leaning a bench up on end against the side of it and climbing over. Kres stayed outside and kept watch. Kres was smaller and not as agile. Additionally, the shot he received still pained him. Jumping the fence was out of the question.

The soldiers inside the Chapel of the Tablet enclosure made their way to the chapel door and found it locked. They started to throw their bodies against the door in an attempt to push it open. It creaked but didn't budge.

"Shoot out the lock," yelled Kres. The Nazis pulled out their weapons and started firing. Then they tried again to push themselves against the door. Still no luck.

"See if there is another way in," urged Kres. Two of the team went around the side of the chapel in an attempt to see if there was another option. They checked the mock windows, but the building was sealed tight. The other three kept working on the door. Eventually the two came around the other side, throwing their arms up in a sign that there was no other option. The front door was the only way in.

Up on the side of the hill, behind some scrub brush, Elliott watched in amusement. He could hardly contain himself from laughing. He sent a text to Greg, "Are you watching this?"

"Wouldn't miss it for the world. The night vision is working great. Do you want me to take any of them out?"

"Not yet. This is too much fun."

"Do you still have sensors on the French Mafia guys? What happened to them?" Elliot had taken Kres' cue that Marcello was a part of the mafia. Neither of them guessed that Marcello was also with the CIA.

"They're still in the area. I'm monitoring them on my heat sensors. I'm not sure how they got away after that barrage of bullets that was fired at them. But they seem to be alright."

"I know I'm asking the impossible, but it would be good to monitor their movements as well as the movements of the NNRL team."

"In the event that they separate, where's the priority?"

"The priority is on Kres and the Ark. Don't lose them even if you have to track them to the other side of the world, which may happen."

"I also see someone hiding in the bushes to the North. They were not part of the group of three mafia members, and they are also not part of Kres' group."

"I wonder if they are the agents that you heard in the hotel."

"Could be, but my ability to watch everyone is getting stretched thin."

In the bushes, off to the North, sat Jano, keeping a close watch on all the activities. After seeing the confrontation between Marcello and Kres, he knew that he was no match for a confrontation with any of them. All he could do was watch, and pray that nothing bad would happen to his treasured Ark.

On the other side of the Chapel, hiding in the shadows of the old church, was Marcello. He had sent text messages to Joe and Conrad and found out that Joe had been grazed by a bullet and received some surface injuries, but that neither of them received any serious injuries. With that knowledge, he watched the show at the Chapel. "A typical bunch of bullies trying to force their way through," was the thought that went through his mind. Marcello didn't really care how all of this shook out in the end. He would prefer to take all these Nazis out and end this right now. But he kept hoping that the IOM would appear, and he can get rid of both groups at once. For now, he just watched and kept Joe and Conrad on standby, ready to shoot if needed.

"Come over here and grab this bench;" Kres yelled as he lifted the bench so that it was partially hanging over the fence. "Use it as a battering ram against the door. There must be some way to break through." Kres was frustrated by the lack of progress. He didn't want to give the mafia guys a chance to regroup and take shots at him and his team. He had already lost too many extremely valuable resources in the last couple of days, and he didn't want to lose any more.

Two of Kres' goons came to the fence and retrieved the bench, which was made of heavy wooden planks. They hauled it over the fence. Rejoining their cohorts, the four men picked up the bench, two on each side, and used it as a battering ram against the door. Each time the bench hit on the door, it made a loud crash. After the third hit, the door gave way slightly. With the fourth hit, pieces of the door broke loose. It only took one more hit before the door gave way and broke open.

On cue, as if triggered by the doors breaking way, there was an enormous explosion. The entire Chapel blew apart, as if it were made out of paper. The roof blew straight up, only to come back straight down. The enormous wall blocks with which the chapel had been constructed blew out in every direction. The concussion from the blast was so strong that Kres was left temporarily deaf with a loud ringing in his ears. Elliott, Marcello, and Jano, who were hidden away at distances of about one-hundred feet, were left stunned. Their ears ached, as if they had just come out of a loud rock concert. And Elliott was afflicted with an immediate splitting headache.

The four Nazis that had been using the battering ram at the door were killed instantly by the collapsing building. One of the large wall blocks, blew directly toward Kres as if it were aimed at him. It hit the fence and, since Kres was standing close to the fence, it gave Kres a severe blast on the side of the head, knocking him to the ground. Fortunately, the fence took the brunt of the blast. Kres would have been killed if the block had hit him directly. But, luckily, he survived with only a severe bruise and gash on the side of his head.

Up on the side of the hill, at a distance of a hundred feet, Elliott was also struck by some of the smaller stones that were able to travel that far. But he only received some bruising.

Marcello and his team, around the side of the old church, were able to pull back quickly enough to take advantage of the protection that the old church offered and avoided getting hit. But the blast was so strong that its repercussion left them momentarily stunned.

Pieces of the building and what appeared to be pieces of the Ark were strewn all over the grounds. It looked like the Ark, along with its resting place, and the guardian, had just been destroyed.

The Chapel of the Tablet was completely reduced to rubble. The largest of the remaining chunks was no larger than one cubic foot in size. It was difficult to see anything. The dust cloud that remained completely encompassed the area of the chapel and a good twenty feet beyond in each direction, and it reached fifty feet into the air.

Elliott, Jano, and Marcello and his team tried to recover their bearings so they could escape this massive scene of destruction.

It wasn't long before sirens could be heard. Elliott and Marcello took this as their cue to get as far away as possible. Before running off, Elliott typed a message to Greg, "Don't lose Kres."

Greg responded, "Will do. Everyone else has already left the scene. What happened?" Elliott was too busy running away to type in a response.

CHAPTER FIFTY-NINE

Stef

Early April, 2025 AD, Axum, Ethiopia

Stef nagged Alan into letting her go to the bathroom. At first, he was resistant, being concerned that she was cleverly trying to escape. He handed her a bucket to use. She did that once. But this time she insisted that what she needed to do in the bathroom went beyond peeing. Eventually Alan gave in and lengthened the ties around her legs so that she would have enough room to walk using small steps. He also loosened her hands.

As Stef shuffled off to the bathroom, Alan became distracted by some messages he was getting on his cell phone. Stef took advantage of his distraction to grab her phone and its battery and take it into the bathroom with her. She powered up her phone and put it on mute. She knew that if Elliott, or anyone else, was tracking her they would be able to find her by triangulating the location of the phone's signal.

Stef returned the phone to where she had picked it up, placing it face down to hide any lights, and hoping that Alan would not notice the missing battery. Then she returned to her assigned seat. At the moment Alan seemed too distracted to worry about reconnecting Stef to her chair. "What has you so distracted?" she asked.

"It appears the Ark of the Covenant and its chapel has been blown up. No one seems to know why or how. The entire town is in an uproar. It's apparently the biggest thing that's happened around here in centuries."

This left Alan and Stef deep in thought. Alan was left wondering how all this affected his mission. What would Marcello want to do now? He knew Marcello was safe, since he was the one who sent him the message. But his message didn't hint at next steps. He was sure Marcello would come to the warehouse. Where else could he go? And he would discuss next steps with him after he arrived.

Stef's immediate concern was about Elliott. "Were there any casualties?"

"It looks like at least five people were killed, including the caretaker of the chapel. An unknown number were injured. Apparently, the chapel has been completely leveled." This did very little to reassure Stef. Was Elliott one of the killed or injured? Would she ever get away from here to find out?

Stef decided to press Alan, hoping that she might learn more; "So how does this affect me? What do we do now?"

"I don't exactly know. We'll just have to sit here and wait for further instructions."

"Instructions from whom?" Stef thought she'd try again to find out who was behind her kidnapping. But Alan ignored the question.

"I'm sure that everyone is rattled at this unexpected event. We will need to rethink our game plan. At this point, I just don't know what we're going to do next."

Alan remembered that he hadn't retied Stef's hands. He went behind her and cuffed her hands together again behind her back and included the seat bar from one side of the metal chair. She didn't complain. She was already working out a plan for her next step and hopefully her eventual escape.

Elliott received a message from Greg. "I have Kres in my sights. He is running for it. He is heading for the airport. Apparently, a private jet has landed, and he is planning to be on it. It looks like the search for the Ark has been abandoned."

This was followed immediately by a second message, "I just got a bleep from Stef's phone. Apparently, it's been turned on again and my satellite detectors have tracked her to the outskirts of Axum. What do you want me to do?"

Elliott responded with, "Hold tight on Stef and keep tracking Kres. I'll get back to you."

Elliott immediately tried to call Stef, but apparently her phone was on silent because no one picked up the call. Giving up on talking to her he sent a message to Greg. "As soon as Kres is on the plane and off the ground, use satellite tracking to follow the flight. Then send the S1 in search of Stef. Send me directions as soon as you have some and I'll start working my way over to her location. I have to see if she is where her phone is."

"Roger that," came back from Greg.

Elliott had already left the area of the destroyed Chapel of the Tablet. He didn't want to be confronted by the police. He made his way to a main street, in hopes that he may get lucky and find a taxi. He considered stealing a car, but that meant he would have to drive, and he had no idea where he was going. In the end he decided to go with his driver and headed for the driver and his car, a short distance from the hotel. Unfortunately, the driver was not sleeping in his car as usual.

About the same time, he received a message from Greg giving the location of Stef's cell phone. Elliott was feeling desperate to see if Stef was safe. Just then Elliott saw a man walking out of a building across the street and heading to his car. He approached the man and asked, "Do you speak English?"

"Little," was the answer.

"Can you drive for me? I will pay well."

"No taxi."

Elliott pulled out a $100 bill, US, which is close to three month's pay for the man and said, "I will pay this if you bring me to this location," and he showed the man the address that Greg had sent him.

"Why so much? Not very long trip."

"Important. Urgent." Elliott had resorted to one-word sentences to make sure he was clear.

"Give me," he said, pointing to the money.

Elliott handed him the money, hoping he would not regret it and the man simply driving off without him. But Elliott was not disappointed. He got into the passenger side of the car and they drove off.

Elliott received another message from Greg while in route. "Kres is off. Diverting the S1 to find Stef. I had my S1 listening ears locked on the plane and I heard something about going to the celebration at Washington DC. They kept mentioning the Pentagon. Something is up."

"Great. First things first. Let me know what you learn about Stef. Then we'll figure this Pentagon thing out."

It took over forty-five minutes for Elliott and his driver to arrive at their destination. After arriving, the driver pointed to a specific building, in a row of warehouses. "Your building," he said to Elliott. Elliott noticed he seemed scared and concerned. The driver acted like he couldn't wait to get away.

"Thank you," said Elliott, as he climbed out of the car, hoping that the driver had brought him to the correct location. The driver immediately took off, as if shot out of a cannon. Elliott could not help but wonder what caused his fear. There must be something about this area that wasn't safe. But if Stef was here, then he was more concerned about her safety than he was about his own. He had to see.

Elliott decided to scope out the area before he made his presence known. He sent a text to Greg, "Are you on site?" Text messaging was quiet and was an excellent tool when talking was not an option. However, the disadvantage of texting was that it created a light which stood out in dark areas, like the area Elliot was in. He had to be careful. The risk was too great.

"Yes;" Greg immediately responded. "And I just saw the car that dropped you off. My heat sensors see four people in the building, but I can't make out who they are. One is in the center of the room sitting on a chair. One is sitting at a desk. And the other two are playing cards off in one corner."

"I'm going to scope out the building and see what I can find. I'm glad you're here to support me. I hate doing this the James Bond way, all alone."

Elliott started to work his way around the building. There were some small windows, used for ventilation, high up in the building, too high to see through. The Building was metal, so Elliott had to avoid touching it and making a sound. The roof was metal as well which meant he couldn't go on the roof. Elliott decided to climb up on the adjacent cement block structure and see if he could get a look through the windows. This took quite a bit of effort because he had to climb over a 10-foot barb wired fence, wrapping his shirt around his hands for protection. Then he used crates to help him climb up on the building. This proved to be challenging as well. The Edges of the building had broken glass pieces cemented along the tops to discourage theft. Eventually he was finally able to look through the window of the garage. But there wasn't much to see.

While Elliott was up on the roof, a car drove up which, from what Elliott could make out, contained at least three individuals. Elliot could only see one person, but he seemed strangely familiar. Then it dawned on him. This was the same guy that was at the Chapel of the Tablet. He was the one Kres tried to kill. He must be a French mafia leader.

The garage door opened, and the car drove in. Then the garage doors closed. Elliott sent a text to Greg, "What do you see?"

"Three more people showed up. The way everyone jumped to attention I would guess these were the bosses. The person sitting in the chair, had something placed over their head, but the other three people in the room got together with the new arrivals and they seemed to be discussing something. I've put on my ears and I'm trying to hear what they're saying. I'm getting some static, possibly because of all the metal in the building. I'll let you know if I learn anything."

Elliott moved around the roof, trying to get a better view through the windows, but his efforts were frustrated. He just couldn't get at the right angle. It wasn't long before he received another message from Greg, "It's definitely Stef in there. She must be the one tied to a chair. They're discussing what to do with her since their original plans have been disrupted. I don't know what plans they're talking about, but it doesn't sound good for Stef. They're saying they don't need her any longer. It sounds like one of the 'bad guys' is Alan. He wasn't kidnapped. He was the kidnapper."

"Then we need to act fast." Elliott thought about his options. Then he sent a second message. "I'm going to take a couple of shots into the building from my side. When I shoot, I need you to take a couple of shots into the building from the opposite side. I want them to think they are surrounded. Then let me know how they react using your heat sensing and listening equipment."

"Will do." Elliott took two shots, followed by Greg taking shots using the S1, followed by another shot from Elliott, and then again from Greg.

The message came in from Greg. "You've spooked them good. In fact, we even got a hit. One of the guys fell to the ground. I'm not sure if he's just hurt or if it was fatal."

Elliott waited. Then he saw one of the men climbing up a stairway and looking out of the high-level windows. Apparently, he didn't think he would be noticed by being high up. However, since Elliott was already trying to look through the window, the man was very noticeable. Elliott took another shot and hit the man in the forehead. The man fell from his observation perch. Then the unexpected happened. Elliott's phone began to vibrate. He was receiving a call from Stef phone.

"Hello," Elliott answered.

"Elliott! Is that you out there?" It was Stef on the phone.

"Six," responded Elliott with a coded response which meant "Yes."

"You're scaring the heck out of these guys in here. They want to know what you want and how many guys you have out there."

"There are a hundred of us out here and I want to know why you're being held prisoner. If any of them want to get out of there alive, they better let you leave the building." Elliott could tell he was on speaker phone and that they were obviously listening to him.

Then a different voice spoke up on Stef's phone. "I'm Marcello Zuniga of the CIA. If you want to see Stef alive, you'll throw down your weapons."

Elliott couldn't resist. He started laughing out loud. "I don't believe the CIA would be randomly kidnapping individuals. That doesn't make sense. Why are you out here in Axum. Let ME tell YOU how this is going to play out. I have two of you laid out. There are four of you left. Alan is obviously one of your traitorous clan. I have sights on all four of you and will take all of you out at once if that's what it's going to take to prove to you that I am in control here. Stef needs to be exiting the front door by the time I count to ten or my team will finish the job. 1. 2."

"Hold it a second. I concede that you have us outgunned. But Stef will be dead by the time you hit 9."

"Then I'll have to shoot you all at 8. Or maybe I'll just get it over with right now."

"STOP. You win. We'll let Stef leave. But first ...." Marcello may be a CIA agent, but he wasn't willing to sacrifice his life for this operation.

"No first! She comes out the front door now. Then we can talk some more if you like. But she comes out NOW. Give her the phone so I can talk to her and make sure she's safe."

"How do I talk to you afterwards?"

A message came through from Greg, "One of the guys is trying to sneak out the back."

"Give Stef your number and I'll call you as soon as she tells me she is safe. Don't try to sneak out of the back of the building, as one of your idiots is trying to do right now. Stay in the center of the building until I call."

Marcello was slow to respond, realizing that he was indeed being watched. He yelled at Conrad to come back. Then he answered, "Stef is on her way."

Greg could see Stef being untied and the bag being removed from her head. He sent a message to Elliott, "She's on her way." The garage door started to open, and Stef came walking out holding her cell phone.

"How are you Stef?" asked Elliott.

"Great, now that you're here. Do you realize that ten minutes ago they were discussing what to do with me? And it didn't sound good." Elliot's heart skipped a beat with excitement. He was truly scared for Stef and that was a new emotion for him. He had never experienced such a strong emotional tie to anyone. And it scared him a little. But he now knew that Stef meant much more to him than just being a fellow agent.

"Get clear of the area. There may still be some fireworks before all of this is over." Stef ran down the street a little way and hid around the corner of a building.

Elliott got Marcello's phone number from Stef and gave him a call. "Tell me your story," asked Elliott.

"What does that mean?" responded Marcello. "We're with the CIA, even if you don't want to believe it. Let me come out and I'll show you the badge and credentials."

"Why kidnap Stef. And how does Alan fit into all this?"

"You may find this hard to believe, but we were trying to protect Stef. We knew there was going to be a showdown between the IOM and the NNRL. We didn't care if the NNRL was wiped out, but we wanted to hang on to someone from the IOM that could explain what was going on with the search for the Ark. And Stef wasn't very cooperative. Alan has been our agent all along. He was turned while a member of the IOM."

"So, you're telling me that the four of you are all CIA. What's the status of the other two guys."

"They were also agents, but you took care of them, so their status really doesn't matter."

"So, you were hoping that the IOM and the NNRL would eliminate each other in a shootout."

"I'm afraid so. But it didn't work out that way."

"So, what's your plan now?"

"I guess the game is up. The Ark has been destroyed. There's nothing else to chase."

"I'm afraid that the Ark was just a small part of the story," Elliott said, wondering if he could trust these guys. He was especially concerned because he felt betrayed by Alan.

"What does that mean?" came back Marcello sounding concerned.

"First you tell me how the French Mafia fits into all of this."

"I'm the French mafia contact. My team did the hit in Alexandria. Kres contacted what he thought was the French mafia, but I intercepted the call. He asked us if we would like to take revenge on the people that executed Barjet. I told him I also had some information that I could trade him for, and I told him Rohit was a double agent. I played the role of the interested Spaniard and we worked out the hit where we were to take out Rohit and the two of you. But I was more interested in targeting Kres and Rohit, and that's why the two of them ended up getting shot and you got away."

"So, you were the guys at the Chapel tonight, pretending to be the French mafia?"

"Exactly." Elliott decided that he needed to get these guys involved whatever was happening in Washington DC.

"There was one other person hiding in the bushes at the chapel. What do you know about him?"

"Nothing."

"So now you're pretending to be CIA. And maybe you really are French Mafia and, for all I know, you're still trying to eliminate the IOM people who shot Barjet. Send Alan out with each of your credentials so I can look them over."

"Will do," came back Marcello. He still wasn't sure how to turn this standoff to his favor. For now, he was going to play along. As far as he was concerned, he was done here in Axum. The Ark was destroyed, and nearly all the NNRL were wiped out. He didn't consider the IOM as big a threat. If it weren't for this complication with Elliott and Stef, he would just leave.

Alan opened the door and came out. "Shut the door," ordered Elliott over the phone to Marcello.

Elliott texted Stef, "Go to Alan and look those credentials over. Let me know if you think they are legitimate."

Stef stepped out of the shadows and walked up to Alan. Alan held out the credentials for her. She accepted them with her left hand, and with her right had she slapped him so hard across the face that he stumbled backwards a couple of steps. Then she proceeded to review the documents. She texted Elliott, "They look good. What do you want me to do?"

"Keep them and disappear back into the shadows. I'll take it from here."

Then Elliott sent a message to Marcello, "Come out here with your crew, unarmed."

The garage doors opened, and Marcello, Conrad, and Joe stepped out onto the street. Elliott had started working his way back down to the street while Stef was reviewing the documents. Elliott was just starting to turn the corner to meet Marcello and his crew out in the street when he received a text from Greg, "They all have pistols inside their pants legs. Now that they're out of the metal building, I can get a better look at them."

Elliott returned the text, "Get ready to shoot if this goes wrong."

Elliott pulled out his pistol and aimed it out in front of him. He started talking when he was still about 30 feet away, "It looks like you may be legitimate. But you're not very smart. I asked you to come out here unarmed and it looks like all three of you have pistols inside your pants legs. I'm thinking it would probably be easier just to give the command to shoot the lot of you, since I obviously can't trust any of you."

Marcello, still believing that they were vastly outnumbered, threw up his hands and confessed, "You're right. Don't shoot. We find it hard to stop using old tricks."

Just then Alan came to the realization that there really wasn't anyone there except Elliott. Who else could it be? And he yelled out, "This is all a sham, a façade. There really isn't anyone else around here. It's all smoke and mirrors. Pull your guns and take him out." But unfortunately, those were Alan's last words, as he crumpled to the ground with a bullet entering in the back of his head and taking out the lower half of his face from his nose down.

Greg felt strange shooting Alan. They had been close working companions and friends. Even though Alan was now an enemy, it was strange to shoot someone who he felt he had gotten to know.

That was enough evidence to convince Marcello, Joe, and Conrad that Elliott was not alone. The shot seemed to come out of nowhere. There wasn't even a building from where the shot originated. It was as if a ghost had shot Alan. Their arms shot up.

"Kneel down," ordered Elliott. "Pull the pistols out of your holsters with two fingers and throw them as far as you can down the street to your left." After the pistols were thrown, Stef came out of hiding to collect them. And, just for fun, she test-fired each of them in the direction of their captives.

"They seem to work fine," she shouted to Elliott, who just chuckled.

Elliott and Stef approached the three remaining CIA operatives. Stef walked directly over to Marcello and gave him a kick between the legs. "That's for trying to decide how to eliminate me a little while ago." Marcello rolled over on the ground in pain but decided not to say anything.

Elliott walked over to Marcello and asked, "I assume you're the boss here."

Marcello was still crumpled up in pain and not quite ready to talk, so Conrad answered for him, "Yes he is."

Elliott continued; "We overheard Kres talking to his team about nuclear weapons being smuggled into the United States, and about arranging for the purchase and shipment of several nuclear fuses. Apparently, these have already arrived in the United States. And Washington DC seemed to feature prominently into their discussion."

"How do you know this," Marcello asked, recovering his strength.

"We had listening devices in Kres' rooms," Elliott stretched the truth. He didn't want the CIA to know the S1 was in the area. That would give away his façade of having several men on site. Also, since Alan was now out of the picture, he decided to limit their knowledge about the IOM.

"Then we need to act fast. Do you know the timetable?" Marcello was obviously concerned about this new information.

"We know that Kres has left Ethiopia by private jet and is probably halfway to Washington DC already. But when they talked about Washington, they kept saying they wanted to celebrate a birthday. I'm not sure what that's all about."

Marcello's concern was obvious. He knew about the NNRL and their strong Nazi ties. "The birthday they're talking about is Hitler's birthday, on the 20th. It's less than a week away."

Marcello started seeing the IOM as a critical partner in this new threat. "I have no reason to doubt any of the things you're telling me;" Marcello attempted to calm the situation and win Elliott over to his side. "Leading us astray at this point wouldn't make any sense. It's obvious to me that I need to ask for your help. You seem to know a lot more about what is happening here than we do. You know the NNRL and you seem to have a track on Kres and his activities. Is there any possible way I can solicit your help in saving Washington from disaster?"

"Unfortunately, you failed the 'trust' test," explained Elliott. "I can't work with someone I don't trust."

"You worked with Kres. He obviously wasn't trustworthy. I'll definitely prove to be a better partner than he was."

"You're right there. But you also admitted that you are actively trying to kill Stef and me. And now you want me to trust you. That just doesn't make sense. And besides, what's in it for us? We're contractors, not a charity organization. We're from Australia, and Australian's think the United States is a big political mess anyway. So why would we want to help you?"

Marcello saw the dilemma. But he also knew that Elliott and his team had better information than the CIA. And he needed the IOM if he was going to prevent a potential disaster. "What can we do that makes sense? What do you want that will get us your support?"

"At this point, we want to get Kres as badly as you do. He put a contract on us in Alexandria, and we don't look at that favorably.

"As far as the IOM – CIA relationship goes; we'll just have to have an arms-length relationship. We'll work by phone and messages. But I don't ever want to see you again. As for what we want out of it, I want your word that from now on the IOM will be treated as contractors to the CIA, and not as terrorists. You won't follow us around. You'll end your surveillance activities. And you'll take us off of the 'most wanted' lists."

"That's all doable."

Elliott continued; "Next time I come into the United States I don't want to be strip searched and investigated. I want freedom to roam. And that goes for Stef and anyone else in my team."

"Agreed."

Elliott gave Marcello a stern and serious look that had the hint of a threat, "Don't disappoint me on this. If I'm coming to the United States to help you, I don't want to be hassled. I want my conditions met immediately, or I'll just turn around and leave and you won't hear from me again."

"You have my word." Marcello knew that this was going to take some effort because it involved several agencies. But he also knew it was critical. He would start the process as soon as Elliott released him.

"One more thing," added Elliott, as he thought about his current situation. "I want a private jet out of here ASAP. They're going to come looking for us after the explosion at the Chapel of the Tablet. And I want to be long gone before they figure out, we're connected."

"Will do," was Marcello's response. "Can I start the process," he asked, reaching for his phone.

"Make it happen," was Elliott's response. "Give me the keys to your van. Have the plane there for us as soon as possible after we get there. Text me with updates as you receive them. And remember, anything funny, and the party's over." Marcello quickly handed the keys over.

Elliott and Stef hopped into the van and headed off toward the airport. Elliott had paid close attention during his drive out to the warehouse. And he thought he would be able to get safely back to the airport.

Marcello barked instructions to Conrad and Joe as the three of them walked back into the light of the warehouse. Then all three of them were busy sending messages to various CIA agencies, to the FBI, to the Department of Homeland Security, and of course to the airports to see if they could line up a jet for Elliott and a second one for themselves. Fortunately, they found one in Addis Abeba, Ethiopia, that was available for charter and they quickly contracted it to come to Axum and pick up Elliott and Stef.

"By the way, where are all these sharpshooters that were shooting at us from all directions?" asked Conrad.

"In the air," responded Marcello, finally realizing that it must have been the work of drone airplanes rather than real individuals.

"Why don't we have anything that sophisticated?" asked Joe.

"Because we're not James Bond. We're the CIA. We can't even organize a decent hit on the NNRL or the IOM. If we would have executed on these earlier hits in Carnes or Jerusalem, as planned, we wouldn't be in this situation now. The CIA has become an enormous, slow moving, bureaucracy."

CHAPTER SIXTY

Heading to Washington DC
Early April, 2025 AD, Somewhere over the Atlantic Ocean

After the explosion, Kres had received a knock on the head which knocked him to the ground. He sat up and took a few minutes to recover. He felt slightly dazed and realized he wouldn't be able to immediately start walking. Fortunately, he wasn't knocked unconscious, but this hit would definitely leave a large knot on his head.

After a while he felt strong enough to stand up. He stood and took a few steps to check his bearings. He didn't want to end up falling over. But everything seemed to be working as ordered. He started walking faster and faster, eventually breaking into a jog. He took a direct route to the hotel, hoping to grab a few things before he headed off to the airport. He knew he had to get away as quickly as possible. He didn't want to be held up by the police for questioning. Any delay might keep him from making it to Washington on time for the Birthday Celebration. Besides, he really didn't know anything about the explosion that might be useful for the police.

At the hotel, Kres' bag was packed, having previously anticipated a quick exodus with the Ark. He grabbed the bag and headed outside of the hotel. Fortunately, a taxi was just dropping someone off at the hotel, and he quickly jumped in.

The cab ride to the airport was quick and uneventful. The driver understood the word airport, but not much else. But it didn't matter.

Kres wasn't interested in a conversation. He just wanted to get out of Axum.

At the airport, the NNRL plane was ready to go. He quickly jumped aboard and ordered a take-off. "I understood we were picking up eleven passengers and some cargo," asked the flight attendant.

"They have been indefinitely delayed;" was Kres' meaningless response. "We need to get going immediately."

"We heard some kind of explosion. Do you know what that was all about?"

"A building was destroyed. And that's why the other men aren't here. It's the reason we need to leave immediately, before someone gets the idea to delay us."

"I understand. We will depart immediately."

"Do you have any ice?"

"Certainly;" responded the flight attendant.

"I need to ice a bump on the head."

"I'll get it for you right away."

The departure of the plane was also uneventful. They were off the ground, and thirty minutes later they were out of Ethiopian air space. A few hours later they were out of Africa and heading over the Atlantic Ocean.

Kres was glad to be on the NNRL private jet heading for Washington DC. He didn't want to miss the celebration. But at the same time, he was furious. Ten agents gone in the blink of an eye. And he barely escaped with his life. The thought reminded him of the hit on the head. It made him run his hand over his head, and he could feel the knot building up. The ice didn't seem to help much. He had waited too long to apply the ice. He was starting to feel like a total invalid. His leg still hurt and caused a slight limp. And now he had a large lump on the head, magnified by a splitting headache.

Kres was frustrated. And the Ark was totally destroyed. As far as he was concerned, this entire adventure was a miserable failure. It couldn't get much worse. Hopefully, the birthday celebration would come off as planned. He didn't want to deal with the frustration of any more failures.

The deadline for his father's birthday, April 20, was only a couple of days away. He had to accomplish his Washington mission on April 20, or the significance would be lost. And he didn't want to wait another year for another birthday to roll around. It would have to happen this year, one way or another.

Kres used his satellite phone to check on the progress of bomb components. The cell delivering the enriched uranium was already in the Washington area. The fuse cell would arrive in Washington DC later that afternoon, along with the scientist who would be able to assemble the bomb. And the cell responsible for the delivery system was scheduled to arrive sometime on the following day. Pieces were starting to come together, and he was getting excited. This would be a glorious day of victory: a kick-off for the Nazi New World Order. He only hoped that the significance of the date would not be lost on the media. Maybe he would need to send out a message to all the media shortly before the explosion. He needed to let the world know so they could unite behind the banner of Arian supremacy. A new world order would begin on the celebrated birthday of Adolph Hitler. April 20 would be a glorious day, making the 9-11 attack seem trivial. Kres had a hard time trying to control his outward composure and ever-growing excitement, as the prospect of such a momentous historical occasion for all the world to witness was imminently drawing to a close. He would be in Washington DC soon and the final preparations can then begin.

CHAPTER SIXTY-ONE

More Heading to Washington, DC
Early April, 2025 AD, Axum, Ethiopia

After leaving Marcello and his team to fend for themselves, Stef and Elliott took the one-hour drive to the airport. As they arrived the lights of a small jet could be seen in the distance, zeroing in on the runway. Marcello had been true to his word, which must have been a little tricky since finding a jet that would land on the short Axum runway could not have been easy. Once landed, Elliott and Stef were quick to confirm that this plane was for them, and immediately after boarding the aircraft without further ado, the jet was on its way.

Before they left, Elliott sent a text to Greg, "Are you still tracking Kres?"

It was Dawn who responded, "You've been running Greg ragged. This is Dawn and I'm taking over while he gets some rest. Yes, we're still tracking Kres. He is in a landing pattern at the Regan National airport in Washington DC. He should be landing shortly. I'm rushing to get the S1 over there so that I can try to monitor him, but it's going to be tough and I'm sure I'll lose him in the crowds. I'll do my best."

"Thanks, and keep us posted," replied Elliott, even though he knew that there would not be much of a signal over Africa and then over the Atlantic Ocean. Even the jet's satellite phone would be hit-and-miss. He probably would be out of communication until they arrived in Washington. DC. He passed word to his pilot that they would need to land at Regan National.

"We may as well settle in and make the best of it," Elliott said to Stef as he reclined his chair. The jet was an executive jet that had come to Ethiopia to deliver several dignitaries from the embassy in London. It had a 3 day lay-over in Ethiopia and when they received a call from the CIA that gave them the opportunity to make a few dollars; the charter company quickly grabbed it. They would be back in Ethiopia in plenty of time to pick up the ambassador.

The interior of the jet was quite lavish. There were six brushed leather recliners that rotated 360 degrees. It also included a sectional couch which faced a flat-screen TV. The plane was outfitted with a full bar, and a self-service snack bar. There weren't any attendants on the plane, only the pilot and co-pilot. Stef and Elliott had the back end all to themselves.

But Stef, now that she could finally relax a little, lost her cool. "Do you realize I nearly got killed back there?" she ranted. "Those idiots wanted to get rid of me. And then you go and negotiate a deal to work with them. We're going to be bosom buddies now. I just want to kick each of them to kingdom come, and you want to be their friend. Who do you think you are? Barack Obama?"

Elliott knew that she was just relieving her frustrations. But he also acknowledged that she had a right to be frustrated. "I did what had to be done," Elliott told Stef, but he knew it would do little to calm her. "It wasn't pleasant, but we need to keep tabs on Kres every bit as much as the CIA does. Besides, you know the saying, 'Keep your friends close and keep your enemies closer.' We need to watch the CIA every bit as much as we need to watch the NNRL."

"Now you're sounding like Alan. He thought being tied in with the CIA was a good thing too. I don't know how we missed that one. How did we get someone on our staff who was tied in with the CIA? That's a big blunder if you ask me."

"I totally agree. We'll need to figure out how that one got missed. But it sounds to me like he joined in with the CIA after he was an IOM team member, not before." Elliott could see that Stef was starting to calm down. But it would still be a while before she would be able to get her mind on the future and forget the past.

"I really trusted Alan. Now I'm wondering about everyone on our staff. What about you? Are you doing anything that you shouldn't be?"

"I want to be," Elliott responded with a sly smile. Stef knew exactly what that meant. She was convinced that Elliot had some type of mental defect that kept his mind focused on sex. And, at the moment, she wasn't interested.

"You have to be kidding. We nearly got killed; me by the CIA and you by some enormous explosion. And all you can think about is sex. Give me a break."

"OK, sorry. I just missed you a lot and was really worried about you. It's not about the sex, that's just a game, it's about being worried about my best friend and about being really glad that you're OK."

"I'm glad that you're OK too;" Stef softened a little after Elliott's explanation. "It was really hard being in there and not knowing what you were doing. I didn't know if you had been captured too, or what may have happened to you. I was thrilled when I finally heard your voice."

Elliott was flipping through some on-board DVDs to see if there was anything interesting to watch on the 60-inch flat screen TV. "Wow, they have some oldies but goodies here. Anything you'd like to watch?"

"Narrow it down to a couple of choices and I'll pick one."

"My two favorites are *Princess Bride* or *Gods Must Be Crazy*. Do you feel like either of those?"

"Put in *Princess Bride*. I loved that movie, and I haven't seen that for a long time."

Elliott knew she would pick the one that had a romantic twist. And he hoped this would help to put her into a romantic mood. Elliott started up the DVD and then sat on the sectional coach and pushed back on the recliner. Stef lay down on the coach next to him and laid her head on his lap. Elliott combed her hair with his fingers and thought out loud; "life doesn't get any better than this. No matter how bad things get, they're always a little better when you're lying here next to me."

It wasn't long before Stef had fallen asleep on his lap, somewhere around the time when Wally Shawn says, "I don't think that word means what you think it means." She could finally relax. Elliott made her feel safe.

The plane took a sudden dip and Elliott, and Stef woke up with a jerk. "What was that?" asked Stef.

Just then the pilot came on the intercom and announced, "We've hit a weather system which is making the air choppy. It shouldn't last long. You may want to fasten your seatbelts just in case we get a big drop."

Princess Bride had ended, and some recorded program was playing on the screen. It was a movie and the theme seemed to involve an overly aggressive young lady that was trying to get a married man to go out with her. She wore sexy clothing and gave him flirty complements. "You know, this whole women's lib thing resulted in the girls losing a lot of their power over men," Elliott said.

Stef sat up and gave Elliott a stern look, "What are you talking about? Are you saying that women shouldn't have the right to vote? Do you think a woman can't be president?"

"Of course not. The right to vote was in place long before this women's lib thing came about. In fact, I think women often put more effort into their selection of candidates than do most men. And I definitely think women could be president. For example, if we had a candidate of the caliber of Margaret Thatcher, I'd vote for her in a second. She's better than any candidate, male or female, that the US has offered up in years."

"Then exactly what are you saying?"

"I'm talking specifically about sex. Women wanted to take on the role of being sexually aggressive, showing that they could take sexual leadership as well as any man. It's the whole 'I can do anything better than you' mentality. And in the end, all they did was give away their sexual power. Now men can get more sex than they know what to do with, and that's what they always wanted anyways. And they don't have to 'put out' – as they used to say. Sure, girls are more sexually aggressive. But what do they have to show for it? They never had a shortage of guys wanting sex before. Now they're just giving it away more freely under the confused assumption that they were somehow getting more or better sex than women of previous generations. I find that incredibly arrogant. The history books are full of stories of women who used sex to manipulate themselves into all sorts of positions. They used sex as a tool. They had power. But today, sex is so freely available, that if a woman were to use the sex tool, the guy would simply go somewhere else where he could get the same or even better sex for free. That's what I mean by saying women have given up their power. And the result is that we're not even sure sex today is any better than it was 'in the olden days'. I would argue that 'in the olden days' girls worked harder at it and, as a result, were probably better at it."

"Well, I kind-of see what you mean," returned Stef. "I have several girl-friends that are frustrated that they can't develop lasting relationships with guys. But at the same time, they say they don't want to be tied down. And I keep wondering what they really want. The funny thing is that they say they are looking for their perfect soulmate, the perfect man. But, at the same time, the way they live their life is far distant from what they want out of their 'ideal' man. They don't understand that in order to find perfection, they also need to be perfect, or the 'ideal' man won't be interested in them when he does come along."

Elliott continued, "I've heard women with breast implants, hair extensions, tattooed makeup, liposuction, and plastic surgery say they don't understand why men are so fake. They wonder why they can't find a real man, the perfect man. They say that men are phony. That they don't really know what's important in life. Yet they are so plastic that any 'real man' would be scared off."

"I've seen that one both ways. But, at the same time, I understand what you're saying about girls and sex. The old saying, 'why buy the cow if you can get the milk for free' definitely fits in far too many cases."

"So, what about you?" asked Elliott. And Stef jumped up into a standing position.

"What do you mean, 'what about me?' Are you saying I'm free milk?" Stef was starting to get worried about where this was going. What was Elliott driving at.

"Not at all. I'm just asking you where you stand on the whole Women's lib thing. How do you feel about sex between a man and a woman?"

Now Stef was really getting worried. What was he saying? Was this some kind of back handed way of getting her to say they shouldn't be having sex so that he would have an excuse to break off their relationship? "Are you trying to break up with me? Give it to me in ten works or less. Don't beat around the bush." She was getting a little flushed and tears were starting to well up in her eyes. She always felt her job would keep her from having a serious, long-term relationship. But she just wasn't prepared for this. Her mind was reeling. Everything seemed so good between them. Elliott didn't seem like someone who would just use her and then throw her away. What was going on here? She stepped backwards and sat down in one of the recliners.

"So, I'm limited to ten words. OK! I'll give it to you in five. STEF, WILL YOU MARRY ME?"

"Oh my gosh!" Was all Stef could think. "Oh my gosh did I ever read this one wrong. Oh my gosh." She leaned backward in the chair. "Oh my gosh."

Elliott could see that he had completely thrown her off guard. He liked it when he threw her off. That always made the recovery so much fun. He stood up, walked over to her chair, and kneeled down in front of her. He folded his arms on her lap, and resting his chin on his forearms, gazed solemnly and deeply into her eyes like a soulful puppy-dog. "I was extremely stressed out when I found out you were being held hostage. It was a lot more than just concern about a fellow soldier. I was scared for you Stef...and I was scared for me. I didn't want to lose you. I want our relationship to go on. I want it to be a lot more than just the artificial boyfriend – girlfriend thing that we've had in the past. I want you to know that I'm interested in making a long-term commitment to you. And I'm hoping you're interested in making the same type of commitment. Please say yes."

But Stef was still at the "Oh my gosh" stage of her thought process. She wasn't anywhere close to processing an answer. All her feelings came to a head. She wanted Elliott close to her, but did she want to make a commitment? The idea scared her, yet at the same time the thought excited her. She didn't want to say no, but she was too afraid to say yes. Finally, after another twenty or so "oh my goshes" she was finally able to pull her thought process together enough to start formulating an answer. But all that came out was "What did you say?"

"I said, Stef, will you marry me?"

Stef knew that she loved being with Elliott more than with anyone else she ever knew. They just clicked. But wouldn't this ruin all that? "Won't this affect our working relationship?"

"It might. But to me it's worth the risk. I've always adored you, enough so that I don't like myself when I 'get the milk for free' as you said. I want to be with you more than anything else in the world, but call me a traditionalist, call me backward, call me anything you want, but I want to be with you the right way. Please say yes."

Exasperated and sounding a little frustrated, Stef replied, "Do you realize that you have effectively made me worthless for the next week, or so. I'm going to be brain dead. I'm not going to be able to think of anything else. Do you realize what you've done to me?"

"Please say yes," begged Elliott, now with even more urgency in his voice than before.

She couldn't hold back any longer; "Absolutely yes, forever and always; 'yes!' You crazy fool. Why did you do this to me? Now I'm going to be worthless. Couldn't you have timed this better?" She laughed excitedly and tossed her golden mane of blonde hair back from her face, not quite sure whether to laugh or cry, or do both at the same time.

"Nope." Elliott laughed, utterly delighted, and pleased with himself for finally having been able to get through to this stubborn young woman, for whom he had come to nurture such deep love, for such a long time coming.

"I wanted to know that we had a long-term future before I crawled in bed with you again. I just had to know. Sorry to have frustrated you, but you just made me the happiest guy *ever!!!* I feel so empowered with my love for you, I feel like I could do anything right now! I'll be thrilled to cover for you while you get your head back on straight." He laughed, unable to curb his own excitement at Stef's somewhat unexpected and enthusiastic reply to one of *the* most important questions he'd ever asked of anyone in his whole life.

"You're crazy." She giggled nervously, still beaming at him through her happy tears.

"Yes, crazy about you, you beautiful sexy wench," he reciprocated, "come here YOU, and let me kiss your pretty face!" Elliott pulled her close to him, squeezing his very own 'squeeze' tightly into his arms. He vowed to himself from that moment on he'd do absolutely anything to make Stef happy and content; and that he would *never* let her out of his sight, ever again.

It took a while to get Stef calmed down from her highly emotional state. Elliott did a lot of hold, kissing, and comforting. Stef kept asking; "Are you sure you want to do this?" and Elliott kept answering; "I've never been more sure of anything in my life."

After she calmed down, she arrived at the point where she was ready to let Elliott do anything he wanted. And Elliott had become aroused to the point where he wanted her naked. Slowly, but lovingly, Elliott unbuttoned, unzipped, and unstrapped Stef till he had her where he wanted her. At first, he just wrapped his naked body around hers, enjoying the feeling of softness and warmth. But finally, he couldn't stand it any longer. The two young lovers conjoined as one, captivated in a long session of emotional and hungry rapturous lovemaking. Each reciprocating their deeply motivated and urgent caring for the other. The peak of their simultaneous ardor culminating into a 'fire-works' crescendo that was able to satiate both their physical, as well as their emotional need for closeness. And above all to simply fulfill a deep yearning, one of being together as a real couple at long last.

CHAPTER SIXTY-TWO

Washington, DC
Early April, 2025 AD, Washington, DC

Marcello had arranged for four agents to observe Kres' arrival. They travelled the short distance from CIA headquarters in Langley, Virginia to the airport, and they were in place when he landed. Two were stationed on top of the main terminals located in the area where Kres would be arriving. The other two agents were on the ground, inside the customs area that Kres would have to work through.

Kres plane arrived close to the time anticipated. He got off the plane alone and headed to the customs desk. It seemed like a long walk on the tarmac. Even though he had a private plane, it didn't exclude him from going through the same customs security checks that everyone else had to go through. He entered the customs and immigrations area. First, he had to show his passport and explain the reason for his visit to the United States. He claimed that he had a sick relative in the DC area and he needed to visit them. Then he proceeded on through the customs process, which was also quick. He only carried a small overnight bag and he had nothing to declare. From there he followed the signs to ground transportation.

Kres noticed the two agents. If they were there for him, who could they be?

He wasn't sure they were tailing him, but he wasn't going to take any chances.

Kres placed a quick phone call, letting his people know that he was ready to be picked up. He also informed them that he was being followed, and that he wanted the pickup to be a surprise. He would act like he didn't know them, and then he wanted to jump into the vehicle quickly and take off.

The CIA agents in place watched him come through the security area. They started tailing him as he headed out the front of the terminal. Kres walked up to the curb, looking around as if he was unfamiliar with his surroundings. Then, somewhat suddenly, a black Sebring pulled up, the door opened up quickly from the inside; he jumped into the back seat and was gone.

Kres' disappearance was so rapid that the agents didn't have enough time to get a license plate, let alone make arrangements to put a tail on him. Kres was gone.

They quickly called the agents on the roof, but it was even too late for them to get any information on the vehicle. It had left the area too rapidly.

They sent a message to Marcello, who they knew was in the air over the Atlantic and updated him on what had taken place. Then they proceeded back to Langley.

Early April, 2025 AD, Washington, DC

"We are coming into our approach to Washington DC. We'll be landing in about 15 minutes. You need to fasten your seat belts and get ready to land." The pilot announced on the intercom,

Elliott hated to do it, but he had to wake Stef up and help her get buckled in. She was snoring so nicely. He felt sorry for her, having lost as much sleep as she had over the last couple of days. But he was thrilled that she said "yes." This was the most exciting thing that had happened to him in years. Even more exciting than being buried alive or being shot at on numerous occasions.

Stef was still a little groggy when the plane finally touched down. But, by the time it came to a full stop, she was ready to go. "I had the weirdest dream. I dreamt that you proposed. And what's even weirder, I dreamt that I said yes."

"That wasn't a dream honey-buns. You're committed."

"Don't start giving me weird nick names, now that you think you have me under lock and key. You still have to be nice to me."

"I intend to spend the rest of my life being nice to you." Elliott laughed, but it was clearly obvious to Steff, Elliott sincerely meant what he said.

The plane landed and slowly taxied to a stop. "What do we do next?" she asked.

"We'll get into a hotel in the Crystal City area. There are lots of hotels there and we can get settled in. It's just one stop on the Blue Line of the Washington Metropolitan Area Transit Authority from Ronald Reagan Washington National Airport. We'll wait till we hear from Marcello and see how this is going to shape up. I'm not sure where any of this is going or what our involvement will be."

Elliott sent messages to Marcello and Dawn, doing a status check. He didn't receive a response from Marcello, which meant he was somewhere over the Atlantic. But Dawn was quick to respond with, "We lost him. Too many people. We did follow Kres until the moment he stepped into the terminal, but we're not sure where he went from there."

Elliott responded with; "Try to triangulate on his cell phone."

Elliott looked at Stef and said, "Maybe, after we're settled in and we don't have anything else to do, we can go visit the Smithsonian Air and Space Museum. I haven't been able to visit it for a long time, mostly because I've been blocked entry in the United States. I hope Marcello has our immigration issues resolved."

"Out comes the real reason behind coming to Washington DC. You have always been addicted to that air and space museum. You must have had withdrawals being away from it for so long." Stef gave Elliott a sly smile. "But we may as well enjoy ourselves until we hear from Marcello. Maybe his people were able to learn more about what's going on around here."

"I agree. We'll just relax until we hear from Marcello. We really don't have any other choice."

Marcello, once again true to his word, had made it so that customs was no problem. Elliott and Stef breezed through without a lot of questions and interrogation. They were just two tourists, who came to Washington to see the sights. After customs they worked their way through the airport and headed straight for the subway system across the street from the airport pick-up area. They hopped the Blue Line and headed for Crystal City. They purchased two tickets at the ticket dispenser, and headed through the turnstiles, and up to the elevated train stop.

Marcello called ahead to the Marriott and arranged for a room. The hotel was a short walk from the Crystal City metro station, and it wasn't long before the two of them were settled in.

Once in the room, Stef pushed Elliott up against a wall and stared him in the eyes, "Did last night really happen?"

"Yes, there really was a last night," Elliott responded, with a smile on his face.

"Don't toy with me. You know exactly what I mean. Are we engaged? Or was I dreaming the whole thing?"

"You're on the hook. You committed to me, whether or not you meant to be, and there's no backing out now. Don't be having second thoughts."

Stef grabbed his face, one hand on each side, and gave him a big fat kiss. But Elliott didn't see any reason to rush this. The Air and Space museum can wait. He grabbed her, picked her up, and threw her on the bed. Then he lay down next to her and suggested, "That was way too quick. How about a real kiss?" Then he went to work.

Elliott was starting to get a little too frisky for Stef and she pushed him up. "Not yet. The first thing you have to do is put a ring on my finger. I need to see if you're financially committed to this, or if you're just trying to soften me up. Also, we have a museum to visit. Besides, you're always nicer to me when you have something to look forward to. Let's get going."

"You're not excited about getting married?"

"Incredibly. Definitely. But I am setting some rules early. First, we do our work. Then we play."

"You consider the Air and Space Museum work?"

"Let's just say that for some of us it's more fun than for others."

"Fine! But from this point on you're a kept woman. And I am planning on keeping it that way for a long time."

"I love it. I've always wanted to be 'kept' by you. I just didn't know if I'd fit into your long-term plans."

"Now you know." Elliott reassured her.

"And I have no idea how this is going to mix with our working relationship."

"I don't either. It's going to get complicated. Especially if we go on assignments. I'm going to be worried sick about you, just like I was when you were kidnapped. I have no idea how this is going to work out." He admitted reluctantly.

"I guess, we'll have to put some thought into how this is going to work." Steff decided.

They both got up, straightened themselves out a little, and Stef went in to redo her facial paint and hair. Then they were off, heading back to the metro station.

Again, taking the Blue Line, and continuing on in the same direction away from the airport, they headed for the Smithsonian station in the center of the DC Federal Triangle.

Leaving Crystal City, the next stop was Pentagon City, followed by the Pentagon. As the metro train came to a halt and the doors opened, Stef grabbed Elliott's arm and squeezed hard. Elliott had a brief grimace of pain and, looking at Stef could see that something had attracted her attention. Looking off in the same direction she was looking, Elliot could see the thing that had her captivated. There, walking in the direction of the Pentagon entrance was Kres and two other men. He may even have been riding the same subway train as Stef and Elliott but must have boarded at a different location.

Elliott quickly moved to get off the train, and Stef rapidly followed, squeezing through the doors as they tried to close behind her. Just then Kres looked up at a mirror, and then he turned and looked back, his mouth opened in surprise. He said something to the two men standing next to him and both of them turned and looked at Stef and Elliott. Then, in a flash, they had their weapons pulled and were taking aim.

Elliott quickly pulled Stef behind a pillar as chips of the pillar blew off in their direction. Neither of them had taken weapons off the plane with them. They would never have gotten them through security. Besides, they weren't planning to use them. And every building in Washington seemed to have security systems, so having weapons would be a constant barrier. Now they were unarmed and under attack. And they had to think quick. The spray of bullets kept coming at them, and they could see that at least one of the guys was walking around to the side to get a better aim at them.

Fortune was with Elliott and Stef. On the pillar was a fire alarm and Elliott quickly pulled the alarm, sending off a blaring sound through the metro tunnel. Then the sprinklers went off, drenching everyone. Elliott peeked around the corner to see what Kres and his men were doing, but they were gone, spooked by the noise and fearful of an army of fire and police showing up any second.

Stef looked up at Elliott. Her hair and clothes were drenched. She had a kind of pathetic, defeated look on her face. The water was freezing cold and she was not happy. "Are you sure that was necessary? Now what?" was all she could say.

"I guess we go back to the hotel and get changed," responded Elliott.

"Oh! I see how it is. I'll bet this was your plan all along. Get me drenched then get me back to the hotel and get my clothes off."

"I guess I've been found out. Did it work?"

"We'll have to see."

"Before we go, I want to take a quick look off in the direction where Kres was headed, to see if I can figure out what they were up to."

"I'll just wait right here," replied Stef shivering. "I'm not in the mood to take a walk right now. Hurry so we can get changed."

Elliott walked down the hall to the entrance of the Pentagon. There were security desks, and numerous guards and detection equipment. Even a little tourist shop. But no Kres. He had disappeared. But Elliott knew there was more to this than just coincidence. He would have to come back and investigate further. But first he had to get dry clothes.

Elliott hurried back down to Stef and they jumped back on the Blue Line heading back to the Crystal City stop and to their hotel. By then Stef was visibly shaking from the cold. Elliott quickly helped her get soaking in a warm tub of water and after about 20 minutes she was back to normal.

Elliott was left wondering about the significance of Kres being at the metro line Pentagon station, right at the base of the Pentagon. Was there some connection between this and his big plan? There had to be.

Surprisingly, the Pentagon station was an area that was relatively unsecured and easy to access. Anyone could take the metro train to the Pentagon stop and simply get off. Then there was a separate security check before you could enter the Pentagon basement. But this security check was simply a metal detector similar to the ones found in most government buildings.

Elliott sent a message to Marcello, saying they had encountered Kres at the Pentagon. He didn't expect a response until Marcello arrived in the DC area.

With Stef still in the tub, Elliott received a message from his boss Malvika back in Alice Springs, Australia. The message was short and to the point, "Call me first chance."

Elliott placed the call immediately. "What's new?"

Malvika sounded irate, "What the heck is going on? You were supposed to protect the Ark, not destroy it. I'm getting calls and messages from 33-degree Masons all over the world and they're extremely upset."

Elliott tried to explain the sequence of events and how there must have been some type of bobby-trap that was set off when the NNRL broke into the Chapel of the Tablet. But Malvika was not going to be consoled. He was angry and he just wanted to vent his frustration on someone. And Elliott was the target.

Elliott listened. He realized that Malvika wasn't really interested in his explanations. And after the ranting was over, they said their goodbyes. Malvika had not even asked where Elliott and Stef were and what they were doing. He was too upset to care. Elliott was left wondering what had just happened. Why was Malvika so upset? There had to be more to this story.

After Stef was warmed up, she dried herself off and got dressed. "Shall we try this again?" she asked.

"If you're up to it. I'd still like to get you a ring and seeing the museum would be an added bonus."

"Of course, but this time let's not take a cold-water shower at the Pentagon."

Elliott had discovered that there was a jewelry shop close to the hotel and he escorted Stef there first. It didn't take long for Stef to find something she liked. For her, it was not so much about what the ring looked like. She wanted the symbolism of the commitment.

Having accomplished their first goal, they retraced their steps to the metro station for what seemed like the hundredth time today, this time the trip to the museum was uneventful. They made it to the Air and Space museum and Elliott was in heaven, looking at all the authentic flying machines. Stef was starting to get worried that here competition may never be another woman. Rather, her stiffest competition would come from Elliott's love of flying.

CHAPTER SIXTY-THREE

CIA

Early April, 2025 AD, Washington, DC

When Marcello and his CIA team finally landed in the DC airport, he checked his messages.

"Those idiots," Marcello said to Conrad. "Our agents saw Kres and then lost him. Don't we have any agents that can do a simple assignment right? Doesn't anyone take their job seriously anymore?"

Then he saw the message from Elliott.

"Kres is planning something at the Pentagon. I wonder if it is connected with this planned celebration commemorating his father, Adolph Hitler's birthday."

He placed a call to other members of the Task Force on Mercenary Activities (TFMA) which he headed and put them to work monitoring the activities at and around the Pentagon. They were to work with the Department of Defense (DOD) to raise the level of security in the area, citing the possibility of a terrorist attack. He also asked them to get the metro security tapes for the Pentagon station during the time when Elliott and Stef had their encounter with Kres.

Next, he called the leaders of the Task Force on Right Wing Revolutionaries (TFRWR) to explain the situation to them. The TFRWR was more directly involved with the activities of the NNRL and other "Right-Wingers." However, the TFRWR considered the TFMA as a second rate, unnecessary and redundant organization. Anything coming from them was considered of minor significance.

"We're in touch with the activities of the NNRL and we have no indication of any activities in the Washington DC area. We see no reason to gear up a security force at the Pentagon. We don't see your concerns as 'reliable' or 'credible,' especially since you're depending on the information of the IOM, a group of assassins who have their own agendas." Was their response.

"Idiots," was Marcello's response, as he closed his cell phone. "I guess we're on our own."

Marcello, Joe, and Conrad had cars at the airport. Marcello sent Conrad to retrieve the security tapes from the metro station at the Pentagon. Marcello and Joe got into their cars and headed directly to CIA headquarters. After arriving at the headquarters, they immediately went to work trying to tackle Kres' activities. It didn't take long before they searched out and found the hotel he was staying at. And Joe was immediately dispatched to observe activities at the hotel. He brought along some additional agents and they set up surveillance in the lobby. They also set up wiretapping and listening devices in Kres' room. And they established an observation van outside the hotel to listen in and monitor activities in the room.

Joe left some agents in the lobby while he went through the security tapes for the last twelve hours. On tape, Joe saw Kres checking into the hotel with two other men. He electronically transferred the images of the individuals and forwarded them off to Marcello, so that Marcello could use them and send pictures of all three individuals out to all the agents watching the Pentagon.

Back at CIA headquarters, Marcello tried to trace any unusual import activities, like thefts or security breaches at the shipyards that may clue him into a possible source for the arrival of dangerous materials. The break-ins that had occurred during the last week had all been explained. Nothing suspicious popped up.

Eventually, copies of the security tapes from the Pentagon metro station arrived and Marcello went through those, watching where Elliott and Stef encountered Kres and his two goons. Marcello was concerned that these heavily armed individuals were able to get so close to the Pentagon security station. It wouldn't take much for them to disrupt the security area and sneak into the main part of the Pentagon.

Marcello was at a loss on what to do next. He had the hotel and the Pentagon under observation. Eventually Kres would show up and they could start tailing his activities. Marcello decided to contact Elliott and update him on what he had learned.

"If you tell us more about the hotel and the room where Kres is located, we could do some of our own observing," Elliott suggested, without stating the obvious. The CIA was restricted in what they could do. Additionally, thanks to the performance enhancements that the IOM had implemented into the S1, the CIA's observation skills weren't as good as the IOM's. Marcello was desperate for the help, since he wasn't getting the needed support from his companions at the CIA. He readily gave Elliott the necessary information. He hoped Elliott would be able to learn more.

Marcello was just starting to relax, feeling comfortable that he had all the necessary pieces in place for tracking Kres, he received a phone call. It was his CIA boss, the director.

"What is this I hear that you are collaborating with the IOM. They're our enemy, not our friend."

"We have a bigger threat with the NNRL," Marcello tried to explain. "They're planning some kind of celebration event for Hitler's birthday here in Washington DC, and we need to be on guard for what that might be."

"Yes, but all that knowledge is based on information from the IOM, which may be unreliable. In fact, the IOM may be planning their own 'celebration' and are sending us off on a wild goose chase, trying to keep us off their scent. I'm sure they have their own agenda. Anyway, we can't be sharing information with our enemies, the IOM. I want you to cease communication with them and treat them as a possible threat. Watch them as carefully as you watch the NNRL."

"But they have the type of surveillance technology that we only talk about. They can be very helpful to our cause."

"The Air Force and the Navy both have remote aircraft. We've been using the Un-manned Aerial Vehicles, UAV drones in Afghanistan for years. For example, the MQ-1 Predator or it's bigger brother the MQ-9 Reaper. And then we have the RQ-4 Global Hawk high altitude spy planes. They have incredible imagining capability. Are you telling me that the IOM has better equipment?"

"Yes. They have close-in surveillance capability for listening and imaging. They have attack capabilities that can pin-point targets. They can shoot out someone's eye or blow up a building. And they have their S1 perfected using scram-jet engines so that it can do long-range reconnaissance anywhere in the world. With its low fuel utilization, it can hover over its target for hours. It's extremely sophisticated."

"That scares me. Anyway, just quit using them and keep an eye on them. I don't trust them.

"On a second point," the director continued, "why are you crossing over into TFRWR territory. You're stepping on their toes. The NNRL is their responsibility."

"They rejected my information and choose not to act on it," Marcello was trying to be straight forward and still be diplomatic.

"Well, if you consider this a viable threat, go ahead and observe, but keep the TFRWR informed, in case they want to jump in and take action. But remember that your focus is on the IOM, not the NNRL."

"Will do," was all Marcello could muster to say as they signed-off on the call. He did his best to hide his frustration. He was trying to do the right thing, but the bureaucracy of the CIA was more concerned about crossing territorial boundaries then they were about preventing a disaster.

"This is ridiculous," Marcello said out loud, to no one in particular. "This is all about a turf war between me and the TFRWR. They call the director and raised a fuss with him. They want me to do the leg work. And then if anything comes of it, they want me to bring them in so they can take credit for it. I can't believe the nonsense that goes on around here."

Marcello stared at a poster of Einstein that he had hanging on the wall. It was the popular picture where Einstein was sticking out his tongue. The quote read: "Imagination is more important than knowledge."

"What happens when you work in an organization that pretends to have both but exhibits neither?" he thought out loud. But it left Marcello wondering if he had missed anything big. Was he so wrapped up in the details, that he was missing the big picture? Was there an "out of the box" perspective that he desperately needed to consider?

CHAPTER SIXTY-FOUR - PART 6

Washington, DC (cont.)
April 19th, 2025 AD, Washington, DC

Kres was excited. He was confident that his birthday celebration would be an overwhelming success, and that the world would recognize him as their salvation. The three key components of a nuclear device, the fuel, the delivery system, and the detonator, were all in place. He had organized three independent cells, each working without knowledge of the other so that if any one of them was compromised, he wouldn't lose everything. He was amazed how easily it all came together. He whispered to himself; "Those stupid Americans, with all their security and military and police, can't even keep a nuclear bomb from being delivered to their nation's capital. It's just pathetic."

The fuse cell had been delivered to Washington DC under the disguise of a VCR. This cell included a high ranking NNRL team member, Joseph Ahuna, and Karl Geisenberger, a nuclear scientist that would be responsible for assembling the device. They were waiting in a DC area hotel waiting to hear from Kres.

The delivery cell included Mohammad Abdullah, known to Kres as Joe Smith, and Moyad Ali, known as Frank Marshall. They would arrive in the DC area in about four hours.

The fuels cell included Krank Markal and Lefty Leviticus who were responsible for the delivery of the nuclear fuel. They were also in the DC area and had stashed the fuel into the bathtub of their hotel room. Kres had contacted them and asked them to come to the airport and pick him up. He asked them to get a new vehicle and to be prepared for a quick pick-up. He told them that he anticipated being followed and that he would need to jump into the vehicle and get away as quickly as possible. Krank and Lefty disposed of the stolen car and proceeded to steal a large four door vehicle which would work well for an easy escape. They knew that this vehicle would be registered on the airport surveillance equipment and that they would need to replace it shortly after they picked Kres up.

After Kres landed in Washington National Airport, Krank and Lefty were ready for him and picked him up. They had arrived in town one day earlier. The first stop was to get Kres checked into the Crystal Gateway Marriott. It was a nicer hotel then the ones the agents were staying at. Instead, the agents preferred a Motel that had outside access, like the Motel 6. They wanted to be able to back their car right up to the door of their room. This allowed them to take things out of the trunk and bring them directly into the room without being noticed.

While Kres was checking in, Krank and Lefty swapped out their car for a new vehicle. Then they returned to the Marriott to retrieve Kres. He wanted to travel the route of the planned "celebration." They hopped the Washington Metro Blue Line and travelled to the Pentagon station. They were just leaving the train and heading through the Pentagon to see both Stef and Elliott standing there. His first reaction was, "They can't see what we're doing here," and he ordered his men to shoot at them, which they did. That turned out to be a disaster. The security system came on and the sprinklers started to soak the area down. Kres, Krank, and Lefty quickly ducked into a bathroom in the reception area, located behind the souvenir shop. Each of them entered one of the stalls and closed the door. Then they waited. After about ten minutes, the alarm was turned off and the noise seemed to settle down. They left the stalls, quickly jumped on the next Metro train, and left the area as quickly as possible.

Kres communicated with Joseph Ahuna and Karl Geisenberger from the fuse cell and give them the details of Krank and Lefty's hotel room where they would find the nuclear fuel. He instructed them that Krank had left a hotel room key resting above the door on the door jamb, and that Joseph and Karl were to go into the room and get to work assembling the bomb. The fuse cell immediately jumped into action and headed for the Motel 6.

Kres, Krank, and Lefty also headed for their Motel so they could observe the assembly of the bomb. On the way they stopped by a Target and picked up a small hard-back suitcase in which the assembled bomb would be contained. By the time they arrived, Karl, the nuclear scientist, was busy working on "celebration" activities. Kres waved Joe, Karl, Krank, and Lefty around him as he pulled out a US one dollar bill. On the back side he pointed to the symbol of the unfinished pyramid topped with the all-seeing eye. "Come here. I need to show you something important. See these Masonic symbols? Now read what's written underneath them."

Karl read, "Novus Ordo Seclorum."

"Do you know what that means?" Kres asked. "It means 'New World Order.' And that's what we will be officially starting tomorrow as we celebrate my father's birthday. As you can see, even the United States is looking for this new world order. They are advertising it on their dollar bill. The Masons have been talking about this since they built Solomon's temple. And look at the mess we're in today. There still isn't any 'order' in this world. Everyone is looking for a 'New World Order.' And we are the ones who are going to help bring it to pass."

Kres continued, waving at the beds; "Come everyone, let's sit on a bed and discuss tomorrow. I want to make sure we do not have any misfires, like we had today at the Pentagon metro station earlier when we were spotted by Elliott."

They went through their delivery plans. Karl would assemble the fuses to the nuclear fuel and set a timer. There would also be a secondary trigger attached to the bomb. This would be a cell phone, which, if it rings it would cause the fuse to trigger a detonation of the bomb.

"How big of an explosion are we expecting?" asked Kres. "I'm not sure exactly how much damage this amount of nuclear fuel can cause."

Karl responded, "The actual explosion will take out the Pentagon and Pentagon City area. The after-shock heat wave will destroy most of the Washington DC area. But the real damage comes from the nuclear fallout, which will contaminate the entire DC and surrounding area for at least six to eight months. The entire area will be useless."

Kres responded with; "And the whole thing fits into a small black roller-bag. How convenient."

"So how are we going to deliver the device to the Pentagon?"

"That's the easy part. I don't want to give you all the details, because we need to keep this on a 'need to know' basis. But what I can tell you is that we'll set the timer for 03:00PM tomorrow. We have a couple of delivery guys that are going to deliver the package tomorrow morning. And they think they're working for God when they do it."

"How are you going to pull that off," asked Karl. "Who are you going to convince that suicide is a good thing?"

Kres continued, "I already have a couple of suicide bombers who think they're working for Al-Qaeda, and they're going to deliver the package to the Pentagon Metro Station, which is directly under the edge of the Pentagon. Then they're going to sit there with it making sure it detonates. We're handing the bomb over to them tomorrow morning. Then we get as far away as possible."

"We're planning on leaving tonight," said Joe. "Karl can set the timer for tomorrow and leave it here with you." He pointed to Lefty and Krank. "Then we'll see you back in Paraguay to have our own celebration."

"Cowards," blurted out Lefty. Joe gave him a dirty look but didn't say anything.

Kres, ignoring the tension, continued; "I'll come by with our suicide bombers in the morning, around 10:00AM. One of you needs to pick us up at my hotel at 09:30AM. We'll drive here and pick up the bomb. Then we'll deliver them to the Metro Station around 11:00AM. The bomb should be set to go off around 03:00PM. That should give us four hours, which should be plenty of time to get clear of the area. I don't want to go so far away that I can see the explosion. I want to go somewhere where we will be able to see the cloud, but still be at a reasonably safe distance." Then, looking at Lefty and Krank he said; "Let's go. You can drop me back off at my hotel and I'll see you tomorrow." To Joe and Karl, he said; "I suppose you'll be long gone by 11:00AM tomorrow so

I'll see you back in Asunción." They shook their heads acknowledging Kres' comment.

Lefty and Krank left Joe and Karl working on the bomb in their hotel room and drove Kres back to his hotel. Back in the hotel, Joe urged Karl along, hoping to get away as soon as possible. Joe had no interest in being around a nuclear explosion. He had already checked for flights out of the area, and he hoped they would be able to catch a flight leaving Washington Dulles airport in four hours. America was great for the Americans, but Paraguay was home, and he wanted to get back as quickly as possible. There wouldn't be anyone trying to blow up Paraguay. There wasn't anything worth attacking.

April 19th, 2025 AD, Washington, DC

Later that evening Kres met with the delivery cell. The delivery cell included two men, obviously Arab, but known to him as Joe Smith and Frank Marshall. They both spoke excellent English, which left Kres confused. He expected Arab radicals. But these guys looked like average college students out on a field trip. They had arrived in the DC area and checked into a nearby Comfort Inn. They took the subway system to Pentagon City where they met Kres in a near-by Subway sandwich shop. It was a small shop, with outside seating, but it was adequate for their little "meet and greet." Each of them stood in line and ordered from the $5-foot-long menu. Kres had a tuna sandwich, and Joe and Frank had turkey.

After their initial greetings, Kres explained; "The world we live in is in rapid decline and decay. I am thrilled that you have decided to join our team. We need to create a New World Order."

Joe spoke up; "We are here to build Allah's kingdom. We want a kingdom founded on the Koran. We need to eliminate the scourge that has been placed on society by those that have corrupted Allah's truths."

Kres listened patiently. In his mind he classified Joe and Frank as fools. But on his face, he expressed concern and commitment to their principles. All he really cared about was the delivery of the bomb. By tomorrow these idiots would be dead and who really cares what they believe or don't believe.

"Exactly," Kres responded. "We need to purify the human race and eliminate its degradation." Of course, to Kres this meant the creation of the superior race. And these fools were imperfections that he was delighted to use for his cause. "We need to take revenge on the evil, morally corrupt West."

The Arabs had no problem telling Kres their feelings. They were very passionate about what they wanted to accomplish. "Sometimes someone has to sacrifice for the greater good," suggested Frank. "And I am committed to doing my part. I want to be one of Allah's soldiers in the pursuit of a righteous world."

Kres, Joe, and Frank were using the same words, but they were both implying entirely different meanings. Joe and Frank were willing to pay the ultimate price to take a stand in their beliefs. Whereas Kres believed he needed to be around to be the leader of the New World Order and that no one would be able to do it as well as he would. So, suicide would be a meaningless gesture if he weren't there to lead the new world.

Kres, trying to appease to their sensitivities, told them that his goal was to create a purified New World Order led and based on the principals of the Koran. And this rhetoric resonated well with the Arabs, even though Kres thought they were idiots, and their ideas were ridiculous. But these suicidal Arabs had an important role to play in his plan.

At this point they were all comfortable working together. Kres saw Joe and Frank's commitment, and Joe and Frank thought they were working for the same goal as Kres. The three agreed to meet again in the morning at 09:30AM, at Kres' hotel. Then Joe and Frank would receive the bomb and head off to the nearest subway station. From there it would just be a short subway ride for the delivery cell to arrive at the Pentagon.

CHAPTER SIXTY-FIVE

Preparing for the Celebration
April 19th, 2025 AD, Washington, DC

Elliott used the hotel information that Marcello had provided about the location of Kres' hotel. He had Dawn dispatch the S1 from the airport area over to the Marriott hotel so he could listen in. He had to use a search algorithm along with a voice print from earlier recorded conversations with Kres to sort out all the communications that were going on in the hotel. Unfortunately, Kres never seemed to have anyone in the room with him, so it was hard to catch any conversations. And he rarely made any phone calls. There wasn't much that could be done until Kres appears. Then they hoped to be able to track his movements. But once he appears, things could get exciting quickly. They would try to listen to his communications and follow his movements. Additionally, Elliott hesitated to trust the information from Marcello, still remembering the experience in Axum.

April 19th, 2025 AD, Washington, DC

Marcello was on the phone with Elliott. He ignored the instructions from his director. Staying in touch with the IOM was the only way he could stay in control of the NNRL movements. Additionally, he had no intention of contacting the NNRL with any information that he learned unless he felt they could directly help his effort. But right now, that seemed highly unlikely. This was way too important to leave in the hands of politically minded bureaucrats who had never been out of their offices. "We watched Kres come into the hotel and go to his room. We got the license plate of the vehicle that dropped him off, but it didn't help much. It was stolen and later abandoned. Apparently, he was alone in his room, and made no calls, so we weren't able to get any information from there either. Were you able to pick anything up?"

Elliott responded by telling Marcello about the incident at the Pentagon subway stop. Then he explained; "We were able to learn quite a lot. We used his cell phone to track him and to track his messages. He keeps talking about preparing for the celebration tomorrow and how he's making final preparations. We weren't onto him quick enough to know where he went after our Metro incident. But apparently, he went to meet with his buddies who were preparing for the 'celebration.' It doesn't sound good. But I don't have any details on who, what, when, where, or how."

"Did you pick up on his meeting this evening?" asked Marcello.

"I just know that he met with two Arabs, but the restaurant was too well buried within a high-rise for us to get much of a signal," Elliott lied. He wanted to see if Marcello would be honest with him.

"We don't know much. They're using false names so that doesn't help either. They were two Arab extremists suspected of being in a terrorist cell. But I thought the NNRL was prejudiced against Arabs. So, the connection confuses me."

"But their prejudice doesn't keep the NNRL from using anyone and everyone for their ultimate purposes."

"So true," responded Marcello. "We tracked the Arabs back to their hotel. We're keeping them under surveillance as well. Perhaps you can see if there are any conversations you can pick up."

"Excellent. They may be instrumental in this celebration. Give me their location and I'll do my best to see what conversations I can pull in."

Marcello gave Elliott the information and he forwarded it on to Dawn.

"Any speculation on what's going on here?"

"The NNRL would not bring in the Al-Qaeda unless they were going to use them in their game. Worst case scenario suggests that they need some suicide bombers to carry out their dirty work. But I don't have any guess on what the plan entails. I hope it isn't what I fear."

"And what is that?"

"A nuclear detonation in the heart of Washington DC."

Just saying the words out loud made both of them hesitate for a minute. This indeed was the worst-case scenario, and it would prove disastrous.

"Well, let's keep observing and tracking, and keep each other informed." Marcello responded.

April 19th, 2025 AD, Washington, DC

Stef was in a daze. It was as if the marriage proposal had finally hit her. She was going to get married, and she had never planned for this eventuality. She had always been so wrapped up in a career, that marriage had seemed like an unnecessary complication. But she also never expected to fall in love. Now, her career seemed secondary to spending the rest of her life with her best friend. Now, she didn't care if either of them kept their job. In fact, it may be less of a worry if they both left their jobs and escaped somewhere where they could enjoy each other's company.

Elliott had literally swept her off her feet. What had started out as a working relationship, and then developed into a sexual and intimate relationship, had now become an involved and caring relationship. She worried about Elliott and his safety, not in an obsessive way, but more of a selfish way. She didn't want to go through life without him. She wouldn't be able to handle it if he ever got hurt. Even now, when he did get hurt, she suffered more than he did. Caring for someone else wasn't something she was ready for. She didn't know how to handle these emotions. It was all quite a struggle for her.

Stef became somewhat irritated with herself. This proposal had made her brain-dead. All she could think about was getting herself and Elliott out of the IOM so they would be safe. The life she had enjoyed, no longer seemed appropriate or relevant. She wanted something else, something more, something long lasting and eternal. And she wanted it with Elliott.

Stef could hear Elliott talking to Marcello, and communicating with Dawn, and sending messages back and forth. These activities, which had seemed so important to her in the past, and where she had wanted to be integrally involved with everything, now seemed trivial and unimportant. Why should she even bother? It no longer fit into the long-term vision for her life.

Elliott had just come off the phone and Stef turned to him and said, "So what are we going to do?"

"We're going to monitor Kres and the Arabs and see what we learn."

"I'm not talking about Kres, I'm talking about us. What are we going to do?"

"Huh?"

"You can't just propose to me and then expect everything to remain the same. What are we going to do?"

"Well, we get married and move in permanently together. Is that what you mean?"

Sarcastically Stef responded, "You're such a man. You totally explode my life and my mind and now you act like 'what's the big deal.' It's an enormous deal! Making a commitment to an everlasting relationship is enormous. You just changed everything that's important to me. You just changed how I look at life. This is a huge deal."

Elliott was a little flabbergasted. He's getting attacked for what Stef thinks he's going to say. He doesn't even get a chance to say anything and he's already condemned.

Stef continued; "I'm talking bigger than that. Are we going to stay with the IOM? I don't like the idea of having a husband that's constantly at risk."

"I was always at risk before, and it didn't bother you."

"That was different. Then you were just someone I worked with; someone I worked for. Now you're someone I plan to have kids with. It's different. The rules have changed. What do you plan to do?"

"Kids?"

"Yes, kids! A family. A life where we grow old together. The active word is 'together.' Not you running off on missions while I sit at home and play mommy."

Elliott had to step back and think about all this for a minute. Had he created some kind of monster when he proposed? But a different side of him was excited because Stef was so excited. He was thrilled that she was so strongly invested in the idea of getting married. But he had always looked at it as him protecting Stef. Now he realized there was more to just protecting her because she was also interested in protecting him. And then there are kids. Where did the kids come from? "You're absolutely right," he started, trying to recapture his composure. "You're just putting it together more than I had. I became really scared for you when you were kidnapped, and I didn't know if you were safe. And I realized I wanted something more long-term with you. Something more permanent. I didn't want to be afraid like that again. It hurts. And it affects my ability to do a good job and use my best judgment. I would do anything to keep you safe. Like you said, 'the rules have changed.'"

"So, what are we going to do? You need to realize that I feel the same about keeping you safe. It's about the both of us, not just about me. What are we going to do?"

"Get married."

"And then what?" She demanded.

"I guess we need to rethink our lives. How do we want to live? Where do we want to live? Etc."

"That's what I meant when I originally asked, 'what are we going to do?' Things can't stay the way they are. It won't work. If we're going to stay with the IOM, we shouldn't get married. But if we're going to get married, we need to change our lifestyle." Stef urged.

"Now that you bring it up, I guess you're right. But I'm not sure I can do anything else, other than playing at being a 'secret agent'."

"So, what does that mean. Does it mean you want to stay with the IOM and not get married. Or do we leave the IOM and get married?" She demanded, unwilling to let go of the issue, as though there was suddenly a huge ultimatum to be considered.

"We get married! I proposed because I adore you, not because it seemed like a fun thing to say. I can't change my feelings just because I may lose my job." He yelled hoarsely, almost to the point of exasperation. Lucky for Elliott it was the answer Stef was hoping for. She jumped up, threw her arms around his neck, and gave him a big kiss. "I guess that was the right answer?" is all Elliott could muster, surprised at his own quick thinking and clearly visibly relieved at Stef's positive reaction.

"You bet it was the right answer. Now you're *really* stuck."

"I guess this means we need to make it work with the cash we already have saved up. We're not going to be rich, but we have enough to live a comfortable life."

"I'd rather live on a homestead in Alaska, then to not be with you." Stef had taken this marriage thing to a new height, much higher than Elliott had ever anticipated. It made him nervous, but at the same time it made him pleasantly excited. This would open up a whole new chapter in his life. Elliott's head was reeling. Under no circumstances would he change his engagement. But the consequences of it had become bigger than he had initially realized. He had committed to a career change and a lifestyle change, not just a relationship change. Oh well, Stef was worth it, and he knew it.

CHAPTER SIXTY-SIX - PART 7

The Day of the Birthday Celebration
April 20th, 2025 AD, 9:15 AM, Washington, DC

"The Arabs are rolling. It looks like they're heading to Kres' hotel," it was Conrad who was watching the Motel 6 in Springfield, VA. He was updating Joe and Marcello.

About fifteen minutes later there was a second call. "Kres just met with two members of his team." This time it was Joe talking to Marcello. Then, almost immediately afterward, he said; "Kres met with the Arabs in the lobby and they were given a suitcase by the two other individuals. Now I see the Arabs leaving. They're walking toward the subway station. We'll try tracking them, but we'll lose them as soon as they get mixed into the congested subway crowd. Kres is now getting in the car with the two guys who delivered the suitcase."

Marcello immediately called Elliott, "We have the Arabs heading for the subway, and Kres driving away with a couple of his agents. Is there any way you can help keep track of Kres?"

"Got it," was Elliott's response. "We have the S1 tracking Kres' car and listening in. I'll update you if we learn anything."

About fifteen minutes later, another call came into Marcello, this time from Conrad. "I think the hotel has been abandoned. I went in and looked around. They left a mess, but I don't think they intend to come back. I think I should call off this surveillance. Where do you want me to go next?"

Then Marcello called Elliott, "Are you watching Kres? Have you learned anything?"

"Yes," was Elliott's response. "The conversation in the car has a slightly different tone. They keep talking about the idiots who think they are serving Allah and a Holy War. I'm sensing that we're talking about a suicide bombing. This doesn't sound good. Kres is using these Arabs to do his dirty work."

"I think you're right," Marcello responded. I hope we can figure out where they're going relatively soon. This is getting scary. Hold it; I'm getting a call from Joe who is tailing the Arabs. I'll call you back."

"Hello?" asked Marcello.

"The Arabs have headed into the Metro station. I'm in trouble here. I tried to follow them, but I think they were on to me and they gave me the slip, which wasn't too hard considering all the people and the congestion. Anyway, they're gone. I think they're headed toward the downtown area."

"Did they take the package?"

"Affirmative."

"Go the route that you think they went and try to follow the package. Do whatever you have to. Let me know if you see anything." Marcello was now convinced that they were following a bomb.

Marcello sent a quick message to Elliott, "We've lost the package. You stay with Kres." That was already Elliott's plan. He knew that using the S1 he would lose Conrad in the Metro, so he had Dawn stay with the easier target, Kres, his two friends, and his car.

CHAPTER SIXTY-SEVEN

Back at the Chapel
April 20th, 2025 AD, Axum, Ethiopia

About twenty minutes after the explosion, the area around the Chapel of the Tablet came to life with police, fire equipment, clergy, and an ever-increasing array of on-lookers. The Chapel was gone. The area where the chapel had been now was heap of dust and rubble, mostly from the roof. The walls had all been blown out. And pieces of the wall and the Ark were blown in about a fifty-foot perimeter. Scavengers were already busily trying to collect pieces of the Ark in hopes that they may bring some spiritual blessing into their home by its presence. Some not-so-noble scavengers hoped to be able to sell pieces of the Ark.

The clergy did their best to prevent investigators from entering the area of the Chapel, declaring it to be sacred ground. But, even without entering the area, it was obvious that the explosion was centered within the chapel, and most probably within the Ark itself. Debris was distributed evenly in all directions, which suggested that the Ark must have contained the bomb which triggered the explosion.

The Bishop of Axum was on site, and he walked up to Jano who was picking through some of the debris. Jano had been sent by the Bishop in Alexandria and had earlier delivered a warning. Jano, because of his monk's robes, was allowed within the Chapel grounds. He was casually looking through the rubble. "What are you finding," asked the Bishop.

"I think we scared off the predators that had visions of stealing the Ark."

"Looks more like you killed them off. I assume that everything went according to plan and that the real Ark is safe."

"I don't see any rubble from the real Ark, only the wood pieces of the fake Ark. And I don't see the body of the Guardian. So, I assume everything went according to plan. But we won't know for sure until we remove this rubble and get rid of these investigators and gawkers. I find it comical that we used the same trick to save the Ark that was used during the Babylonian invasion two and a half millennium ago."

Jano paused for a moment to let that last statement sink in, then continued; "As planned, I was watching those guys last night. From what I could see, there were three groups of people going after the Ark. One group of three people was here early. Two hid away while the third sat on the bench waiting. Then a second group showed up and took some shots at the first group. In the end, one person from the second group was killed, but as far as I could tell no one from the first group was injured. It was this second group that went over the fence and tried breaking down to door of the Chapel. When they broke in the door was when I triggered the explosion. It killed the four that were at the door of the chapel. The last member of the second team, one of the guys who visited us in Alexandria, was knocked down and must have been slightly injured, but he escaped. The five bodies you see came from this second group, one was shot by the first group, and four were killed by the explosion."

"Then there was another guy hiding up on the hill in the bushes. He was also one of the guys that we met in Alexandria. Apparently, he was no longer part of the second group because he was hiding from them. Anyway, he got away as well. It will be interesting to see what the police come up with as an explanation for last night's events. I'm obviously not going to let them know that I observed it all. In the end, it really doesn't matter. All that matters is that the Ark is safe." Jano finally concluded.

The Bishop added; "We plan to construct a new chapel over the site of the old chapel. The guardian and the Ark will stay hidden underground until then. He will need to stay hidden for about six months. I assume that he has what he needs for that period of time."

"Not completely. As soon as we have the area cleared and start construction of the new chapel, enough so that onlookers can't see what we're doing, we can contact the guardian. We have a concealed access hole that we can use to pass small things through, like bread or water, and he can pass notes to us as well. We'll have to be careful to make sure no one sees any of that activity. But I think he'll be fine until we get the new Chapel of the Tablet in place. Then, when everything is prepared, we can bring the guardian and the Ark back out of the hole. We'll consider this new chapel to be a memorial for the Ark. We will keep the knowledge about this being the true Ark a secret from the general public."

"Thanks for your help," expressed the grateful Bishop.

Jano expressed his commitment; "My congregation may be based over at Alexandria, but the Ark is as precious to us as it is to you. If you need any additional help, please call on us."

It would take a week of investigation by the local authorities before the work on clearing the Chapel debris was able to begin. The police and fire departments were convinced that the explosion was triggered by a group of some eleven individuals who were seen going from their hotel to the chapel late on the night of the explosion. Four of those individuals were identified by their bodies, near the entrance of the Chapel. There was a fifth body outside the perimeter of the Chapel grounds with a bullet hole in his head. It was decided that this must have been the result of some dispute between the members of this group. On the day prior to the explosion, three more of this team was found dead in an alley nearby, and two more were found dead in one of the hotel rooms. Apparently the eleventh person escaped by private jet that same evening from the airport. The police were able to put a description together of the remaining individual, and they ran it through INTERPOL, with no success. The police were convinced that this was an attempt to steal the Ark, which had gone terribly wrong. Fortunately, no Ethiopians were killed. The only deaths were from the individuals trying to steal the Ark. They could not explain the absence of the guardian. He could not be found among the living or the dead. That would have to remain an unsolved mystery. After the investigation, the case was closed. The search for the 11th person was suspended. And the site was turned over to the Church for clean-up and reconstruction.

Mourners had gathered throughout the grounds of the Church of Our Lady Mary of Zion, kneeling, weeping, and praying. Some would crawl or walk on their knees from the edge of the Church grounds to the Chapel ruins, a distance of a couple hundred feet. Often their knees would be bloodied by the time they arrived. Then they would fall to their faces in the dirt and cry unceasingly.

Mourners kept pouring in from all around the country and from as far away as Jerusalem to the North, and South Africa in the South. The spiritual impact of the loss of the Ark was devastating to the church community. Their pride and joy were gone. And they deeply felt the loss. This was a tragedy, not only for Axum, but for Ethiopia as a whole, and for the entire Coptic Christian Church.

The Coptic leadership decided to keep everyone thinking that the Ark had been destroyed. At least until they were sure that the threat of anyone trying to steal the Ark was gone. And that threat may not go away for a long time. They were willing to wait generations, if needed, before the truth of the Ark would be made public. The Bishop of Axum shared the information with the other Coptic Bishops and Popes. All agreed that since the Ark was kept secluded anyway, there would be no harm in keeping everyone convinced that it was destroyed.

CHAPTER SIXTY-EIGHT

The Celebration

April 20th, 2025 AD, 10:35 AM, Washington, DC

Kres called Joe and Frank, his Al-Qaeda operatives, "Did you see that you're being tailed?"

"Yes," it was Joe that answered. "I think we gave them the slip. Is there anything in the plan we should change?"

"Go forward with the plan. They have no idea what you're doing but, in the end, even if they follow you, they can't change the results."

"But what if they try to take the package?"

"Don't worry about it. Just do your job." Then he disconnected the phone and told Krank who was riding in the back seat, and Lefty, the NNRL agent who was driving; "Boy those guys are dumb. I hope they don't screw this up."

Kres shifted in his seat, feeling uncomfortable. "I wish you could have come up with something better than this 'piece of junk' that we're driving. Couldn't you have found a Lexus or Cadillac?"

"That would make us easier to identify. We wanted to keep a low profile, so we thought this little silver Honda was generic enough that no one would pick us out."

"You're right, of course. There are lots of these on the road. We look just like any other commuter. I just prefer to have a little more leg room."

"Should we speed it up and get out of here?" asked the driver.

"Let's get as far away from here as possible," responded Krank. They jumped on Interstate 95, heading South towards Jacksonville. Krank had left instructions with his private jet to meet him there in the late evening hours of the 20th, hoping that a departure from this city would be inconspicuous enough not to raise any questions. He knew that the airspace around the DC area would be placed on hold as soon as the explosion rang out.

"Where are we heading," asked Lefty.

"Just stay on 95 for now. I'll let you know what to do as the time comes." Everyone knew this simply meant that Kres felt that this information would be given out on a "need to know" basis. For now, they just maintained their route south, trying to get as far away from the DC area as possible.

What Kres and his team didn't know was that Dawn, using the S1 for surveillance, was tracking their car and listening to every word.

April 20th, 2025 AD, 10:45 AM, Washington, DC

Conrad was frustrated with himself. The job was so easy. All he had to do was follow the two Arabs. But unfortunately, he lost them in the crowd of the Crystal City subway station. There seemed to be no end of people dressed in their business suit best. Most of them were walking at full speed and staring at their cell phones or Blackberries. It was impossible to walk through the area and not get bumped several times. Everyone was so wrapped up in their self-importance, that they hardly noticed Conrad. "If only they knew how unimportant they really were," Conrad said to himself. "They could all be dead within the hour, and they don't even realize the danger they're in."

Based on Elliott's encounter with Kres, Conrad decided that they must be catching the Blue Line and heading for the Pentagon. So, he decided to follow suit. He didn't feel as though standing around in the Crystal City station was going to accomplish anything. He may as well try something. He rode the subway often, so he had a multi-use ticket with him, where he purchased $50 worth of credit and then used it until it expired. He crossed through the turnstile, inserting his card at the front end, and retrieving it at the back end as he exited.

Soon he was on the Blue Line platform, heading toward Metro Center. He knew that the Pentagon station was only two stops, so this would be a short ride. It arrived about five minutes before the next train rolled in. He felt the gush of warm air as the train acted like a circulating mechanism, pushing the air in front of it. If only it could somehow leave the smells behind. But that would be expecting too much.

The first stop was Pentagon City. This stop brought another surge of tie wearing, cell phone staring bureaucrats and politicians. There wasn't a friendly face or a smile amongst them. Conrad was not impressed. Fortunately, there were also several military that seemed like the only people who knew how to speak and not just type messages. They seemed somehow disconnected. They were a part of this crowd, but yet detached from them. One group of four Air Force Captains actually joked and smiled, which seemed entirely out of place.

But Conrad wasn't looking at the suits, or the uniforms. He was on the hunt for two Arabs, wearing jeans and t-shirts, and dragging a roller bag. It was a large crowd to search through, and he would probably miss them even if they were there, but he had to try.

The second stop was the Pentagon station stop. Conrad got out and started scanning the crowd. He noticed them, far off to the left, and almost by accident. And it seemed like they had noticed him as well, but he wasn't sure. He couldn't tell if they had looked directly at him or not. They were standing on the subway train platform, close to where they would have alighted the train, but at the other end of the train from where Conrad had exited.

The Arabs seemed to be unsure of themselves and of what they should do. Then, almost as an afterthought, just as the subway doors started to close, the Arabs jumped on the train. Conrad, reacting quickly, and jumped on the train as well.

Now Conrad was in a dilemma. His jumping on the train just when the Arabs had decided to jump on the train was a dead give-away. Anyone watching would surely know that he was following Joe and Frank. And so, he had to assume that Joe and Frank also knew. What to do next? Does he move forward aggressively, or does he hold back.

It was just a few minutes before the next station, the Arlington Cemetery station, and he had to decide quickly. He resolved to move closer to the other end of the train, toward the end where the Arabs were located. He started to type in a message to Marcello, updating him, but he knew, because of poor connectivity, it wouldn't be transmitted until the train had emerged from the tunnel. Now he felt like he blended in with the rest of his immediate surroundings and was quite inconspicuously able to walk and type a message at the same time. He finally felt like he had made one small step toward being more like the bureaucrats that surrounded him each day here in Washington.

He had travelled about $2/3^{rd}$ of the way to the other end of the train, when it stopped at the Arlington Cemetery station. Conrad proceeded with caution, took one step out of the car, and watched to see if the Arabs had alighted the train yet. He knew he would have to wait till the last minute, because they might just decide to pull another one of their 'last second jumps', as they had done at the Pentagon station. But it was obvious they had no plans to get off, and Conrad jumped back onto the train just as the doors tried to close in on him and turn him into a can of sardines. Conrad continued to work himself toward the other end of the subway train. As he neared the end, he noticed the two Arabs, sitting next to each other on one of the subway seats. They were sitting sideways in the car. He held back and kept an eye on them from a distance. They didn't turn in his direction, so he was sure that he had not been detected.

The next stop was Rosslyn. The Arabs didn't move, and Conrad stayed on the train, watching them out of the corner of his eye, but always ready to jump off the train at the last minute, if necessary.

Then came the GWU station, followed by Farragut West, then McPherson Square, and Metro Center. Conrad was sure they would get off at this station or the next station because they were near the center of town. But there was no action. The next station was the Federal Triangle station and again there was no movement by the Arabs.

The next station was the Smithsonian Station. Just as the doors started to close, the Arabs darted out the door of their car. Conrad similarly jumped out, but this time he was sure he was detected. There was no way they could have missed his last-minute movement. They were on to him, but he didn't know what to do about it. He decided that since they had discovered him anyway, he was going to confront them.

Before Conrad could move toward the Arabs, they slipped into the men's bathroom. Conrad had to decide. Does he wait outside for them, or does he go in after them and confront them. He resolved that confronting them in the bathroom would create less of a public scene, and so he went in after them. The bathroom does not have doors. It has a protective wall that users would walk around. Conrad entered the bathroom, walked around the wall, and then felt a hard thump in his chest. Looking down on his chest he saw a small red circle forming. And that was the last thing he would remember as he felt himself collapsing to the ground.

CHAPTER SIXTY-NINE

Finding the Celebration

April 20th, 2025 AD, 10:55 AM, Washington, DC

Stef lay curled up on the bed, contemplating her future. The fuss and bother about Kres and the Arabs and the Ark seemed insignificant. She now had more important things to worry about, like "should she go through with it?" Of course, she knew she would end up getting married to Elliott. She would be stupid not to. But there was always a nervousness that went with a big decision of this type.

She loved the pile of pillows that you always find in a hotel. There were soft, hard, long, and decorator pillows, and lots of them. She tucked the soft pillows under and around her head, the hard pillows along both sides of her body, and the decorator pillows were only used when she needed something to throw at Elliott. She was all cuddled in and cozy.

Up to now Elliott and Stef hadn't left their hotel room. They needed to stay close to their communication equipment. They were waiting to see how the situation progressed. But now it was time for action. Elliott looked at Stef, who was lying on the bed daydreaming, and said, "Time for action." Up to now Stef had been perfectly happy letting Elliott do all the communication with the CIA and with Dawn and Greg. Besides, he enjoyed the technology more than she did. But she knew that when Elliott said, "Time for action," then she would have to get to work.

"What are we doing," Stef asked.

"I think we better get to the Pentagon. Dawn is keeping track of Kres' movements, but he's leaving the area and I'm pretty sure this 'celebration' is going to come down in the Pentagon. The CIA boys lost the Arabs, and it sounds like they've got the bomb."

"How about we just get the heck out of here?"

"Where are we going to go? This bomb may be strong enough to take out everything from here to New York. We just don't know. Our best approach is to try to stop the bomb from exploding. And if we're going to stop anything, we better get there. We better take our ceramics and leave our other weapons here." Stef understood that Elliott was referring to the ceramic guns that the IOM labs had created, referred to as the C101s. When they knew they were coming to the DC area, Elliott had Greg FedEx overnight, two ceramics and two regular pistols to their hotel. He also sent them fake driver's licenses that they could use instead of their foreign Australian IDs. They had received from them this morning.

The ceramics were automatic pistols made entirely of hardened clay except for the hardened plastic firing pin. The bullet casings were also made from plastic including the bullet itself. This made the weapon entirely undetectable to metal detectors or scanning systems. And the bullet disintegrated upon impact so there would be no ballistics to check.

The ceramics didn't pack the same wallop as a regular lead bullet, but they were still deadly. It also didn't have the same level of endurance as a regular metal gun. It wore out after about 100 rounds. But it was a critical weapon in the IOM arsenal that was used in special cases where detection was an issue. And, since the Pentagon was surrounded by security, their normal weapons would need to be left at the hotel.

Elliott sent a message to Dawn to keep him posted on Kres. He sent a second message to Marcello that he was heading to the Pentagon station just in case Joe, Conrad and the Arabs ended up there. He asked Marcello to keep him informed in case the Arabs reappeared.

Stef slipped on her jeans. Watching her put on her jeans made Elliot wish he had time for a different type of action. And the bulge in the front of his pants gave away what he was thinking, which made Stef smile. She gave him a wink and said, "Later big boy." Unfortunately, Elliot's plans would have to wait till they returned to their hotel room.

Steff and Elliott walked the short distance to the Metro Blue Line. There they hopped onto the underground train for the two quick stops that delivered them underground at the base of one side of the Pentagon. The station wasn't all that impressive, much like any underground subway station. However, it was better maintained than most. Usually, subway stations were known as dirty, tagged with graffiti, and generally undesirable areas. But this station had the flavor of military cleanliness.

What made this station unique was that it contained the entrance to the security area of the Pentagon. Stepping off the train they entered a loading and unloading area, much like any subway station. Off to the back of this area stood a metal detector and several security personnel, much like what you would find at any airport. Here they check visitors for metal and scanned all bags. They also checked for IDs, for which the fake US driver's licenses came in handy.

After successfully passing this screen they were able to walk around the wall and enter the Pentagon proper. At this point you were screened as a visitor to the Pentagon, and security became more complicated. In order to get any further within the Pentagon, you would need someone from the Pentagon, with an official Pentagon ID, to come and escort you. But Elliott and Stef knew that no one with a bomb or a gun would get that far. They wouldn't even make it through the first screening area. So, they waited on the subway platform, outside the secure perimeter. They found a convenient bench and acted like they were intensely interested in the metro map that they had picked up. This would serve to hide their faces as well as keep them from looking suspicious. They knew that the Arabs wouldn't recognize them as a suspicious-looking pair because they had never seen them. They would appear to be lost and confused tourists. Unfortunately, this also made it hard on Elliott and Stef, who wouldn't be able to recognize the Arabs, especially if more than two of them got off the subway.

However, if Joe or Conrad were to appear, they would be able to recognize them from the warehouse in Axum. Both knew that in their current undercover role they wouldn't give away each other's identity.

Elliott and Stef intensely watched every train coming from the direction of the Arabs, Joe, and Conrad. On several occasions they saw a pair of Arab-looking individuals on the subway, but they didn't get off the train. At one point they thought they recognized Conrad. But he also did not get off the train. So, either it wasn't really him, or they had guessed wrong on the station. They sat there a good half hour after the time when the Arabs and Conrad should have arrived. Then Elliott received a message from Marcello, "We have lost contact with Conrad. We're not sure what happened. He sent us a message as he left the Federal Triangle station, so we know he got at least as far as the Smithsonian station. We assume Conrad got off at that station. That was the last communication we received from him. I've dispatched agents to the Smithsonian and the Federal Triangle area and to the next two stations as well, to look for Conrad and to find the Arabs. Joe has also been dispatched to find Conrad."

Elliott and Stef were ready to give up waiting around at the Pentagon station, admitting that they had missed the suspected target. Now they thought that the target must have been downtown somewhere. They were just starting to get up when they noticed two Arabs getting off of a train coming in from the direction of downtown. And they had a roller bag that fit the description of the suspect bag. Elliott and Stef had worked together long enough that they didn't even need to point out the suspects. They knew instinctively and instantly what the other was looking at and what they were thinking.

The Arabs went into a bathroom and Elliott quickly got up and followed them in. They went to the urinals, did their business, and started heading back out of the bathroom, still towing the roller bag behind them. It would have been too obvious for Elliott to walk out of the bathroom behind them, so he stayed in the bathroom a little longer. He knew Stef would pick them up on the outside and watch their activities.

Along the back wall of the subway platform, there is a bank of about twenty rental lockers. These were obviously placed there for people who wanted to get through the Pentagon security system without a problem. It is primarily used to stash knifes and other weapons that wouldn't pass the security screen. Stef watched as the Arabs went over to the lockers, open one of the larger lockers, and put the roller bag inside along with some plastic bag containing something what looked like it could be a gun. Then they locked the locker. Stef paid special attention to try to remember which locker had been used.

Then the Arabs proceeded through the Pentagon screening area, placing only their jackets on the belt for screening. They entered the Pentagon security area. By now Elliott had exited the bathroom and he went over to Stef, holding out his hand as if to help her get up. The two of them, acting like newlyweds, which they nearly were, also proceeded to go through the Pentagon screening area, attempting to see what the Arabs were doing. Stef whispered to Elliott what she had seen at the lockers. Elliott texted Marcello saying, "Two suspect Arab-looking individuals have just placed a roller bag into a locker at the Pentagon Metro Station. We're watching them. Not sure if these are our guys."

About the same time Elliott received a message from Dawn, "Kres and two cohorts are still on the freeway south. They're going fast. I sense they're trying to get as far away as possible. I think something's coming down in DC."

"Great," said Elliott to himself, showing the message to Stef. "Something's coming down and we have no idea where or what. But it does sound like time is growing short." Elliott forwarded the message to Marcello as they entered the Pentagon reception area.

The Pentagon reception and waiting area was a rather large space. The left half of it was seating, where visitors would wait for their escorts. There was also a reception desk along with a line, much like you would find at a bank. The reception desk would process the visitors and call for their escorts. In the area was a loud, and somewhat obnoxious school group that had come for a visit. Some were sitting and yelling, some were playing with their cell phones, and some were jabbing, poking, and horsing around.

There is a souvenir shop off to the right side of the reception area which formed an island in the middle of the room. The shop had a door on both ends. One door faced out toward the waiting area and the guard station, and the second side opening out toward the bathrooms.

Commenting on Dawn's message, Stef said; "Doesn't sound good." Then she noticed the Arabs purchasing a couple of military coins from the tourist vendor and she whispered; "Do you see what I see?"

Elliott, thinking these may just be tourists, said; "I think these two guys may be legitimate as well. They're just doing tourist stuff. Which is frustrating because it's already noon and we still have no idea what Kres had planned."

Suddenly, in a surprise move that caught Elliott and Stef completely off guard, two shots rang out, and two of the Marine guards with automatic rifles fell to the ground, a bloody spot in the center of their heads. It was immediate pandemonium and chaos. The shots came as a complete surprise. If it weren't for Stef noticing puffs coming from the pockets of one of the Arab jackets, no one would have been able to identify the shooters.

"Wooden guns," whispered Stef to Elliott, "and plastic bullets." Wooden guns were also undetectable, but they were more primitive than the IOMs ceramic weapons. The wooden guns were single shot and needed to be reloaded. They still used regular bullets and a metal firing pin. But these could be disguised in watches or jewelry. For the Arabs, the firing pin was taped to the back of their wristwatch and the bullets were buttons on their jackets; visible but not seen.

"Be careful. There may be more to come as soon as they reload." Elliott said as Stef ducked behind a pillar in an attempt to stay out of the line of fire.

There were two more shots, again coming from the pockets of the Arabs, and two more guards fell. By now the entire Pentagon security team was on alert, rifles aimed in the direction of the shots. A command of, "On the ground" was yelled out. There were about a dozen people standing around the tourist shop area and all of them, including the person taking care of the shop immediately fell to the ground. The Arabs, who were heading into the bathroom most likely to reload followed suit, but not before ditching the guns into the garbage bins by the bathroom entrance.

Stef, with her keen eye for detail, was keeping a tight watch on them. She noticed one of them carefully slip something into a garbage can. She was sure it must have been their weapon, but she didn't want to give herself away by looking into the garbage.

The chaos that followed was the commotion that the Arabs hoped would allow them to work their way toward the exit. But the plan was foiled by the immediate lock-down that gets executed as soon as there was any kind of security breach at the Pentagon. No one was able to enter or leave the Pentagon security area. Everyone would be searched until the shooter is found. But, of course, the search would find nothing. And Stef didn't want to give herself away by identifying the hidden weapons in the garbage can.

"Let's do this through Marcello," suggested Elliott. After he had been searched, and he was no longer being watched, he sent a text to Marcello explaining what had happened and instructing him that he needed to report the location of the weapons to Pentagon security. Then he asked, "If we sent you a picture of the Arabs, would you be able to identify them?"

"I'll take care of the message to Pentagon security. Joe may be able to help with ID. Send me a picture."

Elliott pretended to take pictures of Stef with his cell phone. After several shots he was able to get a reasonable picture of the Arabs, now sitting on the ground. Then he transmitted the picture to Marcello. After several minutes, Elliot received his response, "Those are the guys."

Elliott replied, "Then you have a bigger problem. They put the package into lockers on the other side of the security, and we can't get to it because of the lock down. Good luck on finding it."

Marcello, again true to his word, had the Pentagon security searching the garbage cans and it wasn't long before they came up with the two single shot wooden guns in the garbage cans.

"I guess we've done all we can do until they release us," commented Stef. "Let's see if the Pentagon is any more efficient than the CIA."

Apparently, Marcello had gone the extra mile and had also transmitted the picture of the Arabs to Pentagon Security. The two were quickly approached by the guards. The intent was to take them into custody and remove them to a secure area where they were sure to go through some level of interrogation. But the Arabs had other ideas. They stood up, and immediately kicked their military captors between the legs, leaving them crumpled. A second set of guards were more cautious. They dropped their weapons and took aim, ready and willing to shoot. But that didn't happen. Two other guards had worked their way to the back side of the island tourist shop and hit the Arabs over the head, dropping them instantly to the ground.

"But what about the bomb?" asked Elliott. "Or was it even a bomb? But we have to assume the worst case, that it was a bomb. We also have to assume that they won't be able to get any information out of these Al-Qaeda operatives in time to make a difference. They were planning on dying anyway, so why would they give up any information."

Just than Dawn sent in a message to Elliott and Stef, "Kres got caught up in a traffic jam and he said 'we only have two more hours. We need to get as far away as possible.' So, whatever is going to happen, you have two hours to stop it."

Elliott forwarded the message, unedited, to Marcello. Then he added the message, "We're going to take Kres out before we lose him."

"No. He may have valuable information. We may still need him," came back from Marcello.

Elliott and Stef each had their C101 ceramic pistols hidden in the one place they were sure not to get searched: their crotches. The pistols were extremely small, about the size of a cell phone, and so they were easy to hide. They each had magazines which held 4 rounds. Both Elliott and Stef had special pockets sown into their pants that allowed them to hide the pistols. These were zippered pockets which they opened when it was time to conceal or retrieve their weapons, and which were zipped shut when they were being searched.

Elliott and Stef each migrated their C101 ceramic pistols from their private parts into their pockets where they could easily be retrieved. At this point they felt like they were ready. They had done all they could do, and now they had to wait.

CHAPTER SEVENTY

The Celebration Continues
April 20th, 2025 AD, 1:00 PM, Washington, DC

Marcello's team found Conrad stuffed into a bathroom stall at the Smithsonian Metro station. He was shot in the right upper chest. Fortunately, he was still alive. They rushed him off to the nearest hospital. Apparently, he had been left for dead.

It was immediately after that when they heard about the shots being fired at the Pentagon security station. Marcello ordered everyone to go there immediately. Marcello, coming from the CIA, and Joe coming from Washington city center, each hopped into a car and headed there. Joe drove so Marcello could maintain communication with Elliott and with the Pentagon. He had sent the information on the Arabs to Pentagon security. And they were interrogating their captives, but they were unsuccessful in coming up with anything meaningful.

At this point all attention had to be placed on finding and disarming the bomb. Marcello placed another call to Pentagon security, "We think the bomb is somewhere in one of the lockers at the Metro station."

"There are hundreds of lockers down here," was the response from Cornel Fritz, the commander in charge of the security desk at the Pentagon. He was looking at the lockers that were inside the Pentagon security area, a completely separate bank of lockers from the ones outside on the subway train platform. "Can you be more specific?"

"No. We're not even sure there is a bomb, only that we suspect it, and it may be anywhere in the area. We're just guessing that it's in the lockers since one of our sources saw them put something into the lockers."

"What sources?"

"I can't disclose that for security reasons."

"Are your sources still on site?"

"Yes."

"If we talked to them, we may be able to get more useful information. If we start tearing into the lockers, we may accidentally detonate the bomb. There may be some kind of trigger mechanism."

"If the sources reveal themselves, they have to be immune from prosecution and from any record being made of their presence or identity. No identification can be made. Can you give me your assurance of that?"

"Of course. Why do they need to stay hidden? I supposed that's on a need-to-know basis, and irrelevant to the current situation. We may be talking about destroying everyone here. What do I care about someone's identity? Who is your source?"

"Go back to the tourist shop inside the Pentagon security area and I'll have them reveal themselves to you."

Marcello sent a message to Elliott explaining the plan. Since Elliott didn't actually see the bag get placed into the locker, he decided that only Stef would reveal herself, and that he would stay unidentified, in case something went terribly wrong in this process.

The Pentagon Station had gone into complete lockdown. No one was allowed to enter or leave the station. Everyone on the station platform was rounded up into the center of the platform while the security forces went through a thorough search of everything, including purses, bulky clothing, hats, and shoes. A separate group started searching the premises. But for now, they avoided the lockers, fearing that they may cause a premature detonation.

Col. Fritz was quick to march through the screening area and entered back into the Pentagon security area. Walking directly toward the tourist shop, Stef stepped out of the shop, held out her hand, and said, "I understand you're looking for me."

"I am indeed. Can you help us?"

"I can give you the general area where I saw them place their roller bag. But I can't identify the specific locker."

"Did it appear that they had installed any type of triggering mechanism?"

"It took them a couple of minutes to put the bag into the locker, so it is possible that they initiated some kind of trigger. I'm not really sure."

"Come with me," responded Col. Fritz, and the two of them marched back through the security check point and back out to the Metro station platform. "Show me which locker they used," being careful not to use the word bomb so as not the raise concern.

Stef walked him over to the area of the lockers and indicated a section of 4 or 5 possible lockers. Then she suggested, pointing at the people standing in the center of the platform, "Shouldn't we get these people out of here. This could get dangerous."

"Photograph everyone here, including their IDs, and get them out of here as quickly as possible," Col. Fritz ordered one of the guards, as he grabbed a wireless security camera off the wall and handed it to the guard for filming. It wasn't long before the platform was cleared, and the people loaded on a subway train. Similarly, all the people standing in the Pentagon security area were filmed and escorted off to Metro trains and sent on their way. Stef was also forced to leave as well without her picture or ID being photographed. But Elliott was nowhere to be found.

A special train was brought in to haul people away from the Pentagon Station. Other than that, all traffic on the Blue line and the Yellow line, which also ran through the station, had been halted.

A four-member bomb squad had also arrived, and they were given directions where the bomb might be located. Then Col. Fritz had all his security personnel cleared out of the area. At this point he still kept in the dark that this was possibly a nuclear device aimed at taking out the entire city of Washington DC, and not just a bomb aimed at the Pentagon.

CHAPTER SEVENTY-ONE

The Pentagon
April 20th, 2025 AD, 2:30 PM, Washington, DC

Elliott had managed to hide himself in the gift shop behind a rack of souvenirs. It wasn't an ideal hiding place, not totally concealed and extremely uncomfortable, but it worked. Since everyone was distracted by the evacuation, he was successful in avoiding detection. When it finally seemed safe, and when everyone had been cleared out of the area because of the bomb scare, he slowly and carefully snuck through the check point and out onto the Metro platform. The bomb squad was wrapped up in their bomb suits, which hampered their peripheral vision and hearing. They didn't notice Elliott working his way to the Metro station tracks, where he felt he could observe their activities while remaining hidden from view and sheltered from any possible minor explosions.

The bomb squad lacked the master key to get into the lockers, so they resorted to prying the doors open, one at a time, and carefully watching for any wires. Then they would take whatever bags were found and explore them as well. This was a slow process, and Elliott hoped there would-be enough time left to actually defuse any bomb that they found.

As they started prying on the fourth locker, a loud, hi-pitched screech went out. This was an obvious booby trap intended for the bomb squad, since the screech was so high pitched and deafening that it easily penetrated the bomb suits. Initially it exploded camera lenses and some glass panes, but then it started to affect the bomb squad members.

Because of their suits, they were unable to cover their ears and they started dropping to the ground one after another, struck down and knocked unconscious by the sound.

Elliott, when he heard the screech, knew immediately what it was and dove down on the ground. He pushed his right ear into the dirt and covered the left ear with both hands. It didn't totally eliminate the sound, but it dampened it enough so that it didn't knock him out. Elliott realized he was on his own. The bomb squad had been eliminated. And because the cameras had been knocked out by the screeching sound, the security forces can't even see what's going on. There would be no help coming. If someone were going to act, it would have to be Elliott. And time was quickly running out.

Elliott spit into the dirt and used one of his hands to cake the greasy, oily mud together into a clay-like clump. Then he started packing the mud into his left ear. He continued doing this until the thick cake of mud in his ear had successfully dampened the sound. Then he wanted to do the same process for his right ear. He realized that his quantity of spit was limited. He was getting dried out, and it became impossible to choke up any more spit. But he needed more, or the sound would have the same effect on him that it had on the bomb squad. The only other liquid source he could think of was his blood. H pulled his ceramic pistol out of his pocket and fired a shot that would graze the tip of his index figure, just enough to cause bleeding but not enough to break a bone. He pulled the trigger and flinched and yelled. The shot hurt more than he expected, but he wasn't concerned about anyone hearing his scream. The shrieking siren droned out any noise he could make.

The blood worked. Unfortunately, he also got some the oily dirt into the wound on his finger, and it made the finger throb. Once he had the right ear caked with mud, he was able to concentrate on his bleeding finger. He took off his shoe, pulled off his sock, and tied it tightly around his finger, which was a little tricky with one hand. But it successfully slowed up the flow of blood. Now, with his hearing blocked, and his bleeding under control, he could concentrate on the bomb.

The bomb squad had successfully identified the location of the bomb, and Elliott could see the roller bag in the locker. He also saw the booby trap trip wire that had signaled the screeching sound. He quickly wound the wires together, and fortunately the sound stopped. Next, he took the roller bag out of the locker, laid it out on the floor, and slowly started to open it. He feared that there may be a second booby trap, but then what did he have to lose. If the bomb went off, he was a goner anyway. He finished unzipping the bag and slowly opened the cover. He knew enough about bombs to recognize that this was a nuclear device, complete with fuse, nuclear fuel, and a timer which was ticking down with **12 minutes,14 seconds to go...**

With the screeching sound off, Elliott tried his best to knock the dirt out of his ears. He grabbed his cell phone and call Marcello, the only person he knew to call, and quickly gave him and update. Marcello, in turn, contacted the Pentagon security forces and explained the situation to Col. Fritz, who immediately dispatched a couple of security forces team members to the Metro platform. By this time, the timer was down to **9 minutes, 18 seconds...**

Col. Fritz called Elliott directly and asked him, for the sake of time, to take a picture of the bomb and text it to him, and he would relay it to his bomb squad headquarters. This Elliott did, hoping to get some guidance on how to defuse the bomb. **6 minutes, 52 seconds** on the timer.

Elliott was getting extremely anxious; He didn't want to be sitting here cuddling this bomb when it went off. The minutes ticked away as he waited for a response from the bomb squad. **4 minutes 13 seconds...**

Elliott received a phone call. It was the bomb squad. Elliott put the phone on speaker and laid it down beside him so his hands would be free to work. They instructed him to cut the red wire. "There is no red wire," exclaimed an excited Elliott. "All the wires are black. They weren't nice enough to color code it for me."

"Then we'll need to pull the core out of the warhead. Are you ready?"

"Do I have a choice?" Elliott asked, as Col. Fritz's men watched. They felt helpless. There really wasn't much for them to do. And handling the bomb could trigger a detonation. So, they just watched.

"Take out the three screws from the tip of the warhead," directed the bomb squad.

"You have to be kidding. I don't walk around with a screwdriver in my pocket."

"The bomb squad should have one."

"Right." Several of Col. Fritz's men quickly searched the bomb squad team members and found a screwdriver in one of their toolboxes. *2 minutes 47 seconds…*

Thankfully, the screws came out easily and the top of the warhead also slipped off easily. "Now what?" asked Elliott. *1 minute 31 seconds…*

"You need to reach in and slowly pull out the core, which is also the detonator, and then separate it as far as possible from the fuel. The fuse will still go off. It's strong enough to blow your hand off so you don't want to be holding it. Just throw it as far away as possible. Then you'll hear a minor explosion, but don't worry about it. Without the nuclear fuel, you won't get the big boom."

"Great," responded Elliott. Up to now the operation had gone smoothly. But now everything started falling apart. The fuel rod would only pull out so far. Then it caught on something. It was blocked by the roller bag's frame. He tried removing the entire bomb from the roller bag, but it wouldn't come out. It was fastened to the bag. What were his options in the limited time he had left? *0 minutes and 46 seconds…*

He couldn't get the bomb out of the bag, so he decided to destroy the bag. He grabbed the crowbar that the bomb squad had been using to pry the lockers open, and he started beating on the roller bag, doing his best to tear it apart. Col. Fritz's security personnel jumped in to help and they all started tearing at the bag.

The bomb squad heard them beating on the suitcase and assumed they were beating on the bomb. They were screaming for him to quit, that he could accidently set the bomb off. But Elliott was deaf to their screams. All Elliott registered was the timer on the bomb. *0 minutes and 18 seconds….*

He tried again to pull out the core. There was still too much blockage. He yanked one end of the bag while one of the men grabbed and yanked on the other end. *0 minutes and 9 seconds…*

He tried again. He could see that he was closer, but it still did not pull free. Elliott ripped away at the bag's side. *0 minutes and 4 second….*

One more try. This time it finally slipped out. But now he had to get it away from the fuse. ***0 minutes and 1 second....!!!***

He threw the core as hard as he could over the side of the railway platform and it fell down along the tracks just as the timer ran out and the fuse made a loud bang. The fuse had been activated. But there was nothing to ignite. Washington DC had been saved for at least one more day. In his mind Elliott was sarcastically hopeful that it had been worth saving.

"What's happening," was the scream over the phone.

"The core is out, and the fuse has been detonated," was Elliott's exhausted response as he slumped down in a sitting position against the lockers.

Just then one of the groggy bomb squad agents rolled over, groaned, and said, "What's happening? Did we find the bomb?"

"Great timing," was all Elliott could say, but he was hopeful that they would be all right.

Col. Fritz and the remainder of his entire team came charging into the room to see what had happened.

"Nice you could show up," was Elliott's exhausted comment.

The team inspected the nuclear device and looked over the damage done to the subway tracks. The Blue Line would not be running today, but fortunately the damage was not extensive. It would only be shut down for a day or two. As everyone was bustling about, trying to make sense of the situation, and surveying the damage, Elliott slipped down onto the Metro tracks and disappeared into the darkness. He had enough excitement for one day.

CHAPTER SEVENTY-TWO

The Celebration Fails
April 20th, 2025 AD, 2:50 PM, Washington, DC

Kres and company had pulled over at a rest area. They had driven past Florence, South Carolina, and stopped at the first roadside rest area, close to Shiloh. Kres wanted to look back to see the fireworks over Washington DC. "This is going to be the biggest fireworks show they have ever seen in Washington," he said to Lefty and Krank. "Even bigger than the 4th of July. In fact, after today, April 20th is going to be the new 4th of July."

They waited. It was now 03:05 PM. "What's the deal with the timer? I thought it was fairly accurate. Did those scientists screw up somehow?" They continued to wait, looking north towards Washington, and hoping to see a funnel cloud rising in the sky.

It was now 03:15 PM, and Kres was fuming. He realized that the "celebration" had been foiled somehow. ***"Whaaat the bloody hell happened???"*** was all he could muster. Then he remembered the back-up plan. He had a phone number that he could call to self- detonate the bomb. He called the number. Nothing happened. He tried again. Still nothing. He ranted and raved and stomped around the grounds in a fury. ***"Blast! It's going to be a whole year before we can make another attempt at celebrating my father's birthday by taking out Washington!!!"*** he hollered red-faced, as though he was about to explode himself, instead. Lefty and Krank knew better than to get to close to him when he was in one of these moods. There would be no consoling him. All they would do was to get themselves into deeper trouble with him.

Kres stomped and fumed like a bull about to charge. He made such a fuss that other people in the Rest Area started paying attention to him, showing concern on their faces. He kicked a garbage can, then walked over to a big tree and gave it a swift kick. But the tree got the better of him and he bounced away on one foot, holding desperately onto the toes of the foot that he had assaulted the tree with. Lefty and Krank spent another fifteen minutes waiting for Kres to calm down. Then they got into the car and Lefty asked, "Where do we go now?"

"Let's go to Columbia, South Carolina where I'll have our plane sent. I want and get out of here. I can't handle being in this country another minute." Then Kres sent a text to his pilot to have his private plane fly from Jacksonville to Columbia. That would only be about one more hour's drive, and then he could leave.

"You know who's behind this?" asked Kres. "I'll bet its Elliott and Stef, those IOM guys. Remember, we saw them at the Pentagon Subway Station and took a few shots at them. I'll bet they're behind this. The CIA isn't clued in enough to catch us. But the IOM may have figured out what we're up to. We spent way too much time with them. We gave them too much information and trusted them way too much! I'll bet they're behind my ruin, both in Axum at the Ark of the Covenant, and now again in Washington DC when I was trying to celebrate my father's birthday. It **has** to be them. I'm going to get even with them if it's the last thing I do. I'm going to see that they're ruined. You wait and see."

Lefty and Krank remained silent. They knew that Kres had to get this frustration out of his system.

April 20ᵗʰ, 2025 AD, 4:00 PM, Washington, DC

Stef was beside herself with worry. She knew Elliott had stayed behind to make sure the bomb got defused. But was he safe? Did he make it? Or is he shot, lying somewhere? She had been sent on to the Arlington Cemetery Metro Station, along with the other people from the

Pentagon Station. And she heard an explosion coming from the direction of that station, echoing as it travelled through the tunnel. She sent him a message. She didn't want to call him in case the ringing of the phone gave anything away. "Are you safe? Where are you? I'm not ready to lose my husband just yet."

Elliott responded, "I'm still planning to attend our wedding. Have you set a date yet?"

Stef was so excited to get the message that he was OK that she nearly peed her pants. *We have to get out of this business,* she kept saying to herself. Then she sent the message, "Where are you? Can I help you in any way?"

"I'm in the metro tunnel walking to the Pentagon City station. It's dark down here but I can still see the light of the phone. I had to get out of the Pentagon area quick. Too many military guys asking too many questions. Grab a taxi and go to the hotel and I'll meet you there. The Metro tracks are messed up and it won't be running for a couple of days. I'm exhausted and I need a break."

"I'll meet you there. Be ready for a nice bath and rub down."

"And some decent food would be nice. I feel like I haven't had a good meal for weeks."

"You have a date."

Then Elliott received a message bleep from Marcello; "What's happening?"

Elliott sat down on a small ledge at the side of the tracks. He was exhausted and wanted to take a break from his long walk. He gave Marcello a call and explained what had happened.

"So, you saved the day, did you?" Marcello asked.

"I saved our lives, is what I did. But it was teamwork. Without the bomb squad and the security guys at the Pentagon we wouldn't have made it."

"Yes, but there's no denying that you were critical to the success of this operation."

"Whatever you say," was all that Elliott felt like saying.

"I owe you big time."

"And I'm the type of person that will collect. So, don't be surprised to hear from me in the future."

Then Marcello apologized; "I know we didn't have a good start to our relationship. Sending a hit squad after you, and then kidnapping Stef doesn't tend to be the foundation of a strong relationship. But after today, I owe you big and I will do anything to help. Just let me know what I can do. I hope you can forgive my past behavior and see that we can work together in the future."

"Give it some time," Elliott replied. "You still make me a little nervous. But I'm sure time will mend all things." Just then a message beeped on Elliott's phone. "I need to go. I have an important message coming in. I hope Conrad's OK and I hope we can work together again in the future." Elliott didn't really know if the message was urgent, he just wanted to get off the phone. He knew Stef would be waiting for him, and that was a lot better than talking to Marcello.

"Conrad's going to be OK. They took him into emergency surgery, and it will take a couple of months for him to recover, but he'll be back on his feet again." Marcello reassured him.

"That's good to hear, even if I don't really like the guy right now." Elliott confessed.

"Thanks again, until we meet again." were Marcello's last words.

"Goodbye." Elliott replied, immediately checking in with his other caller.

Elliott's message was from Dawn. "Can I take him out yet? I may lose him soon. I already thought I lost him a couple of times, but I found him again. So, can I get this over with?" she sounded determined and very keen at the prospect of removing this particular scumbag of an adversary from off the surface of the earth, with 'EXTREME PREJUDICE'.

Elliott sent Marcello a similar message to which Marcello responded almost immediately, "At this point I don't care what you do. Just don't tell me about it so I can retain my deniability."

Elliott responded to Dawn with the message she had anxiously been waiting for, "Do it."

Dawn and the S1 were still tailing Kres, Lefty, and Krank. It had been a struggle because they were driving such a generic car that she was constantly plagued by lookalikes. Right now, the threesome was travelling in the fast lane heading down the interstate and taking them out wouldn't be good because it may cost other innocent lives. And the IOM was very precise about only taking out the target and minimizing other casualties. Right now, wouldn't be a good time. She had missed a big opportunity while they were at the rest area, but she knew Elliott and the team wouldn't take action as long as the bomb was still active.

So, she waited, getting more and more impatient. Then she got lucky. Kres' car started to migrate across the lanes of traffic to the slow lane, obviously planning to take the next exit. Dawn knew this as her queue to act. She flew the S1 around to the front of the plane and took aim. She was able to see the two men sitting in the front seats of the car. Fortunately, unless these individuals looked up into the sky, they wouldn't see the S1. And, even if they tried to look up, it would be hard to spot. The S1 guns were able to lock on target. What they lacked in power they made up for in accuracy. The first target was the driver. She hoped that taking him out would simultaneously take the entire car out. And she was right. The car had started to take the exit ramp. When the S1 shot the driver in the neck it caused him to jerk and surge. The car missed the exit ramp turn and went flying over the embankment toward the overpass. It was going so fast that it left the ground and took a full sideways spin in the air before landing in the bushes. Then it took three more turns and came to a stop under the overpass. And then it burst into flames.

Lefty, the driver was killed instantly. Krank, who was sitting in the back seat without wearing a seatbelt received a sharp knock on the side of his head and was left unconscious. And when the car burst into flames, there was no hope for rescue.

Dawn, satisfied that she had completed her mission, headed the S1 back to her base in Nevada. Unfortunately, she didn't notice the long bearded and shabbily clothed homeless man who crawled out from under the overpass and foolishly risked his life pulling a passenger out of the car. The flaming car didn't scare him. But, when he heard the sirens, he quickly crawled back into his cove, leaving the emergency medical team from the ambulance to finish saving the passenger.

CHAPTER SEVENTY-THREE

Returning to the CIA
April 20th, 2025 AD, Langley, Virginia

Marcello sent a message congratulating Stef and Elliott for their critical role in diverting disaster in Washington. He thanked them for their help in the name of a grateful nation. And he committed to erasing their identities from CIA and FBI files, thereby returning them to anonymity. He committed to remove the entire IOM from their current "under investigation" status. This turned out to be challenging. The "system" did not allow him to delete an entry. Eventually he realized that by changing the IOM status to "dead" it dropped them out of the active files and dropped them into a deleted status. It's amazing how these "systems" are theoretically here to help you and in the end, you spend more time trying to work around them in order to accomplish what you're after.

Marcello's reception back in Langley was far from congenial. The barrage of e-mails, phone calls, text messages, and message bullets, was enormous. You would think that Marcello had attacked the President of the United States. It seemed as if everyone was hot for his blood. The messages included "deviated from protocol," to "put lives in danger," to "introduced foreign terrorists into national security" and "assisted known terrorists in their arrival on American soil." Marcello could see that his days were numbered. The Secret Service was after him for "not keeping them informed," the FBI was angry that he had "exceeded his authority and interfered with their internal investigation," and internal to the CIA, politics ruled. The Task Force on Right Wing Revolutionaries (TFRWR) took no time in attacking Marcello's activities. They saw this as an opportunity to eliminate the TFMA who they considered redundant and second rate. And they attacked Marcello with full force, calling him a "renegade" and a "loose and uncontrollable cannon." And, of course, Marcello's boss didn't want his name associated with this calamity. Marcello had to be the scapegoat for what the media seemed to view as an unnecessary and uncontrollable disaster in security.

The writing was on the wall. Marcello could see that if he hung around too long, he may even get indicted for criminal activities. Marcello called his wife Julia using his personal cell phone. "The gig is up," he told her. Unfortunately, she knew what that meant. "They're going use me as the scapegoat, or for want of a better word 'sacrificial lamb', in order to get the media off their back. So, either I sit here and take it, and maybe even get indicted for criminal activities. Or we go with plan B." She knew Plan B was "run for it." Unfortunately, "running for it" was always a known alternative when working for the CIA. Politics and the media needed someone to blame, and they could care less about the facts. The media was more interested in commentary and over-dramatization. And the political system needed someone to blame, which would conveniently draw the attention away from them. No one really cared that an enormous disaster was diverted. The focus of the headlines was "Nuclear weapon on US soil" and "Explosion on the Metro shuts down the Blue Line."

Julia had mixed feelings. She knew Plan B would totally disrupt their lives and change everything, but she was also sick and tired of living in stress and fear. And staying in DC would mean that the stress level would only increase. She was ready for a change, and she excitedly responded; "Plan B."

"Plan B it is. I'll be there in an hour. Can you be ready to go that quickly?" Only the basics would be taken, similar to them going on a vacation. Some personal items, like photographs and journals would be brought along. And a few articles of clothing, enough to get them through one week. They would re-establish their home including clothing when they arrived at their new location. Everything else would have to be left behind. Their household items would be left with the house. There could be no trace or clue as to where they went or had disappeared to.

The only thing that she would miss was the kids and the grand kids. She wrote them a letter, which she left on the kitchen table. It explained that they had to execute Plan B, and the kids all knew what that meant. They would be back in touch when the coast was clear.

"I'm already packing," she responded.

Marcello cranked up his lap-top computer and plugged in his wireless air card. He had to do some money transferring, and he didn't want to do it through CIA equipment which would be tracked and possibly raise red flags. After several layers of transfers, the money trail would be lost. He knew which international banks intentionally kept untraceable records. And now was the time to use them. He grabbed his CIA budget, and CIA expense account, and any other funds he could find including extending his corporate and private credit cards to the max. Then he ran all the funds through his money laundering network. They would have plenty of money for a comfortable life, long into the future.

Once he flushed all the bank accounts, leaving the money distributed in a dozen different foreign locations, Marcello called Joe into his office and got Conrad on the speaker phone so he could have a frank and confidential conversation with them. They were his friends, and he felt he could trust them. He explained that he was going to grab his family and "disappear." Conrad had "deniability," because he was in the hospital during the disarming of the bomb. And Joe could claim he had been operating under direct orders of Marcello and didn't realize the "big picture" impact of his activities.

Marcello put Conrad in charge. He explained that he would contact them when the "smoke settled" to make sure they were OK. They were not to worry about him.

"Are you going to be all right?" Conrad asked, with sincere concern for his friend's welfare.

"I'm covered," replied Marcello. "As you know, the TFMA has several million in foreign banks that we keep on reserve for emergencies. This is an emergency. I feel bad for my family, having to separate from the kids and grandkids and pulling my wife out of her job. But we all knew the risks when I took this job. When I explained the need for us to escape her comment was, 'you're alive and I'm tired of getting scared every time I hear about some terrorist activities.' So, she's ready to go."

"I enjoyed working with you," was Joe's comment. "But I understand the politics. Even though I feel bad for you, that you have to leave this way, I feel jealous that you get to disappear from the world. I hope you have a good life."

Marcello stood up and held his hand out to shake hands with his friend. Joe would have none of it and gave Marcello a big hug. And Conrad expressed his gratitude and concern over the phone.

"Give me as much time as possible before you let anyone know I'm missing. Tell them I told you I had to take care of a family emergency and that I should be back in the morning. Good luck with trying to answer the e-mail nightmare. But use me as the scapegoat so that you can keep you noses as clean as possible." And with that Marcello left the office, took the back stairs down toward the car lot, and slipped out the back door to his car, avoiding the normal traffic that passed through the elevators.

His drive home was filled with regret. He wished this could have resolved itself differently. However, he couldn't think of anything he would have done differently. He took the best road possible. And he saved his nation. A nation he now had to flee for his own protection.

When he arrived home, Julia was indeed packed and ready. All electronics had to be left behind, including cell phones, computers, etc. Marcello kept a couple CDs which contained all his family's critical information and documents, like birth certificates, and contacts. Someday this may become important. But for now, these electronic versions would have to be sufficient. He threw a couple suitcases in the trunk. And they were off, heading for Washington National Airport and taking the first flight to freedom. Their first stop would be the Bahamas. Then they would purchase a separate ticket, using false identities that Marcello had saved for just such an emergency, to Havana, Cuba. And where they went from there, only Marcello knew. They were off to their new life.

CHAPTER SEVENTY-FOUR - PART 8

Returning to the IOM

Early May, 2025 AD, Alice Springs, Australia

It took a couple of weeks before Stef and Elliott returned to Alice. They stayed in the DC area and spent a week exploring the Smithsonian before returning home. They were feeling pretty good about preventing a major melt-down in Washington DC. But, unfortunately Malvika, their boss, wasn't quite as cordial. He ranted at them; "What the heck are you guys doing, collaborating with the CIA? You know those guys can't be trusted. And here you are getting in bed with them and saving their hides. Why are we protecting one of our sworn enemies? Didn't they try to assassinate you two? Didn't they hold Stef hostage? Didn't they turn Alan against us? These guys are bad news. Are you guys insane? And how did you get into a position where you were at risk helping these guys out? There's no up-side for us in getting involved here, only risk. I hope you get back out the United States without being arrested." Malvika ranted.

"There wasn't a lot of time for discussion," Elliott tried to explain. "We had to react quickly. There really wasn't any choice."

But Malvika wouldn't listen. He had a strong dislike for the CIA, and this explanation wasn't helping; "I only see risk and cost; no gain. We're not some kind of James Bond hero organization. We have to think like a business. We can't get all moral and self-righteous. You two should never have gone to Washington."

"It had to be done," Stef jumped in, listening in on the speaker phone.

"No, it didn't," responded Malvika emphasized sternly. "No, it didn't. No one won, as a result of your efforts. You didn't do anyone any favors."

"The people that lived sure won," replied Stef.

"But if you didn't save them, someone else probably would have. What's the CIA or the FBI good for? That's their job. They should have been out there saving the day. Not you."

Elliott and Stef were frustrated, but not surprised. Initially they also had some reservations about going to Washington. But they felt it was the right thing to do, and so they went. But "right" isn't always "right." One person's right is another person's wrong. And that appears to be the case with Malvika.

Malvika continued; "And the whole Ark recovery was another disaster. We don't have the Ark. The NNRL leadership is wiped out so we won't get paid. And we just wasted a lot of time and money on a wild goose chase. I sure wouldn't rate this as one of your more successful missions."

"There have definitely been some challenges," commented Stef with a slight hint of sarcasm to her voice.

"Not to change the subject, but we have some news we need to share with you," injected Elliott. He knew that there wasn't much else to be said about the mission. Financially, it had been a disaster. And there had been a high level of risk associated with it. But he still felt good about what they had accomplished, and he sincerely believed that he has saved a million lives. And that felt good.

"I have some news for you as well," reported Malvika.

"You go first," retorted Elliot, not wanting to water down his news.

Malvika punched a button on his phone and announced to someone at the other end of the line, "Send him in." Then looking back at Elliott, he said, "I want to introduce you to the newest member of your team." Marcello walked into the office.

"Well, I'll be darned," was all Stef could say. "This business sure takes a lot of twists. My captor is now going to be my team-mate."

"It just got way too hot for me in Washington," commented Marcello. "And you guys are much better organized than the CIA will ever be. I hope you can forgive me for my past life and let me work with you.' Turning to Stef he continued; "I promise I won't ever try to kidnap you again."

"How about trying to kill me?" questioned Stef, still perplexed at his unexpected entrance.

"I promise I won't ever try to kill you either," added Marcello. "Will you accept me as your partner?"

"No problem," was Elliott's response. It wasn't as trite a response as it sounded. Elliott had earned a lot of respect for Marcello during their work together in Washington. He felt Marcello would be a great addition to the IOM team.

Then, turning back to Malvika, Elliott said, "I don't have a problem working with Marcello. I was impressed with his performance in Washington. But I have some news that may twist this organization into a different direction."

"Well, don't keep me in suspense any longer," urged Malvika. "What's your big news?"

"Stef and I are engaged."

"Engaged to do what?"

"To get married, of course," replied Stef.

"Well congratulations," commented both Malvika and Marcello together. Then Malvika continued, "but how does this affect the IOM?"

"Because we're planning on taking a honeymoon."

"I still don't see how this will affect anything."

"We're thinking about a ten- year long honeymoon."

"Oh! I see the affect," replied Malvika. "I didn't mean to get on your case so badly that you would run out the door." Looking directly at Elliott he said, "This organization needs your cool head." Then looking at Stef he added; "And Stef, we need your clear head."

Elliott jumped in; "Actually, now that you've brought in Marcello, I'm a little less concerned about our leaving. We'll spend a couple of months getting him up to speed. Then we're off. Between him, Greg, and Dawn, you've got a darn good team. And, if you're ever in a tight pinch, you might be able to twist our arm to help you out." Stef gave Elliott a "not over my dead body" look and Elliott made a quick recovery by telling

Malvika; "But we don't want you to consider us regulars anymore. We're serious about taking a break from the business."

"I really don't want to lose you guys. I take back everything I've said about your mission, but it doesn't sound like it will make a difference. It sounds like you've made up your minds even before I chewed you out."

"Afraid so," jumped in Stef. She wasn't going to let Elliott water down their commitment to change. She wanted them to be '*out*'. And the excitement of getting married had gotten the best of her. She was ready for her new life together with Elliott. Just her, Elliott, and maybe one or two mini Elliotts. It was astoundingly obvious to the three men watching Stef's beautiful sky-blue eyes flashing a meaningful and fiery glance into Elliott's direction, that her adrenalin was running high, and she seemed to have miraculously transformed into a fierce lioness taking firm possession of and clearly marking, 'her territory'....

CHAPTER SEVENTY-FIVE - PART 9

Happily Ever After
Mid-August, 2025 AD, Chester, California, USA

Two months became three before Elliott and Stef were finally able to leave Australia. Before they left there had to be a wedding, and it was everything Stef had dreamed of; quiet, simple, and yet elegant, surrounded by their closest friends. About twenty people were in attendance, with Dawn coming all the way from Elko, Nevada just to be her bridesmaid and Malvika as the best man. It took place the first week of August, about two weeks before departing Alice.

When they finally left, it was with mixed emotions. They liked their work but being married put an entirely different dimension on their relationships. To be James Bond, you had to be agnostic to relationships. They knew that their effectiveness would be compromised whenever one or the other of them was in harm's way, just like when Stef was being held captive in Axum. Elliot had started to get a little reckless trying to save her. And that put them both at unnecessary risk.

Elliott had scouted out options for their retirement retreat. He wanted something remote, yet not too distant from civilization. And he found what seemed like the perfect spot in the most surprising of locations, California. About three hours' drive north of Sacramento is Lake Almanor, one of the few privately owned lakes in California. That was important because all the publicly owned lakes had restrictions on land ownership. Private citizens could not own lake-front property. But

Lake Almanor was owned by the PG&E power utility company and private, lake-front homes were available, but not cheap. Lake Almanor was close to 5,000 feet above sea level. It was close to several small communities, the largest being Susanville, about thirty minutes away, which had major shopping centers and two movie theatres. Larger cities like Chico or Red Bluff were a little over an hour away.

They were glad to be on their way. They caught a flight from Alice Springs to Sydney, then on to San Francisco, and from there to Sacramento. In Sacramento they rented a car and started their drive Northward, heading through Yuba City and Oroville, then on to Chico and up along the Feather River to Greenville. The first half of the drive was amongst some of the most beautiful agriculture fields in the world. Everything seemed to grow there, from rice, to kiwi, sunflowers, almonds, pistachios, and much more. The second part of the drive was through mountains along a beautiful river. Eventually, they arrived at the Southern tip of Lake Almanor, a heart shaped reservoir with the bottom tip of the heart being the location of the dam. On the top of the left lobe of the heart was the small community of Chester. It was here where they had made arrangements to meet with a real estate agent.

The top center "cleavage" of the heart was a gated community of private resorts. But Elliott and Stef wanted something a little more secluded and private. Elliott had heard it said that the East Shore of the lake presented *the* prettiest location. It was called the "banana belt" because it was hit by the afternoon sun and the snow melted quicker on that side of the lake. Also, lake front property on that side of the lake would have an excellent view of Mt. Lassen. Lassen was still considered an active volcano that had last erupted in the early 1900's and was said to be due to erupt again sometime in the future.

First, they drove up the west side of the lake, heading to Chester. They stopped in at a small burger shop that had great shakes in at least thirty different flavors. Stef got herself a bacon cheeseburger with a blueberry shake and Elliott ordered Fish and Chips. They were already hooked, before they had even met the real estate agent. This was the relaxed, remote environment that they had always talked about.

After lunch they met with the real estate agent who took them directly to the East Shore to show them a few available properties. As they drove down the East shore along the lake they were totally captivated. The lake was everything they had hoped for; remote, yet accessible. It was beautiful. The lake was calm, is if it were putting on a show to impress them. There were several boats tied up in front of their cabins, but, in spite of the large size of the lake, there was only one fishing boat out on this side of the lake.

"The internet told me this was one of the best fishing lakes in all of California," commented Elliott. "And there's only one boat out there. How is that possible? I guess they're saving all the fish for me."

"I'm sure that's it," responded Stef.

They looked at several lake front houses that were up for sale. One in particular caught Stef's eye. The street was about fifty feet higher than the lake. And the property was about three-hundred feet from lake to the street. The house was on two levels. The upper level was at street height and had a large parking area and a two-car garage. One story level below the garage, and under the garage, was a full workshop, with a one-car garage door, which immediately caught Elliott's eye. The house itself was a separate building, back behind the garage, connected by a covered walkway. And behind the house was a large back yard, leading to the lake.

"I think I'm in love," was all Stef could say. Elliott immediately asked the real estate agent if they could see the inside of the house, and he, of course, was delighted to show them everything.

Early May, 2025 AD, Elko, Nevada

Marcello, feeling comfortable in his new IOM role, placed a call to Greg in Elko Nevada. Greg couldn't attend the wedding. With Dawn attending the wedding, and with Alan no longer a team member, Greg had to hold down the fort. The lab couldn't be left completely unmanned.

"Fire up the S1 and keep an eye on them. Whatever you do, don't lose Elliott and Stef. I need to know where they end up."

"You got it," responded Greg.

Late September, 2025 AD, Lake Almanor, California, USA

It took a couple of weeks of negotiating, and another couple weeks to prepare the closing documents, but about six weeks later Elliott carried Stef over the threshold into what they called their "honeymoon suite." Three hours later Stef and Elliott were out on the lake competing to see who would catch the first fish.

Later that evening Stef and Elliott were unpacking some of their boxes. Stef opened up a box and carefully pulled out a device which looked like the reconstruction of an ancient timepiece. Alan had brought this to Axum, and after Elliott had rescued her, she had grabbed it just as she and Elliott were making their way to the airport. Turning it over in her hands, she looked at it from several sides and, showing it to Elliott, she asked, "I wonder what this thing is supposed to do?"

"Is that the Antikythera Mechanism?" gasped Elliott, eyes wide open with surprise. "I didn't know you had it."

"I didn't want anyone in the IOM to know I had it. But I've been dying to play with it. Any ideas on how it works?"

"Well, I guess that will just have to be another mystery that we'll have to solve."

"What do you say, we crack open that last bottle of 'champers' I saved for a special occasion. I think this is just one of those moments worth toasting to, just the two of us. I think we deserve it, don't you?" Elliott offered, doing his quick 'wink, wink, nudge, nudge routine, and searched Stef's face for a reaction. Then they burst out laughing simultaneously, their eyes reflecting that old familiar expression of hunger for excitement, adventure and the associated adrenalin rush that came from the nature of the work of their chosen profession, and which had been so much part of their very proactive lifestyles. And that only six weeks into their newly established lives together. He filled their glasses; they locked arms and simultaneously called a toast. They savored their champagne, and then he kissed her.

ABOUT THE AUTHOR

Dr. Gerhard Plenert has a PhD in Resource Economics and Operations Management, which are fancy words for "a whole lot of math."

He spent 12 years as a university professor and the remainder of his life living and working all over the world in places like Europe, Asia, the Middle East, Latin America, and of course North America.

He has 8 children, and his grandchildren are just starting to get numbered, the last count was 15. He has successfully published over 32 books and close to 200 articles on various business and academic topics. But his love is Jason Bourne and James Bond.

The Dawn of the New Templars is his first novel.

www.ingramcontent.com/pod-product-compliance
Lightning Source LLC
Chambersburg PA
CBHW072336020726
47506CB00004B/895